All I Want for Christmas

Karen Swan is the *Sunday Times* top three bestselling author of more than twenty-five books and her novels sell all over the world. She writes two books each year, which are published in the summer and at Christmas. Previous summer titles include *The Spanish Promise*, *The Hidden Beach* and *The Secret Path* and, for winter, *Midnight in the Snow*, *The Christmas Postcards* and *Christmas by Candlelight*.

Her historical series, called 'The Wild Isle' and starting with *The Last Summer*, is based on the dramatic evacuation of Scottish island St Kilda in the summer of 1930.

Karen lives in Sussex with her husband, three children and two dogs.

Follow Karen on Instagram @swannywrites,
on her author page on Facebook,
and on Twitter @KarenSwan1.

Also by Karen Swan

All I Want for Christmas

Karen Swan

PAN BOOKS

First published in paperback 2024 by Macmillan
This edition first published 2024 by Pan Books
an imprint of Pan Macmillan
The Smithson, 6 Briset Street, London EC1M 5NR
EU representative: Macmillan Publishers Ireland Ltd, 1st Floor,
The Liffey Trust Centre, 117–126 Sheriff Street Upper,
Dublin 1, D01 YC43
Associated companies throughout the world
www.panmacmillan.com

ISBN 978-1-5290-8433-7

1 3 5 7 9 8 6 4 2

A CIP catalogue record for this book is available from the British Library.

Typeset in Palatino by Palimpsest Book Production Ltd, Falkirk, Stirlingshire
Printed and bound by CPI Group (UK) Ltd, Croydon, CR0 4YY

Visit **www.panmacmillan.com** to read more about all our books
and to buy them. You will also find features, author interviews and
news of any author events, and you can sign up for e-newsletters
so that you're always first to hear about our new releases.

For Sam Burns

The best listener and deliverer of belly laughs

Chapter One

Copenhagen, 25 November 2024

'What exactly are you doing?' Darcy asked as she watched her flatmate type into her phone. She had a growing suspicion that Freja wasn't, in fact, searching for the weather forecast as she had claimed.

'Helping you.' Freja didn't look up. 'It's been three weeks.'

'Is that all?' Darcy groaned, tipping her head back and staring up at the cafe ceiling. It was pitched pine, swagged with some bushy faux conifer branches and fairy lights threaded through.

'You have to get back out there,' Freja said, both aware of and oblivious to her foamy hot chocolate moustache. She was incapable of eating or drinking anything without somehow wearing it too.

'Says who?' Darcy asked, watching as her flatmate bit her lip in deep concentration.

'Your mother, for one. You're twenty-six. She wants grand-babies.'

'She's got Cara for that.'

'Cara's nineteen and white-water river rafting in Thailand.'

Darcy rolled her eyes. Her little sister's gap year antics were distinctly more fun than anything she had going on in her

1

own life. All she had on her horizon was a rent payment, a hygienist appointment and the next deadline for her thesis. If Lars hadn't cheated on her, she'd have gone to Stockholm last weekend, she would have been sitting second row at The Weekend concert a week Friday from now, and she'd have had someone to pull a cracker with on Christmas morning. Instead, he'd kissed a girl he'd known for all of twenty-eight minutes in that bar three weeks ago and two months, five days' worth of emotional investment had been washed away.

Darcy's finger tapped the small square table. 'Well, *I'm* on a hiatus too. I'm going to need another three weeks off.'

'Permission denied. You might be perfectly fine with spending Christmas alone, but I am not. And if you won't come back to my parents' with me, then we're going to have to find you some company.'

'Frey, I have a thesis to write. I'm so behind it's not even funny. If I had time to celebrate Christmas with you, I'd have time to join my own family on their holiday. Believe me, I'd love nothing more than to be lazing on a Thai beach instead of hitting two thousand words a day here.'

'Which is why you need some downtime with a baddie when you hit those word counts.' Freja looked across at her. 'And besides, you're not getting any younger.'

'Or wiser, it appears.'

'They're not all like him.'

'No?' Darcy arched an eyebrow. 'I thought he was one of the good guys. That was supposed to be his shtick – dull, but solid, dependable, decent job, good prospects.'

'Well, perhaps that's the issue. You're setting the bar too low.'

'Oh, because you're the expert now?'

'Yes, I am,' Freja said with a smug smile. 'I have been

sleeping with the same man for a whole month and that means I've crossed to the other side. Suddenly I can see everything so clearly.'

Sarcasm tittered at the edges of her voice, but even though Darcy guffawed as she reached for her hot chocolate, she was struggling to adapt to this worryingly 'in love' model of her flatmate. Freja had never dated anyone for longer than a week – the child of a bitter divorce, she didn't believe in things everlasting; she couldn't even keep their houseplant, Miss Petals, alive, which was alarming for a microbiology PhD student specializing in genomics – and their friendship had been formed through bonding over dating disasters. They had met in the loos of a student bar in the summer, when Darcy – newly arrived in the city and hiding from a bad Tinder date – encountered Freja trying to jimmy the tampon machine with a collar-stiffener found in the bottom of her bag. Darcy had given her the change required and Freja had seen off her date in return, telling him she'd found Darcy in the toilets crying over a positive pregnancy test; the guy hadn't even waited to finish his drink. They'd been partners in crime ever since – or at least, until the past few weeks, when Freja's latest torrid affair had stubbornly failed to cool.

Darcy looked through the window and watched as the lunchtime skaters glided – or in some cases, wobbled – past on the Tivoli Gardens ice rink. Even though it was the last week in November the giant tree was already up, all the little cabins fully stocked with the soy candles, lavender sachets and wooden toys that would grace stockings this Christmas. The trees were threaded with lights, the park filled with dog walkers and staggering toddlers with gloves dangling on strings. Voices, young and old, carried above the whirr of the

3

fairground rides and the sluice of skates on the ice. It was easy for the festive spirit to come early in a place that wore snow like a scarf and boasted the happiest citizens on the planet. A couple stopped on the far side of the rink and posed themselves for a well-practised selfie, his arm slung over her shoulder, her head angled in as he reached down for a long, lingering kiss.

'Ugh, revolting.' Darcy slumped back in her chair as she watched the shameless display of happiness.

Freja glanced up, following her eyeline. 'See what I mean? All the good men are being snapped up. Right before your eyes.'

'Then I'll move to Paris. Or Barcelona. There'll be plenty there too.'

'Too late. I officially declare the mourning period over.'

'But I like mourning,' Darcy mumbled sullenly, still watching the happy couple. 'Black's my colour.' Her hands rose to her long, light brown hair; the blonde highlights framing her face – which she'd had put in in the summer – were still just bright enough to give her some lift, but the long layers had grown out and her olive skin had no trace of Ibiza tan left.

'Here's what we're gonna do.' Freja handed the phone back with a triumphant look. 'Check your homescreen.'

'What did you do?' Darcy frowned suspiciously.

'Open it.'

'Hm. What am I looking for?'

'Raya.'

'Ray–?' Darcy's eyebrows shot up. 'As in, the celebrity dating app?'

'That's overblown,' Freja dismissed. 'There's really not *that* many celebs on there. I mean, there's a few . . . but what there *are*, are plenty of professional, successful, high net worth individuals, just like you.'

'I am not a high net worth individual! I have to split bunches of bananas because I can't afford the wastage!'

'But you are beautiful and brainy, and these men all want a woman just like you.'

Darcy frowned. In her experience, men didn't like a woman being cleverer than them. 'Isn't Raya invitation only?'

'Yes. Tristan referred you. He did it last night.'

'. . . Tristan's on Raya?' She knew Freja's current squeeze was successful but she hadn't known he was *that* successful. She had yet to meet the guy, but Freja – who was doing a work placement as part of her PhD – had told her they'd hooked up after a conference trip. It was supposed to have been a one-time thing but so far, it had been a thirty-one-time thing. To Darcy's shame, yes, she was counting.

'He was,' Freja replied, before quickly catching herself. 'I mean, he is! He is! He's just got it on hibernation mode for the moment. He'll be back out there before you can say . . .' Words appeared to fail her.

Darcy watched, appalled that there was seemingly not yet an end in sight for her friend's giddy happiness. 'Flibbertigibbet?'

'Flibb . . . ?' Freja winced, the word too arcane for a non-native British speaker.

'Hm.' Point made. Was Freja – whisper it – falling for this guy?

Darcy didn't have time to consider it. Freja reached over and tapped on the app for her. For someone who hadn't even known she had it on her phone, it was something of a surprise to find she was already logged in and . . . 'I've got an account?'

'Well, I knew you'd never do it if left to your own devices,' Freja shrugged. 'You're becoming far too cynical in your second quarter.'

Darcy didn't appreciate the reminder that she had entered

the second of the twenty-five-year life stages by which Freja had mapped out their lives.

'Go on, have a look – they're a cut above, right? All solid eights for the main part but . . . if you see a four or a five, just know that means he's rich as fuck.'

Darcy blinked. 'Rich as fuck isn't really my thing.'

'But it can't hurt, right?'

'It can if he's a moose!'

'So you're saying you only want looks?' Freja gasped in mock horror. 'That's pretty shallow, don't you think?'

Darcy laughed at her friend's teasing as Freja reached across and placed a hand over the screen. 'Now, before you start going trigger-happy, there are rules.'

'Rules?'

'Yes. I want you to choose three and only three.'

'Reverse psychology? Really?' Darcy knew her friend too well. Give her a sea of men and then restrict her catch . . . when moments earlier Darcy had been saying she didn't want any?

It worked. Naturally.

'Fine. Let's have a look and see if we can choose only three.'

Freja shuffled her chair in closer, her cheek pressed against Darcy's arm as she began to swipe on the carousel of handsome faces. All of them appeared to have been caught laughing mid-joke or else staring off moodily into the distance with clenched jaws, seemingly unaware of the cameraphone directed straight at them. Some were playing football or Frisbee in a park, shirts untucked to reveal a snatch of hard stomach; one – seemingly a mountaineer – was grinning from a cliff face; another guy was playing a banjo around a campfire with a soulful expression as the firelight threw a golden glow over his cheekbones.

At first glance they all looked like perfect 10s: happy-go-lucky, fit, accomplished – but Darcy wasn't falling for it. Somehow, she had to read commitment issues, mother complex or narcissist from a photo. She had to tell the cheat from the liar from the good guys they all professed to be. She flicked through with – yes – a cynical eye: the guy cuddling a dog? She bet it wasn't his own. Swipe left. The one at a wedding? The dinner suit looked rented. Swipe left. The guy in a Ferrari – who wanted a guy in a Ferrari? Swipe left.

Darcy stopped on a profile. *Aksel. Vet. 29. Rubik's Cube PB 13 seconds.* She smiled slightly at the boast. It was ridiculous and silly, and hopefully intentionally self-deprecating.

'Oooh,' Freja said in an approving tone. 'He's cute.'

'Yeah. And he looks surprisingly normal. Like I might actually be able to talk to him.' He had shaggy dark brown hair and rich brown eyes, a seemingly shy grin. She flicked through his other pictures: on a park bench with two friends, seemingly post-run (good legs); at a bar drinking something suspiciously pink; on a sofa with a Bernese Mountain dog twice his size (might be his dog; he was a vet, after all). He seemed genuine enough, but she made herself focus only on what she knew to be true: he was attractive and 1.2 miles away. She swiped right.

'You want to *talk* to them?' Freja teased.

Milas, 30, graphic designer; 6'2", it said – but he was standing in a door-frame and clearly not that tall. She swiped left – not because he was short, but because he was a liar.

Calvin, 27, broker: he was playing to type, holding up a couple of magnums of Cristal in a club. She swiped left.

Darcy stopped at the profile of a guy staring straight to camera, not quite smiling but not *not* smiling either. He looked mildly bemused, as if suspicious of the intentions of the person taking the photograph. *Max, 32; Copenhagen. Lawyer. Likes skiing, wine, winning. No time for dating.*

To the point, she thought, turned off by the intimation of what he only had time for. It wasn't exactly the charming, witty bio of the other profiles, but her attention snagged on 'winning', and she looked back at his photo again and that direct stare. She could see now there was an arrogance there, bordering almost on contempt. His hair was dirty blond, blue eyes, a chiselled bone structure that suggested his poor mother had had to carve him. He was handsome, but in a cold way, and there was only that one photograph of him – a tight headshot, no backdrop, no narrative, no other moods or angles. Nothing by which to assess him other than that gaze.

'Hm. No, definitely not,' Freja frowned. 'Too hot for his own good.'

'But I thought talking was overrated?' Light sarcasm frilled Darcy's words this time.

'It is – but he looks like he needs to be humbled.'

'True,' Darcy agreed. He had the aura of someone to whom no one had ever said no. She wondered if he regarded every swipe right as one of his precious wins, and she was tempted to swipe left just on principle. She *wanted* to do it on principle, but her finger hovered, unable to commit to the rejection . . . He really was very sexy. Did she need to like him? She certainly didn't need to talk to him. He was good-looking and at least he was honest, which was more than could be said for almost every other guy on here. He wasn't pretending to be nicer than he was and he wasn't offering fairy tales or happy endings. No woman in her right mind would ever trust a man like him, but at least they'd know what they were getting.

She stared into those cold blue eyes, then against her better judgement, swiped right.

Freja gasped at her recklessness. 'Why did you waste a go on him?'

'Because he's a ten and I really am that shallow,' Darcy winked. 'What I see is what I'll get, I know that.'

Liam, 28, professional polo player. In Copenhagen? A marine city? No.

Ben, 27, architect. The second picture was of him playing the piano with a little girl. She had to hope it was his niece and not his daughter, but she wasn't prepared to take the risk. She wanted no complications. None at all. She swiped left.

Erik, 29, property developer. Deep tan, whitened teeth, swept-back hair, no socks in the summer. He looked like he spent his summers in Mykonos and winters in Courchevel. His other photographs showed him jet-skiing on water, kite surfing, standing on the grid at an F1 track somewhere . . . Wait – was that Lando Norris?

What the hell. She swiped right.

'But you hate the Eurotrash vibe,' Freja said in confusion.

'Yeah, but I have a crush on Charles Leclerc and he might be one degree removed from him,' Darcy said, tapping the screen.

'Or he might not be! You're really wasting another of your goes for that vain hope?'

Darcy dropped her phone to the table with a smile and a sigh. 'They're *all* a waste of goes, Frey.'

'Wow, Lars really knocked the stuffing out of you, didn't he?'

'No, he just pulled out the last remaining bit of stuffing. I can already tell you exactly how these guys are going to pan out, assuming they match with me: the vet will be soulful and cute, but not looking for commitment, the arrogant lawyer will be a fuckboy, and Mr Eurotrash will spend longer doing his hair than he spends doing me.'

Freja sat back with a loud laugh, pulling her frizzy blonde hair up into a chaotic bun, before letting it fall free again in a wild mane.

'Tell me I'm wrong,' Darcy grinned.

'Oh God, I wish I could,' Freja chuckled. 'I *wish* I could.'

'Yeah,' Darcy sighed, watching a figure skater spin in a pirouette. 'We've seen this one before. We already know the ending.'

'Maybe – but remember, the fun's in how you get there. And with Christmas coming, you can't stay holed up in the apartment on your own.'

'I wouldn't be on my own if you ever came home!'

'All in good time. The sex is too good, babe.'

Darcy groaned again.

'Don't worry, we'll go down in flames soon enough. But in the meantime, you need to be out in the world and this is the way to do it. These guys will match with you if they've got eyes in their head and a pulse, and you'll have three hot new guys to date before Christmas. You never know, they may even surprise you.'

Darcy picked up her mug and plucked out another marshmallow. 'The only thing that would surprise me, Frey, is if they surprise me. You'll have to forgive me if I don't bother holding my breath.'

Chapter Two

Darcy was draping her coat over the back of her chair when Ida, Otto's secretary, peered around the doorway.

'Ah Darcy, you're back, good. Otto's been asking for you. He says it's urgent.'

'Oh?' Nothing was ever urgent in Otto Borup's world. The head of the fine art department and her thesis advisor, he was a man with a leisured manner who believed that words were often overrated and that as much, if not more, could be conveyed by a well-judged silence. So if Otto said something was urgent, either he was dying or the Royal Academy was on fire.

'Yes. They're all waiting for you in Workroom 3.'

'All?' Darcy felt a shot of alarm that there was to be an audience to whatever this was.

Workroom 3 was where the conservation team were based. As a PhD student and a theoretical academic, Darcy rarely had reason or opportunity to go in there, but she always felt like a child in a sweet shop when she did venture in.

Had she done something wrong? 'Do you know what it's about?'

'I do,' Ida nodded, making no attempt to enlighten her.

'I see . . . Thanks.' With a gulp of trepidation, Darcy headed for the stairs, walking through the corridor where the faculty offices were set. Otto's door was ajar, his desk neatly stacked with paper piles and reference books tabbed with Post-it notes; but she noticed his chair was pushed back at an angle, as if he had risen in a hurry.

Was it her thesis? The committee had approved her hypothesis months ago. Had they changed their minds? *Could* they change their minds?

She walked quickly, with growing dread. The Charlottenborg building, which was the official home of the Royal Academy of Fine Arts, comprised three sides of a square and the workrooms were located on each floor in the central span, the next wing along from here. Long whitewashed spaces, they were usually bright even on the dullest of days thanks to the large graphite-steel windows that ran along either side – but as she pushed on the door into the workroom on the third floor, she saw the black curtains had been drawn so that it was suffused with gloom. Vast tables ran through the centre of the room and workbenches were pushed along each wall. Every surface was piled high with books and papers, a few plaster busts sat on pedestals, canvases were propped on easels and draped with dust sheets. Brushes poked from pots, amber-coloured solutions sat in jars. Stools, chairs, jumpers and bags littered the space, and it smelled of solvents and coffee.

At the far end stood a small group of people clustered around one of the tables. They were standing tightly packed, talking over one another in low voices, but even from here she recognized the redoubtable director of the National Gallery, Margit Kinberg; the Royal Academy's head conservator, Lauge Bekker; and of course, Otto. Even without the presence of the academy director, currently in New York, it was about as senior a gathering as she could imagine and her pace slowed as she approached. This had been the wrong day to choose to run in. She had been anticipating a quiet afternoon in the stacks. What on earth could they possibly want with her here? Had Ida been pulling a prank on her . . . ?

'Ah, Darcy,' Otto said, turning at the sound of her footsteps. He was an elegant man, not tall but very lean, bald, with a close-clipped white beard and watchful blue eyes. He made a point of only ever wearing a sober palette of navy, grey or black; his chunky tortoiseshell-framed glasses were the sole glimpse of personality in his uniform, a snatch of the private man beyond the enigma, for his austere reputation preceded him. He wasn't inclined towards small talk, undue praise or even smiles – but today appeared to be the exception. She felt herself relax a little. He wouldn't smile if this was bad news, surely? Unless . . . pity?

'Thank you for joining us. You know Lauge, of course.'

'Lauge,' Darcy nodded politely.

'Have you met Margit Kinberg?'

'It's a pleasure to meet you,' Darcy said quickly as they shook hands. Kinberg was pale, with a dark bob and glasses; she had a formidable reputation as a straight talker and there was certainly nothing soft and fluffy about her handshake.

'Ms Cotterell, Otto's been bringing me up to speed with your work.' She spoke in English, even though they'd been talking in Danish on her arrival. Everyone spoke English to a high standard here – although Darcy's Danish was impressive too thanks to her Danish mother, who had raised her and her sister as bilingual back home.

'He has?' Darcy looked at Otto with an apprehensive smile, not at all sure why the director of the National Gallery needed to know anything about her PhD thesis – 'Homemakers and Revolutionaries: A Re-examination of Women in the Modern Breakthrough'.

'Have a look at this, Darcy,' Otto said, stepping aside so that she could see a painting set flat upon the table behind him; it had been removed from its frame and an ultraviolet lamp was positioned above it. Her heart beat a little faster, for she recognized the artwork right away – it was *Her Children*, the Johan Trier masterpiece that had been undergoing light restoration ahead of a large retrospective of the artist at the National Gallery in the new year.

Johan Trier was considered the grandfather of the Danish New Masters and Otto had spent the past two years painstakingly negotiating the loans of works from other museums, galleries and private collections to curate this show, the most comprehensive exhibition of Trier's work since his death, almost exactly fifty years ago. The Ministry of Culture wanted it to do for them what the Vermeer tribute had done for Amsterdam's Rijksmuseum a few years earlier.

'Go on – tell me what you see.'

Darcy, seeing how everyone watched her closely, leaned over and peered down at the famous oil. She had seen the painting countless times – it showed a woman standing by the shore, watching as her children waded in the shallows. One hand was perched on her hip, the tip of her chin betraying a watchful gaze over the frothy surf. Her skirt and blouse were pushed back against her body by the strong breeze, the ribbon of her apron flying behind her.

'This is Trier's *Her Children*. One of his most iconic paintings.' It was famous not because of the expert figuring of the children or the tumbling light in the sky, but because in the precise posturing of the woman – her close, watchful stare counterposed with a relaxed patience – he had captured the fierce complexity and intensity of motherhood.

'And what do you know about Trier?'

'Off the top of my head?' Darcy was a little taken aback. Being interrogated on native artists by someone in Kinberg's esteemed position was intimidating, to say the least. 'I know that he was a master draughtsman; he specialized in plein air landscapes, particularly beach scenes later on, although he made his name originally with formal portraits. He was often likened to John Singer Sargent for his renderings of texture in women's fashions and his use of colour. He was especially well known for his strong use of white, and also pink . . . Um, he was very preoccupied with natural light. He was highly influenced by the impressionists and adopted their technique of impasto paint application and rapid brushwork.' She looked down at the oil. To be this close to it, to see it as the artist had, without its frame, was a truly rare privilege. It was a jewel in the crown of Danish art.

Kinberg nodded. 'And now? Tell me what you see.'

Beside her, Otto switched on the lamp and a vivid purple light washed down upon the painting. The image she knew so well remained visible but beyond it, she also saw a face – a woman's face – staring back at her.

She gasped and pulled back with surprise. Seeing the similarly excited looks from the rest of the group, she guessed they had all had exactly the same response. She looked back down again, as if unable to trust her own eyes, but there it was once more – the head and shoulders portrait of a young woman. The colours and details were indistinct, as if the image was being seen through a muddied window, but even with that, there was clear accomplishment in the tilt of the woman's head and the directness of her gaze.

'Oh!' she breathed. 'She's beautiful.'

'Yes, she is,' Margit Kinberg nodded, looking down at the portrait too. 'It was quite a surprise to find her there.'

'. . . You never knew before?' Darcy asked.

'The painting hasn't been touched since '59, when a plumbing leak altered the humidity and affected some of the original paint,' Lauge Bekker said, breaking his silence. 'The remedial work was done but there were no further explorations and the painting's been hanging in a stabilized environment ever since, so there was no need to look. It only came in for a light clean ahead of the retrospective.'

Darcy was no conservator, but she knew ultraviolet light, although first used in fine art conservation from the early 1930s, hadn't become commonplace until the 1980s.

She also immediately understood the importance of the discovery. Johan Trier was Denmark's pre-eminent painter of the twentieth century; his former home was a tourist attraction in its own right and his brand was one of the country's greatest exports. He had come to prominence in the 1920s and many of his paintings were recognizable the world over.

'What a shame he overpainted this,' she deplored, scrutinizing the ghostly image again. Many painters, obsessed with notions of their 'legacy', painted over what they considered to be inferior or lesser pieces.

'Well, that's what's so exciting about this,' Margit said with a direct look. 'He didn't. The portrait is painted on the *reverse* of the board. It's not beneath *Her Children*, it's on the back of it.'

'Two paintings in one?'

'Yes,' Lauge said. 'Unfortunately, initial investigation is suggesting the backing is made up of several sheets of board, which have been glued on –'

Glued? Darcy winced. Otto and Margit too.

'– Meaning the portrait is sandwiched between the board layers.'

16

'Is it reachable?' Darcy asked.

'That is certainly the great hope,' Lauge Bekker said. 'But it's going to be painstaking work trying to remove it. Clearly we cannot risk any potential damage to *Her Children* and if it is deemed too risky, we'll stop. If we have to choose between the two, then of course we'll choose the bird in hand.'

'Of course,' Darcy nodded, staring still at the ghostly outline of the woman shimmering beneath the paint. *Her Children* was a flagship painting, appearing on postcards in the Academy's gift shop, but for this portrait to remain trapped – hidden – under boards, would be such a shame too. There was something special about this woman; Darcy could feel it somehow, even though she could barely see her. 'How long will it take to try to remove the backing?'

'Ordinarily we'd be looking at a couple of months but with the retrospective coming up in the new year, we're under extraordinary pressure to move more quickly.' From the way Lauge's eyes darted over to Kinberg, Darcy sensed tension between the two on the matter.

'We're deciding on a course of optimism,' Margit said firmly. 'It's in everyone's best interests to work towards the best-case scenario: unveiling a newly discovered Johan Trier masterpiece at the retrospective.'

'Margit . . .' Lauge frowned.

'I know. It might not happen,' she said, looking back at him sternly. 'But we will certainly reach for it. We're going to move as quickly as we can on *all* fronts.'

She turned the stare onto Darcy. 'We're making this a cross-organizational project. While Lauge's team here work to release the board backings, the gallery's conservation preparators will be commissioned to design and build a double-sided exhibition mount. We must have a way to display both paintings at once.'

'Yes.' Darcy waited with a gathering sense of anticipation to learn what her role would be in all of this. Clearly she hadn't been called in simply to admire the discovery.

'Which brings us to you, Darcy,' Otto said, interjecting smoothly as if he could read her thoughts. 'You won't have met Ebbe Busk, our chief researcher – she's on maternity leave until mid-March.'

'I know the name.'

'We've got someone covering for her on a part-time basis but they're already fully occupied with prepping for the retrospective. We've put our heads together trying to think who would be next best qualified, as well as available at such short notice, and I thought of you.'

Darcy blinked. 'Otto, I'm incredibly honoured, but I'm not employed by the Academy. From an insurance perspective—'

'You won't be in direct contact with the painting. And given that you are studying for a professorship and you have a special interest in the women artists of the period, you are best placed to take the reins on this.'

'Is that woman an artist, then?' Darcy asked, glancing at the portrait again.

'Probably not, but the fact she was painted by the greatest artist of the day means she's no unknown either. Patrons and artists move in interconnecting circles. I'm sure she's only a step removed.'

Darcy swallowed, knowing exactly what was being asked of her here – and it was no small task. 'But what about my thesis? My next deadline is—'

'Negotiable. I'm your advisor. I'm happy to do the paperwork to push everything back a little, given these extraordinary circumstances.'

Margit cleared her throat. 'Not to mention, this could help

to boost your profile in the sector. Otto tells me you have already rediscovered a long-lost artist from the Skagen group?'

'Yes, Katje Lange.'

'Katje Lange, that's right,' Margit nodded. 'Posterity recorded her as a farm labourer, I understand?'

Darcy nodded. Her entire master's dissertation had hung upon proving that a small portfolio discovered in a farmhouse loft on the northern coast had been created by Katje's hand and not her more famous husband's, as had been the original presumption.

'Her name would have slipped into obscurity but for your research putting her back on the map,' Margit said pointedly.

'And that's what you want me to do here? Identify this woman, find her name?'

'Find her name – and then dig out everything you can on her, Darcy. If we're unveiling a hitherto unknown Johan Trier to the world, then we'll need to work up a thorough biography. The coverage will be global.'

Darcy swallowed. On the one hand, this was a dream opportunity; on the other, with only a month till Christmas and five weeks till the retrospective, it was a giant headache.

'At a first look, does the woman in the portrait look familiar to you?' Otto asked her.

Darcy hesitated as she was put on the spot. She was surrounded by some of the most senior figures in the Danish fine art establishment and they wanted *her* expertise? There had certainly been no obvious, immediate recognition for her of the subject.

'No . . . But I could certainly tell you who she isn't,' she said. Her thesis was focused on the lesser-known women artists contemporary to Trier, and off the bat, Darcy knew the woman in this painting wasn't any of them. 'She's not Anna Felsing,

Ingrid Hjort or Charlotta Juhl. Not Elsa Tobiassen, Dorrit Knudsen or Grete Caspersen. But it's a very indistinct image at the moment. I would really need to get a higher-res version in order to study her properly . . .'

Otto nodded. 'The imaging team is already on it.'

'Okay.' But Darcy was sceptical about the likelihood of it revealing much. How were they supposed to sharpen up clarity until the backings came off? Without a clear view of the painting, it was impossible to tell even this woman's hair or eye colour. She was little more than a silhouette, a shadow from the past. How was Darcy supposed to find her when there had never been any record of this portrait even existing?

Margit must have read her hesitation because she cleared her throat, bringing attention back to her again. 'Darcy, I appreciate that you are only a term into your residency at the Academy and your focus is on your PhD work. But I hope you understand the significance of this find – not only to the retrospective but to Danish culture in general.'

'Of course. It's an incredible opportunity. I feel honoured to be asked to be a part of it.'

'Good.'

Darcy looked down again at the painting. The woman quivered like a mirage until Otto switched off the lamp and she was eclipsed once more, falling back into the depths.

The black curtains were drawn back, daylight falling in with alacrity.

'Okay, well, now that we're all up to speed, let's get to work,' Margit said, checking her watch. 'I've got a press conference announcing the find in fifteen minutes, so brief your departments to direct all enquiries to the press team if you get any calls.'

Darcy watched everyone scatter, the timer already ticking.

'Darcy, I've got some calls to make,' Otto said. 'But come to my office in an hour and we can talk through first steps?'

'Sure.'

She watched him walk calmly across the workroom floor back to his office; the conservators pulling on their white gloves and lifting the Trier canvas with a care reserved for carrying injured fairies. Her own role was clear. She had one thing and one thing alone to do: identify a random woman who had lived a century earlier.

Give her a name. Give her a life.

Just find a ghost.

Chapter Three

Otto was still on the phone when Darcy knocked on his door sixty minutes later, but he beckoned her in and she took a seat opposite him, listening to him 'mm' and 'mm-hmm' down the line as someone else did all the talking.

A colour printout of the portrait lay on his desk and he reached over, handing it to her to study as the one-sided conversation continued.

Darcy stared at the image, trying not to feel dismay at the minimal uplift in clarity. The woman's long hair was, unusually, not worn up in the fashion of the day, but seemed to be simply pulled back; her dress was high-necked and modest, not a society gown; a simple necklace gleamed at her throat. And it was impossible to read actual colours under the ultraviolet light. She couldn't tell if the woman had black hair or brown; blue eyes or green or hazel. Normal identifying characteristics weren't available to her and she was going to have to do this blind. No name. No face. And while she was experienced enough to know that if this woman had been painted by one of the country's greatest painters, then there would be some sort of record of it somewhere, it was nonetheless almost a hundred years old. If the portrait had been hidden for all that time – if no one else had known it existed, even – what supporting evidence might have been destroyed or lost in the interim?

It was another moment before she realized Otto had finished his call and was watching her. Was her concern evident?

'How are you feeling?' he asked.

'. . . Daunted.' It pained her to give a negative answer, but her area of expertise was lost female artists, not their famous male counterparts.

'Good. That's the appropriate response,' he nodded. 'There's no point in pretending it will be easy.' He reached for the top file on his stack and handed it to her. 'This is the standard bio we have on file for Trier. I assume you'll be starting your search through him?'

'I'll have to,' Darcy agreed. 'He's the only fixed point at the moment.' She scanned the material. 'Born 1895 in Aalborg; died 1974 in Paris, aged seventy-nine. Never married, no known children . . .'

'That list shows his complete works – or rather, his *known* works – in chronological order.'

'Okay. It says *Her Children* was painted and sold in August 1922, so he would have been . . .' Darcy quickly did the maths. 'He was twenty-seven when he painted it. Still pretty early on in his career.' She looked up at Otto. 'Logic would dictate that the portrait was painted first, before *Children*. Trier must have rejected it, turned the board over and then produced *Children*.'

'I agree. Which gives us a fixed end date – the portrait was painted before August 1922.'

'Great. So then, we've got our first fact,' Darcy mused. 'And would you agree that if the portrait couldn't have been painted after 1922, it's also unlikely to have been painted very long before that? Artists are invariably broke or tight. I doubt he'd have let the board go to waste for years and years, taking up space in the studio. It was probably painted no more than a few years before *Children*.'

'We can't be as certain of that, but yes, it's more than likely. You should at least start with that narrow scope and widen it if nothing yields from those dates.'

'Okay. Well, I assume Margit Kinberg's involvement means I'm well placed to gain access to the National Gallery's archives?'

'The National Gallery?'

'Yes – they must hold extensive material on Trier.'

'They will, but actually, there's somewhere better. Have you heard of the Madsen Foundation?'

'No.'

'Bertram Madsen was Trier's patron back in the day; a rich industrialist. He gave Trier his big break. His daughter was a noted society beauty and he commissioned numerous portraits of his family for their many houses. He introduced Trier to all the great and good here and put him on the map – until they had a falling out, over *Her Children* no less.'

'What kind of falling out?'

'As patron, Madsen had first refusal on all his work. He had set up a studio for Trier at his summer house in Hornbaek, on the coast, and when Madsen saw an early draft of *Her Children*, he wanted it for the drawing room of his new mansion on Toldbodgade.'

'I sense a *but*.'

'But Trier sold it to a German tourist who was passing by the Hornbaek house – admiring the garden, of all things. Supposedly they got talking and by the time Madsen knew otherwise, *Her Children* was already across the border and in a private collection in Munich. It remained out of the country for the next thirty years.'

Darcy sat back, intrigued. 'I never knew any of this.'

Otto shrugged. 'It ended Madsen's patronage at a stroke and things quickly soured for Trier here. The upper class closed ranks at what was seen as his betrayal. No more profitable society portraits were commissioned and he eventually ended up moving full time to France, where he lived between Paris and Languedoc.'

Darcy bit her lip. 'It seems an extraordinarily short-sighted decision, selling *Children* to a random tourist.'

'He must have made him an exceptional offer. Artists aren't usually known for their long-term financial planning.' Otto shrugged. 'But perhaps Trier was also tiring of being Madsen's puppet. Portraits were his cash cow but it was clear from everything he did afterwards that his heart lay with plein air landscapes. *Her Children* was his key out of those golden handcuffs, whether he had intended it or not.'

'It sounds very bitter. Will they want to help out now? Especially when it concerns the painting that caused the split in the first place?'

'Everything's been long since forgiven. There was a rapprochement of sorts, albeit many years later. It was in the sixties, I believe. Bertram Madsen was long dead by then, but the eldest son, Frederik – I think seeing rising prices for Trier's work on the international market – established an art foundation. They built a gallery on Stockholmsgade and have spent the past fifty years buying every Trier they can get their hands on. It's a vanity project, I suppose: they were the original patrons, and with Trier now held in such high esteem in the Danish canon, they want that connection to be maintained. They're the self-appointed gatekeepers of the Trier legacy once more.'

'So they hold most of his source material, then? Not the National Gallery?'

'Yes. They've got a very good archivist, Viggo Rask. He's

the man to see. I've put a call in already. He's expecting you there tomorrow.'

'Wow. Thanks.'

'Time is against us,' Otto said simply.

Darcy looked again at the printout of the portrait. Her eye kept falling to an indistinct shape on the woman's left shoulder. 'What do you think that is?'

Otto reached for the sheet and studied it too.

'Hmm . . . Possibly a fox stole? They were fashionable at the time.'

Darcy grimaced. The shape was rounded. 'So that would be its head?'

He shrugged. 'They kept everything on back then: paws, head—'

'Ugh, please don't.'

'Different times, Darcy.' He watched as she slipped the printout into the Trier file and went to hand it back to him. 'You can keep that, it's for you.'

'Thanks. Well, I guess I'd better make a start, then—' She started to get up but he shook his head.

'Before you go, there's something else. Margit's hosting an event tonight at the National. I appreciate it's short notice, but you really should attend now you're on this special project. Do you have plans?'

She hesitated. Erik the Property Developer had wasted no time in being first off the starting blocks and had asked her out tonight; he had to go to Dubai on business on Thursday and wanted to meet her before he left. '. . . Nothing firm.'

'Good. It's a private Patrons and Friends benefit – just drinks, but it will be a useful networking opportunity. Some of the executive team from the Madsen Foundation will be there, so it's a good opportunity to show your face.'

'Okay.' She began to move again, but once more Otto shook his head.

'One more thing. You should be aware of the political landscape.'

She frowned. 'What do you mean?'

'Things will appear friendlier than they actually are. Everyone will be all smiles tonight, but you should know there's underlying friction. In any difficult economic climate, arts funding is always the first to be slashed, and the Ministry of Culture keeps announcing budget cuts. Margit's under pressure to raise funds however she can.'

'Hence the drinks party.'

'Exactly. It keeps the benefactors sweet. But of course, the easiest and most effective way to raise a large sum of cash quickly is to sell assets, and Margit is under increasing pressure to compensate for the cuts in her budget. The Madsen Foundation is circling her.'

Darcy's mouth opened a little as she realized where he was heading with this. 'She'd sell them *Her Children*?'

'Not if there's breath in her body – so she says.'

'Well thank God. It's a national treasure. It belongs to the Danish people.'

'On that we all agree. But the Madsen Foundation sees anything and everything to do with Johan Trier as theirs, and this discovery of a new painting is really going to get their blood up.' He inhaled slowly. 'They've worked closely with us on the retrospective, providing access to their collection, but don't think it's out of the goodness of their hearts. The parent company, Madsen Holdings, is preparing to float on the stock exchange in the new year, and they want whatever good publicity they can get to boost their list price. When you're dealing with them, just remember that self-interest lies

27

at the heart of everything they do. Ostensibly we're all on the same side, but that doesn't mean we're on the same team. So tread carefully, and watch what you say. Never forget we have something they want.'

'God,' she muttered. 'I had no idea it was all so cut-throat.'

'The fine art world is a sixty-eight-billion-dollar market. It's not just pretty pictures and sipping on champagne. It's big business.'

'Noted.' Suddenly tonight's drinks reception seemed less appealing. 'Talking of sipping champagne, what's the form later? Can I bring a plus-one?' She didn't relish the prospect of walking in on her own. Perhaps this could be a good setting for a first date, with the safety of a hundred strangers all around them.

'Best not. These events can be conservative. An old-money crowd. You know the type.'

She didn't – not personally – but he clearly meant they were the sort that bankrolled retrospectives, bequeathed gifts to museums and had their own boxes at the opera house. Flirty first dates between Raya matches were not it.

'We're only there to work, not have a good time.'

'Got it.' She got up at last and headed for the door.

'And, Darcy – I take it you have a cocktail dress?' Otto asked behind her, no doubt privately aghast at her mismatched running kit.

'Of course,' she lied.

'Good. I'll email you the details,' he murmured, releasing her fully, and she rolled her eyes as she stepped into the corridor. She had nothing fancier to wear than a black tube dress that was distinctly more clubbing than cocktails. She would need to go out later and buy something suitable. It was another job to add to her to-do list, which was growing longer by the minute – and she still had a seminar to teach at four. She walked back down the corridor, past the faculty offices, the squeak of her trainers on the floor at a distinctly faster tempo than on the way in.

Chapter Four

'Tonight's not going to be possible, sorry. I have a work thing I can't get out of.'

She checked the time. Seven twenty? The day had run away from her and it showed no sign of slowing down yet.

'Do academics have evening work things? Surely the libraries are closed?'

'Ha-ha. I've actually got to attend a fancy drinks reception.'

Did she have her lip liner in her bag? she wondered, rifling through the side pockets.

'Skip it. Live a little.'

'Can't. Important people I have to meet for a special project I'm working on.'

'How about afterwards?'

'No idea when I'll be out.'

She stared at her fingernails: clean, but unshaped and matt. There'd been no time for a manicure.

'I've been to my fair share of fancy work events. They don't exactly kick off. You'll be done by ten. We could still meet for a drink after.'

'I'm not sure. Maybe.'

'Do you always play so hard to get?'

She sighed. She didn't have time for a full-blown conversation right now.

'No, just wary of making plans I can't keep.'

'*I'm prepared to take the risk of a no-show . . . Besides, you'll be all dressed up, won't you? Shame to waste that effort on people you work with.*'

She smiled. Female gaze.

'*Well, that is true.*'

She stared at her reflection in the dressing-room mirror. Like her old clubbing dress, this one was black and strapless – but it was cut from velvet, not jersey, and had an ivory satin bandeau across the top. It didn't show too much boob or back, but how short was too short? she wondered, feeling the skater's hem graze her fingertips. It was expensive – far more than she wanted to spend on a last-minute purchase for work – and she wondered if Freja would go halves on it with her. Plus, if they shared the dress between them, she could get some new shoes too.

'*Where's the party?*'

'*At the National Gallery.*'

'*That is fancy. How will I recognize you? What will you be wearing?*'

She deliberated a moment, then took a photo of her reflection. '*This.*'

'*Wow!*'

'*Thanks.*'

'*I'll definitely be waiting for you outside.*'

'*No. I'm working. If I'm late . . .*'

'*Then I'll keep waiting, don't worry about it. Gtg but I'll see you later.*'

He clicked off before she could argue out of it.

Darcey stared at the text exchange. She'd been on the app for all of half a day and already she had a date. Erik was determined, she'd give him that. Was that what made him so successful? He was decisive, a go-getter; she'd messaged to say she couldn't see him and somehow he'd converted it into a win. He'd outpaced his competition by a country mile.

She clicked on Aksel the Vet's latest message. He'd responded quite soon after Erik, but whereas the property developer had launched straight into action, Aksel had struck up conversation. They'd had a brief text exchange before her seminar as she waited for her students to arrive – nothing exciting and certainly not flirty, just the sort of small talk she always hated at dinner parties. Information-gathering exercises rather than genuine connections.

'Have you ever visited South America?'

Darcy rolled her eyes, feeling herself prickle at the innocuous question. She resented this charade of courtesy, pretending to care about one another's lives when invariably they both knew things between them would end the same way: once he'd got what he wanted he'd either cheat, ghost her or tell her he wasn't ready for something serious. Well, neither was she. This project was going to take all her focus in the coming weeks and she didn't have time to waste on chasing a fairy-tale myth. She would play the men at their own game: take what she needed and reserve her emotional energy for work alone.

She typed quickly.

'Trekked Patagonia in my gap year. Machu Picchu too. Amazing. Would love to go back.'

That was a lie. It was a matter of once and done, as far as she was concerned. There were too many other places to see in the world to spend time retracing her own steps, but if it moved them along . . . Besides, men said what they thought women wanted to hear all the time.

'I was thinking of visiting Stockholm in the next few weeks. Any recommendations?'

It was the perfect cue for him to offer to show her around

himself. A dirty weekend away with a hot vet with soulful eyes instead of her ex would be all the closure she needed.

Max the Lawyer hadn't responded. Was he too busy even to match, or was she just not his type? She prickled at the thought of being overlooked by him. There was no doubt he could have his pick –

She put the phone down, forcing herself not to dwell on the thoughts of a man she had never even met. Right now, he didn't know she existed.

She looked back at her reflection with a sigh. Did she look appropriate for tonight's grandees? Sexy enough for Erik? It would have to be one or the other; she couldn't oblige both. She twisted her hair up into a loose chignon and stood on tiptoe. It definitely needed heels.

She texted her flatmate.

'Want to go halves on this? You'll need something fancy if Loverboy's going to be taking you out.'

Freja's response was almost instantaneous. *'Love it! Done!'*

Time!

She caught herself losing track again and unzipped the dress, throwing her clothes back on. The store would be closing soon and the shoe department was on the next floor up and the drinks reception was starting in ten minutes . . .

'Shit-shit-shit,' she hissed to herself, trying to get her arm through the inside-out sleeve of her jumper. She'd have to do her make-up and get changed in the toilets; a cab would only take ten minutes from here, so that should mean she'd arrive only fashionably late. And by then, hopefully, after Otto and anyone else she might know had arrived there.

A notification sounded, and she glanced at her phone as she threw the dress over her shoulder and darted out of the changing room.

'Nightcap tonight?'

It was from Max the Lawyer. Talk of the devil!

She stopped dead in her tracks, feeling a jolt of euphoria that he had liked what he saw on her profile after all. Darcy had to admit, Freja had done a sterling job of pulling together the most flattering photos of her.

Darcy read the two words swimming before her. It was hardly a seduction, more of a proposition. No 'Have you been to South America?' from him; not even the 'Hello' Erik had managed, and she remembered the arrogance she'd read in his eyes. That air of self-importance. He was playing true to the form set up in his bio. No games here, at least.

Still, it felt nice to have a little win, and she sent back her own two-word reply – *'Busy, sorry'* – before sliding the phone back into her bag with a sense of satisfaction and heading for the stairs.

Her new heels clicked on the limestone floor as she walked through the old galleries, in stark counterpoint to this afternoon's hurried, rubbery squeak. She was a different creature entirely now, her work clothes stuffed into the backpack she had handed over in the cloakroom, her limbs bare, long hair pulled back in a bun instead of a ponytail, a red lip replacing flushed cheeks.

Men in dinner jackets walked past, their eyes travelling over her in silent appraisal as they spoke in low voices. It was well past eight – significantly later than she had hoped, but getting an Uber had proved tricky. The entire city was out tonight, it appeared, the first Christmas parties beginning to swing.

She walked through the Street of Sculptures, a contemporary glass-framed space that connected the original eighteenth-century gallery building to the uber-modern extension at the back. The reception was being held in the double-height events area, set down below a dramatic sweep of steps. It was like being in a Greek temple, everything white, vaulted and pristine, and she stood for a moment, taking in the scene playing out before her: waiters waltzing through the crowd with trays of flutes, guest mingling with apparent ease. The sense of money in the room was distinctive, like a nectar she could taste, a weight like gold. A string quartet was playing in front of the vast glass wall and for a moment Darcy wondered how this scene looked from the outside, as passers-by stared in from the park. Did *she* look like she fit in here? Could anyone tell this was a brand-new dress and that her shoes still had their stickers on the soles?

She saw Margit Kinberg in conversation with a group of men nearby but Darcy didn't feel sufficiently well acquainted with her to walk up to her. She scanned the room, trying not to show her growing alarm that she didn't recognize anyone, then felt herself sink with relief as she found Otto by the steps. His bald head was distinctive even in a room full of seventy-year-olds. Carefully, she picked her way down the stairs and through the crowd towards him. He was standing with a grey-haired woman in a gold jacquard suit and a portly man in glasses.

'Good evening,' Darcy said, catching his eye as she approached, but it seemed to take him a moment before he registered her.

'Darcy,' he said with surprise. 'I was beginning to wonder if I'd missed you.'

'Trouble getting a taxi,' she smiled.

'. . . Have you met Mr and Mrs Albert Salling?'

Salling? She recognized the name from a brass plaque in the university buildings.

Otto addressed his companions. 'Darcy Cotterell is one of our PhD students, on secondment for a year from the Courtauld in London. We're very lucky to have her in the department. Formidable researcher. She's a great asset to the team.'

'PhD, eh?' Albert Salling said, taking her hand and holding it lightly. 'Soon to be Professor Cotterell, then?'

'That's the plan, although I've a way to go yet.'

'What is your field of study?' Mrs Salling asked. There was a sapphire bracelet dangling from her skinny wrist.

'Well, I've a particular interest in re-examining the output of female artists at the turn of the last century. So many were just ignored or allowed to fall into obsolescence. I'm trying to shine a light into those dark corners.'

'How very current.'

Otto nodded. 'Darcy is especially interested in the contradictions inherent in Danish art at that time when the Modern Breakthrough was espousing the rights of women – but it was men talking on their behalf.'

'Well,' Mrs Salling laughed lightly. 'That's certainly always been the case in our family.'

'She has also been appointed as the lead researcher for the new Trier portrait,' Otto said smoothly. 'I'm sure you've heard about the discovery of the painting – on the B-side of *Her Children*, if you will?'

'Indeed. Who could have missed it?' Mr Salling replied. 'It turned tonight into a very hot ticket. Will we be hearing more about it this evening? Margit looks like the cat that got the cream.'

'She does, doesn't she?' Otto agreed. 'But no, there's really nothing more to see or tell at this point. The conservation team have got their work cut out trying to free the portrait.'

'Have you had any luck yet?' Mr Salling asked Darcy.

'Well, today was only Day One—'

'Ah, Otto – there you are.' A manicured hand rested on Otto's shoulder as Margit Kinberg herself came to join them, her cool smile rising like a moon behind him. 'Albert. Valerie. How are you?'

Kisses on cheeks were exchanged with the Sallings. Old friends. Warm smiles. Otto swapped a glance with Darcy, as if reminding her of their conversation earlier.

'*Wonderful* news on the discovery,' Valerie Salling enthused.

'Isn't it? We're delighted.'

'I'm sure. What a thrill!'

Darcy smiled. They all sounded like proud grandparents.

'We shall definitely have to make sure we're back from the Bahamas for the opening night now,' Albert Salling said. 'What more do you know about it?'

Darcy felt her smile become fixed as the conversation retraced its steps. This was going to be a long evening. A waiter came up, seeing she had no drink, and she took a glass gratefully, resisting the urge to down it. The smile on Otto's face had become fixed too and she wondered how many of these he had to attend, schmoozing the great and the good in the pursuit of donations and sponsorships. This was the reality, though – art had always been a rich man's passion, and the deep pockets of people like the Sallings were an essential part of the scene.

Their small group opened up again as another unit of people wandered over to them and Otto was stirred from his inertia.

'Helle,' he said, drawing himself up. 'The very person I hoped to see tonight. I have here the researcher I was telling you about, Darcy Cotterell. Darcy, this is Helle Foss – COO at the Madsen Foundation.'

'A pleasure,' Darcy said quickly, shaking hands with a diminutive woman in grey silk and pearls.

There was a pause before Helle Foss replied, 'You're very young.'

'Lively brain, Helle,' Otto said smoothly. 'She makes connections quickly, researches thoroughly. Certainly one of the best minds I've come across.'

Darcy tried to mask her surprise. If that was true, it was the first she'd heard of it from him.

'Indeed. Well, there's a lot resting on your lively brain, Ms Cotterell.'

Margit and the Sallings were deep in conversation about the Venice Biennale, but Darcy saw Margit's head turn ever so slightly in their direction and knew she wasn't oblivious to the exchange.

Darcy smiled. 'I feel honoured to have been tasked with such a great responsibility. I'm taking it very seriously.'

'As you should. You're English?'

She was taken aback by the older woman's aloof manner. 'Yes.'

'You speak Danish very well.' Helle Foss blinked slowly, scrutinizing her through beady eyes. Darcy couldn't tell whether the woman didn't like her because she was foreign or because she was dressed up. Did it undermine her professional credentials to look attractive too? Should she have covered her shoulders? Worn a longer skirt?

'Thank you. My mother's from here so we grew up bilingual, and of course it meant I was exposed to Danish art and culture from a very young age. It's why I chose to pursue my PhD here.'

'I see. Well, it's reassuring to know that you have some emotional investment in the project.'

'I do.'

'And can you do it? Can you identify her?'

38

'Yes, if I have access to the archives I need. Johan Trier is the key figure to investigate at this stage.'

'Then the Madsen Foundation is entirely at your disposal. Have you met Viggo?'

'Not ye—'

'Rask!' Foss tossed the call over her shoulder, and a man standing in the next group along turned. He was Darcy's height, five foot six, with a thick grey beard, and unlike almost every other person in the room, he had genuinely friendly eyes.

Instinctively, Darcy smiled, but as Rask shuffled towards them, her gaze caught on another man who had been standing beside him. He was close to her own age – far closer than anyone else here – and so handsome, it came as a shock. Her smile died on her lips as their eyes locked.

Was that . . . ?

'Good evening,' said Viggo Rask, coming to a stop in front of Darcy and drawing her attention away. He had a slight stoop, and was looking at her with open curiosity.

'Viggo, this is the young academic who will be leading the research into the identity of the woman in the Trier portrait,' Helle Foss said.

'Darcy Cotterell,' Darcy said, holding out her hand. She was acutely aware of the younger man's gaze still upon her.

'A pleasure to meet you, Professor.'

'Oh, I'm not a professor – not yet,' she said quickly, her eyes flitting in Otto's direction. He didn't stir.

'Otto called me earlier. I understand we're going to be seeing quite a lot of one another, you and I, in the coming weeks.'

'Yes, it appears so.'

'Viggo was the apprentice to the archivist who personally catalogued all our artefacts when the Foundation was established

39

in 1961,' Foss said. 'Whatever you are looking for, he can find it for you.'

Darcy smiled and nodded. She just wished she knew what she was looking for. 'Brilliant, thank you. I thought I'd make a start with you tomorrow?'

'I'm there from seven,' Viggo replied.

'Seven? Wow, okay.' Darcy still slept like a teenager and mornings were merciless to her. Getting to the library for nine felt like an accomplishment.

'Once you get to my age, sleep becomes more a succession of quiet interludes than full-blown oblivion,' he said, seeming to read her mind.

Darcy smiled, feeling relieved that he, not the formidable Foss, would be her principal point of contact. She looked up again to find the younger man still openly staring as his group carried on their conversation around him. She felt a hard buzz of static as their eyes met again across the room, excitement rippling through her at this unexpected flirtation. It was the last thing she had been expecting from this evening. Was she blushing? She wasn't used to such obvious interest.

Reluctantly, she faced her companions again, reminding herself she was here to work.

'How's Lauge getting on?' Viggo was asking.

'They've made a start.' Otto shrugged. 'He's not thrilled by the time pressures. You know Lauge.'

'Indeed I do,' Viggo chuckled. 'I've seen how long it takes that man to finish a beer.'

Everyone chuckled with him, even Darcy, though her mind was not remotely on the conservation.

'And where are you intending to start your investigations, Miss Cotterell?' Viggo asked, turning his attention to her again.

'Well, until we can capture a higher-resolution image of the portrait and take a clearer look at her face, I think my time is best spent investigating Trier in the few years before *Her Children* – identifying his social circle, his movements, that sort of thing.'

'We have a great many of his letters and diaries, which may prove helpful – preparatory sketches and the like.'

'That sounds ideal. I can't wait to get started. It's going to be a fascinating challenge,' she said, glancing back in the direction of the handsome stranger – but he had gone.

Disappointment filled her at his sudden, glaring absence, and she scanned the room in search of him. The spark of excitement he had brought to the evening had lifted her momentarily, but now she found herself crashing back down to earth.

'I assume there have been no similarly exciting new discoveries at the Madsen Collection?' Otto was asking Helle.

'Any more hidden paintings, you mean? Sadly not. We're putting them all under the scanner to double check, but what are the chances?'

'Well, if he did it once, why not again?' Otto said in a reasonable tone, but Darcy caught the look on his face as he spoke and recognized the rivalry that flowed between them.

The conversation drifted onto other topics and Darcy found herself discussing the record recently set at Christie's for a pair of Canalettos and the shift in the general art market from public auctions to private sales. People drifted in and out of their bubble, names exchanged and pleasantries passed, and the minutes began to slide past. Her glass was regularly refreshed, though she took only the barest of sips. When Viggo unapologetically checked the time on his old wristwatch, she was surprised to see it was almost ten.

'Well, it's time for this old man to get to his bed. It's been a pleasure, all,' he said to the group collectively, taking his leave. 'And I'll see you tomorrow, Ms Cotterell.'

'Darcy, please.'

'Darcy,' he nodded.

She watched him go, feeling relief that she'd got through the evening successfully. Small talk wasn't her forte; she wasn't a political player. She liked a small social circle and meaningful interaction, but work demands increasingly meant that sometimes she had to step out of her comfort zone – as tonight.

'I should head off too. I need a clear head for hitting the ground running tomorrow,' she said to Otto, and he nodded his approval of her departure. She looked at Helle Foss. 'It's been a pleasure meeting you.'

'Ms Cotterell,' Foss nodded.

'As you're going to be at the Madsen for the rest of the week, let's regroup in my office on Monday, our usual time,' Otto said. This meant nine thirty, over coffee. He took his coffee, like his art, very seriously and wouldn't dream of drinking from the vending machine. It was Ida who had given Darcy the details of his favourite coffee shop and how he liked it, and they now had a routine in which she would bring their coffees on the way in to the meeting.

'Great.' She was aware of eyes upon her as she ascended the steps and headed towards the Sculpture Street. The reception was beginning to break up, and a few people were already wandering around the statues as they slowly meandered towards the exit.

'Darcy Cotterell.'

Turning her head in surprise, she saw the handsome stranger sitting on one of the benches between the statues. He put his phone away and got up, walking towards her with the same steady expression he'd worn downstairs.

'Yes.' She swallowed, trying not to betray the effect he had on her as he approached. It was like waiting for a tiger to come out from the trees, his confidence seeming to strip her of hers. 'Have we met?' she asked, seeing how he slipped his hand into his trouser pocket. His suit was expensive; well cut, and he moved with a self-assured manner. Was he another rich patron? Used to owning everything he wanted?

'Not yet.' He stopped in front of her. Even though she wore heels, he was several inches taller than her. 'You were very popular this evening.'

'I wouldn't have said so,' she demurred.

'I would. These things are usually like death. You brought the average age down by at least twenty years.'

'As did you.' He couldn't be more than a few years older than her.

He shrugged, holding the eye contact, and she felt the tension between them tighten. On the one hand, it felt odd that they were talking as though they were picking up a conversation that had been interrupted. On the other, it didn't feel strange at all. 'Leaving?'

'Yes.' But she wished she wasn't.

'I'll walk you out.'

She wished he wouldn't. Suddenly she wanted to stay.

'. . . So what brought you here this evening?' she asked as they fell into step, his hand resting lightly on the small of her back so that a blush of goosebumps bloomed over her arms.

'Business.'

She swallowed. There was always a distinction to be made between those who did business and those who merely worked. 'And what is it you do?'

There was a pause. 'I push paper around at Madsen Holdings.'

She glanced at him in surprise, catching an excellent view

43

of his profile. His bone structure was admirable – heavy dark brows, hooded blue eyes, a fleshy mouth. But for his pale skin and dirty blond hair, he could have been Greek.

'Oh! I was just talking to—'

'Helle and Viggo. Yes, I saw.' A smirk twitched on his lips. 'I'm afraid she hates you.'

Darcy was shocked at his bluntness. 'Why would you say that?'

'Because you're young and beautiful and clever, and she's only ever been one of those things.'

'Young?'

'No, clever.' He caught her eye with a sly look. 'I swear she was born sixty years old.'

Darcy gave a sudden laugh and he looked pleased by it.

'Anyway, she'll get over it. She'll have to, seeing as you're going to be a regular visitor now.'

She frowned, hating being on the back foot like this. 'How is it you know so much about me?'

They were walking through the old galleries now: dark-painted rooms with glass roofs, the historic masterpieces moodily lit, uniformed security guards standing at their posts. Her heels tapped on the stone floor, steady and regular.

'Like I said, you were popular this evening. Everyone's talking about the new find and that's put you in the spotlight. All eyes are on you. Daunted?'

She swallowed. 'Yes.'

She hadn't intended to be honest; the admission had just fallen from her, and she felt the pressure of his hand increase on her back slightly. 'You'll do it.'

For reasons she couldn't explain, his confidence seemed to reassure her.

They walked in silence for several moments and she

wondered what was coming next. Because if he led her straight to his car, she would get into it. There was something about him that tore down her usual reserves. A current that ran between them, threatening to pull her feet out from under her.

She didn't believe in love at first sight, but lust . . . That she could go with.

Her heart began to pound in anticipation of his next move. He had clearly been waiting for her, and his body language broadcast the illusion that they were together. They walked over to the cloakroom desk and she handed over her ticket. While the attendant disappeared to get her coat and backpack, she turned to look straight at him, only to find he was already watching her.

'Are you going to tell me your name?'

'Do I need to?' He blinked slowly. 'When you already know.'

She felt the heat come into her cheeks as confirmation was given. So it was him. She hadn't been entirely sure. She looked back at him, recognizing that cocksure stare that had antagonized her on screen. She had sensed arrogance and it had riled her, and yet, in his presence, it came off differently. Confidence, self-assurance . . . 'Max the Lawyer?'

He smiled, bemused at the title.

At what point, she wondered, had he recognized her? Almost immediately – as for her? – or had it only come as her name had carried on the crowd? 'But you said you work at Madsen Holdings.'

'Yes. I'm a corporate lawyer there.'

'Oh.'

'Oh,' he echoed, his gaze falling to her lips. Subtlety wasn't his strong suit and she found she didn't care. In fact, she liked his directness. It was everything Lars – evasive, non-committal, deceitful – hadn't been.

'Miss?'

The moment was broken by the attendant coming back with her coat and bag. 'Thank you,' she murmured, looking away from Max.

'Want some help with that?' he asked, as she looped her jacket – the turquoise puffa she wore for running – over her arm. His eyebrow arched fractionally at the sight of it. It was an incongruous pairing with her cocktail dress but little did he know how her day had unravelled. She had been on the fly since her lunch with Freja.

'No, thanks . . . I ran in this morning,' she said, by way of explanation of the coat.

He nodded. 'Still, it's cold outside and you're not wearing very much.' His gaze fell to the sweep of her bare shoulders before coming back to her again.

'It's fine, I'll catch a cab,' she said, heading for the doors but already waiting – hoping – for his next suggestion to share a car with him.

It came.

'Or we could get that nightcap – now you're no longer busy.' He held her gaze and she remembered her abrupt response to his equally short message. Perhaps they were as bad as each other?

The door was opened by one of the porters. 'Good night,' the man said as they passed out onto the steps. Immediately the northern chill asserted itself and she shivered.

'Here.' He went to shrug off his jacket. Gentlemanly. Seductive.

'Darcy!'

The voice rang out from somewhere in the darkness and she looked down to see a man standing beside a taxi, waving at her.

Oh, God. She had completely forgotten. She looked back at Max, but in that single moment, his jacket had already been shrugged back onto his shoulders.

'But you're still busy, I see.' He held her gaze for a moment and she saw frustration, irritation even, in his eyes.

'I . . .' She couldn't think of what to say. She wanted to tell him it was nothing, that she'd never even met that man before, that she didn't want him – not over Max. She wanted to tell Erik to sling his hook, but Max was already stepping back and reaching for his phone, a distant smile on his lips.

'It was a pleasure meeting you, Darcy. Have a nice night.'

She watched him turn and go down the steps, his phone against his ear.

It all happened so fast. One minute she was in his orbit, the next, flung out with dizzying speed.

'Kristina?' His voice was low, already distant, but she swore she heard him say the name as he headed towards a waiting black car, a driver opening the glossy passenger door as he neared. In the next instant he had disappeared inside, gone from her sight, and she felt again as she had when he had left the party earlier: deflated, as if the sun had been plucked from the sky.

'Darcy!' Erik called, waving frantically again as the car pulled away into the night. 'Over here!'

'Fuck,' Darcy said under her breath, shrugging on the running jacket after all and heading down the steps towards her dreaded date.

Chapter Five

'I can't believe you actually had a date last night!' Freja exclaimed, sitting on the side of the sink in her underwear as they brushed their teeth. 'You wasted no time!'

'That was down to his scheduling, not mine.'

'Was it good? Did you go back to his?' Freja asked.

'That *really* would be wasting no time!' Darcy protested, spraying toothpaste in her indignation. Her brain rattled a little as she talked; she had undone her restraint on the champagne at the National by having some espresso martinis, which were never a good idea. 'We had drinks at Brønnum.'

'Oh, fancy!' Toothpaste foamed in Freja's mouth as she spoke, and she twisted to spit into the basin.

'Yeah. We had a nice time.'

'. . . Nice? *Nice?*' Freja patted the towel against her mouth. 'Oh no. That is not good. I know you Brits. Damnation by faint praise . . . You hated the guy.'

'No I didn't!' Darcy rolled her eyes.

'Was he funny?'

'He certainly thought so.'

'Attentive?'

'Uh-huh.'

'Fuckable?'

'Sure.'

'So then, what's the problem?'

It was Darcy's turn to spit and she stood up, running the tap. '. . . I was on a date with the wrong guy,' she said finally.

'How'd you manage that?' Freja frowned, looking confused.

'By accident, that's how. I met one of my other matches at the drinks reception and the eye contact was off the charts, Frey,' she groaned. 'The chemistry was unreal! I'd have gone straight back to his last night, no hesitations, I'm telling you.'

Freja was looking appalled by the developments. 'So then why didn't you?' she cried, splaying her hands in dismay.

'Because Erik the Property Developer has all the emotional intelligence of a slug! Instead of seeing me standing on the steps with another guy and deciding to hold onto his dignity and slink into the night, he began madly calling my name and waving at me!' She shrugged. 'Max the Lawyer didn't even give me the chance to make a choice. He just said goodbye and buggered off.'

Freja reached for her moisturizer. 'Do you think he was pissed off?'

'Maybe mildly.' Darcy shrugged. 'His sure thing disappeared in smoke before his eyes.'

'So then message him,' Freja urged her. 'Make another date with him – a proper one.' She began applying the cream in long, upward strokes on her neck.

'Ugh . . . I doubt he'd be bothered,' Darcy muttered. 'I think he was calling another girl before he'd even got in the car.'

Freja's hands paused and she winced. 'Oh, really?'

Darcy nodded, reaching for some of Freja's moisturizer too. 'I get the impression he's got a whole . . . routine, down. You know, hookup back-ups.'

'Oh. Well, maybe it was a blessing in disguise, then,' Freja said disapprovingly. 'Man-whore is my type, not yours.'

'Ordinarily I'd agree.' Darcy rubbed the cream vigorously into her cheeks. 'But I've never experienced anything like that before. All bets were off with him. Usual rules didn't apply.'

'Is this some *Freaky Friday* shit?' Freja asked her with an incredulous look. 'Did we swap bodies in the night? How come I've been sleeping with the same guy for nearly a month now and you're ready to hook up with . . . ?'

'Max the Lawyer.'

'Yes. Him.'

'I know,' Darcy shrugged. 'Mental. The universe is messing with us.' She looked sheepishly at her flatmate in the mirror. 'I googled him when I got in, you know. Max the Lawyer, I mean.'

'Yeah?'

'He looks pretty well connected. I did an image search and he came up at a lot of grand, society-type events.'

'Not that surprising if he's on Raya. The whole point is it's for that strata.' Freja squirted some highlighter into her palm.

'Yeah. He seems to know a *lot* of beautiful women. Model types. I'm not sure PhD students quite cut the mustard.'

'*You* are the catch, babe, not him,' Freja said loyally. 'Remember that. If he wants to surround himself with vapid skeletons, let him. You deserve way more than some pretty fuckboy.'

'I know that. But I thought the whole point of this was to provide me with some meaningless diversion over the Christmas holidays.'

'He won't be here over Christmas. His sort never are. He'll be skiing in Gstaad or lying on a Harbour Island beach.' Freja turned to look at her as she applied the highlighter to her cheeks. 'Thing is, Darce, I know we're calling this a post-Lars revenge spree, but fundamentally, you're a relationship girl. You catch feelings – a guy like that would be bad news for you.'

Darcy let her words settle, knowing her friend was right. She hadn't been able to go through with going back to Erik's last night, in spite of the fact she was tipsy and he was clearly keen. Max had been on her mind during every conversation. However much she wanted to see herself as a weapon of seduction, the evidence suggested otherwise.

'Do you want my advice?'

'I sense I'm going to get it anyway,' Darcy said with a wry smile as she pulled on a fleecy hairband to hold her hair back.

'Forget him. If he was calling another woman as he was walking away from you, he's a serious player and he's only going to hurt you. Remove the temptation now, before things can develop, and just move on. You've had enough turmoil lately. Keep things simple. We're not looking for either love *or* drama; just a little festive fun, so you're not completely alone while you get your thesis done.'

Darcy stared at her reflection in the mirror. She looked pale and slightly panda-eyed, traces of last night's mascara remaining in spite of the fact she'd applied her micellar water three times. But last night, by Max's side, his hand on her back as they walked, she'd felt beautiful, seductive; powerful, even. When was the last time she'd felt that? Had she *ever* felt that, in fact? Everything in her world had felt fundamentally different beside him.

'You said Erik the Property Developer's fuckable, right? And attentive and funny. That's all you need. Nothing more, nothing less. Go with that package. Emotional slug can't hurt you.'

Freja stuck her face in Darcy's eyeline, forcing her to look away from her reflection – and deep thoughts – and make eye contact. Take notice.

'Go on another date with Erik.'

'No, he's . . . Erik's . . .' Darcy wrinkled her nose. 'It's just not right between us. He's too . . . flashy for me. He spent half an hour telling me about his watch collection.'

'Hm.' Freja made a disapproving sound. 'Well, what about the third one?'

'Aksel the Vet? He seems . . . sweet, I guess,' she sighed, soaking a cotton wool ball with more eye make-up remover. The conversation with him was dull but ongoing, with a few faint flickers of life.

'Yeah? Show me him again, I've forgotten which one he is.'

Darcy brought up his profile on her phone, watching as Freja flicked through the carousel of images.

'Oh yes, the one with the *gorgeous* eyes,' Freja said encouragingly, ever her hype woman.

'Yeah, soulful. And he saves animals, so he's a good human too.'

'Total winner.' Freja looked at her. '. . . Show me this Max, then.'

Darcy hesitated. 'You didn't like him. He's the arrogant-looking one.'

'I don't remember,' Freja shrugged. 'Show me.'

Darcy brought up his profile, her breath catching as she saw again the haughty stare that had felt so mesmerizing in 3D.

'Oh yeah,' Freja breathed. 'He looks . . . he looks . . .' She swallowed. 'Yeah. No one should be that hot. *Total* fuckboy . . . No. I'm telling you, Darce, he'll wreck you. Block him.'

'But—'

'No buts.' Freja made the sign of a phone with her hands. 'Mr Booty-Call? . . . Unmatch with him now. Let me see you do it.'

Darcy hesitated, then did as she was told. He hadn't messaged her last night or this morning. There had been no 'nice to meet you'. No 'let's have a drink sometime'. There'd been no hello and now there'd be no goodbye. All she had was the memory of walking by his side, his arm looped lightly around her – territorial, protective, proprietary. For a few minutes, she had felt like she was his, and it had been . . . intoxicating.

She closed her eyes, trying to banish the thoughts.

'I *really* think you should give Erik another chance,' Freja said, pumping hair serum into her palms and smoothing it over her split ends.

'I told you, the spark wasn't there. At least, not for me.'

'Yeah, because you didn't give him a chance. You were distracted by the man-whore.'

'Can you please not call him that?'

'I think we definitely should call him that,' Freja said with a pointed look. 'Keep you focused.'

Darcy tried to focus now, but she was profoundly distracted. She'd had a restless sleep, falling into confusing dreams and waking with sudden starts. 'I think perhaps you're the one who's strayed from the path. I take it you're going to be seeing Tristan *again* tonight?' she murmured, trying to change the subject.

Freja met her gaze with a sly look in the mirror. 'I mean, there's no overwhelming reason not to.'

Darcy gave a tut as she began applying some foundation. She needed to look distinctly more alive than she felt. It was eight in the morning and Viggo had already been working for an hour. 'You don't think a firebreak would give you time to control these flames a little?'

'Honestly? It would only fan them,' Freja said, sounding incredulous. 'I don't know what the hell's happened to me but I'm obsessed with him, Darce.' She shrugged. 'At this point, I reckon it's just better that I get it out of my system. But don't worry, I have a plan.'

'Oh yeah? And what's that then?'

'I'm going to overdose on him. Mainline him. I reckon another week, two max, and I'll start getting bored.'

'Well, it's a new tactic, certainly.' Darcy applied some cream blush to her cheeks and lips and a quick slick of mascara to her lashes. 'Mm . . . Better.'

'What are you up to today?'

'*I* am heading to the Madsen Collection archives,' Darcy said with a note of satisfaction. 'It's a day in the vaults for me with a septuagenarian.'

'You really are on a roll!' Freja called after her as Darcy headed for her bedroom to get dressed.

'Aren't I just,' she called back, as her phone buzzed and Erik wished her a good morning.

'My worst meal has to be the moo ping I bought from a street seller in Krabi. Tasted great – as it went down. Ended up on a drip in hospital with severe dehydration from throwing up so much. Haven't been able to look at a pork skewer since.'

Darcy smiled. Aksel the Vet was beginning to warm up.

'Yeah, I had food poisoning once too, although not so glamorous as yours. My culprit was an opened jar of Dolmio pasta sauce when I was at uni. It was no joke. Haven't eaten ready-made pasta sauce since.'

'Ah. So a happy ending then.'

He was a food snob? Interesting.

'Do you like cooking?'

'Love it. De-stresses me. I love Asian especially. You?'

'I like Italian best. The cheeses, herbs. I'm obsessed with the smell of fresh basil.'

All I Want for Christmas

'There's a great Italian on Nørrebrogade called Cicchetti.'

She stared at the comment hopefully. Was it supposed to be the opening line for asking her on a date? She waited a moment for the question to come through, but nothing did.

She groaned. Had anyone checked him for a pulse recently?

'Okay great, thanks for the tip. I'll check it out some time.'

The Madsen Collection was housed in a large single-storey white villa and set on the shore of the lake in the Ørstedsparken. Single-storey in height, it boasted two wings that spread from a central oval folly. The gallery sat elegantly in the landscape with large opaque windows in the walls and skylights in the roof. It was partially eclipsed from the street by what were currently bare-fingered trees, ducks sitting on the steps in the weak winter light.

Darcy wheeled her bike along the path – cycling was prohibited in the park – and slotted it into one of the racks along the back. Her fingers were clumsy with cold. The clouds had come in as part of the northern winter's relentless march, and the grey sky was woolly and slung low like schoolboys' socks.

According to the timings on the door, the gallery would not open to the public for another twenty minutes, but as Darcy peered in, she saw the place was already buzzing with tour guides and cashiers getting ready for the day ahead.

'Hi,' she said, approaching a woman behind a desk who was installing a fresh roll of receipt paper into her till. 'I'm Darcy Cotterell, here to see Viggo Rask?'

'Ah yes, he said you would be coming,' the lady replied, reaching for a laminated barcoded pass on a lanyard and handing it to her. 'Through the door over there, down the stairs. He's expecting you.'

'Thank you.' Darcy headed for the door in the opposite

corner, pressing her card to the scanner pad and hearing a beep. Immediately beyond, a narrow staircase spiralled down to the basement archives and as she went down, she saw Viggo working at an old wooden desk at the back of the oval-shaped room. Several reading tables were set end to end in the space in front of him and covered with papers and folios. He looked up as her footsteps carried through the silence.

'Darcy.' He put down his pen, seeming pleased to see her.

'Morning, Viggo,' she smiled. 'Apologies – I did intend to set my alarm for six in the hopes of joining you here bright and early, but . . .' She gave a grimace, knowing he wouldn't have any interest in hearing about her failed date and point-lessly late night.

'If it's any consolation, it's never bright down here – which makes the early starts a little more bearable.' He rose and she saw he was wearing a white coat, similar to those worn by the Academy conservators. 'Welcome to my world,' he said, holding out his arms.

He gestured to the long, dimly lit spaces that ran either side of where they stood, beneath the length of the two galleries above. In contrast to the cool grey northern light upstairs, down here had a warm, soft-amber glow. Old-fashioned reading lamps were set in the walls every few metres, with a long perpendicular run of antique oak shelving stacks set down the centre of each wing. At the end of every fourth stack was a small reading table with its own lamp and chair. Darcy thought all it needed was a dog, a rug and a fireplace – although it was comfortably warm down there; the temperature no doubt strictly controlled – and she would never have cause to leave. The smell of old papers and old books was her favourite scent, but she could glean wood polish and coffee too, and . . . apple pie?

'I call this my oval office.'

'It's heavenly down here,' she smiled.

'Some find it a little claustrophobic.'

'Not me. It's perfect.'

He smiled too, looking pleased by her response; they were birds of a feather, clearly. 'I've just boiled the kettle. Would you like a cup of coffee?'

'Thank you.'

She watched as he turned to a small table set beside a sink, copper pipes exposed against the old brick wall. He heaped some instant – but organic – coffee onto a spoon and poured the boiled water into two large mugs, one with a chip in the rim. He handed her the unchipped one. 'Come. I'll give you the tour.'

They headed into what he called the east wing first. 'As you can probably tell, the temperature is climate controlled at seventy degrees for humidity stability purposes. This side houses all Madsen Collection artists with surnames from A to K – so, Anna Ancher all the way through to P. S. Krøyer. You'll see there's a reference volume on this desk here –' he pointed to a tall red leather book – 'which lists the artists alphabetically, and then chronological search references in the stacks. Obviously, some have more material than others. Krøyer, for instance, has his own stack entirely, whereas Carl Bille has only a single box file.'

'Ah, so you don't only hold Johan Trier?'

'Not at all. The Foundation was begun with the intention of becoming the permanent home of Trier's work – as far as possible, when some pieces, of course, remain in private collections or public institutions – but our remit has expanded over the years to include his contemporaries as well. We specialize in Danish artists from 1920 onwards.'

'Hm,' Darcy mused, biting her lip thoughtfully. 'So then you may not have the material I need. I specifically want to look at Trier's source material pre-1922. I'm hoping the search period will be 1920–22, but it could end up being before that.'

'Not to worry on that score. Trier is our exception. You probably know our founders, the Madsen family, were his patrons?'

'Yes.'

'So we hold more comprehensive records on him than any other institution in the world. We cover his whole working life until his death in 1974. If we don't have it, then it probably doesn't exist.'

'Phew. That's a relief.'

'Everyone else is a side dish. Trier's the main event here.'

'Good to know,' Darcy nodded, her eyes scanning the space and noticing an absence of something. 'Um . . . I'm not seeing any computers anywhere . . .'

'There's only one, at the end there, just around the corner,' Viggo said, pointing to the furthest stack. She headed towards it. 'I'm in the process of scanning and putting everything online, but it's slow going.'

'Can't they bring anyone in to help you?'

'They could,' Viggo smiled. 'But since my wife died eight years ago, this place has become my world, and I like having a reason to get up in the mornings. If I were to do a nine to five, with no pressure on me, I think I'd be dead within the month.'

'I'm sorry about your wife,' Darcy said. 'I'm glad your work offers some distraction.' She looked around the corner and saw the size of the tower of files on the small desk. She smiled back at him. 'Especially when you have so much of it! I guess you like moving mountains.'

'I do. Even though the old system works perfectly well. Everything has been logged by hand, and there's a brief description of each artefact in the reference volume and its position in the stacks – so you don't need to search through thirty boxes, for instance, to find one specific photograph. Look for it in here –' he tapped the red leather ledger – 'and it will tell you where to find it.'

'Analogue. I like it. That must have been a mammoth task for whoever had to compile it originally.'

'My predecessor, Harald Morgensen,' Viggo nodded. 'And yes, it was. When Frederik Madsen established the Foundation, Harald was tasked with archiving the family's entire collection of art and artefacts. People think primarily of Johan Trier and the Modern Breakthrough masterpieces, but the Madsens were avid collectors of sculpture and furniture too.'

He pointed towards the shelves lining the walls behind her, opposite the stacks. They were laden with bowls and vases, some woodcut panels. Below them was a glass-shelved floor-standing cabinet filled with clay busts. Many appeared to be heads of fishermen in their sou'westers but one was bare-headed too, cropped curls caught in relief; their expressions were somehow captured and held behind blank eyes.

'These are wonderful,' Darcy murmured, crouching in front of the cabinet for a better look. 'Who are they by?' She could just make out some initials at the base of the neck on one piece: *A.S.*

'We believe the initials stand for Anna Saalbach.'

'Anna Saalbach,' she echoed, interested. 'Now, I've never heard of her.' She could have sworn she saw a fleeting moment of surprise pass over Viggo's face, quickly wiped away. It was like a rubber band pinging on her skin; she prided herself on her encyclopaedic knowledge of almost all the major – and many, many minor – female Danish artists working in this period.

'A-Anna?' He cleared his throat, pressing his hand to his

lips for a moment. 'No. Well, few have. The Madsens bought the entire collection. As I understand it, they've never been in any public exhibitions.'

Darcy looked over at him, puzzled. 'So then, why is her work not on display upstairs?'

'There's no public appetite for it. She's, uh, an unknown, clays are out of fashion, and there are so many other artists to exhibit. The Madsens were voracious collectors. We try to rotate the stock, but there's still a lack of space. And Saalbach didn't exactly embrace diversity in, uh, her content,' he added, with a pointed look towards the row of fishermen's heads.

'True,' Darcy agreed. There were some smaller pieces in the cabinet as well, but they were mainly gardener's tools – a wheelbarrow, a spade, trowel . . . unremarkable, everyday items that would be lying around a garden. Hardly revolutionary. The heads too, although beautifully formed, were variations on a theme, she realized as she peered closer.

'They've all got the same face,' she remarked.

Viggo nodded. 'Perhaps there was only one fisherman willing to sit for her?'

'Or it was a *very* small fishing village.'

He chuckled, starting to walk back up the gallery and crossing through the central chamber into the west wing. Darcy followed him. 'As you can see, the set-up is mirrored in here. Artists M through Z in the stacks, and at the end there . . .' He pointed towards a caged-off area at the very end of the room. 'Surplus stock.'

Darcy walked towards it and peered in at canvases stored on wheeled racks across the width of the space. Each rack was a floor-to-ceiling metal grid with the paintings clipped on, still in their frames. Even from here, she could recognize a Marie

Sandholt, which, as far as she was aware, hadn't been on public display since an exhibition in the 1970s.

'We have over a hundred and eighty paintings in there. Mainly minor pieces and those earmarked for conservation work.'

Darcy looked at the locked gate into the caged area. It was the old-fashioned key type – no fancy digital access pad to navigate. She was pretty sure there'd be a TikTok tutorial out there showing how she could pick the lock with a hairpin in under a minute.

Viggo smiled, as if reading her mind. 'Don't worry, the security upstairs is state of the art. Anyone wanting to get down here would have to first navigate the infrared laser system; plus there's a night security team with dogs that patrols seven till seven. And besides, for anyone planning to rob us, there's nothing of interest or value down here. It's all upstairs.'

'Reassuring to know, if I'm working late!' Darcy turned back to him as she sipped her coffee. Like everything else down here, it was old school but good. She looked at Viggo. 'I'm so excited to be here. I feel like I'm in Aladdin's cave.'

'Well, consider me your genie. Your wish is my command. Whatever you need, I can find it for you . . . Is there anything specific you want to start with?'

'To begin with, I just need all things Johan Trier, pre-1922. Whatever you've got, I need to see.'

Viggo nodded. 'He's got one and a half stacks to himself,' he said, walking over to the middle of the racks and placing a hand on one. 'He starts here: T(ii). Then he goes all the way to the end and comes halfway back on the other side of T(iii).'

Darcy peered at the thick storage boxes filed on their ends, floor to ceiling, all the way along. 'Okay.'

'The stacks are grouped alphabetically but sub-referenced

A(i), A(ii), and so on. Each stack is divided into vertical blocks or cells, the shelf level is counted from the top, and then the files are numbered boxes on those shelves.'

'Okay.' Darcy's eyes scanned the system as he talked. So far, so self-explanatory.

'So, Trier was born in 1895 but the earliest letters and diaries we hold on him date to 1915, I believe.' Darcy watched as he crossed to the table and checked the red leather reference volume. He flicked through the pages with practised ease before running his finger down the ledger. 'Yes . . . Stack T(ii), block five, level three. Box nine.'

She walked into the T(ii) stack, following his instructions: block five, level three down from the top. Box . . . ?

'Box nine, that's the one,' Viggo said, coming to stand by her. He was holding the red leather book and a small pad of Post-its. 'Peel off the top one and set it on the box so you've got a quick reference for your start point.'

Darcy set the Post-it on box nine as Viggo looked back at the red book again.

'And 1922 ends . . . Stack T(iii), block eleven, level five, box two.'

She found the spot, following the same method, and placed a Post-it on box two.

'There, that's your preliminary search area,' he smiled. 'It looks so easy, doesn't it?'

'I wish,' she grinned, knowing each box file might contain ten diaries, a hundred letters, a thousand photographs or slides. This could take weeks, if not months. Or she could get lucky and find something in the very first box. But somehow, she doubted it.

'How friendly are the night guards?' she asked archly, looking at him.

'Not so friendly that you can stay here past seven,' he laughed. 'I'll be at my desk if you need me. There's a bell on each table to save you from shouting.'

A bell. She smiled, watching him go. Yes, this was definitely old school.

'You unmatched me?'

Darcy looked up with a start. She'd been so engrossed in her work and become so accustomed to the soft shuffle of Viggo's footsteps in the background – bringing over cups of coffee every few hours – that she hadn't clocked this more strident approach to the table.

Max was leaning against the end of the next stack, watching her. He was wearing a navy suit but no tie, the top button of his pale blue shirt undone. Suddenly she felt vastly under-dressed in her boyfriend jeans, yellow Sambas and navy jumper, her hair pulled back in a messy bun. Last night's glamour was a distant memory. If she'd thought for one second she was going to see him again, today, here . . . She'd have put the damned dress back on. If she'd thought she would *ever* see him again, she'd have been a lot happier all day.

'I didn't think you'd even notice,' she said, finding her voice and wishing he didn't look so good. 'You're not exactly chatty online – and you left at some speed last night.'

She watched his reaction to her words. He betrayed nothing on a macro level but she caught the minute tightening of his lips and the slight narrowing of his eyes. 'Third-wheeling isn't my idea of a good time.'

She wondered what was.

'Good date?' he asked.

'Yes, fine.'

'Just fine?'

63

She shrugged. 'Yours?'

She tried not to think about what he'd done with his date that she hadn't done with hers. He made no pretence at romance on his Raya bio. Any woman in his contacts would know exactly what she was signing up for with him, and Darcy suspected there were many others only too happy to play along.

She saw another micro-narrowing of his eyes as he realized she had overheard him on the phone as he walked away, but he ignored the question by asking another of his own. 'Boyfriend?'

'Now why would I be on a dating app if he was my boyfriend?' She held his gaze for several long moments, wondering what it was about him that drew out this side to her. He made her combative, spiky. Provocative. She sensed he operated within strictly controlled boundaries and for some reason, she wanted to push them. Test him.

She looked away, feeling the intensity colour up between them again and unable to hold his gaze. She felt sure he could read her every thought, that he could see just how much she wanted him. 'What are you doing here, anyway?'

Had he come to ask her for another drink? The prospect of it made her entire body thrill. Erik had been texting all day, pushing for dinner again tonight before he left for Dubai, but she knew she'd have more fun standing in a puddle with Max than fine dining with him.

'I work here, remember? I thought I'd look in and make sure you were finding everything to your satisfaction.'

Oh.

'So far, so comprehensive,' she replied, sitting back in the chair. She'd been here for six hours and only got through one and a half boxes. Fifty-six to go. 'Viggo's been fantastic.'

'He's the best there is. The National's been trying to steal him from us for the past ten years. Luckily for us, he's loyal.'

'Right.' Were they really talking shop? She locked eyes with him again, feeling that primal rush once more. Whatever this was between them, it was undeniable – wasn't it? Did he feel it too? Had she been on his mind all day, the way he'd been on hers, or was she completely delusional? Every time she lifted her head, every time she came back from 1918 to 2024, she had replayed their meeting in her mind, remembered the feeling of his hand upon her back. She had *missed* him, even though she barely knew him.

She saw something stir behind his eyes.

'So look,' he said, clearing his throat. 'Seeing as we're going to be . . . running into each other here for the foreseeable future, I don't think it would be wise to take things any further between us. On a personal level, I mean.'

She stared at him, feeling stunned by the fierce disappointment spreading through her chest at his words. For several seconds, it felt too difficult to speak. She felt sure her cheeks were burning, betraying the feelings she was struggling to keep hidden. 'That's what you came down here to tell me?'

'Yes.'

'. . . Even though I had already unmatched you?'

He fell still and for the first time, he looked on the back foot. 'I just don't want there to be any misapprehensions. We had made private contact before we actually met, but clearly this is a professional relationship now, and we should . . .' His gaze fell to her lips. 'Act accordingly.'

She hesitated. It was like watching him go down those steps all over again, walking away from her. '. . . That's perfectly fine,' she said, as flatly as she could. 'I really hadn't thought

I would ever see you again anyway. There are no expectations on my part.'

He nodded. 'Right . . . Good.'

For a moment, he just carried on staring at her as if he wanted to say something further – or perhaps he was waiting for more from her – but then he straightened up. 'Well, good luck with it all. You're in excellent hands with Rask.'

'Yes. Thanks.'

'Bye, then.'

'. . . Bye, Max.'

Strike one. Her first prospect had been shot down in flames. She watched him go, unable to explain the sense of panic it drew up in her to watch him leave. Again. It felt as if the air was being sucked out of the room.

'That's strange,' Viggo said, coming and standing by her as their unexpected visitor disappeared up the stairs. 'He's never once come down here before.'

'No?'

'No. The executive offices are downtown.' The old archivist looked at her with a concerned expression. 'Is everything all right? He does have a bit of a reputation.'

'Reputation?'

'For being bullish. He's not pressuring you, is he? Obviously everyone's under a lot of pressure with this new discovery in the headlines.'

The comment perplexed her. 'Well, yes – but at the Academy, surely? It isn't a Madsen Foundation issue.'

Viggo smiled. 'Anything to do with Johan Trier is a Madsen Foundation issue. We see him as ours. And Max Lorensen certainly does.'

Darcy was quiet for a moment. 'I don't understand. He told me he's a corporate lawyer.'

'Yes, he is. He's a big cheese at the parent company, Madsen Holdings – but he's also the chair of trustees at the Madsen Foundation. He masterminds the gallery's expansion ambitions and oversees brand partnerships, sponsorships, acquisitions . . .'

'That sounds like a big job for someone so young.'

'Thirty-two. Not that young. And, like I said, bullish. He knows how to throw a punch, as they say – so don't let him bully you.'

'No, I won't,' she said quietly.

They hadn't even had a date, but he'd gone out of his way to dump her anyway. Did that count?

Chapter Six

'I can't believe you changed your mind.' Erik smiled at her across the restaurant table, looking better than he knew in the candlelight. 'I'd almost given up hope.'

'I'm sorry, I wasn't giving you the run-around. It's just been a trying day,' she replied, trying to muster some social energy. 'I wasn't sure I'd be good company.'

'How could you not be? You'd be good company on a silent monastic retreat.'

She smiled. 'Well that's a very kind thing to say.'

He shrugged. 'I'm just happy to hear that was the reason for your hesitation and not something I did or said last night to put you off.'

'No,' she said, trying to look puzzled by the mere suggestion. 'Of course not.'

'Good, because I enjoyed last night; I really wanted to see you again.'

'Yeah. It was fun. I'd not been to Brønnum before.'

'You liked it there? Well then when I get back, I'll take you to Bazaar. That's even better.'

'Really?' She swallowed, already bored. The conversation felt hollow and fatuous compared to the few words she'd exchanged with Max, in which everything had felt charged and loaded.

'They've got a ten-month waiting list for a reservation – they turned away Brooklyn Beckham and his wife not long ago.'

'Oh.' She ran her hands through her hair, but no amount of root lift could override a day without sunlight and she hoped she didn't look as jaded as she felt. She had pulled a ten-hour shift in the archives only to make her way through a grand total of . . . three boxes. 'So then, how would we get in?'

'My father's friends with the owner, so I can always get us a good table.'

'Is he in the hospitality business then, your father?'

'. . . No.' He laughed, bemused. 'You know, your Danish may be excellent but I can tell you're not from here if you don't know who my father is.'

'Should I?'

'He's a pretty big name in the city. He set up his commercial property development business twenty-five years ago and it turned over 125 million krone last year; he started with nothing and now he's a donor to the Venstre party, knows everyone, is respected by everyone. And now he's grooming me to take the helm of the company when he retires in a few years.'

'Oh, I see.' Darcy swallowed, feeling a budding resentment in the pit of her stomach at the casual nepotism he clearly expected her to admire. Her own father was a geography teacher at the local sixth form college back home in Berkshire and her mother a GP receptionist; she felt every bit as proud of them as he was, only she suspected he would see nothing to admire. Money and status were important to him, and his choice in women was no doubt intended as a reflection of his high self-worth. She supposed there was a compliment in there somewhere. 'Well, that sounds like an amazing opportunity for you.'

Erik shrugged. 'My father's an incredible man.'

She took another sip of her wine, trying not to think about whether her own father would be disappointed to see her having dinner with such a spoilt man-child.

'Yeah. This deal we're putting together in Dubai is actually my first solo.' Erik sat back in the club chair, pressing his fingers together. 'I made the pitch, won it, and now I'm going out there to drill into the detail with the client. The budget is AED 90 million.'

'Gosh.' She wasn't quite sure how to respond to the boast. '. . . That is a lot of dirham.'

He looked surprised that she knew of their currency. 'Have you been?'

'To Dubai? No.' She shook her head. 'But I stopped off at Doha once, en route to Bali.'

'It's incredible there too. Even just the airport is a spectacle.' He pinned her with an intense look. 'You never know, if things continue to go well between us, you could come out with me on the next trip. I could show you the sights,' he winked.

'Oh, no . . . I don't think that would be necessary.'

His self-assured look slipped and she wondered if she'd been too blunt.

'I mean, if it's a work trip, you need to concentrate,' she explained quickly.

'Don't you worry about that; there's plenty of time on these things for work *and* play. I think we'd have a lot of fun together.'

He held her gaze at the not-so-subtle intimation and she forced herself to smile back. It was why they were both here, after all: two single, consenting adults looking for something light and casual. She definitely didn't want another relationship so soon, and there was no doubt he was an attractive man; she had caught plenty of women checking him out as they passed by the table. Clearly, they were incompatible on a personal level – but how personal did things really need to be? She was here to have *fun*, as per Freja's instructions.

And yet . . .

'Well, it's not really my scene anyway.' She heard the rejection in her own voice.

There was a missed beat. 'No? Why not?'

'Well, look at who goes there – it's full of oil barons, property developers, TikTokers, social media influencers and *Love Island* people. Everything there's so *shiny* and my life is more . . . dusty.'

'Dusty?'

'Yes. Let's be honest, it's not exactly the natural habitat for a history of art academic. I deal with the dead, I guess. Dead artists. Centuries-old paintings. It's about as different as you can get.' Every word was a rebuff. She could hear it and yet she couldn't stop. Something in him made her turn away. '. . . Unless the beautiful people living in your glossy high-rises will want some old masters to hang on their walls? Then I could be their art advisor, I guess.'

It was only a throwaway comment, but Erik's expression went from wary to intensely focused. 'There's probably good money in that. I know a lot of rich people who are just looking for ways to spend their money. Someone like you could make a killing.'

'Someone like me?'

'Yeah – I imagine academia really doesn't pay so well?'

She swallowed. 'I guess compared to building hotels, no.'

Just then the waiter came over, and she looked away with relief. A slight edge had crept into the conversation and it was her fault, she knew. He was trying to flirt and she was blocking him at every turn. 'Mr Rasmussen, are you ready for me to take your orders?'

'Thank you, Oscar. We'll have the chateaubriand and a bottle of the Puligny Montrachet.'

'Very good, sir,' the waiter said, snapping the menus shut and slipping away again.

'Oh, but—' Darcy had wanted to order the truffle pasta. She watched in disbelief as the waiter retreated without even glancing over at her.

'You're going to *love* the filet,' Erik said with certainty as he sat back in his chair. 'I've never once come here and been unhappy with the choice.' She looked at him, seeing how pleased he was with himself at this show of power. How did he know she even liked chateaubriand, or that she wasn't a vegetarian? He had never asked.

She swallowed back her irritation. 'Is that so? You must come here a lot, then.'

'It's one of my favourites, actually. There's always a good atmosphere and I live just around the corner, so . . .'

He shot her a loaded look again. If he had all the subtlety of a sledgehammer, she also knew this was their second date – drinks last night; dinner tonight – and that expectations were rising . . . She knew when the meal came out, his knee would begin to brush against hers under the table and he would start to lean in on his elbows while they talked, touching her hand with increasing regularity. She was going to have to have made a choice by the time pudding came out.

She watched him as he talked, trying to talk herself into it. He used his hands a lot, made plenty of eye contact and had stories for any turn of conversation. He was not quite as funny as he thought he was, nor as clever, but he was engaging.

Engaging enough for one night.

She could do this, couldn't she?

'So, tell me about the rogue who broke your heart,' he said, coming in again with an intense look. She sensed it was part of the seduction.

'Excuse me?'

'You mentioned him in passing last night when I asked about your last relationship. You said he cheated on you?'

She rolled her eyes. 'He did *not* break my heart.'

'Really? But you said it was your first date in weeks, since the breakup.'

'Not because I was heartbroken, though. I was just done with being lied to again. I haven't got the time, nor the energy for those games. It's so . . . tedious.'

'So it's happened before?'

'I date men. Of course it's happened before.'

'Ouch.' He winced at the sarcasm, but she saw a look of satisfaction in his eyes. 'Well, then I apologize on behalf of my brethren – but I hope you know we're not all like that.'

'It honestly doesn't matter either way,' she shrugged. 'Whoever I date can see whoever else they want. I'm not looking for a relationship right now.'

His eyebrows raised. 'You're not looking to fall in love?'

'I don't have time.'

'Oh, come. Everyone has time for love,' he argued. 'It's what makes life worth living.'

'Not me. I'm twenty-six years old, I've never been in love – and I'm fine with that.'

'You're not looking for marriage, kids?' He looked openly incredulous.

'Not yet. I've got my friends and family; my career comes before any man right now,' she shrugged.

'Huh.' He didn't reply, and she watched as he reached for his drink with an enigmatic smile.

'What?' she asked. 'Why are you smiling like that?'

She watched as he took a slow sip, in no rush to answer. He set the glass back down again before looking back at her.

'I guess because I don't believe you. Women always say they aren't looking for anything serious, but they invariably are. Why else would they be on a dating app?'

'To have some fun,' she bristled. 'Like you.'

'Oh! So that's why you're here is it? To *use* me – as a plaything?' His knee brushed hers under the table.

'I wouldn't have put it like that.' She swallowed, hating the innuendo he'd put into the word, this clumsy, forced charade they were playing. 'I'm here for the entire experience: the conversation, the meal; to be out and about in this amazing city I get to live in for the next year. To meet new people.' She stared back at him. This conversation hardly justified whatever the subscription was. 'And for the record, *I* didn't sign myself up to the app. My flatmate did. She wanted me to get back out there because she could see I had so little interest.'

'Ah. The plot thickens! So, did *she* choose to swipe right on me? Or was it you?'

Darcy blinked. 'It was mutual. We were together when I was looking and we both thought you looked nice.'

He threw his head back and laughed. 'Oh, I've been called many things before, but never nice. I'm so offended!'

'It wasn't intended as an insult.'

'I'm joking! I'm just teasing,' he said, leaning in and touching her hand. Were they talking at cross purposes? 'I'm very pleased you swiped right – whoever did it, for whatever the reason. And if you want the truth, I think it's kind of cute that you're so modest about it all.'

'Modest?' She was confused. It didn't seem like the correct word. In what way was she modest?

74

'Yes, coming in softly and pretending you don't want love; not putting any pressure on things.'

She blinked, looking back at him. Was he being deliberately obtuse? 'But it's true. I don't. I meant it when I said my career comes first.'

He laughed again. So patronizing.

'*Why* is that so funny?'

'Because I hardly think you can call being a . . . perpetual student a career.'

She stared at him, unable to believe what she was hearing. She pulled her hand away abruptly. 'I'm a PhD student on track to be a professor. How does being a world-class expert in your field *not* count as a career? Oh! I guess you wouldn't know, seeing as your own career is just another thing Daddy handed over, along with the keys to some flashy flat and a twatty sports car!'

She stopped, realizing people at the neighbouring tables were staring. Her voice had raised in her indignation and she had caused a scene; the mask had been ripped off and she couldn't pretend to go along with this any longer.

She stared back at him, seeing the anger simmering in his eyes too now. She had humiliated him in front of these strangers – but she didn't care. Her decision had been made before the first course had even come out.

A heavy silence beat between them.

'I think it's best if we just call it a day now,' she muttered, pushing her chair back. She saw panic cross his face at the prospect of her publicly walking out on him, on top of everything else.

'Clara, wait—' he blurted, his hands already reaching for her, but the words died on his lips as he realized his error.

She gave a small snort of disdain that he couldn't even get

75

her name right. 'Wrong girl, I'm afraid. Please don't contact me again, *Erik*,' she said pointedly, feeling heads turn, eyes burning into her back as she left.

Shrugging on her coat, she stepped outside into the damp night and took a steadying breath as she leaned against the wall. Strike two. The second dumping in a single day. Disaster snatched from the jaws of defeat. She ran her hands over her face. *Why* hadn't she trusted her instincts about him and just gone home instead?

But she knew perfectly well why. She just hadn't wanted to face it.

Max's rejection in the archives had stung and she had needed some validation. She had wanted to feel sexy, desirable, worthy of the chase, but she had felt none of those things sitting in there tonight. Worse than that, she was now left facing the even more uncomfortable truth that it was Max's actions that had led to this reaction. Indifference should have been her response, not distraction – but all she had proved, whether she liked it or not, was that Max Lorensen was already well and truly under her skin.

Chapter Seven

'So no breakthroughs?' Freja panted, dodging a Labrador carrying a large stick that spanned almost the entire path. They were on their usual Saturday morning run in Kastellet, and the promise of breakfast at the end of it was the only thing keeping Darcy going.

'Nope. Nada. Zilch. It's painful. I've spent the past three days going through Trier's diaries and letters and it's one thing having to read solidly in Danish but oh my God, his hand-writing! How can someone so proficient with a brush be so hopeless with a pen?'

Freja chuckled. 'I wonder how he'd have been with a pipette.'

'My money's on useless! The man was chaotic. Clearly drank too much, was homeless half the time, sleeping on beaches and getting kicked out of boarding houses.'

'He sounds like that ex of mine – remember Jasper, the musician? Nose ring; tried to snort cocoa powder?'

'Fun times,' Darcy said wryly. 'But painters were actually the rock stars of their time, you know. They could get away with shit no one else could. Creativity freed them from the usual social constraints.'

'Oh! Were they cheating bastards then too?'

Darcy grinned. 'Undoubtedly – although in Trier's case, no

affairs of the heart that I've come across yet. No love letters, no dates – clandestine or otherwise – detailed in his diaries. He used prostitutes, though. He actually lists them as an expense.'

'Ha!' Freja snorted, bemused. 'Why am I not surprised?'

They both jumped a large puddle, landing in sync, their footsteps in perfect unison. Darcy was grateful for the opportunity to be outside, moving. All week she had been crouched over a desk, thumbing through myriad preparatory sketches, receipts, maps and expenses for Trier's travels in Europe. He had left Denmark for Paris in 1919, enrolling with some of the fine art academies there and working primarily on life drawing studies, before moving down through France to Italy. By March of 1920, he had been staying in Florence, painting the silk weavers and goldsmiths and working mainly in charcoal and pencil, with only occasional forays into using oil.

Darcy's gut told her this timeframe was still too early for the portrait. At twenty-five years old, the artist was immature and still very much finding himself as he travelled. It wasn't so much that his hand was underdeveloped – technically, he was already brilliant and had begun the portraiture that would soon attract the attention of his future benefactor Bertram Madsen; but his eye and mind were naive, and although he might have been able to reproduce the woman's likeness, she doubted he'd have been able to capture her essence at this point. The finer details were still obscured beneath the thick board layers, of course, but there was something knowing in the woman's posture, the way she held herself; Darcy sensed it, woman to woman. The portrait was accomplished and sure – and Johan Trier in early 1920 was not.

'So do you think she could be one then, the woman in the portrait?'

'A prostitute? No, I don't think so. He made his name painting society ladies.'

'You mean like John Singer Sargent?' Freja looked pleased with herself for knowing the name.

Darcy grinned. 'Exactly like him. He focused on their fashions and hairstyles as much as their faces and figures. He painted them into glamazons. Queens.'

'So then maybe he glamorized her. Perhaps he painted her after a "session" when the post-coital glow was still strong.'

'No glow would have lasted *that* long,' Darcy chuckled. 'Portraits require multiple sittings.'

'Couldn't he have done it in one sitting? As a one-off?'

'It's possible, but unlikely. The brushwork looks heavily layered, suggesting multiple revisits – spooled out to allow for drying times,' she explained. 'And of course, sittings require scheduling, but there's no reference to anything like that in his diaries for 1919, or what I've read of 1920 so far.'

Freja was quiet for a moment. 'What if he "bought" her time but instead of shagging her, he painted her? That's why he claimed it as an expense.'

Darcy considered for a moment. 'I guess that could be plausible.' She groaned. 'God, I hope not. How would I ever trace an Italian prostitute a hundred years later?'

'Hm. I don't envy you that one. Maybe you should have gone to detective school.'

They split apart, running either side of a young family pushing a buggy, a toddler standing on a board at the back. The track was stylistically designed in the shape of a Tudor rose and was always crowded at weekends, runners vying with dog walkers and families for space on the path. The ground dropped away steeply either side of them, a moat to their right and the red-brick army barracks in the centre to their left. Freja had joked about breaking in many times.

'Thing is,' Darcy panted as they fell back in step again, 'he wasn't really painting society portraits in 1920. Not yet. He didn't have the contacts by then, and at that particular point, travelling around Europe, he was doing lots of vignettes of peasants and workers. He had no interest in the artifice of formal portraiture but wanted to depict the working man—'

'Exactly. And she's a working girl!'

'Except I just don't think she was. Her clothes are . . . modest. Demure. The dress is high necked; she's wearing jewellery. If he wanted to paint a prostitute, why disguise her as a lady?'

'Hm.' Freja mused on the point for a moment. 'Okay then, say she's not a prostitute. She is a lady. Could he have done it as a one-off to earn some money while he was travelling?'

'Yes. But all things considered, 1919 and '20 is definitely feeling too early for him artistically to have done this painting.'

'But you still think it has to pre-date *Her Children*?'

'Absolutely. You wouldn't create something at that level, a national masterpiece, and then turn it around and doodle a portrait on the back.'

'No. That makes no sense,' Freja agreed. 'So then, at least your window is getting smaller. This all means it had to have been painted between mid-1920 and summer 1922.'

'Yeah – except even with that tight timeframe, there's so much material to get through. My main problem is going to be getting through it all in the time we've got. In three days,

I've only managed eleven boxes. I have moved all of three feet, with nothing to show for it.'

'How much is there?'

'Well, right now that stack is looking a mile long,' Darcy panted. 'There are dozens of boxes to go, which is not helped by the fact that I can't work late.'

'Why not?' Freja frowned.

'I can't stay in the gallery past seven. Not allowed. That's when the night patrol team comes in and all the security systems are activated.'

'Oh damn. Hadn't thought of that.'

'Yeah. I got in for seven yesterday morning, which is when Viggo always gets there and opens up. At least I can build in a little more time that way.'

'And there I was thinking you had got lucky after all.'

'Ha bloody ha.' Darcy had regaled her flatmate with all the details of her disaster date the other night with Erik. They both knew perfectly well that luck was not on her side.

'Well, if your back's up against the wall, then I reckon you've only got one option open to you.'

'Which is?'

They were approaching the bridge that reconnected to the rest of the park and Darcy felt her reward getting closer. Eight kilometres down, two to go. They had plans to go to the flower market after this and watch the new *Mission Impossible* this afternoon, before they both went for dinner with Tristan in the evening. Freja had had to plead with Darcy to agree to it. He wanted to 'bond' with her, Freja said – which, to Darcy, suggested an alarming leaning towards commitment.

'You're going to have to ask for an assistant.'

'Freja, I'm looking for a nameless face in a photo, a faceless name in a letter – that means trusting someone else *not* to miss the single clue that will unlock it all.'

'Ah yes, trust. Your favourite quality.'

Darcy rolled her eyes at the tease. 'Besides, Viggo's being amazing. And I do trust him; no one knows the archives better. He's doing what he can to help but he's got a full workload too.'

'Surely he can prioritize helping you while you work on this?'

'Not really. The retrospective is going to mean an uptick in visitor numbers for the Madsen Collection too so they're frantically pulling together *their* new exhibition. They've loaned a bunch of Triers to the National so they've got a lot of blank walls that need filling.'

'You know, hearing all this drama makes me glad I chose to pursue a career in the sedate world of genomics.'

They crossed the bridge and exited the park, on to the home straight for their coffees.

'So, dare I ask how's it going with our Last Man Standing?'

'Aksel the Vet? . . . Oh, it's going, I guess,' Darcy panted. 'We're currently politely discussing climate change and the increase in tsunamis since the 1990s.'

'Wow, tsunamis, huh?'

'Yeah.'

'Just you be careful. A guy like that – one minute you're discussing tidal waves and the next, he'll be sorting your recycling.' They stopped at a pedestrian crossing, jogging on the spot as they waited for the lights to change. 'Has he made any suggestions about meeting up yet?'

'Not yet. I'm beginning to think he just wants someone to talk to. You know – if only they could talk?'

'Ugh, just cut to the chase and ask him directly if he wants to have a drink. There's no point in wasting any more time. You don't need someone to talk to; you've got me for that.'

'Hm, I'm not so sure. There's been something quite soothing about having a rolling quiet conversation after the Erik and Max disasters. He may not be the most dynamic guy but he's intelligent, thoughtful, sincere.'

'He sounds like someone your grandmother would choose for you.'

Darcy chuckled. 'I'll take it. I don't have the bandwidth for drama right now.'

The lights changed and they jogged across the road, turning into the wide residential streets and running just south of the King's Garden. The wind gusted and Darcy felt a newfound appreciation for the feeling of it on her face, the sound of the traffic, bicycle bells pinging and people calling dogs and children in the parks. All the silence and dim light in the archives sometimes made her feel like a mole.

Up ahead, as the roads grew narrow and more winding, she saw the cafe where her reward beckoned. She wasn't a natural runner, unlike her flatmate, and every weekend she had to be either cajoled, bribed or bullied into her running shoes. Her occasional stumble to the Academy couldn't compare to this cross-city trek.

'Oh, thank God,' she panted as Freja steadily slowed to a walk, her hands on her hips and her face turned to the sky. It was the signal that Darcy had survived this weekend's outing.

Her phone buzzed and she pulled it out of her jacket's zipped pocket as Freja led the charge inside.

'Oh! What a result!' Darcy said, reading the message in disbelief as Freja placed their regular orders.

'What is?' Freja, leaning on the counter, looked over at her.

'Viggo's managed to get permission for me to bring some of the material home so I can work on it there.'

'Why's that such a big thing?'

'Because normally, no one's allowed to remove anything from the premises. Historic artefacts? Insurance?' She rolled her eyes. 'Seeing as I can't work late, Viggo said he'd look into it for me but he thought there'd be no chance. He's been pleading special dispensation given the circumstances but he was pretty sure the insurers would baulk on the grounds that this research isn't directly to the benefit of the Madsen Collection.'

'What do you mean?'

'Well, the portrait, as it's conjoined to *Her Children*, will belong to the nation and hang at the National Gallery – so why should Madsen incur any risk to *their* assets?'

'Oh, right.'

'Yeah. It's not an unreasonable position. They're already doing me a favour by giving me unrestricted access to their archives. But this . . .' She pressed a hand to her heart in a soothing gesture; it was still racing from their run. 'Oh God, what a relief. This will make such a difference, being able to put a shift in this weekend. I've been so stressed about it. Otto wants an update on Monday; he's got to report back to Margit Kinberg and as it stands, I have nothing to give him. Fingers crossed I find something – anything – to show him by then.'

She checked the time. Ten forty. Her eyes narrowed as she did some mental calculations. 'Hm. If I head over there now, I could pretty much do a full day and still be able to meet you guys for dinner later.'

'You're going to go straight there? Right now?' Freja cast a sceptical eye over her.

Darcy rolled her eyes. 'I assure you Viggo doesn't give two hoots if I'm a hot sweaty mess. And he says the boxes have just been delivered. I don't want to keep him waiting in case he wants to go out.'

'Where is he?'

Darcy checked the address. 'He lives . . . Oh, he's on the same street as the gallery.' She looked back at Freja. 'Now *that* explains his unfeasibly early starts.'

'I guess.'

Darcy glanced up at her tone, realizing she was torpedoing their day's plans. 'You don't mind, do you? We could see the film tomorrow?'

'It's not the film I'm worried about. Work's got to come first.' Freja handed her the juice and chia pot as they stepped outside again. 'But just be there for dinner, okay? No matter what? Tristan wants to meet you properly and it's important to me that you two get on.'

'I promise.' Darcy kissed her on the cheek. 'And we will.'

'But change! Dress up! He's taking us somewhere posh.'

'Posh. Got it,' she called over her shoulder, one hand in the air in a wave as she headed back up the street they'd just run down, crossing into King's Garden again. She sipped her juice and ate the chia pot as she walked, dodging the tourists heading at a brisk clip for Rosenborg Castle and feeling more aligned with the locals idling on park benches, children climbing on the marble spheres dotted around. Groups of undergrads were emerging bleary-eyed from the university accommodation halls after their heavy Friday night.

She turned onto Stockholmsgade and walked in the direction of the gallery, checking the building numbers as she passed, stopping eventually outside a very handsome period townhouse: the red-brick walls were covered with magenta Virginia creeper, the large blocky windows painted a blackish green.

She pressed the buzzer and waited for Viggo's familiar greeting. In the space of less than a week, in dim light and over strong coffee, they had become new friends, but standing here now, she realized he was still an enigma to her. A house like this, on one of the best roads in the city? She knew he was a widower but had his wife also been an heiress?

She looked back at the park on the other side of the road as she waited, trees denuded of their leaves, the lake twinkling darkly against a dull sky. Traffic had slowed for a troop of blue-jacketed soldiers marching in formation down the centre of the street and proceeding irrespective of the traffic light signals. Trucks, buses, taxis all stopped, waiting patiently, the packs of cyclists bunching up behind them. It was no different to the Royal Household Guards returning to the Hyde Park barracks, she supposed.

She heard the front door click open and whirled round with a smile. 'Hi—'

The word died on her lips as Max Lorensen looked back at her. For a moment, he looked as surprised as she was – but only for a moment. 'Darcy . . . I didn't expect you so soon.' He stepped back to allow her in.

Darcy blinked, utterly stunned. Viggo hadn't mentioned Max would be here. Could he not have given her a heads up? And *why* was he here anyway? On a Saturday? Were they having a meeting?

'. . . Thanks.' She stepped in, now bitterly regretting her decision not to go home, shower and change before coming here. Her sartorial decline from their first meeting had been brutal: from dazzling black tie the first night to work-sensible, slouchy jeans, and now sweaty running kit.

He was wearing jeans and a grey sweatshirt. No shoes. No socks.

No *socks?*

He shut the door and openly looked her over with scepticism. 'Running again, I see. You must be keen.'

'Not in the least. My flatmate bullies me. She does triathlons.'

'She sounds impressive.'

'Oh, she is. She's a microbiologist. Decodes the origins of human life.'

'Whereas you discover the identities of long-dead women.' His gaze was so steady, always so steady upon her.

'Yeah. It's not exactly the same, is it?'

He blinked. 'Both are valid.'

A silence descended as they stood there for a moment; Darcy remembered the crushing disappointment of their last meeting, his casual dismissal of her, and she wondered: if Erik hadn't been standing at the bottom of those steps that night – if she had gone back to Max's for a nightcap instead – how different would things be between them now? Would it be better or worse than this strained, enforced professionalism?

She looked away, noticing for the first time the beautiful hallway. It had antique timbered floors, matt black panelled walls and a verdure tapestry hanging down behind a beautiful round walnut table. On top, a huge pale clay pot had been planted with an extravagant abundance of sprigs of yellow forsythia.

'Follow me. They're up here,' he said, leading her towards the staircase and up to the next level.

Darcy trailed behind him, her eye falling to the few but

special *objets* dotted around the place: the Picasso sketch between two doorframes, a small Diego Giacometti bronze of a bird, a worn and faded Heriz carpet that seemed as old as the building. Was Viggo a collector? He had mentioned in passing that he had lived alone since his wife had died and connoisseurship often could fill a void, she knew that. It was her opinion that most collectors had unhappy love lives. The obsession had to go somewhere.

She followed Max into a room on the first floor. It was vast, spanning the entire back of the house, with a run of huge windows looking out over a mature garden. In contrast to the moodiness of the hall, it was painted a thick ivory with a black open-plan kitchen in the middle of the space and a huge dining table, seating fourteen, set beyond by the windows. Where she stood, in the foreground to all that, a soft seating area had been arranged with dark green velvet sofas arranged in a U. On a low table in the middle sat two marbled burgundy boxes she recognized very well . . . Only two?

She looked around the space again, recognizing a Maria Slavona on one wall, a Max Liebermann on the other.

'Viggo lives here?' she asked in disbelief.

'*Viggo?*' He gave a small laugh as he crossed the room and headed for the kitchen. 'What on earth makes you think that?'

'I . . . He said he'd managed to arrange for some of the boxes to be released and that I could collect them from this address.' She glanced again at his bare feet with a sinking feeling.

'Collect?' Max glanced over at her as he reached for a bag of coffee beans and tipped them into a grinder. '*I* arranged the release for you – and I was only able to do it because I gave the insurers my assurance, as a trustee, that the material would be safe in *my* home, under *my* supervision. The fact that I live up the street from the gallery reassured them, but you won't be able to take anything away from here. Their conditions were strict.'

This was his house? 'You mean I'll have to work here?'

He arched an eyebrow. 'Is that a problem?'

'But this is your home.'

'Yes.'

'And it's the weekend.'

'Yes.'

She gave an astonished laugh. 'You don't want *me* working here, getting in your way.'

'Why should you get in my way? Is this place not big enough for the two of us?'

The two of us. Was it just her, or did the words seem charged? 'You know what I mean. Just because I've got to work overtime, doesn't mean you have to.'

'*I* don't intend to work.'

'But—'

'Darcy, we're all invested in wanting to get this over the line as quickly as possible. If this will help, then I'm happy to oblige.'

She watched as he pressed some buttons and the coffee machine began to loudly grind the beans.

He stared over at her. 'How do you like it?'

'Sorry?'

'Your coffee.'

'Oh . . . Strong and black.'

She began to pace slowly, her eyes grazing over the finer details of the room, noticing the Tiffany espresso cups, an Hermes ashtray, a cashmere fringed throw . . . It was a very grown-up space, completely opposite in style and spirit to hers and Freja's, which was filled with Ikea sofas, takeaway boxes, mismatched underwear drying on the radiators and glitter eyeshadow perpetually on the bathroom counter. 'How long have you lived here?'

'. . . Ten years, thereabouts.'

'You bought this when you were twenty-two?' The question burst from her before she could stop herself and he looked surprised in turn. But who could afford a four-storey townhouse on one of the best roads in Copenhagen at the age of twenty-two?

She remembered the driver outside the museum earlier in the week. Max's supreme ease with the older, sophisticated crowd. As if it had been just another Tuesday night for him. Something of a drag.

Born to it, then.

She turned away, collecting herself. Had it really only been Tuesday that they had met? His presence somehow loomed large in her consciousness now, a second pulse ticking away deep inside her.

'Don't look so impressed. Copenhagen prices don't compare to London,' he murmured, pushing buttons and pulling on a lever. She gave him a surprised look of her own. Was that modesty she was witnessing?

'Have you done much work to it?' she asked, looking up at the plaster cornicing.

'Not really. Mainly just a paint job. And the bathrooms.'

Bathrooms, plural. She wondered how many he had. She wanted to ask if he lived all alone here, but that felt too intrusive – personal – and he had made it clear they were to stay away from that. Although she didn't think standing in his kitchen on a Saturday morning came under the standard definition of 'professional'.

He came over with the coffee and held it out for her. 'Strong and black.'

'Thank you,' she murmured, distracted by his bare feet in her peripheral vision.

A sound above them, like the creak of a floorboard, made her look up. Was someone else here? She looked back at Max but he had already turned away, heading towards the archive boxes.

'So, how long do you think it'll take you to get through these?'

She bit her lip. Three a day was her average – but it was almost lunchtime now. 'Uh, well, it depends on what's in there. If it's some auction catalogues, I can speed up. If it's slides . . .' she shrugged. 'But I'll go as fast as I can, I promise.'

'No, I . . .' He turned back to her. 'I wasn't suggesting you need to rush. I just meant, will these be enough for you today or will you need more?'

'Oh. No. This will be . . . great.'

'I can arrange for more to be sent over if you need them.'

'Thanks, but this will do.' She watched as he took a sip of his coffee, lifting the lid on the nearest box and peering in at the papers. Idly he leafed through the topmost ones. 'I don't envy you,' he said, half over his shoulder.

'Max, are you really sure I can't take them back to mine? I'd be *so* careful, I swear.'

He shook his head. 'It's more than my job's worth. I gave my word.'

She looked away with a sigh. 'Sure.'

From outside the room there came a sound of more creaks, drawing closer now. Someone was coming down the stairs. Darcy's eyes slid over to him, asking the question 'who?' but he turned away again, focusing on his coffee.

'Baby, I thought you said—' A striking brunette stopped in the doorway. She was tall and thin, a model without doubt, wearing leggings and a grey cashmere jumper with micro-Uggs. 'Oh. Hey.'

'Hi,' Darcy gave a stricken smile, holding her hand up in a feeble wave. 'I'm Darcy.'

'Angelina.' But as she said the word, her eyes slid in a question mark towards Max. Darcy's too. She was sure that wasn't the name she'd heard him say on the phone, on the steps, the other night.

'Darcy's a colleague. She's working at the gallery for the next few weeks,' he explained.

'You're a curator?' Angelina asked.

'PhD student at the Royal Academy, actually, but I've been put onto a special project here.'

'Is this about that painting you were talking about?' Angelina asked, walking – stalking – over to Max and looping her arms around his shoulders. Standing at five foot eleven, she was barely an inch shorter than him and she sank onto one hip, kissing him lightly on the cheek.

'Yes.'

'He's been so excited,' she drawled in a sardonic tone, looking back at Darcy, who was standing frozen, clutching her mug. 'Like a little boy.'

'I hardly think so,' Max said, extricating himself from her languid embrace and checking his phone. 'It's simply very relevant for the Foundation.' He looked up and slid his phone into his back pocket, regarding the two women for a moment. Darcy looked down, knowing that even at her best, in black velvet with a blow-dry, she couldn't come out of any comparison with Angelina favourably.

'I'm really sorry to interrupt your weekend like this,' she said, motioning vaguely to the boxes. 'But if there's a quiet room where I can go to work, at least I can get out of your way.'

'That isn't necessary,' Max said.

'I'd feel better if I wasn't in your way here.'

'You won't be. We're going out now.'

'Oh.'

'Socks.' Angelina slapped her forehead with her hand and pointed to his bare feet. 'I forgot to bring down your socks. I knew there was something. I have a mind like a sieve.'

Darcy smiled wanly. *Now* the bare feet made sense. She had interrupted them.

'Nice to meet you –'

From the way her voice angled up at the end, Darcy knew she had intended to use her name but had forgotten it. 'Yes. Nice to meet you too, Angelina.'

She didn't stir as the other woman drifted from the room like a fairy, and the silence that grew in her wake felt heavy with unspoken words.

'You look concerned,' Max said, watching as she bit her lip.

'Aren't you?'

'About what?'

'Are you really comfortable with leaving me alone in your house?'

'Why shouldn't I be?'

'You don't know me.'

'Don't I?' A beat passed at the question, the sound of the floorboard creaking upstairs reminding them they weren't alone. A small smile played on his lips. 'Darcy, relax. I have an instinct I'm not going to come back to graffiti on the walls and the fittings stripped out.'

'Hilarious. But if you knew me at all, you'd know a comment like that would only make me *want* to do it.'

'So you're contrary?' He nodded. 'Worth knowing.'

She sighed. Jousting with him was exhausting; their words

were weighted but the silences were heavy too. 'Do you at least know when you'll be back? I'll try to be gone before you return.'

'No.'

'A ballpark idea?'

'Darcy, just do what you need to do. Stay here till midnight if that's what it takes.'

'God, no,' she said quickly. 'It wouldn't be anything like that.'

'It can be, though, if that's what you need.'

'No.' She shook her head. 'I have to be somewhere for eight.'

His eyes narrowed fractionally and she saw his mouth part as if to say something.

'Socks!' Angelina said, pushing on the door and throwing a pair towards him.

He caught it with one hand, his gaze not lifting off Darcy. 'Great.'

'So, is there anything I should do on my way out? An alarm I should set?' Darcy asked as he began putting them on, one-legged, perfectly balanced.

'It's fine. Don't worry about anything. Help yourself to coffee, whatever you want. There's not much food in, but there's cheese and grapes in the fridge.'

'No, I –' She shook her head quickly. As if she'd come over here and eat his food! 'I'll be fine. Thanks.'

He nodded, standing on two feet again, his hands on his hips. He looked so different in his jeans and socks. Saturday Max. 'Well, have a good day. I hope it's productive.'

'Me too,' she agreed, watching him leave. Angelina was holding out a short navy coat for him and a grey scarf, and he shrugged them on carelessly.

She listened to their steps on the stairs, the withdrawal of their voices and finally the click of the front door. Several seconds passed as she stood motionless, trying to understand how the hell it had come to pass that she was alone in Max Lorensen's townhouse on a Saturday lunchtime. Was this a dream or a nightmare?

She sank onto the sofa with a groan.

It was both.

Chapter Eight

Seven fifty-two.

Darcy sat alone at the table, staring out of the window at the wildflower meadows which were an incongruous luxury in a marine city. The sleek blonde wood room was an homage to eco luxury, with no decoration beyond an antique *shou sugi ban* table, some hides on chairs, and plants and vines hanging from the ceiling. It certainly wasn't the sort of place to sit staring at her phone, the ambient noise level never rising beyond a civilized murmur. Everyone was dressed in a sombre but refined colour palette and she suspected that if she checked labels, all she would find was Massimo Dutti, Loro Piana and Celine; just so much as a ruffle or a hint of pink would disturb the peace.

She was trying not to drink her glass of water too quickly, but after the day she'd had, she could have downed a bottle of wine. The minutes ticked by at half speed. The waiters probably thought she'd been stood up. She had known it was silly to arrive so early, but she'd been propelled all afternoon by a need to get going – to get gone – and she hadn't been able to shake it off when she'd got back to the apartment. Somewhat to her relief, Freja hadn't been there – no doubt getting ready at Tristan's – and she'd been able to shower and calm herself down in peace.

'My God, are we late?' Freja asked, rousing her from her thoughts.

'No, I'm just crazy early for once.' She pressed her cheek to her friend's.

'Don't tell me you're hungry?' Freja asked with mock surprise.

'Always.'

'Of course.' Freja was wearing a dark green silk dress shot through with delicate gold thread which Darcy had never seen before. *New?* she asked wordlessly, with an arch of her eyebrow; Freja winked back in silent reply. Her ringleted hair was blown out and she was wearing chunky gold earrings, also new. Darcy wasn't sure she'd ever seen her friend look sophisticated before. The two of them very much alternated between Hedge Backwards (running/gym kit), Rotting Corpse (PJs), Basic Bitch (jeans) and Club Rat (anything black, cropped or tight).

Freja looked back, holding her arm out towards someone, a smile enlivening her face. Darcy caught the look of pride in her eyes. 'Darce, finally, you get to meet Tristan. Tristan – no pressure, but this is the most important person in my life.'

Darcy looked up to finally greet her hitherto-faceless foe, the man responsible for stealing away her best friend and leaving her alone in an empty flat.

'No pressure at all, then.' Tristan grinned, his face pleating into easy folds as if it was his default setting as they shook hands. 'Hi.'

'. . . Hi.' Darcy was taken aback. He was not what she had expected at all. Freja's usual type was unemployed artist/musician/writer, bouncer or barista. This guy was more barrister. He seemed to be Freja's opposite in every way: neat to her scruffy; formal to her relaxed; large, open features to her doll looks; an athletic, muscular frame to her long, skinny limbs. He was dressed simply in a black suit and open-necked shirt but had a stealth-wealth vibe that Erik the Property Developer could have learned a lot from.

But that wasn't what surprised her most. Freja had somehow failed to mention at any point that Tristan was a good ten, if not twenty, years older than them. Of course he had chosen this fancy restaurant, would order the wine, pay for dinner – all of which Freja had forewarned her about. He could be her dad!

'. . . Thanks for arranging this.'

'I take any excuse I can. The food's very good here. Have you been before?' he asked.

Darcy suppressed a shocked laugh. 'No. Never.' Funnily enough, her student budget didn't stretch to Michelin-starred restaurants. 'But it all looks so good.' She cast an envious glance at the diners already eating. 'I'm ravenous.'

'Why *so* hungry?' Freja asked.

'I've not eaten since breakfast.'

'What? Nothing at all?' Freja asked, looking appalled. She ate hourly and was still somehow stick thin.

'Yeah.'

'But there's leftover curry in the fridge.'

'I know, but I wasn't at home. I had to stay where I was to work. Turned out I couldn't leave the premises with any of the material.'

Freja looked scandalized. 'But surely Viggo could have made you a sandwich?'

Darcy bit her lip, wondering whether to tell her friend the full story. After the way Freja had reacted to Max last time, she didn't relish bringing up his name again – especially not in front of Tristan.

'It was fine,' she demurred, deciding to change the subject. 'I wasn't hungry while I was working. It was only afterwards that it caught up with me.'

'Tch.' Freja looked unimpressed. 'You need fuel, especially after we went harder on the run today.'

'We did?' Darcy asked in surprise.

'Didn't you notice? We knocked six minutes off our PB.'

'That's impressive,' Tristan said, looking at Darcy.

'It was nothing to do with me. I had no idea, I just try to keep up,' she shrugged.

'You were stressed. It was like a jet engine propelling you along.'

'Huh.' Darcy wondered how quickly she would go if she were to run tomorrow, with today's encounter with Max running through her head. Supersonic?

'This is precisely why we run, I keep telling you. Stress management. You need it even when you think you don't.'

Darcy rolled her eyes. 'See what I have to live with? She never gives me any peace. My Saturday mornings are gruelling.'

A waitress came over with the menus. She automatically handed Tristan the wine list. 'Well, she's trying to talk *me* into doing a Tough Mudder competition with her,' he said, taking it mindlessly. He looked perfectly at home here.

'It'd be so fun!' Freja exclaimed, reaching for his hand.

'Tristan, escape now while you still can,' Darcy quipped, reaching for her almost empty water glass instead. 'The next thing you know, she'll have you signed up to Iron Man and ultramarathons.'

'Yeah, that's what my head's saying too,' he grinned. 'On

the other hand, I do like how she pushes me.' He looked back at Freja and they shared a look so private, Darcy had to look away. She stared down at the menu but the words swam in front of her eyes. Having been alone all day, she'd been looking forward to meeting up with them tonight; she hadn't expected to feel lonely in their company.

As if reading her mind, Tristan pulled his hand back and cleared his throat. 'Apologies, we're still at the "disgusting to be around" stage.'

'Darcy doesn't care. Her love life is far more exciting. She's got them lining up,' Freja grinned.

'Now that's not exactly true is it, Freja?' Darcy said in a wry tone, before looking over at Tristan. 'Thanks for the referral to Raya by the way.'

He shrugged. 'My pleasure. I'm glad it's working out for you.'

'That might be a stretch. All I have on my horizon so far is a date booked with a rather reluctant vet.'

'So he finally asked?' Freja gasped.

'No, I did. I couldn't be bothered with waiting any longer.' Sitting alone on Max Lorensen's velvet sofa while he was out lunching with a model and opening a text from Aksel asking her if she could roll her tongue (it was a genetic quirk, suppos-edly) had been her tipping point. Just date me or dump me, she had thought as she texted back: *Let's meet and I can show you.*

'Good on you, girl.' Freja looked back at Tristan. 'This guy's been dragging out the conversation for days,' she explained.

'*Days*? Surely not,' Tristan said, bemused. 'You say that like it's a bad thing.'

'It is a bad thing. This is modern dating. There comes a

point when being endlessly polite is actually just rude. Does he want her or not?'

His smile grew. 'Perhaps he's one of those guys who doesn't want to rush things. I've heard there's still a few of them left out there.'

'Yeah. Well, he hasn't met me, but he *really* respects me,' Darcy said sardonically.

Tristan chuckled. 'He could turn out to be a keeper. You never know.'

'So when are you seeing him, and where?' Freja demanded.

'Tuesday night. At the Bastard cafe.' It was a board games bar, perfectly suited to rainy Sunday afternoons – but he was on call this weekend.

'Quirky.'

'Yeah. I figured if the conversation was lacking, at least we'd have something to do.'

'Good call,' Freja agreed. 'Are you excited?'

Darcy arched an eyebrow. 'Come now – we know better than that. No expectations. No disappointment.'

'This is a tragedy! You're both so cynical,' Tristan exclaimed.

'You would be too if you had to date men,' Freja replied.

He laughed.

'I'm serious. Poor Darce got cheated on in her last relationship. And the one before decided that he was bi, but since then has only dated men.'

'I turned him gay. *I* did that,' Darcy said, thumping her chest with a proud smile and making him laugh harder.

'You've had a bad run,' Freja consoled, patting her hand and also laughing. 'Which is precisely why your luck is about to change. Aksel the Vet is everything those guys weren't. Just you wait. Tuesday night is going to be transformative.'

Darcy rolled her eyes as she looked back at Tristan with a tut. 'I don't know what you've done to my friend, but could you give her back, please? I don't recognize this lovesick puppy sitting beside me.'

'Apologies,' he grinned, looking delighted and not at all sorry.

Two waiters walked past carrying plates, and Darcy's nose twitched at the tantalizing scent. 'My God, what is that?' she asked, unable to place it.

'Reindeer brain jelly, if I'm not mistaken,' Tristan replied.

She suppressed a guffaw of laughter. *What?* 'Of course. How silly of me not to recognize it.'

He grinned. 'As I say, I come here any chance I can get.'

'Well, I can honestly say I've never even seen reindeer brains before, much less eaten them.'

'It's more delicious than you could imagine.'

'I'm counting on it.'

Tristan laughed.

'I still can't believe Viggo let you work without a break,' Freja fumed. 'I thought you said the guy was lovely!'

'He is. And it really wasn't like that.'

'No? How not?'

Darcy hesitated, unable to see an exit strategy. 'Because *he* wasn't actually there.'

'Huh?'

'When I got his text saying the boxes were available, I assumed the address he gave was his, but it wasn't. That's all,' she shrugged.

It was not all, of course. Freja knew her too well. 'So whose was it, then? Where were you?'

'Does it matter?' Darcy replied, as dismissively as she could.

Freja's eyes narrowed. 'Yeah . . . I think it does. Where were you that you couldn't leave and couldn't eat?'

She sighed, knowing her flatmate wouldn't give it up. 'I was at Max's house, but—'

'Max?' Freja looked at her blankly, before giving a gasp. *'Max the Lawyer?'*

'Yes.'

Freja sat back in her chair, her hand plastered over her open mouth.

Darcy rolled her eyes. 'Frey, that's a bit dramatic, even for you.'

'You were in his house? But . . . how? You unmatched with him.'

'Because he was the one who got the approval for the archive material to be taken off site. He lives on the same road and he's a trustee, so it was enough to convince the insurers to allow it – but I couldn't take it away. I had to stay and work there.'

'Who is this guy?' Tristan asked, looking bewildered by the sudden drama.

'A man-whore who she needs to keep well away from,' Freja said. 'He is everything Aksel the Vet isn't. He's trouble. Toxic.'

'Do you always describe everyone by their occupations?'

'It helps keep them . . . one-dimensional.'

Tristan's eyebrows shot up. 'Now who's toxic?'

'That's not toxic. It's sensible. Until they can prove they're trustworthy, they don't get to be fully fledged people in our lives.'

Tristan absorbed this for a moment. 'So what was I? Tristan the Scientist?'

She beamed at him. 'Actually no, you're saved in my phone as Boss Baby.'

'Boss Baby?' He laughed. 'I see.'

'You're her *boss*?' Darcy asked in shock.

Tristan froze, his eyes sliding over to Freja. 'You didn't say?'

'. . . It hasn't come up!'

'How not?'

Freja swallowed. 'Because I didn't anticipate us getting to this point where we would be meeting each other's families and friends.'

Tristan reached over and placed his hand over Freja's. 'How can you be so young and yet so cynical?'

'Because a lot's changed since you were young,' Freja quipped.

Tristan grinned and Darcy saw again the teasing energy between them.

'What exactly is the age difference?' Darcy asked, seeing as they were being frank.

'Sixteen years,' Freja answered. 'He's forty-two.'

'Forty-two and your boss,' Darcy murmured. 'Right.'

'It's not ideal, I know. On paper it looks bad,' Tristan said, his smile disappearing for the first time since he'd arrived. 'But Freja's twenty-six. She knows her own mind, and neither of us was looking for this or expecting it to become what it's become. We're more surprised than anyone.'

I doubt that, Darcy thought but didn't say. She wondered how her flatmate's parents would take the news when they heard. If they heard. 'So are you divorced, or . . . ?'

'No. Never married. I was too focused on building the business to have time for relationships before now.'

'Building the business?'

'Black Circle Labs is Tristan's company. He's the founder.'

It was Darcy's turn to gasp, as she heard the name of the company where Freja was doing her work placement. 'So then you're the boss's boss. The *big* boss.'

'I'm the boss of everyone *but* Freja. I've yet to win an argument – or to steal the duvet back in the middle of the night.'

Darcy had to smile. '. . . Any kids?'

'No kids either. Not even any pets.'

'Oh, well, that's just worrying,' she rebutted. 'Anyone who willingly chooses to live without dogs is clearly sociopathic.'

'Then I shall get a dog,' he said, not missing a beat. The man radiated charisma. 'How am I doing? Do I pass, in spite of my very obvious flaws and dogless state?'

'I guess you're passing muster,' she grinned back.

'Is that it? Is the interrogation over?' Freja demanded. 'Can we get back to the crisis in hand now?' She turned back to Darcy. 'How was it, seeing him again?' She looked at Tristan. 'He dumped her before they could be a thing. Said they need to be professional because of working together.'

'Usually I would wholeheartedly agree with the sentiment,' Tristan said, reaching over and squeezing Freja's thigh.

'Well, it was a shock, obviously, given I thought I was going to see Viggo.' Darcy shrugged. 'But he was . . . very nice about it all. Generous.' She tried to make her words as neutral as possible.

'Wasn't it awkward, though, being in his house?'

'Not really. He wasn't even there after the first ten minutes.'

'He left?'

'Yes, he had plans with his girlfriend.'

Freja's jaw dropped open as the hits kept on coming.

'She's another model,' Darcy said quickly, anticipating the questions before they came. 'Angelina or something. Stunning. Exactly what you'd expect for him. Anyway, they went out and left me to it, and I just worked until about six and then went back home, and that's it.'

She drew a breath.

'Wait, wait, wait – just back it up,' Freja said bossily, holding up her hands. 'He left you *alone* in his house, *all day*?'

Darcy felt relief that she wasn't the only one to have found it odd. 'Yes. Working.'

'But not eating.'

'He did actually say I could help myself to whatever. But obviously I wasn't going to do that.'

'So what, you just starved for seven hours?'

'I had a glass of water. Two glasses, actually.' The coffee machine had looked too expensive to use. What if she did something wrong and broke it?

Freja stared at her, analysing her every breath. 'What's his house like?'

'Stunning. It's a townhouse on Stockholmsgade.'

'Oh, I've got some friends who live along there,' Tristan said, interested.

Of course he did, Darcy thought. Millionaire's Row.

'There are some special properties on that road.'

'Yes. His is definitely one of them. Ivy-clad, windows over-looking the park; antiques. A few Picasso and Matisse sketches in the downstairs loo.'

'You went to the loo?' Freja gasped.

'Obviously.' Darcy rolled her eyes. 'I just told you, I had two glasses of water and was there all day.'

'Where else did you go?'

'Nowhere. That was it.'

'That was it? You didn't have a quick sneak peek at his bedroom?'

'Of course not!'

'The sitting room, then?'

'Freja! I wasn't going to go snooping around the place!' She shot a sideways look at Tristan, who was listening interestedly.

Freja's eyes narrowed. 'You think he has cameras?'

'I mean, maybe,' Darcy shrugged. She dropped her voice. 'I couldn't take the risk, you know?'

'Yeah,' Freja agreed, sitting back in the chair and tapping her fingernails thoughtfully on the table.

Tristan chuckled, as if amused by them both.

'I don't know how you could bear it, all those hours sitting there . . . alone,' Freja commiserated. 'The temptation to just *see* his stuff – his life, his world – you know?'

'Are you getting this?' Darcy asked Tristan.

'Oh yeah.' He nodded. 'This is why women are terrifying.'

Darcy laughed, but Freja was still on her riff. 'It could have told you so much about him, though. Homes are so revealing.'

'Well, it definitely revealed he's rich. Likely born rich. He's been there for ten years, he said.'

'And he's with a supermodel!'

'Well, she's just a model – but she was pretty super,' Darcy conceded. 'They definitely looked right together.'

'Yeah,' Freja agreed, even though she hadn't laid eyes on either one of them.

'Is that a thing, then?' Tristan asked. 'Looking right together?'

'You don't agree that some people just look like they belong together?'

He looked across at Freja and gave a shrug. 'Not really, no. I'm not sure you and I are a visual match. And yet . . .'

'You're so sweet,' Freja murmured, looking into his eyes, her features softening as his gaze held hers.

Darcy cleared her throat to remind them she was still there, still third-wheeling. 'Well, anyway, it's none of my business. I was there to work and that's what I did.'

Freja drew herself back into the moment. 'But weren't you

distracted? Didn't you spend the whole time thinking he'd be back any minute?'

Darcy didn't want to admit it. '. . . Yes. It sort of defeated the point of working the weekend.' She had somehow made her way through both boxes, leaving a piece of paper on top with a note. *'All done. Thanks, D.'*

Strictly speaking, she could have done with looking back over some diary entries for June 1920 one more time, but the spectre of his – his and Angelina's – imminent return had her nervous to the point of feeling sick, and she had bolted as early as she could. She *really* hadn't wanted to still be there when they got back.

Freja's eyes narrowed again. 'Would it have been better or worse if he'd been there?'

'Oh, worse. Infinitely. I couldn't have concentrated with him in the vicinity.' She gave a shudder.

'Bet you wish you'd gone home and had that shower now, huh?'

'Yep,' Darcy agreed. 'But at least it's over and done with now. And I won't have to see him again. He doesn't work in the same building, so this was a one-off.'

'Yeah, right.' Freja's eyes slid over to Tristan's and he gave a shrug.

'What?' Darcy asked.

'Nothing,' Freja shrugged back.

'No, what?'

Tristan caught the eye of the waitress, and she came towards the table to take their orders. 'I just feel sorry for the vet.'

'Interesting case today. I had a hamster brought in that had swallowed a marble. Never seen that before.'

Darcy lay in the dark, staring at her screen. It was well after midnight, and she was home alone; Freja had gone back to Tristan's after dinner. Why wouldn't she? He had a penthouse apartment in Islands Brygge. *'Were you able to get it out?'*

'Yes, eventually. Costly though.'

'How much?'

'13,000 kr.'

'OMG. For a hamster?'

'People do crazy things for their "fur babies".'

She smiled, turning onto her side and pulling the covers up over her shoulders. It was a cold night, frost forming on the outside of the window. *'What's the strangest medical emergency you've ever had?'*

'There's been a few: had a rabbit that accidentally got stoned a few weeks back, eating a joint.'

'No! That's terrible.'

'The owner swore blind it wasn't theirs [shrug emoji] And we have a dog who keeps swallowing bees and keeps getting stung. Repeat offender. Doesn't seem to learn.'

'Poor thing.'

'Yesterday a cat was brought in with concussion. It ran headlong into a wall, chasing an infrared laser.'

'No! Was it okay?'

'Will be. No lasting damage.'

'I never knew being a vet was so diverting.'

'Rarely boring, that's for sure. How was your day?'

'I ended up having to work too. But it was nowhere near as interesting as yours – sifting through boxes on my own. I did manage to get a run in with my flatmate this morning though, so that was something.'

'You like running?'

'Hate it, but she bribes me with food.'

'How far do you run?'

'Usually 8–10k. Depends on whether we have hangovers.'

'Sounds like you get on well.'

'We're very close. She was my first proper friend in the city. Do you live with anyone?'

'My sister. She's three years younger and training to be a nurse.'

'Medical family.'

'Yes. My father's a doctor too . . .'

They chatted for a while longer before saying good night and she switched off her phone, staring across her room and out of the window. She never drew her curtains here. It would be dark until her alarm went off in the morning – not that she had set an alarm for tomorrow. Sunday mornings were sacrosanct and with Freja over at Tristan's, she had the place entirely to herself. She might bake a cake. Or read that book she'd bought at the airport on her way over in the summer and still hadn't had time to read. Or go to the gym. Or try dry-slope skiing at CopenHill. Or finally see the Vilhelm Hammershøi painting *Interior in Strandgade* at the Kunst . . .

Or, most likely, sit on the sofa watching Netflix, eating cereal from the box.

What time was it?

Darcy groaned, reaching for the phone, her hand patting around blindly for it on the bedside table. She found it eventually on top of her covers, which meant two things: she hadn't stirred in her sleep. And she had drifted off to sleep too quickly last night, forgetting to plug it in to charge. She opened one eye and checked the time: 9.48 a.m.

The green WhatsApp icon was still banded across her home screen. Was that what had woken her? She clicked on it, though there was no name attached to the number. Not a contact of hers.

110

All I Want for Christmas

It was a photograph – of three archive boxes. She could see from the codes on their labels that they were the next ones along to the ones she'd worked on yesterday.

There was no hello, no goodbye. Just four words: *'Ready when you are.'*

Chapter Nine

'It's eleven thirty.'

Darcy looked back at Max leaning against the door, somewhat surprised to hear the fleck of annoyance in his voice. Was he irritated that she was here? Or here late? 'It's Sunday.'

'Sleeping in?'

'Washing my hair.'

His eyes roamed over her fresh blow-dry, distinctly bouncier than yesterday's limp ponytail. She was wearing her 'no make-up' make-up and after twenty minutes of agonized staring into her wardrobe, she'd pulled on boyfriend jeans, chunky loafers and her best cream rollneck. It was of vital importance that she didn't look like she cared about how she looked.

'Come in.' He stepped back, and she moved past him into the beautiful entrance hall. 'How are you today?' he asked. He was wearing jeans and a blue marl knitted sweater with navy stripes on the cuffs. Socks, too, this morning. Sunday Max looked cosy, an open invitation to cuddle.

Only that wasn't on offer – only the use of his sofa.

'Fine, thanks. Did you have a good day out yesterday?'

He glanced at her as he passed, as if hearing the stiffness of their formal conversation. 'Yes.' He climbed the stairs, offering no details. 'When did you leave?' he asked over his shoulder.

'About six . . . When did you get back?'

'Six twenty.'

She rolled her eyes with relief. She'd escaped in the nick of time. 'Ah. Well that's good, then.'

'Good?'

'That I was out of the way.'

He glanced at her again as he headed into the luxurious kitchen. It was the same size as Darcy and Freja's entire apartment. She noticed a huge, fresh bouquet of black tulips on the dining table; it scented the space, along with the coffee that was being freshly ground in the fancy machine. The Sunday papers were scattered on the table beside the boxes, open to the business pages.

'When did the new boxes come over?' she asked, not moving past the sofa as he made a couple of coffees.

'Nine, thereabouts.'

He brought them over a few moments later. 'Strong and black.'

'Thanks.' She wrapped her hands around the mug, grateful for its heat. She had decided against cycling over, not wanting to arrive looking dishevelled like yesterday, but there had been a hard frost overnight and vanity had dictated no socks with her rolled-up jeans. 'You know, I hadn't planned on coming back here today.'

It was intended as an apology, a way out for him, even, but he frowned. 'Why not? Have you found what you needed?'

'No.' She rolled her eyes. 'God, I wish. No—'

'So then . . . ?'

She hesitated a moment. '. . . Can I really not take one back with me? Just one? I'd be so careful. I'd protect it with my life.'

He frowned. 'Why are you so determined to get away from here?'

'I'm not.'

113

'No? Could have fooled me.'

She stared at him, trying to find the right words. How could she tell him it felt like a punishment to be here, both with him and without him? It wasn't easy for her to be in his presence, as it seemingly was for him to be in hers. He wasn't neutral to her. 'It just doesn't feel right, dominating your weekend like this.' It was as honest as she could get.

'You're not dominating. I barely saw you yesterday. It made no difference one way or the other that you were here.'

She swallowed. The words felt rough, even if he was trying to reassure her. 'Well, even so, it's a Sunday now and . . . Are you going out again today?' she asked hopefully. At least, sitting here alone was something she knew she could do.

'No.'

'Oh.' Her eyes flickered around the room, skating over the ceiling as she listened for signs of Angelina upstairs. She was probably still in bed. Beauty sleep.

'She's not here,' he said, as if reading her mind.

'Oh?' But he offered nothing further and she tried to decide whether it was better or worse that they were alone here together.

'Have you eaten?'

'Uh . . .'

'I noticed you didn't seem to have anything from the fridge yesterday.'

'Of course not. I'm not going to come over here and eat your food,' she muttered.

He rolled his eyes, a small groan escaping him. 'Darcy –' But he stopped again, staring at her with an inscrutable look. He turned away and walked back to the kitchen counter, pulling some pastries from a brown paper bag. 'Come over here.'

She hesitated, then did as instructed. It was the furthest she had moved into the room and it felt like she was stepping out of the 'professional' realm that had brought her here and into the private one. She saw paperwork on the marble counters – stiff invitations, bills, letters – an Acqua di Parma scented candle, a pair of brown leather gloves. He had apples and pomegranates in the fruit bowl and when he opened the Wolf fridge, she saw an unopened bottle of Krug and a whole wheel of Brie. He retrieved a plate of cold, crisp grapes, ribbons of prosciutto and some sliced gouda.

'Hungry?'

She nodded, knowing she had no business being famished. She had eaten well last night but in her haste (and panic) this morning, food had been the last thing on her mind.

He carried the food over to the table, setting the plates down at the far end. He took the chair at the head, pulling out the one beside it for her. 'Sit. Eat.'

'Yes, sir,' she quipped in military fashion, drawing a quick look from him. She smiled, breaking the tension, and he gave a half-smile back. They seemed to be rare with him, these lighter moments of emotion.

'So you were out last night?' he asked, motioning for her to fill her plate first.

'Yes, dinner plans,' she replied, forking some of the cheese and ham onto her plate and breaking off a clump of grapes.

'Where?'

'Noma.'

His eyebrows shot up. 'Did you have the duck feet candies?'

The what . . . ? 'No.'

'Shame. They're excellent.'

'Oh. Maybe next time, then.' She could sense he wanted to ask who she'd been with. Somehow the question hovered, like the feeling of being watched – distinct but intangible. And she found she didn't want to tell him – but she did. Just like she didn't want to be here – but she did. And she didn't want him to be here – but she did. It was confusing, this constant sense of conflict. 'You like it there?'

'That's rhetorical, right?' She wanted to ask who he'd gone with, too, but she didn't. She felt a silence bloom between them filled with questions they couldn't ask, conversations they wouldn't have.

'Is that really a Liebermann?' she asked instead, looking over at the huge oil on the wall above the sofa. She wondered idly what other artworks were hanging in this beautiful home.

He half smiled again, looking impressed. 'Yes. Everyone always assumes it's Manet.'

'Well, it would be pretty poor if I didn't know.' She sighed. 'It's really sensational.'

'It's always been my favourite,' he murmured, twisting in his chair to look over at it.

'Always?'

He hesitated, turning back to her. 'My parents owned it first. It used to hang in the music room.'

Music room? Who had a music room?

'My father was determined I should be able to play piano to a decent standard, even though I detested it and clearly had no natural talent. My teacher would rap my knuckles with a wooden ruler whenever I got anything wrong. Which was frequently.'

'Really?!'

'I know. Old school.' He shrugged. 'I would try everything to get out of the lessons. That painting hung on the wall opposite and I would just stare at it, wishing I was inside the canvas. Anywhere but there. Sounds crazy, right?'

'Not at all. I always used to do that too.'

'You did?'

'Oh yes. Depending on my mood, I was either the girl on Fragonard's swing, or Millais's Ophelia . . . I was a very dramatic teenager.'

He grinned, taking a sip of his coffee. 'Did you always know you wanted to be in the art world?'

'Pretty much. Paintings have always spoken to me, somehow.' She looked down quickly. 'Sorry, I know that sounds pretentious. I just don't know how else to describe it.'

'I get it.'

'You do?'

'I've always had an affinity, I suppose. I grew up surrounded by beautiful things.'

'So then what made you choose law?'

He looked back at her, his eyes roaming over her face as if studying her. 'Expectations.'

'Your parents' expectations?'

He shrugged, clearly not wanting to be drawn, but as she looked around the impressive home, it was clear their instincts had been correct. As Erik had said, there wasn't the same kind of money to be made working in the art world as in commercial property development – or law.

'So who's your personal favourite?' he asked, watching as she ate. He had put a croissant on his own plate but didn't seem terribly hungry and she began to feel self-conscious, as if she had come into his house and was just taking from him.

'Artist?'

He nodded.

'Well . . . Max Liebermann is right up there, actually. But I'd probably say Joaquín Sorolla.'

'Oh . . . I've got a Sorolla.' He glanced towards the ceiling.

She stopped chewing. 'Here? You've got a Sorolla *here*?'

He gave a hesitant smile. 'You're not going to rob me, are you?'

She sat back in her chair, staring at him. 'You just left me, a perfect stranger, alone in your house all day yesterday with a Sorolla hanging on your wall?'

'Well, I might have thought twice if I'd realized you were such a fan.' He cocked a half-grin as her bewilderment persisted. 'Don't worry, I have good security. Why do you think the insurers are happy to go along with this?'

She shook her head, tearing off the tip of her croissant. 'I just don't understand how you could do that.'

'Clearly.'

'What's the title of it? Would I know it?'

'It's called *Bacante*.'

'Not *Bacante en Reposo*? You mean the one with the girl on the bed?'

'Yeah, that's the one.' He looked impressed.

Her eyes shone with excitement as she stared at him, open-mouthed. 'His brushwork in that . . .'

'I know.'

'And his colours: the pink, the reds, that flash of white.'

'I know.'

She couldn't believe he had that actual painting in his house. Right here. She hesitated, wanting to ask where it was in the house but not wanting to ask, either. The line between professional and personal, polite and personal, was constantly shifting.

'It's upstairs,' he said, as if reading her mind.

'Oh.'

There was a pause. 'If you'd like—'

'No,' she said quickly, sensing he'd only asked out of politeness, and wasn't it enough of an intrusion that she was eating breakfast in his kitchen? 'I know it. I've seen it hundreds of times. It's wonderful.'

'Yes.' He didn't point out she'd never seen the real thing; that seeing it in a book or on a screen couldn't possibly compare to standing right in front of it hanging on a wall. But to go upstairs with him, into the truly private part of the house, wasn't an option. They both knew that.

A small silence bloomed.

'Was that also a gift?'

'No. I bought it at auction in Madrid.'

'Ah.'

She ate a little more of her breakfast but her appetite had deserted her as the chasm between his life and hers widened with each passing comment. After a few more bites, she sat back. 'I should really get on.'

'But you haven't had—'

'I didn't come over here to hijack your day and have breakfast with you, Max. I need to work.'

He looked up at her as she pushed her chair back and quickly rose. 'Okay.'

'Thanks for the sustenance.'

'Anytime.'

She hesitated as he reached for an iPad on the table. Was he going to stay sitting here while she worked at the other end of the room? '. . . You're sure there's not somewhere else I could work? A study? Broom cupboard?'

'Darcy.' He pinned her with a steady look. 'I'll do my own thing. I'll ignore you. You ignore me.'

Ignore him.

Right.

*

'I'm not here,' he murmured, sinking onto the opposite side of the U-shaped sofa arrangement and picking up the sports pages.

Darcy listened to the rustle of the pages, aware of his sprawling frame in her peripheral vision. She reached for the next envelope in the box, pretending his proximity was of no consequence to her, even though her eyes had followed him every time his back was turned.

She opened the envelope to find newspaper clippings of reviews of an exhibition in Turin in 1920. It appeared Trier had managed to get three paintings included – a shoemaker's workshop, a beach scene and a marketplace. She knew nothing in these reviews was likely to contain the information she needed – a woman's name, something to get going with – but she couldn't discount them out of hand either. What if the woman in the portrait had been a rich buyer at the exhibition? Or a collector? Of course, most women hadn't been in control of their own money back then, but if she'd been a wealthy widow or an heiress . . .

She tried to keep her eyes on the clippings and her mind on the task, but she could hear him breathe. Just like when he'd gone downstairs an hour ago, she'd heard the whirr of a running machine, the clatter of weights on the presses, faint grunts, the beat of a Spotify playlist.

Other sounds, too, announced his presence. Stretching, clearing his throat, clicking his fingers distractedly. The room above this had very creaky floors and she heard him on the phone up there, his voice a low bass through the ceiling. Angelina? Darcy wondered where she was today. Whether she had stayed here last night or left early this morning.

She redoubled her focus on the clippings. The paper was yellowing, the font tiny. No names were mentioned bar those of the artists.

Her phone buzzed and she glanced at it, seeing Aksel's name.

'I take it back. A new record for strangest veterinary incident.'

She smiled, picking up the phone.

'Oh?'

'Emergency admittance of a dog. Owner tried to castrate it by putting rubber bands around the testicles. Led to urinary infection and two-hour surgery this morning.'

Darcy gasped, her hand flying to her mouth.

'What's wrong?'

She looked up, to find Max already watching her. 'Sorry.'

'What is it?'

'It's nothing. Just a slightly shocking anecdote from a friend who's a vet.'

'Oh?' He looked intrigued.

'He's been regaling me with horror stories in his clinic.'

'I see.'

She looked back at the screen, typing quickly.

'Will he be ok?'

'Yes, just very sore.'

'Poor thing.'

'I've had to put him in the cone of shame. Now he's really feeling sorry for himself.'

She smiled. Aksel was warming up nicely. Much more of this and she might actually start to foster some hope for their date on Tuesday.

She glanced up, thinking of a reply, to find Max still watching with an intense stare.

The doorbell rang, breaking his focus, and he got up. She watched him disappear downstairs. He had changed into grey trackies and a t-shirt after working out. Sunday Max, part II. He returned a moment later with some steaming bags of food.

'Lunch,' he said, walking past, but she sensed a twinge of irritation beneath his usual brusque demeanour.

She got up and joined him, watching as he put the bags on the counter and lifted out some boxes with a distinctive name on the side. Noma might be iconic, but Geranium had just been voted the number one restaurant in the world . . .

'Geranium does takeaway?' she asked in amazement.

'No.' He shrugged. 'But I have a friend who works there.'

He didn't look at her as he set out the boxes, a sharpness to his movements. He was definitely being testy with her. Had she done something wrong? Outstayed her welcome, in spite of her best efforts to be invisible? She bit her lip at the contradiction; it wasn't like she'd asked for lunch.

'Max . . . do you want me to go?'

He sighed, planting his hands down on the counters as he fixed her with a hard stare. 'No, Darcy, I don't want you to go. I want you to eat and I want you to stop apologizing for being here.'

She looked back at him, wanting to leave now more than ever. She sensed they were having an argument and she didn't even know why. 'Okay,' she shrugged, bewildered. 'No more apologies, then.'

'Good.' He reached into a cabinet below and brought out some plates and bowls. He was silent for a moment as he began decanting the dishes. 'I wasn't sure what you'd like, so I asked for a selection.' It was more considerate than Erik had been at dinner the other night, ordering with impunity.

'It looks incredible.' It smelled even better. She couldn't believe Geranium had delivered to him. Was this who she'd heard him talking to on the phone earlier? 'But you really didn't need to go to this trouble. I could have popped out and got a sandwich. Or burger.'

He smiled at her then, as if she'd said something funny, and she felt the bubble of tension that had floated up between them so suddenly burst just as quickly. 'No. I wanted you to try the scallop.' He opened up the smallest box – it had been secured with a ribbon – to reveal a tiny cake sitting atop a small white fluted porcelain dish.

'Oh! That's making my mouth water just looking at it.' The top of it was a shiny glazed marble of vanilla into red.

'It's good. It's a cake made with seeds, apples, elderberries and apple brandy.'

She looked up at him with a conspiratorial smile. 'It would be wrong to try that first, right?'

His eyes locked with hers. 'Very wrong. You have to wait, Darcy.'

'But it looks so good. What if I can't?' she protested, jokingly reaching a hand towards it.

He caught her hand with his. 'Sometimes we have to.'

The joke was gone as she looked up at the word *we* to find him openly – hungrily – staring at her, at her mouth. She was transported back to their first few moments in the National Gallery, when the flirtation had been open and strong; not something to deny or repress or pretend wasn't happening. Would it be so terrible if he were to kiss her? After all, Freja and Tristan worked together, and *they* were making a success of it.

But he dropped her hand and turned away, decanting the boxes, before carrying the plates over to the table.

She followed him, the two of them taking their places again, as at breakfast. In silence, she helped herself to a little of everything.

'This is what you should try first,' he murmured, pushing towards her a singular white scallop wrapped with a lacy, deep red vine. Like the cake, it too was sitting on a small white fluted dish, as if they were dining in the restaurant itself. 'It's a scallop, gently grilled and served with blackcurrant and a dried scallop roe infusion.'

She peered at it. 'The lacy bit is blackcurrant?'

He nodded.

'So not only do you have world-class art on your walls, your food is art too?'

'Not every day, but I thought perhaps you'd appreciate it.'

For a moment she had thought he was going to say it was a special occasion.

She watched as he carefully split the scallop with a fork and held it out towards her. 'Try it.'

She looked at it, hesitating as she saw that he wasn't handing her the fork to take from him. It felt intimate to her but his gaze was inscrutable and she leaned forwards, her mouth opening for him as he gently fed her. Automatically her eyes closed as the flavours hit her tastebuds.

'Well?'

'Oh my God,' she groaned, not wanting to swallow but to savour the taste for as long as she could. She opened her eyes again. '. . . Bastard. You've ruined me.'

He grinned. 'Have more.' He held up the other forkful.

'You're a feeder,' she muttered, taking it with more hunger this time.

He arched an eyebrow. 'You clearly don't eat enough.'

'Oh, I eat plenty,' she shrugged. 'Just in fits and starts. Some days I'll eat like a fairy and others, like a trucker.'

He laughed at that, his shoulders shaking, and she realized it was the first time she had seen him actually let himself go, even for a moment. It made him seem younger.

They ate with appetite after that, sharing the dishes, her

eyes closing at the profusion of flavours, little sighs of happiness escaping her as he forked different samples onto her plate for her to try. 'Oh God, this is so good. *So* good.'

He looked bemused, watching her.

'What?'

'You do a little nod of your head every time you like something,' he said, doing an impression of her.

'No I don't.' Did she? She had never noticed.

He shrugged.

'Well, you smoosh your mouth to the side when you're reading,' she countered.

He looked scandalized, his brows coming together in a deep frown. 'I don't *smoosh*.'

'Oh, you do.'

He paused for a beat. 'Darcy, I don't smoosh.'

'You were doing it just now, reading the sports pages.' She smooshed her mouth to the side in her best impression.

He laughed again, but this time shooting her a look as if she was drawing something from him against his will.

They sank into a small silence as their teases died down.

'So, who's your team? Let me guess – Copenhagen?'

'Actually, AGF.'

'Really?'

'I went to school in Aarhus.'

'Ah. Best days of your life?'

'I sincerely hope not,' he quipped. 'Do you support a team?'

'Not actively. My brother is a Chelsea supporter so I'm a proxy fan, I guess.'

'You have a brother?'

'Younger, by three years. And then a sister, seven years younger.'

'So you're an eldest child,' he mused.

'You say that ominously, the way people say they're a Scorpio. Or a witch.'

He chuckled again.

'You?'

'. . . Just me. Can't you tell?'

She supposed she could, now it was pointed out to her: the self-sufficiency, conspicuous maturity, self-possession . . . He didn't look like someone who'd ever had to fight over sitting in the tap end of the bath.

Unless it was with a model.

She sighed, suddenly depressed again by the image, and he glanced at her. 'Good?'

He meant the food, she knew. She nodded. 'Great.'

Max was watching the match on his iPad, on the sofa, wearing his AirPods. Every few minutes he would wince at a foul, gasp at a bad tackle, groan at a referee's decision, unaware of the sounds he was making into the silence.

She had moved onto the third box and was almost through it. Most of the material had been bulky but unhelpful – more auction catalogues that she could move through quickly and discount. A sense of worry was beginning to build. She had been wading through resources at the gallery's archives for almost a week now and hadn't unearthed a single clue as to this woman's identity.

She sighed and sank back against the cushions. Her meeting with Otto was tomorrow morning. How could she tell him that a week into a five-week deadline, she had achieved precisely nothing? She hadn't found a single useable fact.

'Everything okay?'

She looked up. Max was watching her, one of his AirPods out.

'Yeah, I guess.'

He glanced at the box, correctly identifying it as the source of her despair. 'Still nothing?'

'Nope.'

'It'll come.'

'But will it come in time? I've got a meeting with Otto tomorrow and absolutely nothing to give him.' She sighed again, running her hands down her face and keeping them planted on her cheeks as she stared at the boxes. They might as well have been empty for all the good they were doing her. 'Oh God, what if he pulls me off the project and gives it to someone else?'

Max was quiet for a moment. 'He won't do that.'

She raised an eyebrow. Her advisor was a demanding and ambitious man. 'You don't know that. I'm only on the job because the official researcher is on maternity leave and her replacement is too busy with the rest of the retrospective.'

He didn't reply but got up from the sofa, moving into the kitchen and returning a few moments later with a bottle of wine and two glasses.

'Oh . . . no. I need to keep a clear head,' she protested weakly as he poured.

'One drink won't hurt. You need a break. You've been working non-stop all weekend. Tell Otto I can vouch for that. You can call me as a character witness.' He handed her a glass and collapsed back onto his side of the sofa with one for himself.

'It won't help. Otto needs information, not excuses. The clock is ticking and—'

'Drink.'

She obeyed. '. . . Oh, that's good.'

'Yeah.'

She looked at the glass, taking in the deep claret colour, before looking back at him. 'Do you always have to have the best of everything?'

He hesitated. 'Is that a bad thing?'

'No, of course not.'

His eyes narrowed as if he didn't believe her, but she wasn't sure she believed herself either. *Was* he spoilt, pampered, over-privileged? Did he know how to do anything for himself, or was it all done for him – meals delivered by the best restaurant in the city, housekeepers, assistants and security guards on tap to keep all the plates spinning? Was his world so vacuous and empty that he had to fill it with bright, shiny things: Liebermanns and models and premier grand cru?

He put the AirPod back in and returned his attention to the match. Darcy resumed her final trawl through the last box of the day: some letters Trier had received from a French artist called Louis Moreau. By this time, Trier had moved on to Rome and was living and working in a tiny studio in Trastevere. Her French was decent, but her eyes narrowed as she struggled to decipher the handwriting, which was tightly scripted, with frequent ink blots that made the job of reading markedly harder.

She sipped her wine, tucking her knees up to her chin as she read: *'The heat was unbearable . . . peace conference . . . Versailles . . . proposition Dessoye . . .'*

She yawned, unable to suppress it in time. French politics was not what she needed to know about . . . She needed a woman's name. She forced herself to focus, envisaging Otto's face across the desk from her tomorrow. She just needed something, anything.

She frowned, stumbling upon some sentences that she couldn't decipher at all. She tried again.

'What is it?'

She looked up to find Max watching her again. 'Oh . . . I just can't understand what this says,' she said, holding up the letter. 'It's in French.'

'I speak French. Let me see.' She went to hand it over to him, but instead he got up and sank down on the cushion next to her. 'Which bit?' he asked, peering over her shoulder.

Darcy fell very still at the sudden proximity. Their legs were pressed together as the cushions splayed and she was close enough to smell a faint woody scent on his skin – cologne or body wash, she wasn't sure.

'This,' she murmured, pointing as he read it a few times. On the face of it, he was simply being helpful, but she detected a deeper shift, something far more fundamental changing between them.

'It says they're proposing a bill for electoral reform embracing the *scrutin de liste* method and a system of proportional representation.'

'Oh. Well, no wonder I couldn't understand it. I can barely understand that in English; that's definitely beyond my A-level French.'

He smiled at her. 'Riveting stuff.'

'I know. Aren't I lucky?' His face was just inches from hers, and she saw his gaze openly drop to her mouth. All day – all weekend – the tension had flickered quietly beneath every word, every look, though they had resolutely ignored it; but as his eyes rose to hers now, she knew this time it was no good. No matter what he had said about them having to keep things strictly professional, this mutual attraction wasn't going to go away. It was going to just keep sitting between them like a giant black cat – determined to be acknowledged – and she made no attempt to pull back as he leaned in at last and finally kissed her.

His lips tasted of wine, like hers, as he pressed his mouth to hers softly, at first. She felt his scent envelop her; what had been faint at a few inches away was now distinct and intoxicating. The pressure lessened on her lips for one moment, two, both of them breathing quickly, knowing that this had been a question and the next kiss would be the answer. The passion flooded her, running like a riptide between them, coming in at sharp angles, tugging at her feet and trying to upend her. Both of them.

It was better even than she could have imagined and as he came in again, the kiss grew stronger and deeper, his mouth beginning to open, his head to move, the tip of his tongue finding hers. Her heart rate had already accelerated to double time and—

The doorbell rang.

For a moment, as his hand moved to her hair, she thought he hadn't heard it; but when it came again thirty seconds later, he pulled back slightly, though still didn't get up. Instead, they sat face to face in their own world, breathless with passion, his gaze reaching deep into her and finding what he wanted to see; what she wanted to hide, but couldn't.

He kissed her again, their urgency growing even as the doorbell rang once more.

'Hadn't you better get that?' she breathed, her lips still against his, not wanting to break apart.

'No,' he replied, refusing to release her. The kiss had made prisoners of them both and this intrusion, this threat, only increased their desperation. She felt his grip around her tighten as her body pressed against his, touching at every point.

The bell rang again. '. . . They sound insistent.'

'I don't care.'

'. . . It could be important.'

'No.' He increased his hold on her, but this time she did pull back.

'You don't know that.'

He sighed, pressing his forehead to hers in frustration. '. . . Someone had better be dying,' he muttered under his breath, breathless too. '. . . Don't move. I'll get rid of them.'

He got up, striding over to the door, and looked back at her with open want for a moment before disappearing down the stairs.

Darcy sat in silence for a moment, grateful for the brief reprieve. She needed to get her breath back. She'd never been kissed like that before. She'd never felt her own edges blur, her body so completely overrule her mind . . . Not that she needed talking out of anything. He had been the one pushing for boundaries, not her, and if the dinner with Tristan and Freja last night had proved anything, it was that it was – somehow – possible to sleep together and still maintain a professional relationship. Why not them, too? In his arms just now, everything had felt so natural between them – effortless and inevitable – it was as if she was simply allowing water to flow downhill. Letting Nature take its course.

In her mind, she heard Freja's voice telling her he was everything she didn't need. And it was true that the more she saw of his life, the more she saw the differences between them. He came from and belonged in a different world to hers.

And yet, she would deny him nothing. She didn't care if they didn't match or suit. Freja hadn't seen the connection between them. The chemistry was too strong to ignore.

She reached for her glass of wine and took a deep slug, her

nerves rising as she anticipated his return and everything that would follow. Him, in that doorway, coming towards her. For her . . .

His voice drifted up the stairs and she strained to hear, but the words were indistinct. Until, suddenly, they weren't. She heard a woman's voice rise with . . . frustration? Anger?

She heard the low bass of Max's voice, also getting louder: '. . . didn't agree this!'

'Can't we be spontaneous? . . . was missing you! . . . you'd call!'

Darcy caught her breath. Angelina.

'. . . come back!'

Her heart pounded with sudden guilt and shame. They were together, she knew that. What was she doing, allowing herself to be seduced by a man she had seen with his girlfriend, only the day before?

Hurriedly, Darcy put down her wine glass and picked up the letter again as she heard footsteps running on the stairs. In a panic, she perched herself on the front edge of the sofa cushions to look less at home. She cupped her chin in her hand and was reading intently when, moments later, the door was pushed open.

She readied herself with a polite smile, but the woman stopped in her tracks at the sight of her.

'Hi—' Darcy's voice trailed off.

Max came up behind the woman a second later, looking tense. There was a taut silence. Darcy felt as if her heart was about to fall from its perch to her feet. She saw Max slump a little as he recognized the look of shock – and dismay – in her eyes. He swallowed.

'Darcy, this is Natalia. Natalia, Darcy,' he mumbled.

Wow. It really was a revolving door policy he had going.

And she had been right on the cusp of stepping into it. She felt stupid. Humiliated. Meaningless.

'Hello, *Natalia*.' She smiled benignly, as best she could, at the woman: tall, blonde. Model.

'Darcy and I work together,' he said as the woman spun on her heel to look back at him accusingly. And rightly so. 'She's researching a project at the gallery.'

'Oh, really?' Her words were heavily accented with Russian and sarcasm. She didn't sound like she believed a word of it.

Good for her, Darcy thought, replacing the letter in the box with a shaking hand and setting the lid on top.

'Yes, but I had just finished up,' Darcy said, not even sure why she was covering for him. She owed him no loyalty. Clearly he didn't know the meaning of the word. 'Max kindly gave me some space to work here –'

The blonde looked back at her – and the wine glasses – with outright suspicion.

'I can't access the archives when the museum's shut, you see. Security. Insurance . . . But I'm done for the day, so I'll get out of your hair.' Darcy tried to move naturally, but even breathing felt forced. Her upset was so fierce, the only way her body wanted to express it was in tears – but she would *not* allow that to happen. She just had to get out of here. 'These are ready to be sent back, Max,' she said officiously, without looking at him.

Natalia watched her as she got up, smoothing her jeans and reaching for her bag; the model loosened a moment later, as if recognizing there was no threat here. She even almost smiled.

'Nice meeting you, Natalia. Thanks, Max,' Darcy said, still managing to avoid making eye contact as she headed for the door.

'I'll just see –'

She heard him start to follow her and she whirled round, holding up a hand, forced to make eye contact now. 'No, no need,' she said, her cold look stopping him in his tracks. 'You've got company, Max – and I've stayed far too long as it is. I should have left long before now.'

Her eyes told him this had been a mistake. A grievous error. He had played her as one of the many, but it wouldn't happen again.

'I'll see myself out.'

Chapter Ten

Otto sat behind his desk, staring back at her, his fingers interlaced in a steeple. 'It's going to be very difficult going back to Margit with this news, Darcy,' he said with an unhappy look.

'I know, and I'm sorry. I'm really doing everything I can to try to unearth a lead. I just need *one* thread to pick up. Once I get a name or find a clear photograph of this woman, I'll be able to run with it.'

'But there's nothing of interest *at all* so far?'

She shook her head. 'Trier was on the road straight after the war. He went to Paris, then down into Italy. I've been keeping an open mind whether the woman could have been a prostitute. We know he used their services, and it would fit his focus at that time, which was depicting peasant life and the working classes. It could be that he painted one of them and used his paid-for slots, so to speak, as sittings?' She was reaching, she knew.

Otto frowned, thinking about it for a moment. 'I don't think I buy that hypothesis. If he wanted to paint a whore, why present her as a lady?' He made a gesture with his hand. 'Forgive the crude language, but you take my point.'

'I do. And I agree,' she sighed. It was exactly the point she had made. 'I'm just trying to keep an open mind and consider all possibilities.'

He looked out of the window, deep in thought. 'Trier's own personal interests always lay with the common man. He was a lifelong socialist. He didn't move into society portraiture until Frederik Madsen became his patron in 1921 and painting the portraits of the great and the good became his bread and butter. But he never had any real love for it. He more or less stopped after their falling out in '22.'

She bit her lip thoughtfully. 'That's what keeps niggling me . . . the portrait just doesn't appear to be his typical society commission. There's no interior backdrop, it's not full length, she's not formally attired . . .'

'It could have been an early piece, before he found his feet with the style. It might even have been just a preliminary study. It might have been an exercise in finessing her hair or nose or attitude.' He looked at her. 'I assume you've gone through the list of his officially recognized works, to see if any of the women could be a match?'

Darcy stalled. It was such an obvious suggestion, and yet . . .

She looked down, feeling sheepish that she had jumped straight into researching Trier's life before his actual work. 'Not yet, no. I'll get onto that straight away and cross-check his verified portraits to see if anything correlates.' She sighed, sinking back in her chair. 'I'm sorry, Otto . . . I should have done that first, as well as tightened the search frame from the outset . . . I'm an idiot.'

Otto watched her beat herself up. 'Due diligence is never a bad thing, Darcy. And if the timings weren't so tight, it wouldn't ordinarily be an issue. But we're a week down now with nothing to show for it, and Margit's under a lot of pressure.'

'I know. And I promise I'm going as fast as I can. I'm doing the full twelve hours every day in the archives – seven till seven. And I'm going to see if Viggo can tweak the arrangement we had this weekend so I can work longer then too.'

Otto frowned. 'This weekend?'

'Yes. He managed to secure a special arrangement for working out of office hours. It was unorthodox, but it worked pretty well.'

'Unorthodox how?'

'He arranged for some of the material – just a few boxes at a time – to be delivered to the house of one of the trustees, who lives along the same road as the gallery. It means there isn't the same security concern of transporting stuff across the city, plus the trustee's given a personal reassurance to the insurers about keeping eyes on the material at all times.'

'Who is the trustee?'

She swallowed, not even wanting to say his name. She was doing her level best not to think of him at all. 'Max Lorensen.'

'Max. I see.'

'You know him?'

'Yes, of course.'

Of course. She remembered how Max had mingled at the museum drinks reception last week, speaking with the benefactors as if they were old friends. His job required him to be socially adept and well connected; not to mention the Madsen Foundation's involvement with the retrospective meant he was bound to have crossed paths with Otto at some point.

'And so that's the ongoing arrangement, is it? Any work undertaken outside of office hours is conducted at his house? Evenings and weekends?'

'As it stands,' she nodded. 'But I'm going to lobby Viggo as soon as I get back over there, after this. Clearly there are still time limitations working in someone else's home – I can hardly work through the night! – whereas if I could have them at home, I could work as late as I needed.'

She had absolutely no intention of returning to Max's house, no matter how tight the deadline. Natalia's arrival might have been badly timed for him, but it had been a godsend for her, stopping her in the nick of time from losing herself and becoming just another one of his conquests. Freja had been right. He was bad news for her. She wasn't cut out for a player like him.

'Will that be possible?' Otto asked sceptically. 'Insurers are known for being fastidious.'

'Yes, but if the *principle* has been established that the material can be released from the gallery – under strict conditions – then there's surely room for negotiation on what those conditions can be. The precedent has been set, so . . .' She held up her crossed fingers.

'I see. Well, then, I hope something can be worked out along those lines; it would certainly be helpful for you. And if anyone can make it happen, it's Rask. He's very highly regarded.'

'Yes, he's been a tremendous help.' She sipped her coffee, her fingers still red from cycling over here in the cold. 'Has there been any development with the extrication?'

'Only that it's coming away slowly, slowly. I believe Lauge's feeling more confident than he was this time last week.'

Darcy winced. 'I'm glad it's not my job to get it out.'

'It's painstaking work. Lauge has been pretty stressed.'

'But nothing can be seen yet?'

'No. They obviously have to preserve the integrity of *Her*

Children first and foremost. It appears the portrait is pretty bonded to the backboard.'

'Are they any closer to knowing how long the removal might take?'

'They're saying three weeks now.'

'Oh? Well, that's an improvement.' It was still no help to her, though. She would be working blind for all that time.

'Provided they don't hit any stumbling blocks, of course.'

'Of course.' Darcy's eyes traced the sharp-edged shadow of a tree branch on the floor and she sighed, knowing that another long day in the twilight of the archives awaited her. She was leaving home in the dark and getting home in the dark too at the moment. 'Well, I'd better get on. I'll obviously let you know the second I find anything with potential.'

'Do that,' Otto nodded, watching as she got up. 'And good luck with Viggo. I hope he can help.'

'Mm, me too,' she said, rolling her eyes and feeling her stomach lurch at the alternative. 'Me too.'

'Good morning.' Viggo's smile was wide as she came down the stairs. 'And how was your weekend?'

'Very productive, thanks to you.'

He looked pleased. 'Yes? You found something?'

'No. Not yet. But at least I got through another level of boxes.'

'Indeed.'

She shrugged off her coat and hung it on the hook beside his. 'I've just come from my weekly meeting with Otto and let's just say, I'm not in the good books. He's pretty disappointed I've not found anything useful yet.'

'But you are doing all you can.'

Darcy pulled a face. 'I might have been too fastidious,

starting at the beginning of your records rather than the time frame we had previously agreed on. Time's not on my side. I'm going to have to work around the clock from here on.'

Viggo got up and retrieved the kettle, taking it over to the small sink and filling it up. 'Well, at least now we have a solution that will help with that.'

'Yes, about that . . .' she said, stretching out the words so that he looked over at her.

'Is something wrong?'

'No, not at all. And I'm so grateful for what you managed to do with such little notice.'

'But?'

'But there must *surely* be a way to get permission for me to do the work at home?' she pleaded.

'It is out of my hands, Darcy,' he shrugged.

'But why should the material be any safer at Max Lorensen's house than mine?'

'Because it is up the road.'

'Okay, apart from that. I mean, what if there was a fire? He has got a *lot* of wine that would . . . act as an accelerant! . . . And he's much more likely to be burgled than me! He's got a Max Liebermann on the wall, and some Picasso sketches and God knows what else in there!'

Viggo made a little sound and gave a little shrug as if to say 'of course'. 'That is why he has a good security system.'

'Not that good,' she scoffed. 'When I had to leave on Saturday, he wasn't there, in spite of what he said about promising to keep his eyes on the material at all times. *And* I didn't even have to set an alarm code on my way out. The house was no more protected than my place.'

'Hmm.' Viggo frowned, looking perturbed by that information.

'Please can't you try to talk to the insurers again?'

'Darcy, I cannot argue convenience over risk.'

'But it's not convenience. It's productivity. If I want to work through the night, I can't, obviously. If I went straight from here to Max's house this evening, I couldn't stay more than an hour or two. Think about it – working in his kitchen after nine would be just unacceptable, wouldn't it? And every single day? I wouldn't feel I *could* go there every day or every weekend! I mean, he was really kind to help out this weekend but the man's got a life to live.'

'He certainly has that,' Viggo said with a wry chuckle as he spooned coffee into their mugs and sloshed in milk from a small jug shaped as a sitting cow. Darcy wondered whether he too had seen the pictures of Max in the society pages.

'. . . It's an ongoing intrusion of his privacy and we'd be taking a liberty with his generosity.'

'I see,' Viggo nodded, pouring the boiled water from the kettle and looking thoroughly bemused.

'So you'll try again with the insurers? Because I think the chances are good. By letting the material off the premises, they've established a precedent for . . . letting the material off the premises. The *where* it goes to is simply academic.' She was aware she was talking faster than usual, her voice at a slightly higher pitch.

'Precedent, eh? And I thought he was the lawyer.' Viggo handed her the cup with a smile and a look that made her feel as if he could see right through her excuses. She had felt it with Otto, too. Max Lorensen had a reputation in this city. Did they suspect her reasons for trying to avoid him?

'Please, Viggo.'

'I'll see what I can do, Darcy. Leave it with me.'

*

141

'Do you need a box sent over tonight?'

Darcy stared at the message. She had read it on notifications so that it wouldn't mark as read. She put her phone back down again and tried to pretend she hadn't leapt at the sight of the number; she refused to enter Max's name into the contacts. There was no need to. He was not a person in her life.

She went back to her file – August 1920: pencil sketches, studies and vignettes. Trier was in Puglia, exploring the deep Mediterranean landscape and light that was so different to northerly Denmark. She scrutinized every scribbled face or profile, checked the women's dresses for a detail he might have carried through . . .

The phone buzzed again and although she tried to ignore it, she only lasted eight seconds before having to look.

'I won't be there.'

She bit her lip and texted back. Just to get rid of him.

'No thanks. Not necessary.'

He hadn't chased after her last night, no apology explaining things (because what was there to explain? No promises had been made or broken), and his lack of concern at the way things had played out only made her feel more relieved that they had been interrupted after all. Maybe it had been a relief for them both. A cold shock of water to bring them to their senses when they'd threatened to succumb.

Another message came.

She lasted three seconds.

'Don't cut off your nose to spite your face. I won't be there. Viggo's got a key.'

She gasped indignantly, angered by the message. How dare he think she would sabotage her work just to avoid seeing him!

It was true, but how dare he think it.

She didn't reply and went back to the charcoal sketches, desperately trying to pretend he didn't exist as she scanned over olive trees, the Dauni mountains, a pack donkey, trulli houses, a blacksmith at the anvil . . .

Still hunting a ghost.

And now dodging her own.

Chapter Eleven

Darcy stopped stirring her sauce as she heard the front door close, turning to find her flatmate rounding the corner a moment later. Freja had run back from the lab – her running kit was a migraine-inducing combination of teal leggings, bright blue padded jacket, Barbie-pink socks and yellow trainers – but she had clearly stopped en route, for she was carrying a shopping bag.

'Well, fancy seeing you here, stranger!' Darcy drawled. 'I thought I lived alone these days.'

'You should be so lucky. Did you miss me?'

'Miss you? Miss Petals and I could talk of nothing else.'

Freja grinned, plonking the bags down on the counter and peering into her saucepan. 'What are you cooking?'

'Pasta a la Darce . . . But there's enough for two if you want some? Or are you just passing through?'

Freja groaned, sagging slightly against the worktop. 'Girl, I need a full night's sleep. I've not slept more than a four-hour stretch in over a month.'

'Great! Thanks for that,' Darcy quipped. 'Way to remind me I'm single.'

Freja dropped her head onto Darcy's arm and groaned. 'Now I know how new parents feel.'

'I have no sympathy. If you want endless hot sex with your rich, older boss-boyfriend, it's going to come at a price.'

'Just you wait,' Freja tutted. 'You've got your hot date tomorrow. We'll see how lively you're looking on Wednesday morning.'

'Hot?' Darcy gave a bemused shake of her head. 'Tepid, perhaps.'

Freja straightened and walked over to the fridge, pulling out the opened bottle of wine. She poured herself a glass and topped up Darcy's. 'I thought you said he'd got better?'

'Well, yes, but it was a pretty low bar to begin with.'

'What are you going to wear?'

'I guess whatever I wear to work tomorrow.'

'You're going straight from there? You're not coming back here first?'

'No time. We're meeting at seven thirty and I need to wring out every single minute available to me in the gallery. In for seven. Leave at seven. That's all I've got to work with, and leaving work early is not on my horizon until after Christmas.'

Freja frowned, emptying her shopping bags and decanting food into the fridge. 'Dare I ask how it's going?'

'You do not.'

'Oh.'

'I had my meeting with Otto this morning and let's just say, I'm not his star pupil right now.'

'Oh.' Freja dropped some oranges into the fruit bowl, then jumped up onto the counter. '. . . And how did it go at Max the Lawyer's yesterday?'

Darcy swallowed, stirring faster. '. . . It went.'

'Nothing to report?'

She shrugged. 'No breakthroughs.'

'That's not what I'm asking and you know it.'

Darcy stopped stirring and looked back at her. She bit her lip. '. . . Did you know Geranium does takeout?'

'Huh?'

'Yeah. He ordered it for lunch.'

'He ordered Geranium for takeaway lunch?' Freja's tone was incredulous. 'Wait till I tell Tristan.'

'I wouldn't. Apparently Max has a friend who works there. I think he was just showing off because I mentioned we'd gone to Noma the night before.' She rolled her eyes. 'He's such a narcissist.'

'Well, we knew that on sight,' Freja said, watching closely as Darcy chopped some peppers with careful savagery. 'So he was actually around, then, yesterday?'

'Yep.'

'Was the girlfriend there too?'

'No. At least, not till much later. And it was a different girlfriend that turned up. Seems like she broke the date schedule or something. He was pretty pissed off.'

'He has a date schedule?'

'But of course, Freja! How else could he possibly manage all these models otherwise?' Sarcasm dripped from the words as Darcy lifted the chopping board and scraped the vegetables into the pan.

'Sounds like you really dodged a bullet, deciding to keep things strictly professional.'

'Mm.' She looked away quickly, but something in the movement alerted her friend.

'You *did* keep things professional, didn't you? Darcy?'

Darcy swallowed, knowing she couldn't keep this from her friend. Knowing she didn't want to. 'Okay fine – we kissed. But that was it.'

'Oh my God, you kissed him?'

'But that was all.'

'Because . . . ?' Freja asked in a leading tone. 'You stopped it? He did? What happened? I need the details.'

'The model turned up. Unannounced. It rather threw a spanner in the works.'

'Shit.'

'Yeah. So I left, obviously.'

'Obviously.'

'And that's it.'

'That's *it*? He hasn't called? Begged your forgiveness?'

'Of course not. He just WhatsApped this afternoon asking if I needed another box to be sent over to his house for working late tonight.'

'No! . . . That's cold.'

'Even colder – when I said no, I wouldn't need it, he told me that he wouldn't be there anyway and – get this – not to cut my nose off to spite my face!'

'He did not!' Freja gasped. 'Oh my God, I hate him so much!'

Darcy nodded furiously. 'I know! The arrogance is astounding!'

'So then what did you say to that?'

'I just aired him,' she shrugged. '*Obviously* I'm not going over to his house again, whether he's there or not.'

Freja took a sip of wine, her legs swinging freely. '. . . But don't you need that extra time?'

'Viggo's going to get it sorted for me. We had a chat today, and I made my case for having stuff released here. He gets it. Hopefully he'll have some good news for me in the morning and in the meantime, I can have tonight off at least.'

'Fingers crossed, then.'

'Yeah.'

Freja watched as Darcy turned over the chicken breast and stirred the sauce. '. . . So was it a good kiss?'

Darcy spun on her heel and pinned Freja with a look. 'Why would you ask me that?'

'Why wouldn't I? We always do a post-mortem.'

'Yes. But in this instance there's no point in thinking about it, much less talking about it.'

'Okay, just give me a show of fingers, then. Rate him on a scale of one to ten.'

Darcy shot her a look but Freja batted it right back to her. Slowly, Darcy raised both hands – and a foot.

'Oh shit – it was that good?'

'Well, it would be, wouldn't it? He's well practised. This is what he does.' She shook the pan violently. 'You having some?'

Freja gave a nervous smile. 'Only if you're sure there's enough. I don't want to add *hanger* to the mix.'

Darcy took out two bowls and divided the meal between them. She was slightly short of 'enough' but she had little appetite anyway and she gave Freja the larger serving.

Her flatmate noticed. 'You have the bigger one.'

'I'm not that hungry. Besides, you obviously need to keep your strength up.' She winked.

They took the bowls and wine over to the sofas and sat cross-legged in their usual positions, opposite one another. Darcy ate without appetite, barely registering the flavours. 'So what's Tristan up to tonight?' she asked dully.

'He's on a trip to Antwerp. Back tomorrow, but seeing as a firebreak is being enforced tonight anyway, I'm going to make myself go *two* nights without him. Just to prove I can.'

'Wow, a whole two nights. You're hardcore,' Darcy quipped. 'He's not driving you nuts yet, then?'

'No, but give it time,' Freja said, jabbing the air with her fork. 'I'm optimistic that in another few weeks . . .'

'You said that a few weeks ago!'

Darcy's phone buzzed. 'Aksel,' she said, looking down. '. . . Oh no,' she groaned.

'What is it?'

'He's got to cancel tomorrow night. One of the senior partners at his practice has called a town hall meeting.'

'Damn.'

'He's asking if we can do Wednesday night instead.'

'Well, that's okay, isn't it?'

Darcy shrugged.

'You look disappointed.'

'I guess. I was looking forward to . . . overwriting yesterday's events.'

'You mean, the sooner you kiss someone else, the better?'

'Exactly.'

'Well, at least it's only switching up the days. He's not bailing altogether. And it's good you're feeling a bit mugged off. Shows you do actually like him a bit.'

'I haven't *met* him yet.'

'But you've connected. You've been talking every day for a week now, getting to know one another. By the time you do actually meet in person, you're going to feel like old friends.'

'Maybe.'

'Definitely! Plus, Wednesday is a sexier date night than Tuesday. It's basically the start to the weekend.'

Darcy grinned. 'Is it, though?'

'Optimism, my friend,' Freja said, tapping her temple. 'Aksel's going to come through for you, I can feel it.'

*

'What news, Viggo?' she asked brightly, walking into the gallery on the dot of seven the next morning. It was still as dark as midnight outside and she hadn't expected to find the old archivist upstairs. They didn't open to the public for another two hours but he was armed with a small electric screwdriver and was attaching a clear plaque, inscribed with a painting description, onto the wall.

He straightened, moving stiffly but looking pleased to see her. 'Darcy – another early start for you.'

'Needs must,' she shrugged, unwinding her scarf. She had cycled in again and her hands and cheeks were pink with cold. 'Every minute counts at the moment.'

'Yes . . .' He gave an apologetic smile. 'About that.'

'Oh, no,' she groaned, guessing what he was about to say next.

'I called through to the head office yesterday afternoon and pleaded your case.'

'But they said no?'

'It's a no. The material is either escorted a short distance up the road and overseen by one of the trustees – in this case, Mr Lorensen – or it doesn't go at all.' He spread his hands and gave a shrug. 'I'm sorry. I did try.'

She groaned, pulling her hands down over her face. 'I know. And I appreciate your efforts.'

'It's not so bad, is it? Max Lorensen has left a spare key here so you can let yourself in whenever you need.'

'No, I won't be doing that,' she said with a slow shake of her head.

Viggo hesitated, as if not sure whether to go on. 'I appreciate it must be a little strange working in someone's house, but if it helps, I heard he would be away this week.'

Darcy straightened. 'Really? Where is he?'

Viggo shrugged. 'His PA didn't say.'

'Well, when will he be back?'

He shrugged again. 'Apparently he is away for a few days this week. That's all I know.'

Darcy considered it. It was one thing not wanting to have to work in his presence, but if he really wasn't there . . . If it was guaranteed that he was gone for a bit, it would be an own goal – face-spiting – to miss the opportunity to put in a few more hours.

She watched as Viggo pottered over to the next display. They were in the Madsen Heritage room, a small parlour at the back of the gallery giving a potted history of the philan-thropic family which had done so much for Danish art. A timeline had been painted on the walls, sepia and black-and-white tinted images showing old family photographs. From a distance, they looked like every other rich Danish dynasty of their time – the men neatly bearded and in three-piece suits, the older women still wearing their hair in the old Gibson Girl pompadour style . . .

She walked slowly behind Viggo, looking at the photographs with vague curiosity. She hadn't looked around upstairs at all since coming to work here – either because the tourists were always jostling about or she was in too much of a hurry to hit the stacks. But it felt soothing to wander up here in the calm quiet before the doors opened and any of the other gallery staff arrived.

Viggo attached the plaques to the small brass posts already positioned in the wall; everything had been measured up weeks ago, the copy checked and double checked before it had been sent off to print.

She stopped in front of the giant black-and-white photo-graph that dominated the room and stared at it in silence, wishing the people she saw there could talk. Did they have the answer she was looking for?

The photograph showed the family arranged as a group in an orangery. Vines trailed the walls behind them, the women sitting on fashionable Lloyd Loom chairs, the men behind them looking straight to camera. In the very centre of the photograph sat an older man in a rocking chair. He had white hair and a monocle, a gnarled hand gripping the hand-rest and a small leather book on his lap. Darcy checked the information plaque to the side, her hunch confirmed: Bertram Madsen, 1918. The two young men either side of him were his sons, Frederik and Casper.

According to what Viggo had told her over one of their coffees, Madsen Senior had been a brilliant chemist, once nominated for the Nobel Prize for Chemistry; he had made the family's fortune. But it was his eldest son, Frederik, who had turned the family into a social tour de force, not least by setting up the Foundation. Frederik wasn't a handsome man, with his slightly goggly eyes and lantern jaw, but he had a stern, proud look which Darcy suspected had made him impossible to ignore. His brother, Casper, was slighter in build and darker-haired with watchful eyes. The reserved, recalcitrant younger brother? Spare to the heir?

Seated on a sofa beside Bertram, in front of the brothers, sat the mother and daughter – Gerde and Lotte Madsen, their hands demurely clasped in their laps. The girl looked to be in her mid-teens, doll-like and so pale she could have been fashioned from porcelain. Like her mother, she had fair hair and light eyes and looked so mild-mannered in demeanour that Darcy suspected neither one of them had ever encountered anything more violent in their lives than a runny egg or dropped hem.

She wandered to the next picture. Again it showed the mother and daughter, in a garden, but Lotte looked slightly younger here: June 1915, said the plaque. There was a young girl in the image with them, too, and Darcy could see a gardener working in the background, a pair of shears in his outstretched hand as he tended a flower bed. Gerde was sitting in a canopied deck-chair, the girls on a picnic blanket at her feet with books around them. The photograph had a reportage feel to it as the girls were slightly blurry, as if they had glanced up at the call of their names. They were barefoot, wearing cotton summer dresses and making flower crowns. Was midsummer approaching? Darcy knew from her mother's stories of her own childhood that Sankt Hans Aften – Midsummer's Eve – was a big deal here: bonfires were lit on the beach, an ancient Viking tradition . . .

The photograph showed an idyllic scene, with no hint whatsoever that at the same moment, Europe was at war and men were dying in the trenches. Darcy's own great-great-grandfather had been killed at Ypres; he'd been one of five brothers in a family of nine, cut down in his prime. And meanwhile, these rich little girls had made flower crowns in the garden.

Darcy turned away, feeling agitated by the unfairness of it all even now: why some should suffer so horribly, and others prosper. Others play.

But life wasn't fair and it never had been. Some people simply had all the luck.

The day passed with its usual gentle rhythm – the constant shuffle of papers, Viggo's low voice on the phone, soft-soled footsteps, the background hum of the visitors upstairs. Darcy had worked straight through lunch, on a roll with Trier's diaries now that she had established that none of the women in his official catalogue of work bore a resemblance to the woman in the hidden portrait. It had been a huge relief to realize she hadn't wasted the past week after all.

'Time's up,' Viggo said, coming to stand by the table at the end of the stack where she was working. He had put on his long overcoat and was setting his trilby on his head.

'Really? Already?' she asked, surprised. Another time slip. It had felt more like five o'clock to her, but it was so difficult to tell without daylight.

'Jens is here I'm afraid.' Jens was the chief security officer and oversaw a team of three others, plus two dogs.

'He's always so punctual,' she complained, tapping her papers back into a neat pile and replacing them in the archive box file.

'How did you get on today?' he asked. 'I didn't hear any eurekas.'

'No, sadly none of those. I *did* find a very rude pencil sketch that's made me look at Mr Trier in a new light.'

'Really?'

'Yes. Homoerotic, you might say.' She glanced at Viggo. 'Was he gay?'

'If he was, he wasn't publicly. Same-sex relationships weren't legal here till '33.'

'Mm. It might just have been a doodle, of course. If he did like men, it certainly didn't stop him consorting with women too. I think he paid more for prostitutes than he did for food.' She replaced the box in its position in the stack. She was one column away from the end of the first stack now. Progress, if not achievement.

She grabbed her coat, scarf and bag and they walked up the stairs together. The gallery had closed at six and the shop and reception staff never stayed longer than half past. All the lights had been switched off so that the only light coming through was the early evening twilight through the glass-domed roof.

It always felt special to Darcy, walking through a gallery after hours; maybe even sacred. The space had a pristine quality to it – no litter or mess, of course; nothing so fallible and human as that. But in the silence and darkness, the space breathed, somehow, as if the souls of past lives were caught behind the paint in the canvases. Eyes followed her footsteps. Smiles hovered on lips. Washing on lines billowed mid-blow of the breeze. The gallery was not dead space, but merely sleeping. It had its own slow pulse. Immortality could be captured within these walls, for the long departed were not truly gone for as long as they were looked upon.

'Got any plans this evening?' she asked him as they walked through the hallowed rooms.

'Tonight is my chess club.'

She hadn't been expecting an answer in the affirmative. 'Oh? I didn't know you played.'

'Oh, yes. It's my obsession. I attempted a Bird's Opening last week but it rather backfired on me. I've decided to open with an Elephant Gambit this week instead.'

'You've completely lost me, I'm afraid, Viggo.'

Jens was sitting at the reception desk, his dog curled up in its bed. Darcy didn't know its name and there was little point in asking. It wasn't a pet. The animal lifted its head at the sound of their approach, eyes following them, but it made no move. Not without Jens' instruction.

'Good night, Jens,' Viggo said with a nod as they passed. 'We'll see you in the morning.'

'Good night, Viggo. Miss Cotterell.' The security guard had

a deck of cards laid out before him and was setting up for a game of patience. '. . . Oh, by the way, Miss.'

She stopped and turned at the door.

'Is the other box ready to come back?'

'Back?' she asked in surprise.

'Yes, from Mr Lorensen's. Only we didn't receive the remittance form yet.'

She stared at him. Hadn't her message to Max been clear enough that she didn't need it there? 'But I told him—'

'Ah! This is my oversight, I fear.' Viggo spoke with a slightly frozen look as he turned towards her. 'I apologize. When we drew up the working plan at the weekend, Max Lorensen asked for a box to be delivered each evening after closing up here. I'm afraid I forgot to cancel yesterday's delivery after I learned you weren't intending to go over this week.'

'So you mean it's been sitting there all last night and all day today?'

'Yes, but . . .' Viggo looked shaken and suddenly every single one of his seventy-three years. 'Oh. Oh dear.'

'Viggo, it's fine,' she said, touching his arm and seeing how he paled. The material in the archives was treasure to him and he took its safekeeping seriously.

'I'll go over there right away.'

'No,' she said, shaking her head. 'I'll go. You've got chess club.'

'But this is not your error.'

'I know, but I'm free this evening. I'll check everything's okay and I'll get the form signed and then it can be sent back. No one will ever know.' She gave a careless shrug.

The old archivist looked pained by the oversight. '. . . You're sure?'

156

'Of course. No harm will have been done.' She turned back to Jens. 'How should I communicate to you about when to collect the box?'

'Text me.' He scribbled a number down on a piece of jotting paper and handed it to her. 'Please allow half an hour from the time you send it. Arrival time will depend on whether I'm on patrol.'

'Okay. I'll be in touch.' She and Viggo stepped outside. It was brisk, and Viggo pulled his coat closer to his frame. 'And you're sure Max is away at the moment?'

'Yes. Why?'

She looked down the street, past the tail-lights of the rush-hour traffic as everyone made their way home. 'I'll do another hour or so over there,' she mulled, before looking back at him. 'May as well, seeing as I'm looking in anyway. And if I'm not going to be in his way . . .'

'Here.' Viggo reached into his coat and pulled out a key. 'He gave me this. The code is P-E-D-E-R.'

'Peder?'

'Exactly.'

The Danish form of Peter? 'Okay, well . . . enjoy your chess. Don't worry about a thing. It'll all be fine.'

'You will call me, of course, if there is any issue?'

'Of course,' she smiled.

'Very well. See you in the morning, then, Darcy,' he said, turning right onto the pavement.

'Bright and early,' she smiled, turning left.

She walked at a clip, her breath hanging in cold plumes. Every so often she blew on her hands to keep them warm; cycling would have warmed her up better, but the nearest rental bike rack was a hundred metres in the opposite direction, and it wasn't worth getting a bike for such a short distance.

Within ten minutes, she was standing outside Max's house. It was becoming a familiar pilgrimage. She didn't want to go in – just being there again felt like some kind of defeat – but she reminded herself that she was doing it for Viggo. And there were no lights on inside; the house was reassuringly empty. Max would never even know she'd been back.

She walked up the steps and slid the key into the lock. Almost immediately, an alarm began ticking, but she saw the digital keypad set high on the wall and entered the code Viggo had given her. Immediately, the ticking stopped. No fuss. No drama.

She switched on the lights as she closed the door behind her and found herself returned to the scene of the crime. Cold beauty. Hard elegance. Much like the women he dated, she supposed.

She walked through and straight up the stairs to the kitchen, turned on the light and stood for a moment as the majestic room was revealed again. It really was a dazzling space. She tried to imagine Max hosting dinner parties at that vast table, but it was impossible for her to fathom; she couldn't imagine what his friends must be like. International bankers? Hedge funders?

The box was sitting on the low coffee table between the sections of the green velvet sofa; a form atop it.

'See? No harm done,' she muttered to herself. And why should there have been? What, really, were the chances of a burglary or a fire? Everyone's paranoia about the safekeeping of the archive material was slightly on the hysterical side, in her opinion, and if it weren't for the fact that Jens was going to collect the box from here himself, she would have taken it home and worked from there.

She sighed, looking around the kitchen with a more relaxed

eye now. A navy jumper dangled over one of the stools; a pair of running shoes had been kicked under the cabinet. The Sunday papers were still lying in a pile on the sofa from when she'd left the other night. A silk tie was coiled up on the kitchen counter . . . There were tiny signs of his life here, but all they really told her was that his housekeeper didn't come in daily. Unlike the gallery, there was no pulse in this building.

Her tummy rumbled, and she realized she was starving. Starving and thirsty. She thought of the bottle of sauvignon blanc wedged in her fridge door, just ready for her to come home to tonight – whereas he had a wine fridge with tinted glass, full from top to bottom. She could hear him even now, in her head, tutting and ordering her to 'just have a glass', impatient with her mannered reserve. Instead, she shrugged off her coat and scarf, ordered dinner on Uber Eats and sat down to begin work. These little acts of resistance were a small rebellion against his largesse. A rejection of the man who'd played her.

The box, when opened, revealed a medley of material. Topmost were some letters, bundled together with a brown shoelace. She read as quickly as she could – these were letters to Trier's mother in Odense – but the handwriting was sloppy and rushed as ever and his colloquial language made it difficult for her to gather speed. It was November 1920 and he had returned to Denmark now; he mainly seemed to complain about the cold, having become used to the Mediterranean heat, occasionally asking after Sannie, whom she guessed to be a pet, and whether they had heard from Uncle Malthe.

When the doorbell rang – bringing back bitter memories – she was surprised. Immersed in her work, she had felt like she had only been settled for a few minutes but according to her phone it was actually forty-five. She took her dinner from the courier – a burger, chips and a half bottle of sauvignon blanc – and ate perched on the edge of the sofa while she worked, hoping the smell wouldn't sink into the velvet and betray her presence here. The wine necessitated fetching and using one of his glasses but she grabbed the first she could find – a water tumbler on the side – rather than rummage through his cabinets. Stepping into his kitchen felt like stepping into his life, and she was resolved to stay well out of that now.

She balled herself up in the corner of the sofa, her legs tucked under as she sipped the wine and continued to trawl through the letters. For all his creative genius with a paintbrush, Trier had been no wordsmith and his letters were turgid and uninspiring. She read without interest, hoping that the next sheet, then the next one, would be the one to give her the break she craved.

But none of them were.

She flicked through an exhibition catalogue from a gallery in Aarhus, but it didn't appear to be one he had exhibited in himself. Had he been a guest? Below was a sheaf of papers: more sketches, but they were watercolours this time. Botanical studies. Darcy frowned. Obviously, artists would explore different mediums and themes with varying levels of success, but these felt out of character for Trier as an artist: not just generally but at this juncture especially, where he had begun working more in oils than charcoals.

She spread them out on the cushions, hoping to get more of an objective overview. He had done A4-sized studies of lilac, marguerite daisies, European beech leaves, pedunculate oak . . . Marguerite daisies were Denmark's national flower. Tokens of home? Had he been homesick?

And what did it matter anyway? It still didn't give her a name.

She sank back in the sofa, staring mindlessly at the Liebermann on the opposite wall as she felt her hopes fade and her frustration rise. It was difficult trying to piece together the movements of a man from a hundred years ago by sifting through the dregs of his life. If he had been able to foresee that the complaining, banal letters he wrote to his mother would one day be used to judge him as a man, would he have made them better, brighter, kinder?

She was tired by the endless sitting and constant silence and, with a full stomach and drowsy with wine, her gaze began to grow heavier, sinking into the bold oil colours like toes in sand. She could feel herself almost disappearing into the paint. Escaping.

She was so weary.

She allowed her eyelids to close.

For just a minute.

Chapter Twelve

Darcy blinked. The lights were still on but a pervasive silence, inside and outside the house, gave her the distinct feeling it was the dead of night. She checked her phone with a gasp. One twenty-seven.

'Oh my God,' she gasped, sitting up and trying to orient herself. The botanical studies were still on the sofa cushions but several were creased from where her arm had fallen on them while she slept. She smoothed them as best she could. How long had she been asleep for? How could this have happened? She had to get home. She couldn't be *here*.

And yet neither, she realized, could she simply just go.

Hurriedly she texted Jens and signed off the form, ready to hand over to him.

'Please be quick,' she said to the phone screen, cursing herself for having been so stupid as to fall asleep; an extra half-hour's wait, being awake, was everything she didn't need right now. She debated ordering an Uber but with Jens' arrival time outside of her control, decided against it. Better to hold off until he was here.

She washed the glass, put her coat on and carried the archive box and the paper bag with her dinner boxes inside back downstairs, turning off the lights as she went. She sat on the bottom step and waited in the darkness of the all-black hall.

She waited and waited, her chin cupped in her hands, her elbows on her knees. Her eyes kept closing, sleep wanting to claim her again. She just had to get home . . .

Had she drifted off again? She heard the sound of footsteps outside and stirred. 'Thank God,' she muttered to herself, standing up and lifting the box – just as she heard the sound of a key in the door.

There was no time to react. In the next instant, it opened and Max walked through.

If she looked stunned, he was even more so, and she saw him jolt on realizing someone was standing in the shadows at the bottom of his stairs. He was carrying a holdall and suit carrier, wearing a heavy overcoat and scarf.

'Max, it's me!' she said quickly, worried he might mistake her for an intruder and run at her. Or something.

'. . . *Darcy?*' he asked in disbelief.

Oh God. This scenario was everything she didn't need.

'I fell asleep working here. I'm sorry – I didn't mean to. I'm just leaving. I'm waiting for Jens to take the file. He should be here any moment.' The words came out in a rush, as if she was speaking in cursive.

He looked at the box in her arms and, without a word, put down his bags, walked over and took it from her. 'I can deal with that.'

It was the first time she had seen him since their kiss and up close, she saw he looked tired too. 'You're sure?'

'Yes.'

She shrugged. The sooner she could leave, the better. 'Okay, thanks.' She moved past him, but he turned with her.

'Where are you going?'

'Home?'

'Darcy, it's the middle of the night.'

'Precisely. I need to go home. Like I said, I didn't mean to still be here. I fell asleep.'

'Darcy, I'm not letting you walk the streets at this time of night!'

Her eyebrows shot up. What was he, her dad? 'I'm not walking. I'm about to order an Uber.'

He looked back at her with a sigh. 'Well, wait in here till it comes, at least.'

'No, I'm fine outside,' she said dismissively, immediately making her way down the steps.

There was a silence as he watched her go.

'. . . You have no right to be angry with me,' he said, standing on the top step and watching as she ordered the cab, her back turned to him.

She half turned over her shoulder, incredulous. 'I'm not angry at you,' she said, feeling angry.

'You've ignored me ever since Natalia came over.'

'That's funny – I don't recall receiving a text from you afterwards that I *could* have ignored,' she said tartly.

'. . . I meant you ignored my message about the box.'

'No. I responded to your text.'

'Eventually. And only when I made plain I wouldn't be here.'

She didn't reply.

'. . . Besides, you said you weren't coming over. Yet here you are.'

She glanced back, wanting to tell him that coming here had been the last thing she wanted to do – but she couldn't drop Viggo in it. 'My plans changed last minute and it made sense to push through, seeing as you were away – okay? You're supposed to be away!'

'And I was. For two days. Monday. Tuesday.'

And now it was the early hours of Wednesday. She rolled her eyes, turning away again. What did it matter anyway? She checked her screen. The small circle was spinning. *Looking for drivers*. Hurry up!

'. . . So you'd only come over if I wasn't here?'

Darcy just shook her head. She was too tired to argue at this time of night.

'So then you *are* angry.'

'I'm not,' she lied, because how could she admit to anything she was feeling? She wanted more from him than he was offering, that was the crux of it. She wasn't the one who had wanted to keep things professional between them in the first place, and when they'd kissed, she'd felt all the things she'd been trying not to feel. It had felt so good, natural even, but that was the danger, she saw now: she was going to fall and he wasn't.

'You're avoiding me, even though the thing with Natalia was before I met you and . . . it's not like you and I are—'

She whirled around, knowing exactly what they weren't. She wanted him, even though she knew she would just be another conquest. Natalia's arrival had merely confronted her with that fact and given her a . . . firebreak. Freja had been right from the start: she had to stay away from him, even if she didn't want to.

'I know, Max, it's strictly professional between us. You've gone to great pains to make that clear. I have got the point! . . . And I'm not avoiding you, I just don't *know* you. We're not friends.'

He frowned. 'You don't know me? You just spent the weekend in my house!'

'No, I sat on your sofa and worked. But it could just as easily have been a park bench. Or a desk in the library.'

He came down a step. 'We had breakfast and lunch together!'

She gave a small guffaw. 'That was not breakfast and lunch.'

'Excuse me?'

'That was some stylized version of it.'

He looked exasperated – and very tired. 'I don't even know what that means.'

'It means that you live your life like it has a filter on it!' she burst out. 'Nothing's real in your world. Everything's perfect. You're perfect! Your girlfriends are models! You live in a showho—' She stopped herself, but it was far too late. She'd said too much.

There was a silence and she could see he was taken aback by her outburst.

'Hello?' They both looked along the road to see a figure coming along the pavement. Jens was walking towards them at a brisk march, but his pace visibly slowed as he approached, looking between them with concern. It was the middle of the night and they were raising their voices. There was no way he hadn't heard them.

'Oh Jens, great, you're here,' Darcy said weakly. 'Max has . . . he's got the box.'

'You worked late,' Jens said to her, as Max came down the steps and handed him the box with a mutinous look. 'I was expecting to hear from you hours ago.'

'Yes. I never intended to be here this long,' she said again, for Max's benefit. 'I accidentally fell asleep. But Max has only just got back and he said he'd hand it over to you so I could get home . . . If my Uber would ever get here,' she muttered through clenched teeth as she looked down the street again.

'Ah.' Jens looked between them again, reading the tension. Neither she nor Max was capable of hiding it at this time of the night. '. . . And shall we deliver the next one tomorrow?'

'No,' she said quickly, drawing a sharp look from Max. 'No, that won't be necessary . . . Thank you, though.'

'Okay,' he said, stepping back with an awkward expression. 'Well, good night then.'

Neither Darcy nor Max spoke as Jens headed back towards the gallery. He was in his mid-fifties and overweight, wearing a dark grey uniform with a baton in his belt, but no further weapons; if someone were to launch a raid on the museum, it would be the dog alone stopping them. It seemed strange that the insurers considered Jens an adequate last line of defence for the Foundation's treasures.

Darcy looked at her phone again. The search session had timed out. She lifted her arm and checked the signal here – three bars – and put in a fresh request. 'Just go inside, Max. It's cold and it's late and this isn't your problem,' she said, turning away.

There was a pause, but a moment later she heard his feet on the steps and the door closing sharply behind him. The sound of it made her wince; she knew she was face-spiting again, but she couldn't help it. She hated how it was all nothing to him when it was everything to her.

She sighed, pulling her coat closer to her and shivering as she waited; it had to be minus five, six. Every few moments she checked her phone. A car had been found. Eleven minutes away.

Eleven? At this time of night? She groaned.

She sat on the kerb and waited, hugging her arms around her body, her chin tucked into her coat collar as if she was a roosting pigeon. A light fell onto the ground, over and around her, and she glanced back to see the lights on in one of the rooms on the second floor. His bedroom?

She quickly turned away, not wanting to be caught looking.

Let him go to bed. He had looked tired, a heavy stubble on his jaw making him appear less AI-generated than usual. A chink in the armour.

The coldness from the ground was chilling, seeping through her coat and numbing her bottom as she sat there, waiting for the minutes to tick past. She would have watched the map showing the car's progress, but it was too cold to keep her hands out. Instead, she huddled as best she could, tucked into her own layers.

Eight minutes passed.

Nine . . .

She was shivering constantly. This was ridiculous. It was gone two in the morning and she was sitting on the pavement in sub-zero temperatures. She was supposed to be in the gallery again in five hours. She would have been better off walking home after all; she'd be halfway there by now and at least she'd be generating some heat.

She didn't hear the car approach – it was electric – and the first she knew of it was when the beam of the headlights appeared on the road in front of her. She looked up with relief.

'Oh, thank God,' she whispered, getting up stiffly.

She opened the passenger door and went to climb in, just as she heard another door open. She glanced back.

Max was standing in his doorway, his mouth open as if he'd just said something – or was about to. He was wearing tartan pyjama bottoms and a white t-shirt. Bare feet. Private Max.

He closed his mouth again as Darcy slid onto the back seat. The car door shut with a thunk and she dropped her head back, looking away from him as the cab slunk into the night.

*

'I was getting worried,' Viggo said as she came down the stairs. It was almost nine and the gallery staff were busy upstairs, preparing to open.

'Sorry, I overslept.'

'Yes, Jens said you had a late night.'

Darcy swallowed, wondering what else the security man had said as he clocked off from his night shift. Had he relayed her arguing with Max on the steps in the moonlight? 'I fell asleep on the sofa. My bad.' She shrugged off her coat, grateful for the cosy, stable temperatures down here. She was still chilled from last night; the cold had got into her bones. 'How was chess?'

'Well, I didn't disgrace myself. I took his bishops, rooks and queen, before he stole a march on my king.'

'Sounds . . . tricky,' Darcy nodded, her mind still snagged on last night's showdown.

'Yes. But more importantly, all was well with the box?'

'Absolutely fine. The housekeeper hadn't even been in.'

'That is a relief,' he sighed. 'I can't believe I forgot something so important. I think my memory . . .'

'Viggo, your memory is fine. It was an oversight; it happens to everyone . . . But I do think these "security concerns" are overblown,' she said, taking the opportunity to push back again. 'The chances of some sort of mishap are incredibly low.' She looked at him meaningfully. Could *they* not come to a private arrangement? Max Lorensen and the insurers didn't even need to be involved. She could take a box back with her to her apartment and who needed to know? Surely Viggo trusted her?

'Now don't look at me like that,' he said, wagging a finger at her. 'Max Lorensen's position is clear.'

Darcy frowned. '. . . Max's? You mean the insurers, surely?'

Viggo hesitated. 'Exactly.'

'But you just said Max.'

'He's the one liaising with them.'

'I thought you were?'

'Me and him. We both are.'

Darcy's frown deepened – why didn't she believe him? – but the archivist got up and made his usual trek to the kettle.

'So was last night's shift another dead end?' he asked.

'Yes . . . and no,' she said, thinking back.

'Oh? A development?'

She watched as he spooned instant coffee into their mugs. 'Viggo, there isn't any way someone else's work could have ended up in Johan Trier's files, is there?'

Viggo straightened up with the sharpness of a man fifty years his junior. 'Absolutely not. Harald Morgensen arranged the files when the Foundation was created and he was an utterly scrupulous man. To the point of obsession.'

'Right,' she sighed.

'Why do you ask?'

'It's just that there's a handful of watercolour studies in there that don't fit Trier's MO. I was just wondering if they belonged to another artist and were accidentally misfiled? I mean, that must happen occasionally, surely?'

'Never. Only two people have ever filed these archives: Harald and myself.' He fixed her with a stern look, as if his integrity had been called into question.

'Well, then I wouldn't doubt either of you.' She received her morning coffee with a smile, sliding her hands around the mug for warmth, and gave a little shiver.

'Cold?'

'A little chilled.'

'If there's one thing I can assure you of,' Viggo said, taking his seat again, 'it's that no mistakes have been made down here. Everything is where it should be. If those watercolours were in his file, they're his. Why do you feel they're not?'

'Because I've never seen any other botanical studies by him, for one thing. Nor watercolours.'

He considered these points. 'You're right – neither are his metier. Perhaps he experimented with them and felt he couldn't achieve the level he wanted in those fields?'

'Mm; they were accomplished, though. It wouldn't have been for lack of talent he abandoned that path.'

'Lack of interest, then? Did you come across anything more encouraging?' he asked hopefully.

'Sadly not,' she sighed, already weary even though the day had barely begun. 'The more I dig, the further away I feel I'm getting. You know that game kids play when they're looking for something and the closer they get, you shout "hotter"?'

'Yes.'

'Well, I'm approaching freezing.'

Chapter Thirteen

Darcy checked her reflection in the window of the restaurant. Her hair was hairing and she'd successfully achieved a smooth winged eyeliner in the tiny mirror of the downstairs toilet in the gallery. Remembering her much-anticipated date with Aksel, she had had the foresight to pull on her new winter white jeans this morning, brown jodhpur boots and a chunky moss knit jumper beneath her coat.

'Cute but cosy,' she had said in the bathroom mirror as Freja brushed her teeth; she only came home each morning for fresh clothes.

'Cute but cosy doesn't exactly scream "fuck me in the club toilets",' Freja had said, spraying toothpaste everywhere.

'We're going to play board games. I'll be lucky if he kisses me with tongue.' Darcy threw her hands up. 'With my luck, I'll be lucky if he kisses me at all!'

She skipped down the basement steps of the yellow building and pushed on the door of the cafe. Freja had first taken her there soon after they'd met, saying that if a good mood could be a place, this would be it. It had the convivial pub vibe Darcy missed from back home, crammed with sofas, chairs and tables of assorted sizes, and the walls lined with shelves groaning under the weight of almost two thousand board games. It was always heaving and Darcy had prudently reserved a table.

The ambient noise level was already high as she walked in and she stood taking in the scene, trying to locate her date.

It appeared she'd arrived first and she checked them in, a slight sinking feeling in her stomach. She'd pushed for the date, booked it, he'd cancelled once and now he was late? It wasn't boding well.

'Here you go,' the guy said, leading her to their table. It was set between some bigger tables with groups on. They were already rowdy, pushing their chairs back and leaping with shouts as the die were rolled.

At least they'll mask any awkward silences, she thought, sinking into the chair and opening up the app to order a drink while she waited.

'Darcy?'

She looked up in surprise. He must have been almost right behind her. 'Aksel,' she smiled, cross-referencing the man before her with his photos. Freja always told her that men on dating apps added two inches' height to their bios and a zero to their incomes. She'd once turned up for dinner with a guy sporting beach blond surfer-boy hair in his photos, only to be met with a man fifteen years older and completely bald. She had walked out on the spot – not because she objected to the baldness, but to the lying about it.

But Aksel, if anything, was better than his pictures had suggested. He was olive-skinned, with dark, tousled hair, a slight underbite, ultra-white teeth and those soulful eyes that had first drawn her in. And he's kind to animals, she thought, as he leaned in and kissed her cheek lightly.

'I only just got here,' she said as he took off his coat – flashing a strip of toned abs – and sat down opposite her. He was tall, too, she realized as he banged his knees on the table.

'I know, I saw you ahead of me on the street. When you

173

turned in here, I was hoping you would be . . . you.' He gave an awkward smile. 'Sorry – I really wanted to get here first, but I had a walk-in at the last minute.'

'Do you get many of those?'

'All the time. But never more frustrating than when you're trying to get out the door.'

'I can imagine. Was it anything worrisome?'

'For the owner, yes. Her dog had swallowed her engagement ring she'd left on the side of the sink.'

'Oh no!'

'A two-carat diamond, apparently.'

She winced. 'And so you treated it by . . . ?'

'Putting the dog on a high-fibre diet for the next three days.' Darcy grinned. 'Oh. Nice.'

'It happens all the time,' he smiled, shaking his head. He looked around the room. 'It's great here. I can't believe I've never been.'

'Yeah, good for rainy Sunday afternoons too.'

'Noted,' he nodded. He looked over at the bar. 'Let me get us some drinks.'

'Oh, it's okay, I'll order on the app. It means we don't have to queue and they bring the food and drink over to us here. The nachos and chilli fries are to die for.'

'Yeah? I'm starving. I ended up working through lunch. An epileptic cockatoo.'

She gave a small guffaw. He was amusing without realizing it. 'Well, let's order food at the same time then.'

'You're sure? I don't want to rush us through this.' He smiled at her. 'Now I'm here I feel like I wasted too much time already.'

Darcy smiled at the unexpected compliment. 'Well, I'm really glad we could make it happen.'

'Yeah, I'm not that good with the whole online thing. It's my first time on a dating app.'

'Oh? How did you end up on Raya?'

'My best mate works at Goldman Sachs. He sorted it out for me, although I don't think I'm really what most of the girls on there are looking for. I think they want hedge fund managers, not a guy who spends his days with his fingers in a cat's rectum.'

Darcy spluttered. '. . . But you're a professional. Veterinary school's how many years?'

'Six years.'

'There you go, then. You're more qualified than any banker. Everyone knows they're just winging it.'

He grinned. 'How about you? Who put you on Raya?'

'My flatmate's boyfriend. They did it without telling me.'

'Yikes! And did they swipe on me for you too?'

'No,' she said, throwing hm a coy look. 'I did that all by myself.'

'Well, that's a relief,' he smiled. 'I wouldn't want to think you were here under duress.'

'*I* suggested the date, remember?'

'I do.' They held eye contact for a moment and Darcy felt a small pulse of relief that they were actually flirting. She hadn't held out much hope, especially after the run-ins with Max had left her feeling flattened.

'So tell me your dating history,' she said. 'Let's get it out of the way. What's brought you to be sitting here with me tonight, about to embark on a fierce game of Scrabble?'

He shrugged. 'It's a pretty short story. I was in a five-year relationship, almost all the way through vet school.'

'Was she a vet too?'

'No. She's a data analyst now.'

'Five years is a long time. What happened?'

He hesitated for a moment. 'If I'm being really honest, I think I always had an instinct we weren't going to go the distance. I loved her, but I knew I didn't want to marry her.'

'Ouch.'

'Yeah. It was rough. I felt like a scumbag, of course, even though I was only trying to be honest. I really did – and do – believe it was the best thing for us both, but it put me off getting too involved again.'

'I'm not surprised. That's a long time to be with someone. Are you still in touch with her?'

'A little . . . Not really. She's with someone else now. They're engaged.'

'Are you cool with that?'

'I was a bit sad when I heard, but I didn't want to be him, if that makes sense. It confirmed for me that I'd done the right thing.'

'Yeah – far better to call it quits before you get to marriage and kids. I've already got a friend back home getting divorced.'

'Really?'

'Yeah. The marriage lasted ten months. And the sad thing is, we all knew it was coming. No one thought they should get married. She just wanted a wedding, I reckon.'

'There's a lot of that,' he said, rolling his eyes. 'Do you want to get married?'

She pressed a hand to her heart. 'Gosh, I mean we've only just met but sure, why not?'

He laughed, sitting back as the waiter came over with their drinks. 'Food will be twenty minutes,' the man said.

'Great, thanks . . . Well, cheers,' she said and they clinked

176

beers. She drank, feeling relaxed already, although Aksel seemed to betray some nerves as he gulped his down in deep swallows.

'Tell me your story, then,' he said, putting down a half-drunk pint a moment later.

'Oh, it's a little more meandering than yours,' she sighed. 'I was in a three-year relationship at uni. Then I was single for a bit, doing my master's; then I got into another relationship for eighteen months. After that I rebounded into what was supposed to be a fling but turned into a year-long thing. I moved over here in the summer and was *determined* I'd be single but I met a guy I worked with in, like, my second week and we were together for two months. I keep trying to have my Hot Mess moments but it never quite happens that way. Somehow I always end up in a relationship.'

'Yikes.' He made a face. 'Will I get a warning or just wake up one day married to you with three kids?'

'I'll try to warn you,' she grinned.

'Great. Thanks.' He looked at her again and she felt an ease with him she hadn't felt with Erik or Max. Erik had made her jumpy, pushing too hard for an ending she wasn't ready to give; and Max . . . she couldn't relax with him. He made her feel like her soul was on fire. 'So why did these relationships end?'

She grimaced. 'I wish you hadn't asked that. At least, not before I've had a few drinks.'

'Why not?'

'Because it doesn't reflect well on me.'

'No?' Aksel frowned, waiting.

She sighed and held up a hand, beginning to count off her fingers. 'Uni guy – cheated on me. Master's guy – turned out to be *married*. Yeah, that was great! Year-long guy – decided he was bi, with a strong preference for men. Copenhagen guy – cheated on me.'

'Oh.'

'Yep, I know how to pick 'em.'

'Well, it does sound like your radar might be off a little,' he said falteringly. 'Although you're sitting here with me now, so you obviously have *some* taste.'

She grinned.

'You do know, them cheating only reflects on them, not you?'

'Well, thanks for saying that. But when it keeps happening, you can't help but feel that you're the one doing something wrong.'

'It's not you, Darcy.'

They held eye contact again. It was so easy to look at him. He was unguarded, direct, safe.

'And so you've been in Copenhagen since the summer?'

'Yes, five months now, I can't believe it.'

'Do you like it here?

'I love it. I just wish time would slow down a little. I feel like I'm going to be back in London before I'm ready.'

'Can you extend your stay?'

'Possibly. I've been diverted onto a special project, which means I can't actually get on with my thesis at the moment, so it will probably mean an extension to my deadline.'

'Oh, that's right. You mentioned it – the hidden painting that's been in the news?'

'Yeah, it's down to me to discover the identity of the woman in the portrait. There's this big Johan Trier retrospective coming up at the National Gallery in the new year, so they're throwing everything at it to have the big reveal then.' She pulled a face. 'Nothing like a deadline to deliver to the Danish general public to sharpen the mind.'

He winced. 'How's it going?'

'Oh, it's not.' She rolled her eyes. 'But it's early days still; I'm trying not to be impatient. Such is the life of an art historian. The dead can be reluctant to reveal their secrets.'

'It sounds so different to my job. I deal with what's on the table. Right there, in the moment.'

'Is it what you hoped it'd be, being a vet?'

'It definitely involves more client management than I'd reckoned on. It's not the animals that are tricky, it's their owners.'

'Are you ever scared? You must have dangerous animals coming in?'

'Frequently. And even the most docile pet can become unpredictable and aggressive if they're in pain or scared. I probably get bitten a few times a week.'

'Wow.'

He shrugged. 'There's tricks of the trade that can help; the senior partners are especially helpful there, that's where the experience shows. But I really don't like snakes, so my heart sinks whenever I see that on the log sheet.'

'Do you build up a rapport with animals if they come in regularly?'

'For sure. I've got a soft spot for a particular dog that was brought into us when she was a juvenile. She'd been abandoned by her owners, who'd tied her up to a stake in a remote field. She was just left to die there which, to this day, I still find unbelievable. Luckily some walkers saw her and brought her in. I don't really know how she survived, to be honest. She was completely dehydrated and malnourished when we first got her. Just a bag of bones. She wouldn't look at us, wouldn't eat. I would go into her crate during my lunch hour and whenever I had any free time to read out loud to her . . . It soothes them.'

'That's cute. What would you read to her?'

'Whatever was lying around: old copies of *National Geographic*, the sports pages, medical studies.' He shrugged. 'It didn't matter. She just got used to my voice and began to understand I wasn't going to hurt her. Eventually she came and sat against my legs and started to eat from my hand. She made a full recovery, but man, it hurt when we had to hand her over to the shelter. No disrespect to my ex, but I think it was harder having to let go of that dog.'

'She must have been so bewildered when she was taken away.'

He shook his head, looking pained. 'I lasted four days before I went to the shelter to adopt her.' He pulled a face. 'Only to be told she'd been chosen by a family the day before.'

'No!'

'My fault for hesitating. I'm a chronic procrastinator.' He took another sip of his beer. 'But it was for the best and I do get to see her occasionally. The family registered with us, so whenever she comes in for her annual jabs, I'm the one to do her. All the nurses know to book her in on my shifts.'

'That's so sweet.'

'It's a peril of the job, falling in love with the patients.'

She grinned. 'Well, I definitely don't have that to worry about!'

'No? No hot co-workers, then?'

The image of Max, standing in his doorway last night, flashed through her mind. He didn't count as her co-worker. He didn't count as anything.

She shook her head. 'I'm currently spending all my days with a seventy-three-year-old widower. Don't get me wrong, he's fantastic company and I'm really enjoying it, but no – my heart is quite safe.'

'Good to know,' he smiled, putting his pint down and leaning forward. 'So . . . what shall we play?'

'I'll call you,' Aksel said in the half-second before the cab door shut and she turned back to wave him off, standing staring after the car until it turned out of sight.

Had that gone as well as she'd thought it had? She had a strange sense of abeyance. They had talked and laughed easily all night, the conversation never faltering. In fact, it hadn't really felt like a first date. He was intelligent and seemingly honest. He had flirted just enough and there were no glaring red flags that she could see; his romantic past was far less chequered than hers. He had been respectful – but had he been *too* respectful? He hadn't made any attempt to touch, much less kiss, her. Unlike Max Lorensen, who had acquired a proprietary stance within seconds of meeting her . . . No, he was a gentleman. Decent. He'd paid for their dinner without any hesitation, but unlike most men who did that – Erik – he hadn't followed it up with an equally unspoken expectation that they would go home together either. He'd simply kissed her on the cheek and told her he'd had 'a great time' as the Uber pulled up outside her apartment.

She fished her keys out of her bag and walked into the building, her mind in full evaluation mode. On paper it had been a great date. Not a thing had gone wrong. She had gone in expecting precious little and come away pleasantly surprised. She wasn't going to pretend it had set her world alight; there weren't scorch marks on the ground between them, but it felt like they were on the same page. Their values aligned. It was a solid start.

She slid her key into the apartment door and stepped in.

Freja was brushing her teeth in the bathroom, a charcoal face mask on and her hair braided and stowed under a sleep cap in an effort to control the frizz. Her head popped around the doorway, eyes wide.

'You're back early,' she said after a moment, seeing that Darcy was alone.

'You're *here*!' Darcy fell against the doorframe in mock shock.

'Day two of my firebreak, remember?' Freja gave a thumbs-up. 'I told you, I'm going strong!'

'Good work.' Darcy shrugged off her coat and boots.

'So how was it – dare I ask?' Freja held her thumb up again, but this time side-on like a Roman emperor.

Darcy did a thumbs-up. 'Great.'

'Yay! . . . So where is he then?'

'In an Uber back to his place. He's a gentleman.'

Freja scowled. 'Did you ask him back here?'

'No, and he didn't suggest it either. Which suits me just fine.' She remembered how Max had asked her for the nightcap on the museum steps. So confident, self-assured. So practised . . . 'There's no rush. We talked really easily – like we'd known each other for years. He's a good listener, too. It was great.'

'Was there any awkwardness at all?'

'No. None.'

'Hm.'

Darcy frowned. 'Why do you say it like that?'

'A bit of awkwardness is good. It indicates tension, you know? Sexual chemistry.'

Darcy hesitated. 'We had tension.' She sounded defensive.

'You did?'

'Yes, he's really attractive. And so clever.'

'Well, he is a vet.'

'Exactly.' Darcy leaned against the doorframe as Freja

ducked back into the bathroom and spat in the sink. 'We're going to go for drinks again tomorrow night.'

'Ooh, that's keen. Setting up the next date while you're still on the first one.'

'I told you, it went well.'

Darcy's phone buzzed – already? – and she gave a smile as she checked it. A flirty little 'good night' text was always welcome . . .

But she frowned as she saw the Revolut banner come up and an invoice for 392 kr.

What?

It was for half of dinner! She blinked in disbelief. She had assumed by the way he'd grabbed the bill and didn't even look her way as he handed his card over that he had wanted to cover it himself. She had thanked him for paying! He'd made no mention—

'So, he's a gentleman. Clever and attractive. What else?' Freja asked, patting her mouth dry with the towel.

Darcy looked back at Freja and groaned, slumping against the wall. 'He's a bloody feminist.'

Chapter Fourteen

Another envelope.

Darcy had moved from her spot at the table at the end of the stack and was instead sitting cross-legged on the floor, the latest box open beside her. She had turned the corner, quite literally, coming to the end of the first stack and moving over to the other side of the aisle. Such were the pigeon steps by which she had to mark progress.

She turned the envelope over. It was unsealed and she untucked the flap . . .

'Nice top . . . That colour suits you.' She looked up to find Max standing at the end of the shelves, watching her. He was softly backlit by the library lights above the end tables. Even his silhouette was handsome. 'You forgot this.' Her scarf was bundled in his hand. 'It was on the sofa.'

'Oh . . .' She hadn't even noticed it was missing. She got to her feet as he came down the aisle towards her and held it out. 'Thanks.'

She swallowed, remembering their latest tense interaction – the altercation on his doorstep the other night. She felt embarrassed now. They'd both been tired. '. . . I'd make a rubbish burglar,' she murmured, aiming for levity.

He gave his half-smile, stuffing one hand into his trouser pocket. 'Yes . . . There were other signs of your presence.'

She looked at him questioningly.

'Some fries on the floor.'

'. . . Really?'

He nodded and she winced, appalled. She reached for something to deflect from her embarrassment. 'Well, there wouldn't have been if you had a dog.'

He looked surprised – as was she – by the comment. 'You think I should have a dog?'

'Free hoovering,' she faltered. '. . . Not to mention, it might add a little life to the house.'

There was a perplexed silence. It was a wholly unexpected turn of the conversation. 'I work long hours. It wouldn't be fair.'

'No, probably not,' she muttered, looking down and squeezing the scarf in her hand. She had absolutely no idea why she'd even brought up the topic of dogs. She stared at her pale blue sweater instead. He really thought this colour was good on her?

'A cat might be better?'

Was he trying to rescue her? She looked up at him. 'If you like cats.'

'I take it that means you don't?'

She shrugged. 'It's generally accepted that you have to pick a side, and I'm Team Dog.'

He crossed his ankles as he leaned against the shelves, watching her. 'I see.'

At least they hadn't picked up from the argument on the step. 'Thanks for this. But you really needn't have gone out of your way. It's only a scarf.'

'Well, I know you would rather have lost the scarf than ever set foot in my house again.' He caught her eye and she felt her stomach drop as she saw the look on his face.

'Max . . .'

'We should talk.'

'No. There's really nothing to—'

'I think there is, Darcy.' He stared at her for a long moment. 'I shouldn't have kissed you on Sunday. It was wrong and I'm sorry.'

She swallowed. Each word felt like the snap of an elastic band on her skin – because it hadn't felt wrong to her. This wasn't the apology she wanted. She didn't want him to be sorry for kissing her; she wanted him to be sorry for having Natalia in his life, for having let her leave and Natalia stay . . . But he didn't regret those choices, only kissing her. 'It's really fine.'

'It's not, though. We had agreed to keep things professional and I crossed the line.' He opened his mouth as if to say something else, but closed it again. 'I won't make excuses. I did what I did –'

As far as she recalled, they had both done it.

'– And I don't blame for you not wanting to work in my house again. I know I've made your job more difficult when you're already under pressure.' He swallowed, looking uncomfortable. 'So I came here to say that if you do need to work late, I'll stay out until you're ready to leave. You can text me when you're done. I'll steer clear till you're gone.'

She stared back at him, seeing how ready he was to avoid her. 'That doesn't seem reasonable. It's your home,' she replied. 'We're both adults, both professionals . . . And besides, it was only a kiss.'

'Yes, but –' He stopped again, and this time she knew what he had been going to say: it wouldn't have been *only* a kiss. It had only stopped there because Natalia had turned up; they both knew that a couple of moments more and they would have completely lost themselves. 'I just should have had more self-control. I assure you, it won't happen again.'

She looked away with a small snort. 'Oh I believe you. I'm sure you'll be a paragon of virtue.' She hadn't meant to sound so sarcastic, but she couldn't hold back her pain at his words and it made her feel exposed: could he see that she felt everything, while he felt nothing? She stood still for several seconds, trying to compose herself. '. . . I need to get on,' she muttered, going to move past him, but he caught her elbow.

'Wait.'

She felt the scarf and envelope fall from her grasp.

'What?' She looked back at him, seeing the same look that was always in his eyes, even though his words told different stories. '. . . What is it, Max? You've said what you came here to say.'

His mouth opened to speak but he couldn't seem to find the words, for once.

'It's all fine between us. Honestly,' she said. Another lie. 'If I need to work the extra hours, then I'll do what needs to be done. You don't have to stay out of your own home to accommodate me. I'm a big gir—'

She looked away from him, her words faltering as she glanced down and saw the contents of the envelope, spilled out on the floor. A necklace lay there like a snake.

What . . . ?

Seeing the abrupt change in her focus, Max released her arm. 'Darcy?'

He watched as she bent down to pick it up. The necklace was made of red wooden beads; they were tiny, the necklace's diameter small, with a loop closure and a single bead in the centre painted gold.

She blinked. What did this have to do with Trier? Had he bought it as a gift? For his mother, perhaps? . . . She frowned, her grip closing around the necklace as something stirred in her brain. A memory.

A memory . . . of an image. She lifted her hand and stared at the necklace more closely.

'What is it?' Max asked.

'. . . I feel like I've seen this before.' Her voice was barely more than a murmur as she sank into her mind, sifting and dredging through all the material she had waded through in the past ten days. So many photographs, slides, etchings, studies . . .

'Wait,' she whispered. It was a command to herself, she wasn't talking to him, but he stayed where he was nonetheless as she suddenly stirred. 'I need . . .'

She ran back down the aisle towards her worktable at the end and opened up her file of notes. It was pathetically paltry still, little more than a timeline of Trier's movements during 1918–1920; a list of names of the women in his officially recognized works . . . but the colour printout Otto had given her was still folded in half. She opened it, staring down at the portrait. It was like peering through muddied bottle glass – the ultraviolet light could only reveal so much through such thick materials as board backing, and the colours were an indistinct, brownish smudge. There were only contrasts of tones and shades from which to work, but against the woman's neck, partially obscured by the high neck of her blouse (or dress), there was the suggestion of a delicate necklace. Darcy might have assumed seed pearls from the shape and size of them, but the brightness of a singular bead at the throat indicated a tangible difference in material or colour.

Darcy looked again at the necklace in her hand. She set it down on the printout. The scale was off, of course, but . . .

She looked at Max, who had come to stand by her. 'Do you think it is?'

He squinted, leaning down for a better look. 'I mean, it could be . . . Hard to say for sure without any colour reference, but the gold bead does make it quite distinctive.'

Darcy looked down the corridor. Was Viggo at his desk? 'Viggo?' she called, grabbing the necklace and printout and running down the room. 'You need to see this!'

The archivist, who was working at the computer in the east wing, peered round a shelf. 'What is it? Have you found something?'

'This necklace just turned up.' She hurried over to him, showing him the image and beads. 'See this here,' she said, pointing out the bright gold bead. 'Do you think this could be the same necklace?'

Viggo repositioned his glasses on the end of his nose and scrutinized the image, just as she and Max had done. He took the necklace from her, running his fingers over the small red beads almost meditatively, a small frown beginning to furrow his brow as he straightened slowly.

'Do you recognize it?' she asked, watching him. 'Have you seen it before?' There had been no identifying information on the envelope; nothing to indicate to whom it had belonged – or been intended to belong – nor who had ever worn it.

But if it was the woman in the portrait's . . . it was a *thing* they could link to her. The first sign that she had been in Trier's life.

Darcy felt hope spring for the first time. Finally, was this something to work with?

Viggo was still thinking hard, staring at the shelf opposite but not seeing it. He wasn't here, downstairs in the dim light, below the gallery where tourists trod; he was . . .

'. . . Upstairs.'

'What?' Darcy asked, but he was already moving towards the staircase. She went after him, followed by Max. Viggo used the security card on his lanyard to open the door, and they emerged into the bright daylight. The galleries were as full as ever but Viggo moved like an old cat, sure-footed and silent, through the crowds, knowing exactly where he was headed.

Darcy felt her heart pound. They had their first clue! Something to give to Otto and Margit.

Viggo led them towards the Madsen Heritage room where he had been working the other morning. He walked over to a corner where some black-and-white images of the family were displayed and stopped in front of one, peering at it closely, then pulling back with a satisfied nod.

Darcy went closer, her gaze travelling over the foursome depicted. She recognized the younger Madsen men immediately – Frederik and Casper in summer linens, playing croquet – but the two women, a blonde and brunette, were unknown to her. *July 1921*, said the plaque beside it.

'Who are they?' she asked, her gaze already fixed on the dark-haired woman's throat.

Viggo pointed with great deliberation. 'Sofia, Frederik's wife,' he said, pointing to the blonde woman. 'And Lilja, Casper's.'

Darcy stared at Lilja Madsen. She was wearing a loose white cotton dress with pintucks and dark embroidery on the skirt, and a neckline that cut straight across the clavicle, dropping to little capped sleeves. She was thin, her long hair worn down but for a pearl comb holding back the front strands. A dark, beaded necklace could clearly be seen at her slender neck, the gold nugget winking brightly at her throat.

Darcy pressed her hand to her mouth. She couldn't believe what she was seeing. After days and days of no progress, suddenly they had it? Just like that? The riddle had been unlocked with a string of red beads and a photograph that had been hanging on the wall above them all this time?

She gave an astonished laugh, locking eyes with Max, who had brought up the rear. He looked as disbelieving as her. 'Can you believe it?' she asked him.

'. . . No.' He looked stunned, his customary self-assurance absent for once as the situation developed at pace.

Darcy looked back at the photograph, studying the details of a face that had been little more than an impression till now. A silhouette and the attitude of her deportment – the tucking down of her chin, the slight angle at which she held her head – had been the only indicators of this woman's demeanour and from those, she had been expecting a sophisticated society lady. But the woman in this photograph was far younger than she had expected; in fact, she looked little more than a girl. She had delicate, fine features but there was something in her eyes that was somehow challenging. She was holding the croquet stick with careless insouciance, as if the outcome of the game was of no consequence to her. Or perhaps she had already won, or lost? 'She's really his *wife*? She looks so young!'

'Different times,' Viggo shrugged.

Darcy's eyes roamed the image. The garden was mature, with orchard trees and clumps of silver birches dotting the further reaches of the lawn; a brick gate pillar was just coming into shot and a body of water – a lake? – shimmered at the top right edge. Lilja's companion, and sister-in-law, Sofie was looking to camera, like the men, but Lilja's gaze was slightly averted towards something over the photographer's shoulder. A child? A dog? A car? The possibilities were endless and even here the woman, captured in a still, seemed to move somehow. Elusive.

'Of course, we must not rush to conclusions,' Viggo said cautiously. 'Lilja, in this photograph, may not be the woman in the portrait simply because she is wearing the same necklace. They might have been friends.'

Darcy nodded. It was indeed conceivable Lilja could have loaned the necklace to the woman to wear during the sittings, or given it to her following a chance compliment. Or it could be that everything was the other way round and it was Lilja who had been gifted or loaned the necklace by the woman in the portrait. If Lilja was married to Casper Madsen, the son of Johan Trier's patron, she had surely come into contact with many of the women he painted? She might even have recommended him to her own friends.

'I agree,' Darcy murmured. She had to consider all hypotheses. 'We mustn't get carried away. This might not be an ending to the mystery, but a middle. We'll need to see where the evidence leads.' She looked over at Viggo and gave an excited smile. 'But at least we're no longer stuck at the beginning.'

'Indeed.'

The necklace had led her to a name, and that was a solid start, but she needed more information to help build the story. She wondered where that garden was – clearly not Copenhagen. She would have to find out.

'I must tell Otto.'

Max, standing behind them, said nothing. He didn't share

their academic fervour; he was a businessman, concerned with profits and gains. To him, this woman's name simply added to the legend of a painting that was a national asset. But to Darcy, this was a whole life found again. A woman who'd been quite literally locked in the dark for a century was feeling air on her painted face once more. Darcy remembered something she'd read once: that the dead are only truly forgotten once their name is uttered for the last time.

Well, this woman wasn't dead yet. She was coming alive again. And it might just be that Johan Trier was going to give her the gift of immortality.

'Pleased to meet you, Lilja,' she murmured. 'It's about bloody time.'

'Thanks, Christoff,' Max murmured. 'To the Royal Academy.'

The driver nodded, closing the door with a sedate *thunk*.

Darcy looked around at the plush interior – blonde leather, tinted windows, walnut trim. The two back seats were separated by a console with bottled water and a control suite that wouldn't have been out of place on an A380.

Max checked his phone quickly before slipping it back into his jacket pocket. 'Helle's going to meet us there.' He'd been making calls too while Darcy had been talking to Otto.

'Really?' Her nerves were beginning to rise as it was; she hadn't expected a full-on meeting to be called on the back of the potential identification. It was bad enough that Otto had called in Margit, without Helle Foss's scrutiny too. Max was accompanying her because she was taking source material off site. 'Why?' she had asked him, holding the file Viggo had given her on her lap. 'It's not a Madsen issue. And nothing's confirmed yet; Lilja Madsen may not be the woman in the portrait. This could turn out to be a false alarm.'

'Or it might not – in which case the Madsen name is implicated, and we have a right to know.'

Darcy glanced at him, remembering Otto's warnings. They all wanted the same thing – but were on different teams. 'You want the portrait?'

'I want whatever will continue to grow, drive and protect the Madsen brand name. No one can deny this discovery – with or without *Her Children* – is pertinent to our interests,' he said, holding her gaze without even blinking. His manner – so calm and unruffled – was quietly intimidating and she didn't want to imagine what it must be like sitting opposite him at a conference table; but then she remembered him in his kitchen, drinking coffee and reading the papers; in his sweats and socks, watching the football on his iPad . . . She tried to remind herself he had his human moments too.

'So that's why you've been so unduly interested in my progress on this project, is it?'

'. . . Unduly?'

She swallowed. 'I know it's not the insurers insisting on the working arrangement at your place. It's you.'

His gaze was steady. 'What makes you think that?'

'Viggo slipped up when we were talking.'

He looked away again, staring out of the window. 'I see.' It wasn't a denial.

'. . . So is it true? You've been keeping an eye on me because you can't do your job until I've done mine?'

He was quiet for another moment. '. . . Exactly, Darcy,' he muttered. 'That's what it was.'

They sank into silence as the car pulled out into the traffic and Darcy stared out of her own window, trying, for once, to move her mind away from him. She had to focus. She needed to plot her next steps for researching the young Mrs Casper Madsen. Margit would want not just details, but a plan.

She watched the city slink past, muted and tinted bronze. Everything felt different inside here, as if she had been hermetically sealed in a parallel world.

Beside her, Max checked his watch.

'We've got half an hour before we need to be there,' he murmured, seemingly thinking out loud. 'Any objections if we make a quick pitstop?'

'Where to?'

'The Christmas market. I need to pick something up for Sara.'

She swallowed at his audacity. *Really?*

'She's my PA, Darcy,' he said, as if reading her mind. 'She's sixty-three, married for thirty-eight years and she has seven grandchildren.'

'It makes no difference to me what she is to you,' she said quickly, even though the rapid clatter of her heart told a different story. Was her dismay really so obvious? 'Stop if you like. If you're sure there's time.'

His eyes narrowed ever so slightly at her dismissal. '. . . To Højbro Plads, please, Christoff.'

'Of course, Mr Lorensen.'

The silence in the car seemed to thicken but Darcy didn't feel compelled to speak. There was no neutral ground between them, it seemed; saying nothing was the only safe option.

The car pulled up at the square several minutes later and Max looked across at her. 'Coming?'

She looked out across the Christmas market. Dusk was already falling – she would never get used to the short days here – and the red wooden huts and trees were all picked out in glittering fairy lights so that the entire square glowed with a golden light. It made for a beautiful scene. The place was filled with shoppers and tourists, music was playing through speakers . . .

'No, it's fine. I'll just stay here.'

He blinked but gave no reply, although a tiny sigh escaped him, barely audible. She winced as his door slammed shut.

She swallowed, squeezing her hands into fists, knowing she was being petty and face-spiting again, but—

Her door suddenly opened and he peered in. 'Just come with me . . . What else are you going to do?'

She wanted to reply that she would check her emails, but something in his look told her not to toy. He held his hand out for her and silently she took it, giving a small shiver as she adjusted to the biting chill.

'I see you forgot your scarf again.'

Had she? In all the drama and haste . . . 'Oh.'

He tutted, shaking his head at the trail of mild chaos that surrounded her. '. . . This way.'

He turned left, heading towards the upper end of the square. The crowd was slow-moving as people ambled, in no rush – certainly they didn't appear to have meetings to go to – but from his leisured pace, seemingly neither did Max. He walked alongside her, not striding ahead, his hand hovering lightly on the small of her back, and she felt exactly as she had the night of the drinks reception at the National Gallery. She glanced across at him, just as he looked at her too. Was he thinking the same thing? She had no idea. He was almost impossible to read, his emotions never breaking past a certain pitch. Even when he would contradict himself – say one thing, do another – his surface still never cracked.

Perhaps he was just being gentlemanly, she told herself as

he guided the way – protecting her in the crowd. He'd do it for anyone . . . Kristina. Angelina. Natalia. Sara.

They passed by stalls selling knitwear, wooden toys, *flødeboller* cookies, colourful glazed ceramics, even artisan chocolate moulded as tools: cogs, padlocks, scissors and wrenches . . .

'So random,' she said with a puzzled smile.

Max seemed to know exactly what he was heading for and came to a stop a few minutes later at a stall selling felted Christmas tree decorations. There were terriers on skis, polar bears in Santa hats, gingerbread men holding Christmas stockings. Darcy looked at him, surprised. She wouldn't have thought this was his bag.

'It's a tradition,' he said, as if sensing her stare while he viewed the assorted goods. 'I get Sara a new one every year for her tree.' His eyes roamed for several moments before he picked up a teddy bear dressed as a Nutcracker and looked at her questioningly.

Darcy couldn't help but laugh. 'You want *my* opinion?'

'Of course. Do you think she'll have a desperate need for a teddy bear dressed as a Nutcracker hanging on her tree this year?'

She grinned at his tone. 'Well, I've never met Sara, so it's hard for me to say, but . . . who wouldn't?'

He broke into an open smile. 'So then we're in agreement – for once.' He handed it across to the stallholder, who began wrapping it in tissue as he reached into his suit for his wallet.

'Aren't you going to get one for your own tree?' Darcy asked wryly as he handed over his card.

'I don't have a tree,' he murmured.

Darcy's eyebrows raised up. 'You don't have a Christmas tree?'

'No.'

'What? . . . Never?'

'No.'

The card machine beeped as the payment went through and the vendor handed back his card and the toy, now tissue-wrapped and placed in a paper bag.

'How can you *not* have a Christmas tree?' she asked in astonishment as he started to move along again. She had to skip to catch him up.

'Because I don't celebrate Christmas.'

'Why not? Religious reasons? Lack thereof?'

He turned to look at her. 'Because I don't do Christmas. That's all.'

It was no answer, but clearly he had no intention of opening up to her on his opinions of the Holy Trinity. They walked past some more stalls in silence, but if he was emotionally distant, he remained close by her side, his hand ever hovering behind her but never quite touching.

She gave a shiver, and he noticed. 'Cold?'

She nodded, seeing he was wearing the scarf Angelina had passed to him at the weekend. Cashmere, no doubt; it probably still smelled of her perfume.

'I know how to warm you up,' he said. She looked at him sharply, but he was already heading for a hot drinks stall. 'A hot chocolate,' he said to the stallholder. He glanced back at her. 'Hold the cream?'

She shook her head.

'What are you? Ten? . . . You want the sugar dump?' he asked, surprised.

She shrugged. 'Sugar. Tequila. Crystal meth . . . My days are long at the moment.'

He grinned as he looked back at the stallholder. 'With cream *and* marshmallows.'

Darcy's gaze fell to the neighbouring stall and she drifted over while the drink was being made to admire some ceramic lamps she saw there – they were matt white domes studded with tiny pinpricks, tracing the shapes of angels and stars, through which the light shone.

'Here,' he murmured, joining her a few moments later.

'Thanks.'

They began to walk again, but more slowly now; ambling past the stalls, along avenues punctuated with Christmas tree sellers and small fairground rides. They passed larger-than-life-size reindeer figures, completely made of lights. Max pointed at an elaborate Cinderella coach – as round as a pumpkin and lit like a birthday cake – where people were paying to have their photograph taken.

'You should get a picture. Remember this day for ever,' he said drily.

'I'm not sure this should be the memento of my only Christmas in Copenhagen,' she replied with equal cynicism.

He looked at her sharply. 'What do you mean, only?'

'Well, I'm here for a year. I'll be heading back to London come the summer . . . You knew that, surely?'

He was quiet for a moment. 'Yeah. Of course . . . I wasn't thinking.'

She watched him, wishing she could see inside his head, wondering if even then he would remain an enigma to her.

'Watch out,' he said suddenly, hooking his arm around her and pulling her out of the way of a man coming towards them at pace with a beer barrel on his shoulder. '. . . You okay?'

'Sure,' she nodded. But as they resumed walking, his arm didn't drop from her waist and she fell into the daydream she'd been trying to ignore – being with him here, not on an errand but out of choice, the two of them wandering around together on a Saturday, in their jeans and not their work clothes, his arm slung lazily over her shoulder, kissing her hair as they shopped for the quiet Christmas they'd enjoy together at his place . . . Why was it such an impossibility, when she knew he was drawn to her too?

She finished her drink and looked around for the nearest bin. Reluctant to leave his accidental embrace, she nonetheless headed over and dropped the cup in, her eyes catching on another lamp stall; these projector lamps were wooden and revolved slowly and she dropped into a half-crouch to watch, enchanted for a moment.

He came and stood beside her. 'You like those?'

'Love them! I had a little carousel light when I was little. I haven't seen one of these for years.'

She looked at the display: they were all unpainted larch with the wooden figures set in the round, 360 degrees. There were some with woodland animals: bears, deer, rabbits; a seascape with crested waves and ships at full mast; ponies on a fairground carousel . . . She crouched further in front of one of a winter wonderland scene with reindeer, Christmas trees and stars.

She reached a hand forward to turn over the price tag. *Ouch.* Withdrawing her hand, she straightened up.

'What was yours like?' he asked, watching her watching it.

'Oh, it wasn't anywhere near as lovely as these. It was a silvery metal and had butterflies sort of springing from it. You'd put a tealight in the middle and the heat would make it revolve and the butterflies would spin round . . . I was a bit of a wired kid and I used to have trouble falling asleep some-times; but I could always drop off watching the butterfly shadows on my wall.'

'Do you still have it?'

'God, no,' she scoffed.

'What happened to it?'

'My brother pulled the butterflies off the wires after we had a fight. Mum couldn't get them back on again.' She shrugged but she could still remember how upset she'd been as she had watched it go into the bin.

'. . . Brothers, huh.'

'Yeah.' She shot him a look. 'Consider yourself lucky you don't have one. He was the bane of my life till I was about sixteen.'

There was a pause. 'What changed at sixteen?'

She shot him a wry look. 'He started to fancy my friends. He had to be nice to me.'

Max gave a small smile. 'Why don't you get it, if you like it so much?'

Her eyes fell again to the price tag and she shook her head quickly. 'No.' But she bent her knees again to get a last look at the revolving scene. She could just imagine how dazzling it would be at night, in a dark room, throwing golden light shadows onto the walls. It was hypnotic, the steady, relentless turn of the shapes, and it triggered in her strong memories of childlike wonder, when Father Christmas had still been real and there was such a thing as happy ever after.

A pair of hands came into her field of vision and she looked up with a start as the vendor plucked it from the stand. She straightened, remembering herself. 'Anyway, we should probably get g—'

She turned just in time to see Max handing over his card once again.

'Max? What are you doing?' she asked, looking back to see

the carousel being set inside a box, which was then put in a bag.

'Buying it for you.'

'No! You can't do that!' she protested.

'Why not? You obviously love it.' He frowned and shrugged. 'Happy Christmas.'

'But you don't do Christmas.'

'No, but you do . . .'

She stared at him until he threw his hands out. 'What?' he asked.

'I don't understand you! How does this come under "being professional"? People who are just colleagues don't buy each other Christmas presents.'

He held up Sara's felted teddy bear.

'She's your PA. That's different. She runs your life.'

His hand dropped back down and he didn't reply immediately. 'Fine . . . Then consider it an apology.'

'An apology?'

'I don't want you to hate me.'

'. . . I don't hate you,' she said, baffled.

'No?'

'Max, you're the most frustrating man I've ever met, but that doesn't mean I hate you. This isn't necessary. You've already apologized for the kiss.'

'It's not about that.'

She frowned. 'Then what?'

He stared at her and she could see conflict in his face – thoughts he wouldn't express, whole conversations she would never hear, running behind his eyes – even as she felt the pull between them again, tugging . . .

The vendor cleared his throat, intruding, and Max looked away to take the bag from him.

'We should start heading back,' he said, checking his watch again. 'Shit, now we're going to be late,' he said brusquely, and for the first time he walked ahead of her in the crowd, setting such a brisk pace that she had to fall into a trot to keep up. They wove through the bodies with a haste that had been missing earlier, until the car came into sight, parked illegally on the kerb.

'Here.' He got to the car first and reached back with the bag for her, but she made no attempt to take it from him and he looked back in puzzlement.

'Tell me what you're apologizing for, if not the kiss.' She willed him to say Natalia's name.

'Why don't we just say it's for everything I've got wrong with you?' he shrugged.

'Because that's not an answer.'

'It's the best I can give.'

She rolled her eyes. He made her want to scream! 'Then I don't want it.'

'*What?*'

'You heard.'

They glowered at one another, fighting over she didn't even know what.

'Unbelievable.' He gave a small snort as he opened the car door for her, resting one arm on the car roof, waiting for her to get in. 'You know, you're the first and only woman I've ever known who's *not* wanted a gift by way of apology.'

'A dubious distinction. Perhaps you should reconsider the kind of women you know,' she clapped back.

He cracked a half-smile. 'No.'

'No?'

'They're predictable.'

'And that's what you want, is it? Predictable women?'

'Absolutely.' His gaze was steady. 'I like known entities and managed outcomes.'

'Wow. Life lived by spreadsheet.' She rolled her eyes as she went to slide in past him. 'Do you even have a pulse?'

He caught her wrist and stopped her with a look. They both knew the answer to that.

A moment beat between them as he stared at her the way he had on Sunday night. But instead of kissing her, he held out the bag for her instead. 'Just take it, Darcy. It can be a Christmas present, an apology – whatever you want it to be.'

She just couldn't be what *he* wanted.

Predictable.

Chapter Fifteen

'They're in the meeting room. Go straight in, Darcy. Hello Mr Lorensen. They're expecting you both,' Ida said brightly, half rising in her chair. Darcy noticed how the young woman's eyes lingered on Max as he passed.

As they approached the door she took a deep breath, flexing her fingers. It was a nervous tic.

'Are you okay?' he asked, seeming to notice even as he moved with the comfort of a man in his element, walking beside her with a relaxed stride.

She nodded, but she was nervous. He reached an arm out towards her.

'You'll be fine,' he said quietly, his hand brushing over hers. 'This is your moment.' His gaze tangled with hers as he pushed on the open door.

'Ah, Miss Cotterell. Max,' the National Gallery director said, looking up as they walked in. Margit and Otto were sitting forward, their elbows on the conference table, as if they'd been deep in conversation. 'Take a seat. Take a seat.'

'Apologies for running late, Margit,' Max said, shaking her hand. '. . . Otto.'

'Max,' Otto said, the men shaking hands too. They all seemed very well acquainted with one another.

Margit had taken the chair at the head of the table. Otto

was sitting to her right and it seemed politic that Darcy should sit beside him. Max took the empty chair on Margit's left and Darcy was aware of their splitting into camps.

Darcy smiled at Otto as she settled herself, laying the bag with the wooden carousel by her feet and the folder flat on the table. Viggo had given her a lockable box file for transporting the source material here. It made her feel like a cabinet minister with the classified red box.

'Helle's on her way. She said she'd be a couple of minutes behind us,' Max said, unbuttoning his suit jacket as he took his seat. He didn't look like a man who, fifteen minutes earlier, had been buying a felted teddy bear Christmas tree decoration.

'Helle too?' Margit smiled. 'This must be an exciting discovery!'

A slight sardonic note rang out in her words. Darcy glanced at Max to see if he'd picked up on it too, but he was sitting with an impassive expression on his face.

'Well, we're trying to remain cautious at this point,' Darcy said, remembering Viggo's prudence. 'But it's great to have some news to share at last.'

'It has indeed felt like a long couple of weeks.' Margit's smile was fixed, merely a formality; there was steel in her voice and Darcy was under no illusion just how much she wanted this mystery to be resolved. Fast. Press releases had been issued and the mystery portrait had led to a surge in ticket bookings.

The door opened. 'Ah, thank you, Ida,' Otto murmured. 'Just set the coffees down there.'

The PA did as she was instructed, sneaking another look at Max as she reluctantly turned to leave again. If he noticed, he gave no sign of it, but Darcy still felt a stab of jealousy. She supposed this must happen to him a lot.

Margit 'played mother', though only Otto reached for his cup and saucer on the desk. Darcy was too nervous to drink and Max seemed unbothered, adjusting his cufflinks.

'I understand you were at the gallery, Max, when the discovery was made?' Margit asked him.

'Yes.'

'What a happy coincidence.'

Darcy fell very still, hearing a buzz of undercurrent to the words. Had word somehow got back of a less-than-professional relationship between them? Had Jens relayed their midnight argument as a lover's tiff? If it wasn't right, it also wasn't wrong.

'It was,' he said evenly. 'I just happened to be looking in at the pertinent moment.'

Darcy kept her gaze down, the tissue-wrapped carousel by her feet. To think a forgotten scarf had led to all this.

'How is the recovery process coming along?' he asked back.

'It's coming slowly,' Margit sighed. 'The bond on the backing is almost like glue. And of course, they mustn't warp or pull on the board. They think now the portrait went in wet—'

Darcy frowned but, just then, the door opened again and Helle Foss bustled through. She was carrying a leather bag bulging with paperwork. 'Traffic.'

'I hope you didn't put yourself out, Helle,' Margit said, watching as the short woman took the seat beside Max.

'Not at all. Not at all,' she replied, appearing to miss Margit's sardonic tone.

'. . . Right,' Margit said finally, pulling back. 'Well, seeing as we are now *all* here . . . over to you, Darcy.'

Darcy took a steadying breath as everyone's gazes settled upon her, trying to ignore the one that carried more weight than the rest. 'This morning, I came upon this necklace.' She unlocked the box file and lifted it out. 'It was in an envelope with no distinguishing notes or records at all. At first, I thought it must have been a gift Trier had intended to give to someone – or that he himself had, perhaps as a memento. But this gold bead in the centre seemed distinctive. It reminded me of this.'

She held up the printout of the portrait taken under ultra-violet light. 'Obviously, we can't yet gauge colours in this image – but we can clearly see the contrast in tone on this one bead, suggesting a different material or colour. In and of itself, that probably wouldn't be enough to go by, but when I showed the necklace and the printout to Viggo Rask, he was reminded of this photograph in the Madsen Heritage room.'

Darcy then held up a printout of the black-and-white photograph of the Madsens playing croquet. She pointed to Lilja in the picture: delicate and defiant all at once. 'Again, we have no colour to go by – just differing shades of light and dark – but we can clearly see she's wearing a dainty bead necklace with a contrast bead at the throat. Now, by virtue of this being a photograph and not a painting, this is not a likeness but an actual representation of the necklace so we can accurately assess the shape, size and even the number of the beads; we can identify the singular gold bead in the centre, and we can definitively conclude that the necklace I'm holding is the same one in the photograph.'

Margit Kinberg's knuckles were blanched as she interlaced her fingers, listening hard. 'So, then, who is that girl?'

'Her name is Lilja. She was the wife of Frederik Madsen's younger brother, Casper.'

Margit stiffened. 'She's a Madsen?'

Darcy glanced at Helle, who was listening intently too, her eyes narrowed in concentration. She seemed pleased.

'Yes. However, at this stage it's too early to be certain that she is also the woman in the painting.'

'Well, it's obvious, surely, if they're wearing the same necklace?' Helle pushed.

'It's certainly likely. They both have long dark hair, but we can't get an exact facial match from such a low-grade black-and-white image and a portrait currently buried under board. We have to be mindful of other scenarios that might alter the findings.'

'Such as?' Helle frowned.

'She could have borrowed the necklace she is seen wearing in the photograph. It may not be hers.' Darcy held up the images of the painting and the photo. 'Or it could be that the necklace is hers and she loaned it to the woman in the portrait. A dash of colour as a finishing touch, perhaps . . . A prop. It may be that there's one necklace, but two women. Or two necklaces . . .' She looked at her audience, all of them listening, rapt. 'But I agree the odds would suggest Lilja Madsen is our girl.'

Helle and Max looked at one another. Margit sat back in her chair with an inscrutable expression; she had her elbows splayed and her hands locked together as she ruminated on the news. 'Well, that really is something.' She was quiet for a moment, deep in contemplation. 'So – Lilja Madsen. One of yours,' she said, looking at Helle. 'Perhaps you can shed some light on her for us, seeing as we're all here?'

'Oh, very little really, I'm afraid,' Helle said with surprising dismissiveness. 'Only the broad strokes. As Miss Cotterell rightly says, she was the wife of Casper, the younger Madsen brother, who was something of a renegade and . . . an outlier in the family, I suppose you would say. He made his own small fortune during the Great War, but . . .' She let the sentence trail away, as if there was nothing more of significance to add.

'How did he make his fortune?' Darcy asked, her interest piqued by the way the woman's nose had started to wrinkle with disdain.

Helle looked irritated by the question. 'He was a goulash baron,' she said, as if it were a dirty word. 'But of course, it was Frederik who set up the Foundation in '61 and really drove the family's philanthropy and patronage of the arts. Casper was long dead by then, so we've never paid too much attention to him – or his wife. They both died young.'

'What happened to them?' Darcy asked.

'Well, she drowned.'

'Oh!' Darcy startled. It felt tragic somehow to discover that this young woman had perished in such an untimely, distressing manner, when she had only just found her.

Helle, and Max, looked surprised by her emotional response. '. . . Yes. A tragedy made even sadder by the fact that Casper himself died three days later. Broken heart syndrome. He'd been besotted with her.' Helle gave a shrug. 'But that's really about all I can tell you about that side of the family. This all happened forty-odd years before the Foundation was set up and, as I say, it was Frederik who was the driving force behind it. Casper's really only a footnote in our operations.'

'Not to worry,' Otto said, in his usual placid tone. 'It's Darcy's job to find the details. She's an exceptional researcher. Sometimes I think she could be a detective.'

Darcy shot him a puzzled smile. If she was flattered by the compliment, she was also bewildered by it; he wasn't usually prone to high praise. She suspected this had more to do with communicating a point to Foss, rather than espousing her virtues.

'Well, thank you for that overview,' Darcy said, looking back at Helle. 'I'll make Lilja the focus of my attentions from here and hopefully, now that we have an identity to work with, we can get confirmation quickly and a full bio worked up.'

'Great.' Margit pushed back into her chair as if that was that. She appeared keen to bring the meeting to a close. Unlike Max and Helle, she hadn't seemed pleased by the reveal.

Max cleared his throat. 'Of course, if it should prove to be the case that Lilja Madsen *is* the woman in the portrait . . .' His attention was focused on Margit. 'This would only strengthen the Foundation's claim upon *Her Children*.'

His words were met with a confounded silence.

'Claim?' Margit's voice was hollow.

'Yes. You know we've made no secret of our ambition to buy *Her Children*, but new information has since come to light and we intend to file for restitution in the coming weeks.'

What? Darcy's head whipped round. He had made no mention of any legal case in the car just now. Max was still looking directly at Margit.

'Darcy's discovery today means the hidden portrait is now of great interest to us, as a separate acquisition of course – it is a Johan Trier and the subject, we are now given to believe, is a Madsen family member. If we must proceed under the assumption that the portrait cannot be successfully extricated from *Children*, then we will argue in court that these *two* paintings should come back into the Madsen Foundation fold.'

'Back?' Margit countered with a scoff. '*Her Children* never belonged to the Madsens. You surely don't need me to remind you Trier refused to sell it to your benefactor?'

'Of course not,' Helle said, interceding. 'But artists are temperamental sorts; highly irrational, as we all know. Trier had a tantrum and sold it to a passing stranger because he wanted to prove to himself that he wasn't Bertram Madsen's puppet.' She shrugged. 'He made his point – but at what cost?

211

He sold the painting out of the country, not knowing at the time that he would never surpass it; that it would prove to be his greatest work and masterpiece.' Her mouth tipped at the side. 'We believe tempers have cooled since then and that he would have wanted *Her Children* to sit alongside the rest of his body of work.'

'Well, whatever *you* believe he would have wanted is immaterial, I'm afraid,' Margit said dismissively. 'As I have made plain to you on countless occasions – and no matter which politicians you lobby – *Her Children* is not for sale. And as for this assertion of restitution . . .'

Helle reached for some paperwork in her bag as Max rested one arm on the table. He looked incredibly calm. Too calm.

'I've just returned from some meetings in Zurich,' he said.

Zurich? Was that where he'd been at the beginning of the week? Darcy watched him, listening to his strategy unfold and feeling as if she were underwater – breath held, her perspective skewed. She had thought he was closer to her than he ever really had been.

'We've had a forensic specialist looking into the provenance of *Her Children*.'

'The provenance?' Otto asked, looking disbelieving. 'But that's been well established for years.'

'To an extent.'

Margit gave a bark of disagreement. 'To the full extent! Trier sold it directly to Walter Fleishman, a German banker, in August 1922. It remained in his possession until it was sold in 1940. It was then held in a private collection for twelve years before selling again at auction in Dusseldorf in 1952, where we repurchased it on behalf of the Danish state.'

'That's right.'

'And there's a paper trail to prove all of that.'

'I agree.'

Margit blinked, perturbed. 'So, then, I'm afraid I don't understand what your issue is.'

He took his time replying, in no rush to explain himself. 'It has long been our belief that the transaction in 1940 was a forced sale. That Walter Fleishman was "obliged" by the Nazis to trade the painting for travel permits to Switzerland.'

'What?' Otto interrupted, looking outraged. But Max only slid his eyes briefly in his direction; Margit was his target. 'The paperwork was fudged to make it look like a legal sale – but to all intents and purposes, Fleishman had a gun to his head. Under those circumstances, and under the auspices of the Washington Principles, we believe the transaction should be considered null and void.'

'Absolutely not,' Margit said flatly. 'That is a hypothesis at most.'

'Our specialist has put together a very persuasive – we would say convincing – case for this scenario.'

'How?' Otto demanded again. 'Nothing of this nature has ever been suggested before.'

This time, Max looked at him. 'He has been able to establish that the SS officer who oversaw the sale was implicated in at least two other forced sales, around the same time.'

'*Implicated* is still not proven,' Otto said coldly.

There was a silence as everyone considered his words. Margit was staring at Max like a lion assessing a tiger. 'Even if it *were* proven that the sale was forced, the Madsen Foundation would be no more entitled to the painting than we are. In that scenario, it should be returned to Fleishman's heirs.'

Max gave a single blink. 'Our thoughts exactly. Which is

why I've already met with them,' he said, as if he had been hoping she would say exactly that. He looked to be relishing every point scored. '*They're* ready to file a claim for restitution.'

Margit sat back in her chair with a hard look as his meaning became apparent. This was a *fait accompli*. 'Ah. And if they get it, they're prepared to sell it on to you' She didn't take her eyes off him, as if she could read his every thought. 'The deal is already done. You've agreed a price.'

Max gave a minuscule shrug. He was half Margit's age, but Darcy sensed they were seasoned adversaries.

For several moments, no one stirred at all, the tension in the room as thick as paint.

'Of course, it would make for far better optics if this claim didn't have to be filed at all,' Helle said into the silence, setting down the papers she had pulled from her bag onto the table. 'We would all be tied up in expensive litigation for years, which would only benefit the lawyers. A terrible wrong was committed against an innocent man, even if everyone further down the provenance chain traded in good faith. But now the injustice has come to light, wouldn't it be better if everyone did the right thing, rather than having their hand forced?'

'*Her Children* belongs to the Danish people,' Margit said firmly.

'That is nationalist romanticism, Margit.'

'Says the capitalist advocate of the Foundation of the artist's patron's family,' Margit snapped.

Helle blinked slowly, like a cat deliberating whether to sleep or strike. 'Ethically, it still belongs to the family of the man who bought it directly from the artist with honest coin. And I don't believe the Danish people would support you choosing to go into a costly and lengthy court battle for something that you know to have been sold under duress, threats of violence and even death. Is that who we are? Surely to choose to uphold

214

that corruption would mean becoming corrupt ourselves? Let's right the wrong and do the right thing.'

'This has nothing to do with right and wrong!' Margit spat. 'That's spin for the press release you want to put out! You know, I might find this all rather more palatable if you hadn't already agreed your price with the Fleishmans.'

'They will finally get the compensation they are due, after all this time,' Max said simply. As if this was simple.

'Think about it in real terms, Margit,' Helle said. 'Ownership is just paperwork. All it really means is that the painting will hang a mile down the road from where it is now, still in the public domain. Isn't that better than it going back into a private collection in Germany?'

'Don't pass this off as public service,' Otto said coldly. 'This is about you getting your full flush.'

Max spread his hands appeasingly. 'I don't deny it – our founder's mission would be accomplished, to have Trier's greatest work restored to his namesake collection. But that doesn't make us villains. It's every artist's dream and every patron's ambition.'

Margit gave a small scoff of disgust. 'You've been lining up your backers for years, waiting for precisely this moment.'

'I've never made any secret of our hopes, Margit, but this particular moment – with the link to Lilja Madsen – could not have been foreseen. In that, we have simply been lucky.'

His head inclined fractionally towards Darcy, acknowledging her unwitting role in all this. He'd been in the right place at the right time because of her – returning a scarf, apologizing for a kiss, just as she made the discovery that toppled the dominoes.

'I would like us to resolve this amicably, Margit, but you should know the Fleishman heirs would like to see *Her Children* within the Johan Trier collection at the Madsen Foundation. They are prepared to engage their lawyers to file the claim against the state as soon as next week.'

'Next week?' Margit almost barked the words.

Darcy looked between them all in dismay, feeling like a child in the middle of an adults' argument. She watched as Otto ran his hands down his face. They were hemmed in from every side, and she realized that while she had been calling her advisor to excitedly tell him about her discovery, Max must have been calling not just Helle, but his syndicate of backers. He had their approval to issue his threats with full sanction. They had check-mated the museum's queen.

She stared at him in dismay. 'This is your moment,' he had said to her as they were walking in – knowing full well it was about to be his.

Helle leaned forward and patted the papers on the table. 'Read this, and then let's talk, Margit,' she said in a quiet voice. 'I do believe we can reach a mutually satisfactory resolution.'

Margit gave her a hostile look. 'I beg to differ.'

'The evidence is compelling,' Helle said, undeterred, closing up her bag again. 'In the meantime, while this is all under review, we wish to be involved with all further developments in this project.'

'Absolutely not!' Margit snapped. 'It's not your painting yet.'

'No – but it is our archives you are using for research,' Max said coolly. 'Not to mention we are generously loaning you a very substantial number of paintings for the retrospective.'

Darcy gasped. Was he seriously threatening, on top of everything else, to forbid her access? To pull their loans for the exhibition? She saw Max flinch at her stunned response, but he didn't look her way.

Margit's eyes narrowed. 'Are you blackmailing us, Max?'

'I'm simply reminding you that this project is a collaboration. Work with us and we'll work with you. Whatever Darcy discovers, she must share. I don't think that's an unreasonable request, given we all have our vested interests.'

Darcy stared at his profile as she understood now what it was she had read in his eyes at the market. He had known exactly what he was coming over here to do. Viggo had warned that he was bullish; bullying was more like it. She had thought she'd caught glimpses of the real man, the softer flesh and blood beneath the veneer – but she saw now that he was hard all the way through, his soul shellacked. He had betrayed her trust and she felt awash with guilt that she had brought him here with her today. She had brought the wolf into the sheep's pen.

'As Helle said, let's talk again when you've had a chance to read the file.' He pulled his feet in and readied himself to stand. 'Darcy, you've got my details. I'll expect to hear from you,' he said, meeting her gaze briefly. But she couldn't hide her feelings the way he could and she watched, silent and pale, as he got up with his colleague and left the room.

She saw Ida in the corridor trying to catch his eye again as he left and this time, his head turned slightly in her direction. The girl blushed, throwing an excited, wide-eyed look at his back in his wake.

Darcy looked away.

Known entities. Managed outcomes. She looked down at the carousel in the bag by her feet. It hadn't been an apology for what had already passed, but for what was to come. *I don't want you to hate me.* He couldn't do his job until she did hers.

We're not friends, she had said to him that night on his steps. But until now, she hadn't realized they were enemies.

Chapter Sixteen

Darcy paced outside in the courtyard. The silence that had pulsed in the long moments after Max and Helle's exits had been deafening and Margit had – unsurprisingly – wanted to talk to Otto alone. Darcy had been glad of the opportunity to escape and catch her breath. The cobbles were slippery with frost, but she didn't care. The aftershocks of what had just happened hummed through her bones and she couldn't shake it off. She had to move, shunt the news around her body, not let it settle or stick. Her good news had been hijacked in a way she could never have foreseen, tacked onto a bigger plan with consequences far more significant than putting a name to a face and a biography on a wall. *This is your moment*, he'd said, mere seconds before switching from ally to enemy. His smooth volte-face had felt personal to her, but she knew it had never been that for him. It was simply how business was done at the highest level: take every opportunity without hesitation. Make the kill. Backstabbing and plotting, threats issued behind dead smiles – it was all just part of winning. Too late, she remembered his bio: *'Likes skiing, wine, winning.'*

She felt like an idiot. She felt small; a minnow to Max's shark. She thought back on the hours she'd spent in his company over the past ten days. While she'd been preoccupied with unprofessional thoughts about what could and couldn't happen between them, his mind had only ever been on the job. He'd been spying on her all along. It really was why he'd insisted on her researching in their archives and at his house after hours. It was why he'd lain in wait for her the night of the drinks reception, his hand on her back, fast-tracking her body ahead of her mind. He'd manipulated her attraction to him from the start. He'd seen right through her.

The door swung open and Otto emerged, looking like he'd aged a decade overnight, his usual bluff manner thrown into red-cheeked bluster. Darcy took one look at him and knew better than to interrogate him. He immediately began striding through the courtyard, heading towards the road. She had no idea where he was going but probably neither did he; like her, he just needed to move.

Otto walked with a vigour that betrayed his anger and she had to lengthen her stride to keep up. He reached into the pocket of his navy coat and pulled out a cigarette, lighting up. Darcy hadn't known he was a smoker, but perhaps they all were today. Something had to take the edge off.

'So?' she asked trepidatiously, as they walked along the street.

'So, Margit's more pissed than I've ever seen her. She's making calls to the Ministry of Culture, taking this as high as she can . . . She wants to fight them.'

'Really?' Darcy had expected capitulation.

He glanced at her. 'Why does that surprise you?'

Her mouth opened as she hesitated before saying the words. 'Well, only that it changes things, doesn't it – if we know the painting rightfully belongs to Holocaust victims?'

He shot her a furious look. 'But we *don't* know that. Those are simply their accusations. Don't think the Madsen Foundation's above lying to get what they want. Don't think they wouldn't pay someone to put their name to a falsified report. They have deep pockets, and pretty much everyone has a price. This is just how they like to initiate a negotiation.'

He took a long drag on the cigarette, beginning to slow his walk just a little. 'Besides, we have only ever acted in good faith – our conscience is clear, because we know *our* acquisition was legal and fair. It'll be for the lawyers to argue a debate on the statute of limitations for such matters. Almost none of the original victims are alive now, so the loss is no longer viscerally personal, but more of a principle and a compensation issue. It's been almost eighty years since that sale, after all – where does the moral responsibility end?'

Darcy shrugged. 'If the Elgin Marbles question is anything to go by, it doesn't.'

'Well, that's a national heritage issue,' he muttered. 'Returning something to its rightful home. But *Her Children* is already in its rightful home. It's right here, in Copenhagen, in trust for the benefit of the Danish people. If the Fleishman heirs have struck a deal with Madsen before they've even filed for restitution, then their main interest in it is financial – and we cannot rule out the risk that they might change their minds on their deal with the Madsen. Someone else could well come in with a bigger offer to them. And then the painting could end up leaving Denmark for a private collection elsewhere.'

Darcy wondered what sort of numbers they were talking about. Fifty million? A hundred million? A sum like that could patch a lot of holes in the Culture budget.

Otto sighed. 'As it stands, *we* are the rightful guardians of this national treasure and for all their big talk in there, the last thing the Madsen Foundation wants is for this to go to trial. Lorensen was doing what he does best and bullying us, but he knows as well as we do that it would take years for the case to be heard; and if there's one thing financial investors don't like, it's open-ended speculation where their money is concerned. And with the parent company looking to list publicly, they'll want a swift outcome.'

'So you think he's bluffing?'

'He's just turning the screws. He's good at it.'

They were walking along Nyhavn now, with its famous, brightly coloured harbour houses and tall rigged ships docked in the canal, tourists bundled in coats as they ate and drank in the waterside cafes.

'Is there any chance *we* could approach the Fleishmans and counter-offer the Madsens' bid?' Darcy asked.

He shook his head. 'Madsen will have gone above market value to secure the deal. Plus, the heirs have probably bought into the idea they were sold of seeing it reunited with most of the rest of Trier's body of work. It'll help them persuade themselves that their intentions are altruistic.'

'. . . Do you really think Helle would sabotage the retro-spective?'

Otto glowered at the question. 'I think that's highly doubtful. If they followed through with that, it would threaten the viability of the entire show and that would make the press. You can imagine how bad they'd look if it got out that they were trying to blackmail us.'

'Maybe it should get out, then,' Darcy murmured.

'Tempting,' he agreed. 'But far too messy. The last thing any of us need is sensation around this. No, Max and Helle were just flexing their muscles – but they play dirty and won't back off, you can be sure of that. We'll all need to keep our wits about us.' He glanced at her. 'Don't let Max fool you, Darcy; he's charming when it suits him, but I'm afraid you won't be able to trust anyone associated with them. And that includes Rask, too.'

'Viggo?' she gasped. 'But he would never—'

'Oh, he would. He's a nice old man and a very good archivist, but at the end of the day, he works for them, not us,' Otto said firmly. 'And after all these years of service, there's no question his loyalty is to the Madsen Collection first.'

'But I can't hide from him what I'm doing. It's just the two of us down there. He can see what I'm working on at any moment.'

'And that's fine – just don't include him in your further speculations. If Helle and Max think Lilja Madsen, as the woman in portrait, strengthens their claim to *Her Children*, they'll use any advantage they can get. You can be sure Helle will be briefing him as we speak.'

Darcy sighed, hating the idea of subterfuge. She was an academic, not a spy. Their collaboration, Viggo's help, had been invaluable up to this point.

'Don't look so worried. I know Viggo helped you today with making the identification, but you would have got there sooner or later without him anyway,' Otto said, as if reading her mind. 'Trust your abilities, Darcy. You're a brilliant researcher. You were the one who connected the necklace to the portrait.'

'Do *you* think it's Lilja Madsen in the painting?'

'Unfortunately yes.'

'Me too,' she murmured. They paused to allow a man to cycle past; his two toddlers were huddled inside a large wooden box affixed to the front: part pannier, part pram. '. . . Otto – what's a goulash baron?'

'It's the term used for those who profiteered during the Great War.'

'But I thought Denmark maintained neutrality?'

'We did, but political neutrality doesn't mean there were no financial gains to be made. It's a generic term, but largely it refers to producers who made their fortunes supplying cheap tinned meat to the German troops.'

'What's so wrong with that?' Helle Foss's disgusted attitude had struck Darcy as excessive.

'The quality of the product was shameful. It was produced for soldiers fighting on the front line and they were served intestines, cartilage, ground-down bones in gravy . . . Sometimes rats, too. Their welfare really didn't matter – only the profit margins.'

'Oh!'

'Yes; not exactly a noble endeavour. But then again, great fortunes are rarely made prettily, and the Madsens were not the first or only ambitious family to use art and culture to whitewash their reputation. Look at Vanderbilt and the Met Opera.' He glanced at her. '*Never* underestimate the importance of reputation, Darcy. The Madsens are top tier here now, but that wasn't always the case. You can be sure Helle will not like the prospect of this portrait shining a light on the ignoble son.'

They took another left and the grand Charlottenborg Palace, home of the Royal Academy, sat before them again. They had walked around the block at speed, but Otto seemed somewhat calmer now.

'How do you think the Academy director will take the news?' He was still in New York, but this update on the discovery was beginning to look more like a liability that might need his personal attention.

'Like I did. But at least I can tell him we're not going to roll over and take it. If Max Lorensen wants a fight, then that is what he's going to get.'

Max was, in effect, going to war with the Danish state – and yet she sensed he wouldn't be losing sleep over it tonight. He would probably sleep soundly. Or else not sleep at all, twisting sheets with a supermodel through the twilight hours . . . Darcy squeezed her eyes shut, banishing the image that had immediately popped up, perfectly formed, in her mind.

He was the enemy. She'd do well to remember that.

'Hey.'

Viggo looked up from where he was working. He was standing by the glass cabinet, replacing one of the clays. From the way he straightened stiffly at the sight of her, she knew he'd received the call, as Otto had predicted. 'Darcy – hello.'

She walked into the room with a stilted smile. Were they to act as enemies too? When she had left here, just a few hours ago, they had been friends. Colleagues. Collaborators, putting their heads together and pooling resources. 'So . . .'

'So.' He swallowed, looking at a loss, watching as her hand trailed idly over the leather tabletop, neither one of them knowing what to say or do. They weren't built for big business. They were in this for the love of the subject.

She looked straight at him, seeing something in his eyes that almost looked like fear. Who exactly had called him and what had they threatened? He was an old man, quietly doing a quiet job. The consequences of his actions weren't supposed to bleed into lawsuits against the Danish state.

'Well, that turned into an eventful day,' she said finally, breaking the tension with a little understatement.

He laughed with relief. 'Indeed . . . I'm glad you came back. I thought perhaps I might never see you again.'

'To be honest, I have been loitering upstairs for the past hour.'

He looked hurt. 'You were too scared to come down here?'

'No, not exactly,' she admitted, knowing he would never be her enemy, whatever Otto said to the contrary. 'I stopped in at the Madsen Heritage room on my way. I wanted to look at the photo again, the one showing the necklace, but I ended up getting distracted by another.'

'Oh? Which one? Does it show the necklace too?'

'No. But . . .' She showed him the picture she had taken on her phone just now, of the photograph she also had seen the other day – of Gerde and Lotte Madsen in the garden. 'That girl with them.' She pointed to the dark-haired girl on the blanket. 'Do you know who she is? The bio on the plaque only lists mother and daughter: Gerde and Lotte Madsen, June 1915.'

He pushed his glasses up his nose, his customary frown of concentration coming onto his face. 'You know, I've looked at this photograph many times over the years, but I've never thought to question her identity.'

'Why not?'

'Because it was only the Madsens that mattered,' he shrugged. 'This is their gallery, their foundation. She is just a nameless child in a photograph.'

Darcy bit her lip. 'Do you think she could be Lilja?'

Viggo looked surprised. He hesitated for a long moment, peering more closely, before he replied. 'Well, now you say it, yes – there is a likeness, although it's rather blurred to say with any real certainty. And one little dark-haired girl looks much the same as another little dark-haired girl. At least to my eye.' He looked at Darcy. 'What makes you think it's her?'

'There's just something in her demeanour. It's in the way she holds herself . . . I'm wondering if perhaps she was Lotte Madsen's friend first.'

'They do look to be around the same age.'

'Maybe they went to school together?'

'No, Lotte had a governess.'

'. . . So, then, perhaps she was a companion?'

'Yes, maybe,' Viggo nodded. 'Alternatively, this is just a local girl from a good family, or perhaps even one of the estate workers' daughters.'

'How old do you think they are there?'

Viggo pushed his glasses higher again, peering more closely at the image on her screen. 'Ten? But I *would* be able to confirm that, certainly for Lotte. What date did you say is placed next to the photo?'

'June 1915.'

Viggo walked down the room towards the red ledger on the table. He consulted it, running his finger down the page, before disappearing into the first stack. Darcy followed after him, watching as he opened a box file. It was filled with certificates – births, deaths, christenings, marriages.

'These are the family files,' he said, pulling a sheet with Lotte's name on it. 'Yes, see here – she was born in May 1904, so she was eleven there.'

Darcy looked at the picture on her screen again. The other, dark-haired, girl was smaller, thinner . . . she was possibly a little younger? Her dress had none of the lace trimmings of Lotte's, but was nonetheless a beribboned cotton with cross-stitch embroidery at the shoulders. If Lotte was eleven, this girl was definitely no more than that, and quite possibly she was ten.

Darcy bit her lip, scrutinizing the child's tiny, bird-like frame and dark hair. If the picture had been in colour it might have been more revealing, but the gentle grey and white tones washed out her features so that the image gave an impression of the girl, rather than a direct representation. Just a little dark-haired girl, one of many, as Viggo pointed out. If she only had a missing tooth or a hooked nose, or a third ear; something distinctive about her . . .

She lapsed into her thoughts. If this was Lilja and she had been Lotte's friend before she had been Casper's wife . . . might this have been an arranged marriage?

'Could I have a look at those?' she asked him, pointing at the box file in his hand.

'Of course.' Viggo put a hand on her arm. '. . . Coffee?'

She grinned at him gratefully. 'I'd love one.'

As he filled the kettle and she heard the *ting* of the spoon against the mugs, she flicked through the certificates for the family, pulling out anything with Lilja or Casper's names on.

She spread them all out on the small worktable; there were more than she had expected. A frown grew on her brow as she studied them, trying to compile a straightforward chronology from what they told her. But as the facts lodged in her mind – one marriage, two births, three deaths – there was no simple narrative to glean. Instead, more questions arose, like bubbles floating up from the bottom of a still pool.

She bit her lip, trying to understand what the collection was showing her. Tragedy. Suffering. Horror . . . ?

My God, Lilja, she mused – keeping her thoughts to herself as Viggo shuffled in the background. What happened to you?

Chapter Seventeen

22nd November 1918

Everyone is in buoyant mood now that the house is full again. It hasn't stopped raining for days but it is as though the sun is shining inside the walls. Mama is so happy that I heard her singing in the parlour this morning and she promised we could look for some new ribbons for my blue hat when the weather clears.

Of course Papa is always so busy, I think sometimes he does not realize the war is over. He rarely leaves his office, but I can tell from the way he looks down the table at dinner and nods to himself that he is happy to have his sons home again. He is always talking to Frederik about the running of the company now that we are in better times again but Mama wishes they would stop talking business all the while.

There is talk of throwing a party. Casper is very keen and trying to persuade Mama to choose a date although I have been told not to get my hopes up. Mama says there is much to sort, and Miss Holm disapproves, I think – she says some people are sensitive to celebrating peace when so many have died.

I'm very sad about the dead people but I think they would want us to be happy and have the party. If we do, I want to wear my new pink dress. It has been hanging in my closet, just waiting for a happy occasion, and we have worn our day clothes for so long now, they are almost rags. Mama says Lilja needs some new garments too. She is growing fast; she's so tall and skinny she's like a stick doll. I have asked Mama if we can have a yellow dress made for her because it's her favourite colour and it would be so pretty against her hair.

Her mother has written at last and believes they will be allowed back here once the confusion is cleared up. This made Lilja really happy. She misses her family a lot and I often hear her crying at night but sometimes I think I don't want them to come back. I know that makes me selfish and in my prayers I ask God to forgive me for such wicked thoughts, but I know that when they return, she will leave here and I will lose my best friend in the whole world.

What would I do without her? We tell each other everything. I told her about Henrik passing the message to me in church, and she says she has seen him looking at me when I'm turned away. She sees everything. We call each other sister, which makes Casper laugh. He says I should be careful what I wish for and that two brothers is quite enough. He thinks much has changed since he went away and sometimes I find him watching us while we are in our lessons and he looks sad. The war made lots of people sad, but it made some people rich too, so we must be grateful for our blessings.

29th November 1918

The party has been agreed! Papa said yes and the invitations were sent out yesterday morning. Mama took us to the dressmaker's where Lilja was fitted for a dress and I was allowed some new lace socks to go with my pink dress. Lilja has chosen yellow, as I knew she would. She was twirling and laughing as poor Mrs Harlang was trying to make the calico with pins in her mouth.

Mama has ordered a four-tier cake for the centrepiece and the flowers are being ordered specially from Rotterdam. She wants everything to be beautiful again. There is a famous band in Paris who are going to travel here just to perform at the party and Frederik keeps saying anyone who is anyone in Copenhagen will be there. I *think the only person who is not happy about it is Miss Holm, but Casper says not to worry about her and that all governesses are miserable by nature; it is why they become governesses, because their own families do not want to live with them and no man wants to marry them.*

Also, Casper has bought a new motor car and he took me and Lilja on a ride. People stopped to look as we went past and we waved just like the King and Queen. He says we can go again tomorrow if it is not raining.

13th December 1918

Everyone is in a frenzy. Mama has cried two times today because the dahlias were the wrong shade of lilac and the blueberries have bled through and stained the cake icing. Papa is in a furious temper saying such things should not concern us, but what does he know of the feminine world? Mama asks him this all the time and reminds him he has his sphere and she has her own. He was frightfully cross and has been in his office ever since. He even took lunch in there too, which made Mama wring her hands.

Lilja and I have been careful to keep out of the way. If they think we are too excitable, they might change their mind and say we are too young to attend after all. That would be a calamity after all the effort we have gone to for our outfits, and Lilja is desperate to be there. She has not heard from her mother since the letter last month but she said it would be just like her to arrive at the party as a surprise. She loves surprises and grand entrances!

We are only allowed to be present for the first hour but Casper thinks no one will care once the dancing starts. I reminded him it was Miss Holm's duty to oversee us but Lilja and I think she is sweet on Casper and he has promised to flirt with her and perhaps even to ask her to dance so we might stay longer. He also said we could try our first taste of champagne, but Frederik overheard and said no. He's such a spoilsport. He thinks just because he is engaged to be married now to Sofie that he must be serious like Papa.

Frederik has arranged for a photographer to take pictures of all the guests as they arrive and a special book has been laid out so everyone may sign their names and we can remember tonight for always. I hope our pictures will be taken too. Lilja's dress is so pretty and if her mother does come back from Germany and make a Grand Entrance, this will be our last night as sisters. (I hope she doesn't.)

I can hear Mama calling for me but I will write again tonight, after the party!

13th December 1918

Was it all a dream? I never knew such happiness till now. All my wishes came true. My dress was much admired and Miss Holm forgot the time, thanks to Casper refilling her champagne coupe, so that I was able to stay in the salon for over an hour more. I danced the foxtrot with Frederik and Papa, and Casper danced with Lilja so she was not left out. Mama looked radiant in her gown and anybody who was everybody was there. There were so many compliments, I was obliged to blush all evening. I overheard some of the ladies talking about the coming out season in London so the debutantes can make good marriages. I shall ask Mama about it tomorrow. I have always wanted to go to London. Perhaps I shall marry a duke or an earl.

Of course, Lilja's mama and papa did not make a Grand Entrance. It was no surprise to me, but she clung to hope until it was apparent it was in vain. She ran away during the foxtrot. I can hear her crying through the wall now and wish I could comfort her, but she always prefers to be left alone when she is sad. I will pick her some Christmas roses in the morning to put on the table for breakfast and I will ask Casper to take us for another ride in his motor car. As Mama always says, tomorrow is a new day.

I am tired now and Miss Holm will be angry if she catches me awake. I only hope I can sleep . . .

Darcy put the diary down, leaning back in her chair and staring into the wooden grain of the stack-end as she let the images conjured by Lotte's diary fill her mind. She had her answer, at least. Though Lilja had seemingly not kept a diary, it was nonetheless useful to read her movements by proxy. Both girls were fourteen in 1918 (Lilja possibly a little younger) and excited for womanhood to start. Parties, dresses, boys . . . The war was over and life was for living again.

Darcy still didn't know if Lilja was the woman she was looking for in the portrait, but she was on the road now to finding out. Photographs and diaries already proved to her that Lilja had been friends first with Lotte Madsen – and now Casper was back from the war, her love story was about to begin . . .

Thread by coloured thread, her tale was being woven together. There were going to be holes in the retelling – without Lilja's own voice, the material Darcy had to work with was patchy, fractured and imperfect, other people's truths. But Lilja Madsen was coming alive again.

She could feel it.

'You look great.'

Darcy blinked at the unexpected compliment. 'I do?' She had come straight from the archives and, unlike for last night's date, she'd gone to no effort, unless a fresh application of lip balm counted. Aksel's stealth invoice when she got home last night still bothered her – not because she objected to paying her half for the meal, but because of the way he'd gone about it. There was something small about sneaking half the bill under the table like that and she had already decided she would only stay for one drink.

'Yeah, your cheeks are flushed.' So were his, she noticed. 'Did you walk here?'

'Cycled,' she said, slipping off her coat and scarf – the scarf that had unwittingly led to Max's lucky break earlier. It smelled slightly unfamiliar, as if it had absorbed his scent as it lay in his house like a treacherous cat.

Aksel smiled as she stuffed it out of sight, under her coat. 'You look so fresh.'

Was this part of a charm offensive? Did he sense he'd messed up? 'Thanks,' she smiled, reservedly.

He had nabbed a table in the far end of the bar and was sitting on the banquette. She had been brought up on the dating etiquette that the woman should sit on the banquette, the man on the chair, but perhaps he had chosen it for the better view of the room so he was able to see her when she arrived? She sat opposite him, noticing the already opened bottle of sauvignon blanc and two glasses.

'I ordered us a bottle,' he said, reaching for the empty glass and pouring into it. 'I hope that's okay? I thought it would save us countless trips to the bar.'

'Good idea.' She angled her glass as he poured for her, but he slightly overshot, splashing wine onto the table.

'Oops,' he said, pulling a face and dabbing it with a paper napkin. 'Are you hungry? They do light bites and snacks here too.'

'Actually, I can only stay for one drink.'

He looked so disappointed his face actually fell. 'Really?'

'Hell of a day,' she apologized. 'Not sure I'm the best company, to be honest . . . I probably should have cancelled rather than subject you to—'

233

'I'm glad you didn't,' he said quickly. 'Tell me what happened. Was it something to do with your research project?' He looked genuinely interested, but she couldn't utter a word about the real drama: Max Lorensen's behind-the-scenes manoeuvrings around the ownership of *Her Children* were strictly confidential.

'. . . Well, in part. I found a necklace that was the same as the one being worn by the woman in the painting, and from that there was a bit of a domino effect: the necklace could be linked to a photograph in the collection, which then gave us a name, so I've spent all afternoon starting to piece together the woman's life story.'

'So then, it sounds like it was a good day?'

'Well, there was other stuff too, but . . .' Her voice trailed off. The diversion at the Christmas market felt like a lifetime ago and she had left the carousel, still wrapped, on her work-table at the archive. She hadn't wanted to bring it out here tonight and she wasn't sure she wanted to bring it home, either. The last thing she needed was memories of *him* in her own bedroom.

'Yeah, but a necklace, a name . . . ! You're practically done.'

Darcy was taken aback by tonight's passion. There'd been no sign of this excitement in him last night.

'Well, I still don't have complete certainty that the woman I'm now researching is the woman in the painting. It's probable that she is, but I have to stay open-minded; go where the evidence leads and not just surmise what happened.'

'You sound like a pathologist.'

'That's funny, I was likened to a detective earlier too. Good options to bear in mind if the professorship doesn't work out, I guess.'

'Of course it will. Brilliance awaits!' he said confidently.

She looked back at him. He seemed different tonight. More assertive, almost cocky. 'Actually, I've got a question perhaps you can answer,' she said, remembering something she had seen earlier in the files. It was the sole reason she hadn't cancelled on him tonight. 'It's something medical – and I know you're a vet, but you have to learn the biology for humans first, don't you?'

'Yes . . . shoot,' he said, making gun fingers at her.

'Okay. So, very sadly, she drowned, my lady.'

'Oh,' he winced. 'Plot spoiler.'

She hesitated, her gaze falling to the wine bottle. It was well under half full. 'I know, sorry. But then, apparently, her husband died three days later. Well, no – not apparently. He did die three days later. A seemingly otherwise healthy, youngish man . . .' She tapped her finger on the table. 'Don't you think that's a little too much of a coincidence?'

'How old was he?'

'Thirty-four.'

Aksel pulled a considered face. 'That is pretty young to just drop dead. Do you know what was given as the official cause of death?'

'On his death certificate, it's down as stress cardiomy-opathy.'

He looked genuinely surprised. 'Really? Interesting.'

'What is that? Did he have a heart condition?'

'It's otherwise known as Broken Heart Syndrome.'

Her eyes widened. Helle Foss had been right? 'So that's actually a thing?'

Aksel nodded as he drank more wine. 'It's rare, but it can happen – sudden, acute stress weakens the heart muscle. I had a golden retriever suffer it once when her companion dog was killed in a car accident. She became deeply depressed and passed away a few days later. The owners were distraught.'

'Oh no.'

He shrugged. 'Grief shouldn't be underestimated; it can place a huge toll on the body.'

Grief. Reputations. So many things not to underestimate, she thought. 'When I was told this originally and it was insinuated he'd died of a broken heart, I thought that was just the person making up fairy-tale endings.'

'Is someone dying ever a fairy-tale ending?'

'Touché,' Darcy smiled.

'. . . How did the woman drown? Domestic?'

'You mean, did it happen in the bath?' She shrugged. 'Um, good question – I don't know yet.'

'It all sounds very sad.'

'Yeah.' She was holding her glass, but only now did she realize it was empty. Research was thirsty work.

'Another?' he asked, holding up the bottle hopefully.

She met his gaze, those soulful eyes – guileless. Kind. Nice. What was a little penny-pinching compared to arrogance, ruthlessness, emotional vacuity and obsession with power?

'Sure,' she smiled, settling back in the chair. 'Why not?'

They staggered along the streets, puddles reflecting Christmas lights, bursts of conversation falling through opening and closing doors as they passed by restaurants and bars. It was late, the moon thin but bright in a dark sky. There was a sense of festivity in the city, as if no one was ready to go to bed. But Darcy was. They passed a couple kissing in a doorway, and she looked over at Aksel hopefully. They had finished the bottle of wine, then another one too, nibbling only on olives for 'sustenance', and she felt giddy as the cold night air hit her. She felt playful and loose-limbed, all her tension from the day gone at last. Max Lorensen was just a footnote in her day now.

Aksel's smiles had grown increasingly lopsided. He was a sweet drunk, clearly unable to hold his drink and swaying a little. An Uber sluiced closely past – too closely – on the narrow street. Vaguely it crossed her mind that she was walking on the outside of the pavement, when etiquette dictated he should be on the traffic side. Not that that stuff mattered, she knew. It just would have been nice . . .

'Fuck, it's *freezing*,' Aksel slurred, pulling the collar of his padded jacket tighter around his neck as they reached the end of the street and were hit by the wind at the intersection. They stood at the lights, waiting to cross into King's Square.

'I know,' she groaned, hoping he'd take the opportunity to pull her in to him. But he didn't. The man was blind to hints. 'D'you want to wear my scarf?' she asked, pulling it from her neck and looping it around his before he could reply.

'You're sure?' he asked as she tied it for him.

'Yes . . .' she slurred, looking up at him. 'You can keep it. I don't want it back.'

'Why not?'

The lights changed and they crossed the road together.

'I just don't like it,' she said dramatically. She was definitely drunk. 'It's yours now.'

'Won't you get cold?'

'. . . There are always other ways to get warm,' she said provocatively, sidling closer to him and slipping her arm between his so that their bodies were pressed together. She stopped walking. There was clearly no point in being subtle with him. 'Kiss me.'

'Here?' He looked surprised by the command. They were

opposite the extravagantly lit Hotel D'Angleterre, the square bright with festivity, a huge Christmas tree shimmering with lights in the middle. The front beams of the traffic moved around them slowly, other lives moving past her on the way to other places, other destinies. She had a feeling of life pulsating around her but somehow not touching her, as if a force field kept it back, and she suddenly felt a desperate yearning to be touched, to be kept awake all night. She wanted to be reckless. Thoughtless. Free from responsibilities. She spent her days with the dead – but was she really any more alive?

He leaned in and kissed her, uncertainly at first. His lips were cold but she quickly warmed him up and she felt his arms move around her, drawing her closer.

It was a good kiss. Not the best she'd ever had. Not like the one with –

She put her hands in his hair and traced his lips with her tongue, tasting the wine they had both drunk. She pulled back. 'Call an Uber and take me home,' she whispered, slurring in his ear.

He seemed to wilt a little. '. . . M-my place? Or yours?' he asked, fumbling in his pocket for his phone.

'Yours.'

The car came within four minutes and she was in his bed within eleven. It was unmade, navy sheets, pants and socks on the floor. 'I wasn't expecting this to happen,' he apologized as they staggered into his room, shedding clothes.

'Even better,' she smiled, unhooking her bra as he began kissing her neck. She closed her eyes and sighed, feeling her body submit to pleasure. She was starving hungry, drunk and lonely, and he was a good man. A nice man.

It would have to do.

Chapter Eighteen

The city had woken up dusted white. Snow was falling; fat, dry flakes of the sort that stayed perched on her nose for a few moments before body heat worked its magic.

Body heat.

Aksel's flat had been cold and for most of the night she had slept curled around him. The big spoon. At least he slept hot, a heat stone under the duvet.

She had woken before him this morning – roused by a headache that was only getting worse – and she'd left before he could even turn over. She figured a discreet exit would be a mercy for them both after last night.

It was almost half eight; too late to get back to the apartment to change, but she didn't think Viggo would notice, or even care, that she was in yesterday's clothes. She just needed fresh air, some coffee and toast and a painkiller to shift this hangover.

She walked up the steps to the gallery with a heavy tread. The lights were on, the reception staff already setting up the tills with fresh rolls of receipt paper and readjusting their stool heights as they chatted.

'Good morning,' Darcy smiled wanly, a familiar face now as she stamped her feet lightly on the mat and unbuttoned her coat.

'Heavens, it is snowing hard now!' one of the ladies said,

her gaze falling to Darcy's hair. Darcy glanced down and saw it was thick with flakes.

'Oh yes.' She hadn't really noticed, walking through the parks blindly, lost in her thoughts. 'I guess it is . . .'

'You must be perished! You're white as a sheet.'

'Oh . . . I'm okay . . .' she protested feebly. Nothing Viggo's hourly coffees couldn't fix. 'Have a good day.' She walked across the reception area, looking down and reaching for her pass in her bag, so that she didn't notice the door was already opening –

She fell back as it swung towards her, almost hitting her. 'Oh!'

It missed her by millimetres and she saw Max on the other side, looking just as startled. 'Darcy!'

She swallowed, the events of yesterday coming back in a rush. Of all the people to have to see, this morning of all mornings.

'I didn't see you there.'

'Evidently.' She looked away, catching sight of the tips of his leather-soled shoes: beautifully polished. No scuffs, no cracks. As the shoe, so the man. 'I take it you've just had your daily briefing on what work I got up to yesterday afternoon?' she asked coldly, making no attempt to hide the hostility in her voice or the hardness in her eyes.

A moment pulsed as he read the situation between them now. Not colleagues. Not friends. Certainly no possibility of something more . . . Had he really thought that carousel was going to stop her from hating him for what he'd done?

She was in no fit state for a conversation, much less an argument, and she went to move around him. He stepped aside to allow her to pass, his gaze fixing upon her pale cheeks, then travelling down the length of her.

'Nice top,' he said in a low voice. 'The colour suits you.'

Darcy's head whipped back at the echo of yesterday's words. She knew exactly what he was saying – what he knew – and her cheeks burned as he stared at her in silence for several long, drawn-out moments. But his look wasn't cold. It was hot. A roiling boil.

He was angry.

She watched him walk away without another word. A bad start to both their days.

Freja was already at their favourite table by the time Darcy barrelled up for the late lunch. As ever, the place was packed, the hanging rail at the top of the stairs laden with coats, windows steamed from hot chocolates and non-stop conversation. There was no 'quiet' time at Paludan cafe – breakfast service merged seamlessly into brunch, lunch and mid-afternoon tea, students congregating at every hour for much-needed caffeine and carbs. Darcy was grateful to be back on university turf, away from the reach of the Madsens.

The snow was falling heavily now and small puddles of water collected on the strip wood floor where coats were shrugged over chairbacks.

'I already ordered chilli for us,' Freja said, as Darcy hugged her and took her seat opposite.

'Thanks. I am *ravenous*.'

'Hangover?'

'Of course.'

'Another good date, then?'

'We went to Bar Poldo. Know it?'

'Sure,' Freja nodded. 'Buzzy there. Good olives.'

'Yeah, exactly. The olives were good,' Darcy agreed a little too enthusiastically.

Bu Freja wasn't interested in the snacks. 'And?' she asked, cutting to the chase. 'Did you seal the deal?'

'We went back to his, if that's what you mean,' Darcy hedged.

'How was it?' Freja's eyes twinkled with mischief. 'Don't tell me . . . after all that playing coy, he's an absolute animal between the sheets!'

Darcy bit her lip. 'If by animal, you mean a sloth hit by a tranquilizer dart, then yes.'

'. . . Huh?'

Darcy looked around furtively, to make sure no one was listening. 'Let's just say the mind was willing, but . . .' she whispered, raising an eyebrow.

'The flesh was weak?' Freja gasped.

'We drank way too much,' she shrugged. 'And then he basically passed out.'

Freja gave a slow blink. 'Please tell me that's a joke?'

'The only joke around here is my love life, Frey.'

There was a long pause. 'This is the saddest thing I've ever heard.'

'I know. I'm destined to spend Christmas alone – if not, in fact, my life.'

'Stop,' Freja admonished. 'I'll not tolerate despondency. For as long as there is breath in our bodies and padding in our bras, there's always hope . . . He didn't bill you this time, did he?'

It had clearly been intended as a joke but Freja caught sight of her expression. 'Fuck off! He didn't do it again?' she gasped.

'Oh, but he did.' Darcy felt a laugh begin to bubble up inside her. It was so ridiculous it was funny. She had hardly been able to believe it when the invoice had come through as Viggo was handing her the first of her many daily coffees. 'But get this – he'd had a bottle to himself before I even got there and he billed me for that too!'

'The cheek!' Freja screeched. 'I hope you didn't pay it?'

'Ugh, I couldn't be bothered not to. He was so wasted, I don't think he even remembers who had what.'

'Does he remember . . . ?' She pulled a face.

'Not sure. I left before he woke up and he hasn't texted me yet. I don't know if he's annoyed that I snuck out, or if he's embarrassed?' She shrugged.

'I don't understand why he's so sneaky about it? Why not split the bill like any normal person?'

Darcy shrugged. 'I don't know, but now it's like this . . . weird thing. It's the pattern he's established between us. He invoices me, I pay without quarrel, and neither one of us ever mentions it.'

'It's a *taboo*,' Freja whispered.

'It is. The last taboo,' Darcy agreed, giggling. 'So I'm afraid that's the end of your great experiment. The Christmas deal is off. I've had three strikes, I'm out.'

'No! Really?'

'Of course. Erik went out for a duck.'

'And Max—'

Darcy rolled her eyes. 'Don't get me started on him.'

'I'd rather not – but from your stricken look, I'm suspecting something else has happened? What's he done now?'

'What *hasn't* he done? Just this morning, he called me out on my walk of shame. As if he can talk!'

'I hope you didn't tell him you were shame-less?'

'Of course not.' Darcy gave a satisfied smile. 'He looked really pissed about it.'

'So it bothered him, then?'

'Such is his ego, he can't imagine that what's good for the gander is also good for the goose.'

The waitress came over with their lunch and they both allowed the hot steam to warm their faces for a moment.

'Anyway, he'll be in my rear-view mirror soon enough. I've had a breakthrough on the portrait.'

'No!' Freja gasped.

'Yep. We've got a name so I can work at pace now, and the sooner I'm done, the sooner I never have to see his face again.'

'Well hooray to that!' Freja said, toasting her with a forkful of chilli. '. . . So who is she, our mystery lady?'

'She's the wife of the younger Madsen brother.'

'Oh.' Freja's face fell. 'After all that? She turns out to be just another Madsen?'

'Yeah, I know what you mean, although if there's one thing she seemingly isn't, it's boring. I've been going through the family archives since yesterday afternoon and that woman may have been rich, but lucky she was not.'

'No?'

'She doesn't warrant her own file because she only married into the family with the "spare" son. He was the black sheep, so they're trying to play down his existence – although he seemingly did them a favour by dying young.'

Freja frowned. 'Harsh. What was so terrible about him?'

'You've heard of the goulash barons?'

'Sure. The Edwardian version of the brokers who shorted 9/11. Profit from tragedy.'

'Well, he was one of those.'

'Okay. Morally questionable, sure – but talk about pot-kettle-black. That's nothing compared to what his old man did!' Freja said, her mouth full. 'He was by far the worst of the bunch.'

'What do you mean? Bertram Madsen was a Nobel Prize nominee.'

'Absolutely he was. A brilliant scientist. His fertilizer helped farmers produce more crops and feed millions of people; he was shortlisted for the Nobel Prize for Chemistry – in 1912, I think it was – on the back of it. That's what made his *name*. But not his *money*. Not the serious money. That only came when he "diversified"' – Freja made sarcastic speech marks with her fingers – 'during the war.'

'Diversified how?'

'His chemical engineering company produced the poison gases that were used for military deployment.'

Darcy's mouth dropped open. 'You mean – mustard gas?'

'Yes. And ammonia, chlorine and bromine gas too.'

Darcy stared at her. 'How do you know this?'

Freja rolled her eyes. 'Darce, I'm a scientist. This is my world. Old Bertram Madsen was the godfather of chemical warfare.'

Darcy stared at her in astonishment. 'So why doesn't anyone else know this?'

'They do,' she shrugged. 'It's not a secret per se. I know it; science geeks know it; it's just that the world has moved on. Joe Public doesn't care any more about who exactly did what. They whitewashed their reputation, made themselves into a brand. When people hear the Madsen name now, they associate it with a famous art collection, a gallery in the capital, a wing in a kids' hospital, a chemistry building at the university . . . not trench warfare in the Somme.'

'Right,' Darcy mused, taking all this in and remembering Helle Foss's evident disdain for Casper.

'Anyway, you were saying . . .' Freja prompted her bossily. 'Our tragic heroine. Tell me more about her. Why so sad?'

'Oh, well I think she was abandoned with the Madsens during the Great War, when she was a young girl. She was a friend of the little sister, Lotte. There are various photos of them together and from reading Lotte's diary, it seems Lilja's parents and the Madsens were all friends. According to the marriage certificate, her maiden name was Von Braun, which is German, and I think her parents moved back there to support the Kaiser after the outbreak of war. I've managed to find one reference to some Von Brauns – in a court circular – who were part of the Kaiser's circle.'

'Von Braun is a High German name,' Freja nodded. 'Von tends to indicate the aristocracy.'

'Right, well, if those same Von Brauns are Lilja's parents, then they ended up on the wrong side when the war was over and were imprisoned. Lilja was left over here with the Madsens. From what I can gather, she never saw her parents again and went on to marry the younger brother.' She paused. 'Note, I said young*er* brother, not young brother.'

Freja looked up.

'Your sixteen-year age gap with Tristan doesn't seem so bad, seeing as you met him when you were twenty-six. But our girl was . . . wait for it . . . *fourteen* when she was married off to a guy sixteen years her senior.'

Freja's fork clattered into her bowl. 'That's gross! You can't tell me it's not.'

'I have no intention of it – but Viggo says it wasn't that unusual for the time. Apparently, *twelve* was the age of consent here until 1971! He reckons it was an arranged marriage. You know, the merging of fortunes; maybe some lingering feeling of guardianship, the Madsens owing it to her parents to see her looked after and giving her their younger son?'

'But a fourteen-year-old girl and a thirty-year-old man?' Freja winced.

'Could you imagine being with Tristan back then?'

Freja pulled a face. 'Please don't.'

Darcy shrugged and they ate in companionable silence for a few moments. 'Are you seeing him tonight?'

'Not tonight. I've got to pack.' She looked up with a wink. 'He's taking me to Amsterdam for the weekend.'

'Ugh, he's not!' Darcy groaned, sitting back in her seat in protest. 'You kept that quiet!'

'He only told me yesterday. He wanted it to be a surprise.'

'. . . Can't I third-wheel?' She pressed her hands together in a prayer pose. 'I've always wanted to go to Amsterdam.'

'I haven't told you the best part yet.'

'There's more?' Darcy tried not to wail.

'He also gave me his credit card and told me to buy a dress. Like, a *really* special dress.'

'Freja,' Darcy objected. 'We are modern women. We don't take men's credit cards and go dress shopping with them! This isn't *Pretty Woman*. We're not—'

'He told me to go to Valentino.'

Darcy's jaw dropped. '. . . He said what now?'

'There's a big industry awards dinner next week and the lab is up for prizes in three categories. He wants me to be his date.'

Darcy's eyebrows shot up. 'So he wants you two to go public?'

'Public. Official. In front of the whole company – go with him, sit beside him, the whole caboodle.'

'*Fuck*,' Darcy hissed.

'I know.' Freja's eyes were wide.

'Does your boss know? Like, your immediate boss?'

'Not yet.' Freja pulled a nervous face. 'We've been *so*

careful about keeping it quiet but Tristan says it's time to stop hiding.'

Darcy looked at her with concern. 'Freja, I know this all sounds exciting, but you've only been together a few weeks.'

'Almost six.'

'Okay, yes, exactly. That's a big bloody statement to make in front of the entire company, especially when you're there on a placement. It will complicate things with your manager. Why rush into this?'

Freja shot her a sheepish look. 'Because it's *not* actually as rushed as you think . . . There were mutual feelings for a while before anything happened between us.'

Darcy's eyes narrowed. 'Define a while.'

'Since the first day I got there.'

'In September?' Darcy was shocked. 'But you never said anything.'

'Of course not! He was the top dog, and I just figured it was a crush. I never for a minute thought anything would happen between us –' she leaned in closer, dropping her voice – 'but any time I would see him, my body would go into full blue light mode – sirens in my head, lights flashing. I could hardly *breathe* in his presence, Darce.'

'Please do. I prefer my friends breathing.'

'Then when we first got it on at the conference, I still just assumed it'd be a fling. I figured I'd just enjoy it for whatever it was. You know me.'

'I certainly do,' Darcy nodded.

'But the thing is . . . it's not a fling. I actually think this is the real deal.' Freja looked nervous as she spoke, as if she was admitting to a dirty secret. 'He's the one, Darce.'

'Stop that Hallmark talk!' Darcy scoffed. 'There's no such thing as The One. *You* told me you can have plenty of Ones.'

But Freja looked at her pityingly. 'It's true what they say: when you know, you know. The body knows. It always knows. This –' she pointed to her heart – 'knew long before this did.' She pointed to her head.

'It's called lust. It'll pass.'

'Darce, you know me. I'm a scientist. I'm a logical person. I live by rules and metrics. I'm not "that girl". And yet . . .' Her voice trailed off.

'And yet, now everything is puppies and poems?'

Freja grinned. 'Exactly. Shoot me already.'

'I fully intend to,' Darcy muttered, eating her chilli with appetite. '. . . Well, just so long as you don't want me to be happy for you both.'

Freja laughed. 'I'm worried your heartbreak and celibacy are going to kill my vibe! We could always hit up another three guys on Raya for you?'

'No!' Darcy said quickly. 'Uh-uh. I'm far too busy now, and this first trio have caused me quite enough drama already.'

'True . . . I still can't believe you struck out on all three.'

'Thanks!' Darcy gave a sarcastic thumbs-up. 'So, the dress, then – did you get one?'

'You better believe I did. I was in the changing rooms before he could say -*lentino*.' Freja gave an excited squeal.

'Describe.'

'Long. Red silk. Tight. It sort of drapes a bit at the front and drops off on one shoulder.'

'So . . . quiet and discreet, then? No one will notice you in that.'

'If I'm going to have a Valentino dress, it may as well be a Fuck-Off Valentino dress. I'll probably never have another one for the rest of my life.'

'Well, unless you marry the g—' Darcy looked up before

she finished the sentence and met Freja's gaze. '. . . Oh God, you don't think . . . ? . . . Amsterdam?'

Freja's mouth had fallen open. '. . . No.' Her brow furrowed. '. . . No . . . I mean . . . he wouldn't . . . Would he . . . ?'

'He might,' Darcy breathed. 'He is old, remember.'

Freja lobbed a kidney bean at her.

'Has he said anything else to get your radar going?'

'No . . . I don't think so? . . . But it's not like I've been making notes.'

'Okay so, then . . . he probably won't,' Darcy shrugged. 'We're worrying about nothing. Getting ahead of ourselves. It's just a lovely dirty weekend away. A city break.'

'. . . Yeah,' Freja murmured, staring into her chilli bowl, but seemingly forgetting how to eat.

Chapter Nineteen

Darcy stood by the window, watching tourists and lovers walk past in the street below as she watered Miss Petals. The snow was coming in fits and starts, not so heavily that it settled on the roads, but roofs and park benches, statues and bobble hats were frosted white. Her day had passed quietly and dusk was now deepening, lights beginning to flick on in the neighbouring buildings.

Music played quietly around her, and her fresh pedicure winked as if fishing for compliments as she padded around the empty apartment in clean sweats. With Freja away in Amsterdam with Tristan, she had the place to herself, guaranteed. It was a rare luxury – her first time, in fact, being here alone all weekend – and she had decided to make the most of it after working through last weekend and all the early starts and late nights which had preceded and followed it. She had slept late this morning, skipped the weekend torture run for a Pilates Reformer class instead and, after treating herself to the pedicure on the way home, she had done a meditation and finished up with an 'everything' shower which had taken almost two hours from start to finish: hair mask, face mask, body scrub, a fresh shave with new razors . . . No inch of her body had been neglected and afterwards, she had applied fake tan and blow-dried her hair with Freja's new Airwrap. She was primped and pampered, buffed, polished and glowing, and an evening on the sofa beckoned, with nothing more taxing to consider than which series to binge.

She was pulling a sea bass fillet from the fridge when her phone rang.

Darcy stared at it in surprise. It never rang. Even her parents never called – they WhatsApped. She wasn't even sure that was her ringtone. But it continued to ring, insistent and demanding.

'. . . Hello?' she asked, bewildered.

'Darcy? Thank heavens you picked up. Where are you?'

She frowned. 'Otto?'

'Yes. Where are you?'

'. . . I'm at my apartment—'

'So then you're in the city?'

She frowned deeper, hearing the stress in his voice. 'Otto, is everything all right?'

'Not really, no. Tell me, have you got plans for tonight? And if it's a yes, can they be changed?'

'I . . .' She didn't know how to answer that until she knew what she was signing up to. It was unlike him to sound so harassed. 'Otto, what's wrong? What's happened?'

She heard him take a breath. 'I apologize for calling with such little notice, but we're a man down for the royal gala fundraiser tonight at the Hotel D'Angleterre. Can you step in?'

'Royal gala?'

'Yes – the King and Queen are going to be there. It's an important charity fundraiser for the new children's hospital at Rigshospitalet and Margit always takes a table. It's black tie, obviously: auction, dinner, drinks, dancing . . . Surprisingly fun once the formalities are out of the way. My wife was supposed to come, but she's just had a fall—'

'Oh God, is she all right?'

'She's fine. Just a twisted ankle, but she can't put any weight on it and I can't get crutches now till tomorrow. We really can't have an empty seat at the table. Each table costs fifteen thousand euros. So Margit suggested you.'

'She did?'

'Of course. She's been pleased with your progress this week. She thought you might appreciate the exposure. But if you've already got plans . . .'

'Uh . . .' Darcy hesitated. This was not how she'd seen her evening unfolding. Having dinner with Danish royalty hadn't figured in her line-up. Then again—

She caught sight of herself in the mirror. She was, by some stroke of luck, show ready. And it would be a perfect opportunity to wear again the black velvet dress from the other week. *Do it for the plot!* she could hear Freja cheering her in her head.

Otto seemed to take encouragement from the lack of an outright no. 'I could send a car to pick you up. It would be with you in half an hour.' She could hear the desperation in his voice.

'Okay, Otto,' she said, shaking her head at herself even as she agreed to go. 'I'll be ready in time.'

'Great! That's great news! . . . I'll wait for you in the lobby. Security is tight, as you'd imagine and there's no time now to change names on the guestlist. You'll have to moonlight as Mrs Borup until we get past them.'

'No worries. I'll see you in a bit.'

'Oh!' Darcy said as the footman held the hotel door open for her and she had a first glimpse of the spectacle hidden within. Outside, the city lay grey and starkly urban, but here the lobby had been transformed into a winter wonderland, with a white carpet laid across the floor and fake snow piled into drifts. There were groupings of bent-willow reindeer figures – some standing, some kneeling – arranged in small herds through the space, and potted fir trees had been grouped into stands and sprayed with instant snow. She half expected squirrels to leap from the branches and birds to fly overhead. In fact, it felt just like stepping into her carousel – the one she had left wrapped in its tissue paper since getting home. She refused to take it out, as if to enjoy it would be to somehow forgive Max for what he'd done, and she didn't forgive him. She wouldn't.

She saw her advisor standing by the staircase, texting, and she walked over, aware of the whirr and click of a photographer somewhere recording her progress. 'Hi, Otto.'

He looked up, his eyebrows shooting up a moment afterwards as he took in the sight of her – so very different to her workaday student look. Her hair was pulled into a sleek bun, her make-up minimal with a red lip. 'You pulled *this* together in half an hour?'

'Let's just say we were all lucky with the turn of events today.'

'Red is clearly your colour.'

'Thanks.' She kicked nervously at the hem by her feet, feeling sick at what she was doing. The red dress was a narrow column, with the slightly draped neckline Freja had described and one twisted strap falling off her right shoulder. It was simple and yet by far the most incredible item of clothing Darcy had ever pulled on, and she couldn't imagine what it had cost. Five thousand? Ten? She had only tried it on out of sheer desperation when she had realized Freja had taken the shared black velvet dress to Amsterdam. There hadn't been anything else, at all, in either of their wardrobes that would stand up to a black-tie royal gala dress code.

Darcy had tried calling Freja but it kept going to voicemail; her friend was apparently 'otherwise engaged', and with just minutes to go before the car arrived, she had been obliged to make a decision. She didn't like doing it without her friend's permission, but either she wore this dress or she'd have to call Otto back and cancel on him. Not quite *Sophie's Choice* but a sticky wicket, as her father would say, nonetheless. She had carefully slid the sales tag down inside the dress and on the taxi ride over, she had lain out as straight as she could to avoid creases. She intended to move with all the care of a porcelain doll tonight and with a little luck, Freja would never even know she'd worn it.

'Well, you look very beautiful,' Otto said gallantly as he offered her his arm and together they headed towards the Palm Court doors. Black-suited security officers wearing headsets were standing at their posts, looking into the crowd with watchful, openly suspicious expressions. Between them stood a couple of women in long, plain black dresses, holding tablets.

'Mr and Mrs Otto Borup,' Otto said, squeezing Darcy's hand against his arm briefly, as if in apology for the little white lie.

Their names were found and they were waved through almost immediately, Darcy vaguely aware of heads turning as they walked in. Otto relaxed his grip on her and she felt like he was a father escorting his daughter to her prom. He was chatting lightly to her about some of the people she could expect to see here tonight. No mention was made of their woes with the Madsen Foundation earlier in the week.

A waiter stopped before them with a tray of champagne

glasses, and he let go of her arm completely as they took one each and moved deeper into the crowd.

Darcy looked around, trying to absorb the visual feast that had been carried through into this space: a jumbled confection of brightly coloured satin, velvet and silk gowns were reflected tenfold in a mirrored room. Extravagant sprays of silver birch branches stood splayed in giant urns before each mirror, twisted with delicate white fairy lights. It was like walking into Narnia, an enchanted winter garden.

People milled about as if they were on wheels, feet hidden below long skirts, jewels twinkling. Round tables were dressed in white linen with profuse floral displays perched on tall, fluted pedestals. Candles threw out a warm, flickering light, mellifluous music from a string quartet undercutting the languid buzz of conversation and snappy laughter.

Security personnel stood to attention along the perimeter, watching the guests closely as they drank and made merry. Darcy sipped her champagne nervously as she recognized plenty of faces of people she didn't know. People from other worlds: politics, show business, high finance, as well as the elite art world. Many of those who'd been at the museum drinks reception were here. She saw the Sallings deep in conversation with the Minister for the Interior and Health.

'Otto, so lovely to see you.'

Darcy looked back – and down – to see Helle Foss standing before them with a man she took to be her husband.

She immediately stiffened. It hadn't yet crossed her mind that *she* might be here.

'Helle, Mikkel, how are you?' Otto replied. 'Mikkel, I don't think you've had the pleasure yet – Darcy Cotterell? She's over with us from the Courtauld for a year.'

'A pleasure,' Mikkel nodded, shaking her hand lightly. Helle and Darcy nodded at one another in cool greeting.

'But where's dear Martine?' Helle asked in bafflement, as if she hadn't been issuing threats of court cases and drawing up enemy lines during their last meeting.

'Incapacitated, I'm sorry to say,' Otto said. 'Tripped over the dog earlier and sustained a nasty sprain.'

'Oh dear.'

'Yes. She'll be fine in a few days, but we felt sitting with her foot elevated in the presence of the royals would be suboptimal.'

Helle cracked an amused smile. 'Indeed. And that's why we have the pleasure of Ms Cotterell's presence, is it?' She was like an aged black cat, wizened but still well able to deliver a sharp sabre-swipe of her claws. She smiled as she slowly looked Darcy up and down. 'What a beautiful gown. Is academia paying better than I recall, Otto?'

It struck Darcy as a crass thing to say. Otto must have thought so too, for he merely smiled in reply.

Helle frowned, catching sight of something over Darcy's shoulder. 'Oh dear, he doesn't look happy,' she sighed. 'What's happened now?'

'Who?' Otto turned.

Darcy followed suit to find Max moving through the crowd, almost upon them. His gaze was wholly trained upon her and she automatically straightened, caught off guard by seeing him here. He was dressed in the dinner suit he'd been wearing the night they'd met and he looked so handsome, she caught her breath. If she'd had any idea he was going to be here tonight, would she have come?

Of course not.

He looked angry, and she braced as he wove his way

towards them, bridging the gap until finally he was right there.

'Max—' Otto began in a pleasant tone.

'What is she doing here, Otto?' he asked bluntly. 'Her name isn't on the list.'

Darcy swallowed, feeling pushed back by his abrupt words. No hello, obviously.

'I asked her,' Otto replied. 'Martine has a sprained ankle and cannot stand. Darcy kindly obliged by stepping in at *very* short notice.'

Max swallowed, as if recovering himself a little. 'I'm sorry to hear that; I hope she recovers quickly—'

'Thank you.'

'. . . But obviously there are security protocols in place with the guest list tonight, and as the chair of the event—'

'I'm aware that this puts you in a difficult position, but there wasn't any time to inform you beforehand. I thought it better, under the circumstances, that we have a full table than a glaring omission. And as Darcy is a member of the team who is currently working closely with the Madsen Foundation, I felt certain you would be comfortable with the last-minute switch.'

Darcy bristled, hating that her presence here somehow rested on Max's say-so. If she'd had any idea – 'I can just go, Otto,' she said quietly, lowering her chin. 'I don't need to be here.'

'Yes, you do,' Otto said quickly. 'It would be a breach of etiquette to have unfilled tables in front of the King and Queen. And besides, it isn't an issue. If Max trusts you enough to give you unrestricted access to his own home, why should you taking a seat at a table here be cause for concern?'

He was talking to her, but they all knew the question was

directed at Max. It was patently clear that Darcy posed no threat to the guests of honour. He just didn't want her there, his objections personal and not professional.

She remembered their sharp exchange at the gallery yesterday morning. He had no right to be angry with her – wasn't that the very accusation he'd thrown at her on his steps? – and yet from the way he was looking at her now, it clearly had riled him. She stared back, seeing that any attempt at a fragile amity had completely fallen away; he no longer cared if she hated him. Their efforts to be 'professional' had failed and there was only hostility left.

To her surprise, she wasn't sorry. That felt more solid to hold onto, somehow. Pretending they could be anything otherwise had been an exhausting charade.

'We're here tonight to raise money for the Children's Hospital – and apparently to enjoy ourselves,' Otto said, his gaze flitting questioningly between the two of them as their stare-off persisted. 'So why don't we do that?'

'Here you are,' a voice purred, and Max was accosted by a woman who was neither Angelina nor Natalia coming to stand by his shoulder. She had deeply tanned skin, as if she was straight off Ipanema Beach, and was wearing a gold silk dress so tight and skimpy, Darcy could see she had a belly button piercing. She was stunning – and vaguely familiar. 'I've been looking all over for you.'

Max's jaw pulsed with irritation. 'Sorry,' he muttered, not looking sorry in the least as he inclined his head back fractionally towards her, his eyes still never leaving Darcy. It was like standing in his kitchen last Sunday night all over again, but this time, she refused to look away. Another night, another woman? He was pathetic. He had been a bully in Margit's office the other day. He had ridden roughshod over her

259

moment of celebration. Nothing and no one mattered to him. Over and over again, he had told her what he was; he had showed her – but only now did she believe him. She wouldn't hide her contempt.

The woman's hand grazed up his arm, stroking it. '. . . They told me to tell you they're ready,' she said in an almost intimate voice. 'They want everyone to take their seats.'

'Right.' But he still didn't move.

The woman frowned and followed his stare, her gaze dragging down over Darcy's gown as she recognized it for the designer trophy it was. 'Great dress,' she said, without warmth.

'Thank you . . . Yours is beautiful too. You look just like a model,' Darcy replied, flatly.

'I am.' The woman's beautiful hazel eyes narrowed slightly. *'Really?'* Darcy breathed, sarcasm dripping from the word. She deliberately didn't look at Max, though she felt the flare of anger from him. He knew precisely the point she was making.

Otto reached for her arm. 'Come. If there are no further objections, we'll take our seats,' he said stiffly. 'We all know how tightly this needs to run to schedule tonight . . . Good luck, Max.'

He quickly led her away, back into the safety of the crowd. *'What* is going on between the two of you?' he asked, his voice so low it was almost a growl.

'I don't know what you mean.' Darcy realized her heart was pounding from the encounter but it had felt so good to finally challenge Max. She had shown him she wasn't a pawn to be used in his game.

'The two of you were at each other's throats. You looked like you loathe each other.'

She swallowed, turning away slightly. 'I suppose we do . . .'

'But why? Has something happened between you?'

Darcy gave a small laugh of astonishment. 'Are you honestly asking me that, after what he and that poisonous woman did in the meeting the other day?'

Otto sighed. 'It's a highly disagreeable way to do business, I agree, but it isn't personal, Darcy. They have an objective and they'll try to achieve it by whatever means they can. It doesn't mean they'll win. Personally, I try not to be drawn into their games.'

It was a clear rebuke. She had bared her teeth just now, but was this really the time or the place?

They had reached their table and, without missing a beat, Otto introduced her to Margit's husband, a mild-mannered-looking man who looked like he'd rather be playing golf. Right now, so would she. Realizing her champagne had sat untouched in her glass all this time, she downed it quickly before taking her seat.

Everyone fell into making small talk as they awaited the royal entrance, and Darcy tried to put Max Lorensen out of her mind. The wine glasses were filled and she sat, sipping quickly, as she listened to the conversation bouncing around the table, not caring for a word of it.

A trumpeter's call brought silence to the room several minutes later and everyone was asked to 'please rise' as the national anthem was played. The royal couple walked in, accompanied by a man and a woman Darcy guessed to be senior executives of the Children's Hospital. In spite of her agitation, Darcy felt a small thrill at all the pomp; she had never been in the presence of royalty before. She watched as their Majesties took their places at the table in the centre front of the room, her excitement immediately abating as she realized Max and Helle were sitting at the top table too.

Of course they were.

She reached for her wine and took another gulp.

Otto, sitting to her left, leaned towards her. 'Are you okay?' he murmured.

Was she drinking too much – too fast – she wondered?

'Why are *they* sitting up there?' she whispered back.

Otto followed her eyeline. '. . .The Madsen Foundation is the main sponsor for tonight.'

'Why? What does a fertilizer company have to do with building a kid's hospital?' she hissed.

'Madsen Holdings isn't just a biochemical corporation, Darcy; they branched into the biomedical space years ago,' he whispered. 'This is one of the Foundation's marquee events—'

'They're white-washing their reputation you mean,' she hissed back, prompting a stern look, just as the hospital chairman rose and began giving a speech. He talked at length about how the $350 million project was only possible through the generosity of their sponsors and everyone gathered here tonight.

Darcy looked away, refusing to believe Max and Helle could ever be painted as 'good guys'. She tuned in and out as she glanced around the room, taking in the famous faces, the beautiful dresses, anything to divert her attention from the one person lodged in her mind . . . But it was impossible when his date was sitting a few tables away, swinging a shapely crossed leg impatiently. Darcy tried not to think about Max taking her back to his house later on and slipping that scrap of gold dress off her –

'. . . round of applause for our Chair this evening, Mr Max Lorensen of the Madsen Foundation.'

She watched him stand to a loud round of applause. Otto

glanced back at her, an eyebrow lifting as he saw that she wasn't joining in, but Darcy didn't care if it was rude. Max had had no qualms in being rude to her earlier when he was threatening to throw her out of here.

His voice came through the microphone, filling the room, and she closed her eyes, hating the sound. He didn't have any cue cards, but he talked eloquently and calmly to the dignitaries in the room nonetheless, thanking them for their continued support, particularly in the fight against Kaposi sarcoma, the rare and aggressive cancer that had . . .

Oh God.

. . . That had claimed the life of his brother, Peder.

Darcy watched in dismay as a film began playing on a screen, images showing the transformation of a freckled young boy – playing in the surf with his brother, competing in an athletics meet, cuddling with his dog – to a gaunt and hollow young man lying on a hospital bed with tubes coming out of his arms and throat.

Darcy looked over at Max in horror, seeing how he had his face turned towards the screen, as if he were watching too, but from this angle she could see his eyes were averted to a spot beyond it. He couldn't look. Was this why he hadn't wanted her here? He didn't want her to be privy to anything less than perfect in his life? The photographs were replaced with mathematical graphics – bar charts, pie charts, graphs, all showing statistics and percentages, a worrying rise in the rates of the disease. They couldn't stop here. They needed more funding for further research. No one else should suffer the way his brother had suffered.

She saw the way he moved as he talked, skating over the pain as if it was buried beneath ice, the emotion taken out of his voice as if he had never known that little boy or young man himself. She saw the upward tilt of his chin, the distant remove of his gaze; she saw what she had taken for arrogance the first time she had laid eyes on his profile. He was beautiful, but now he was also bulletproof.

The images were switched off and he looked back to the room, throwing the guests a dazzling smile that was at odds with his frozen demeanour of a few minutes earlier, telling them to bid 'with furious abandon' in the silent auction. The lots would close in an hour; tablets for bidding were to be found on each table.

Nils, the man sitting to her right – a Friend of the National Gallery – was already flicking through, and she glanced over to see the prizes: a fully staffed villa for eight people on Harbour Island for ten days . . . a week's unlimited use of a helicopter . . . a private tour of Bill Koch's wine cellar . . . a holiday on Necker . . . a recording session with Coldplay's producer . . . dinner with former Victoria's Secret model Veronique Huillier . . .

Veronique Huillier? Darcy looked over at Max's date. She had thought the woman looked familiar.

Another wave of applause jolted her attention back onto him and she looked up in time to see him take his seat again. He immediately turned his attention to the woman on his left – a companion in her sixties, bedecked in emeralds – and his expression settled into that charming but impenetrable demeanour Darcy had become accustomed to seeing in recent weeks.

She watched him, feeling conflicted by what she'd learned here tonight. She didn't want to understand why he was the way he was; she didn't want to feel sad for him that he'd lost his brother. (She also didn't want to remember what she'd said to him at the Christmas market: *You're lucky you don't have one.* She could remember the silence that had followed.)

Neither would he want her pity, she knew that much. But she also couldn't pretend it didn't account for certain things.

'Good speech, as ever,' Otto said begrudgingly, reaching for a bread roll. 'Whatever your opinions on him, no one can deny he's a pro.'

'Otto, you never said his brother died,' she said in a low voice.

He seemed surprised by the accusation. 'Why would I?'

What could she say? That it explained so many things about him? 'When did it happen, do you know?'

'Nine or ten years ago now.'

'It's so terrible.'

'Yes. I believe they were very close.'

Darcy swallowed, trying not to think about Max's pain. She adored her own brother. She couldn't imagine losing him. 'It's amazing that he's doing this in his memory.'

Otto nodded. 'Grief affects everyone differently, of course, but Max appears to have decided on action. He set up a research grant in his brother's memory and, through the Foundation, he uses events like this to raise millions for the hospital every year . . . I'm not saying the guy's not a bastard in the board-room, but something like this makes it difficult to dislike him completely. Sometimes I even pity him, ridiculous though that may sound for a man seemingly with every gift and privilege at his disposal.'

'What do you mean?'

'Well, he has nothing else *but* this. It's what makes him so good at his job. His career is his life now.'

'But what about the rest of his family?'

Otto shook his head. 'Helle told me once – during one of

her milder moments – that his parents died in a car accident when the boys were young. Max and Peder were raised by an aunt – they have a fair few cousins – but she sent them off to boarding school.' He looked directly at Darcy. 'You can see why he's a very private man these days.'

Nils, on her other side, leaned towards them as he pointed to the tablet. 'I need your opinions,' he interrupted, unapologetically. 'What do you think, for my teenage son? It's his seventeenth birthday coming up. The session with the Coldplay producer? Or dinner with a Victoria's Secret model?'

'That's easy – dinner with an Angel has to be every boy's dream, surely?' Darcy replied after a beat when Otto offered no opinion.

'Man *and* boy's dream,' Nils chuckled, placing a bid as he talked. 'I wonder if I could tag along too?'

She smiled back, even though she knew exactly who would be living out that particular dream tonight.

She settled in with a polite look of interest as Nils and Otto began debating the merits of the wine being served, but she felt the weight of a stare settle upon her and looked up to find Max watching her from across the room.

Her instincts quivered from his scrutiny, having somehow known it would be him.

The body knows. It always knows.

People were dancing. The silent auction had closed and the royal couple had left suitably soon after dinner ended. The business of the gala had concluded and this was the fun part of the night, where the good wine and good food took effect. The mood had quickly stepped up as royalty exited and manners were relaxed. A band was playing and the dance floor was full, with Veronique putting on a show by shimmying her hips and tossing her hair around like a wildcat.

Darcy had fallen into conversation with a man who had been on the table behind theirs. He'd rather boldly tapped her on the shoulder as soon as they were 'released' from dinner – Nils had gone off to see whether his bid had won – and now she was slightly trapped. The man was a television producer, in his mid-forties, and as an attempt to keep her with him, he was trying to formulate a pitch on the fly for a series around the Old Masters. 'It's about making it . . . relevant and . . . and alive,' he kept insisting, very much the worse for wear. 'And who better than someone who looks like *you*?'

'It's not really about what I look like, though, is it,' she said. 'It's about reaching an audience who thinks fine art is only for the rich and showing them that there can be—'

She didn't get to finish her point. Someone behind her companion went to move past him and he startled, far too focused on her and nothing else in the room. Darcy watched as half a glass of merlot leapt from his crystal glass, flying through the air in a slow-motion arc, before landing in a long splatter down the front of her dress.

There was a horrified moment of silence as even the drunk man recognized the calamity of what he'd done.

'Oh—' he began as Darcy instinctively stepped back, her arms held out as she looked down at the ruined gown. She froze, unable even to breathe. 'I'm so sorry,' he said as she backed away. What had she done? What had she done? 'Let me—'

He reached for the water jug on the table, but she had already turned and was pushing through the crowd. People parted for her, reading her panic, some of them seeing the source of her distress, others looking on in bewilderment as she clamoured to get out of the room.

She felt herself released from the throng and ran down the hallway, looking for the restrooms.

'Oh, my dear!' an older lady in pearls said as she passed, understanding immediately. 'Down there, on the right.' She pointed the way and Darcy burst in to the ladies' room, having to weave her way around a gaggle of women who were heading out.

'Oh no! Her beautiful dress!' she heard one of them say behind her.

'It's ruined!'

The doors closed behind them and, seeing that all the cubicle doors were open, Darcy realized she was alone. She stood back and stared in horror at her reflection in the mirror, seeing the full extent of the damage now. It was even worse than she had thought. Besides the heavy stain over the torso, splashes had dripped all the way down the skirt too. She looked like she'd been stabbed. Like she was bleeding.

Salt, white wine – they were the remedies for removing red wine stains, she knew, but this stain was too large and irregular, the fabric too delicate. Even specialist dry cleaning wasn't going to come back with a spotless result, and on a five-thousand-euro dress like this, there was no room for flaws.

Oh God. What had she done, coming here tonight in someone else's treasure? There was no way she could afford to replace it.

Her hands reached for the counter, her head dropping as she felt the full disaster of the situation descend upon her. Tears began to gather, her breath to roll . . . This dress was supposed to have been for Freja's big moment, when she stood by Tristan's side and they announced their official together-ness – and now Darcy had taken that from her!

'Oh God,' she moaned, feeling her heart racing. Too fast.

'Oh God.' Her hands were beginning to tingle. What was she going to do? 'Oh . . . no . . .' She felt the first tears gather and fall, and she straightened up, her face tipped to the ceiling as she strained for self-control.

But the tears continued to slide. There was no way to stop what was coming, to undo what had already been done. Freja would never forgive her!

She began to pace in a tight figure of eight, her hands twisted in her hair as she walked in continuous loops; no way out.

The bathroom door opened as she had her back turned and she halted in her tracks, waiting for the sound of footsteps into the cubicle. But they didn't come. A sharp sob, escaping her efforts, made her shoulders judder as she waited.

'Darcy . . .'

What?

She spun round at the unexpectedness of her name, the deep timbre of the voice, in here.

'. . . No. Not you.' She shook her head as Max stared back at her, taking in the full scope of the stains across the dress, her smudged mascara as tears skimmed her cheeks. Of all the people she didn't want to see . . . 'Go away,' she said roughly. 'You shouldn't be in here.'

He looked pained. 'I saw what happened—'

'I don't care. Get out!'

'I want to help.'

'I don't want your help!' she cried. 'You're the last person I want to help me! . . . Just go!'

He watched as her tears became sobs and she hid her face in her hands, trying to hide from him. 'It's just a dress. We can sor—'

'You don't get it!' she cried. 'It's not just a dress! It's my friend's dress! Her beautiful new dress that she bought for something special. Only she's away, and I was trying to help Otto! I was trying to do someone a favour and I had no other options. I thought it wouldn't matter, that she'd never even know!' She looked down at herself, her face falling all over again at the sight of it, sobs beginning to roll through her like a stormy wind.

Oh God. How was she going to tell Freja what she had done? How could she ever make it up to her?

She knew she had to get out of here, but she couldn't . . . she couldn't slow down her breathing. Another sob escaped her, unstoppable, and she realized her breath was coming too fast, too shallow and the sound was . . . strangled. He rushed over as she sank forward, her hands reaching for the counter again as she stared down between her locked arms.

She felt his hand on her back then, pulling her back. Protective. Territorial. Safe.

'Darcy, you're panicking,' he said quietly. 'You need to breathe more slowly, okay? Try to control your breathing.'

She heard his words, she knew he was talking sense, but her body wouldn't obey. It was like a runaway train, steaming down oiled tracks.

He took her hands off the counter and turned her towards him, pulling her into his arms. 'Sshh,' he murmured, taking her wrists and holding them both in one hand so that she was pinned to him, her head against his chest. Instinctively her eyes closed. She could feel his heart; it was pounding too, but slower than hers, and the rhythmic beat soothed her somehow. A pulse she could follow.

She was grateful for the help, but why did it have to be his? Why was the ground constantly shifting between them: lover, villain, hero?

He was doing something with his other hand, but she

didn't know what until she heard the bass of his voice against her ear.

'Christoff, bring the car round.'

She felt him slide his phone back into his pocket and then his other hand went to her head as he began stroking her hair softly. 'It's going to be okay, Darcy. We'll get it sorted. Just breathe slowly for me. Breathe slowly.'

Her breathing began to fall into rhythm with his hand on her hair, a conductor's baton controlling her speed, slowing her down. Her body responding to his.

She didn't know how long they stood like that for; the door seemed to open and close several times, but no one else came in, though she could hear the murmur of voices out in the hall.

Eventually, when he felt she had calmed enough, he pulled back. 'Good,' he murmured, looking down at her. '. . . Did you bring a coat?'

She hesitated, unable to think clearly. Had she? She shook her head.

'No? Not your running jacket?' He gave a crooked smile that surprised her and she realized he was teasing her. A memory from the night they'd met. A moment of kindness. Hostilities on pause. '. . . Okay, so then we're going to walk out of here and into the lobby. My driver's waiting. He'll take you home.'

She looked at him. The panic was still flushed in her blood. 'Not you?'

He swallowed, shadows moving behind his eyes. He was close and far away, all at once. '. . . I have commitments here tonight . . . I have to stay.'

She recoiled, feeling exposed – like she'd shown something she shouldn't in her moment of weakness – and she went to pull away but his grip tightened around her wrists, holding her there.

'If things could be different . . .' he whispered, before gently kissing the top of her head.

The touch was so light, so tender, she might have thought she imagined it, had she not glimpsed their reflection in the mirror. Their eyes met in the glass, holding, holding . . .

The door opened again, a quiet *shush* that announced they weren't alone, and his hands dropped away. He turned towards the door. 'Time to go.'

He averted his gaze as she passed by him and they walked out and down the hall in silence, past the gaggle of women she had seen coming out of the toilets earlier, past red candles on polished side tables, evergreen swags looped along the walls, waiters hurrying back and forth with trays.

'Everyone's staring,' she whispered, seeing how people stopped talking mid-conversation as they passed. Max's polished composure only seemed to heighten the contrast with her wrecked make-up and ruined dress.

'You're still the most beautiful woman here,' he murmured back.

She looked over at him in surprise, but his gaze was dead ahead as they approached the snowy lobby, where his driver was already waiting for her. He was protecting her the only way he could – or knew how – and she felt his hand hover, as ever, at the small of her back.

It was a heat that promised to warm her, if only it would land.

Chapter Twenty

'Hi.' Aksel stood in the hallway, smiling back at her trepidatiously.

'Aksel!' she said in surprise, her heart plunging to her feet as she took in the sight of him clutching a bottle of wine, some flowers and a bag of unpopped corn kernels. 'What are you doing here?'

'. . . I decided to be spontaneous for once and see where it would get me.' He looked back at her awkwardly. 'I, uh . . . felt really embarrassed about the other night. That's why I haven't called. I'm sorry.'

'Oh – no, really, it's fine. I get it,' she said quickly, feeling his difficulty. 'We both had *way* too much to drink.'

'Yeah . . .' He shot her a shy grin. 'Would you believe me if I told you nothing like that's ever happened to me before?'

'Of course!' she lied. 'But it didn't matter anyway. It's always a much bigger deal to guys than it is to us.'

He shrugged his shoulders and rolled his eyes. 'I should have known you'd be okay about it. I know I should have called. I just—'

'Stop,' she smiled, desperately trying to reassure him; desperately trying to get off the subject. 'It was really fine.'

'Okay, well good then.'

They stared at one another in awkward silence for a

moment and she felt her despair grow. The apology was sweet but she was in no mood to socialize. But he had come all the way over here, with gifts, and she couldn't imagine how hard it must have been for him to come here and face her after the disaster on Thursday. '. . . Do you want to come in?'

He looked back at her with relief. 'I mean, only if you're free? I wasn't sure you'd even be in . . .'

She stepped back for him to come into their small entrance hall, taking his gifts with an appreciative smile. 'My flatmate's been away for the weekend so I've been enjoying having the place to myself . . . God, I must look a state,' she muttered, realizing she hadn't even looked in a mirror today.

'No. You look . . . cosy,' he said, taking in her bare feet (at least they were pedicured), tartan PJ bottoms and the old, soft blue shirt Lars had left and which she had no intention of returning; she considered keeping it a cheat's tax he had to pay.

She knew he was being kind. She hadn't slept, of course, all of yesterday's well-being exercise undone. She was so tightly strung she couldn't settle; so wired she couldn't eat; she was exhausted but couldn't rest; the apartment had never been so clean. Freja had finally returned her calls with a single text – 'Sorry! Been busy [winking emoji] Will update you when back' – and Darcy had spent the entire night staring at the ceiling, wondering how on earth she could make this right.

Her only solution – to extend her overdraft and buy another dress – was an imperfect one. Nothing could be done today, on a Sunday, and the overdraft would take a day or two to arrange, meaning there was no chance of switching the dresses before Freja got back. She would have to come clean about what she'd done and *then* make it right. It solved 50 per cent of the problem.

It was the other half that was the worst half. The real issue was the breach of trust, and this solution meant Freja would know what she'd done. Darcy had worn her dress without permission; to all intents and purposes, she'd stolen it, taken something precious like it was nothing and destroyed it.

It didn't help that she had no idea when her flatmate would be back. Tonight? Tomorrow? Rest was impossible, and Darcy's attention leapt to the door any time there was a sound outside in the hall, as if their neighbours' comings and goings suddenly carried threat.

'I'll open this, shall I?' She held up the wine bottle with a degree of apprehension. This was either the last thing she needed, or the very thing. Would it distract her from her troubles? Would he?

'Great.'

'Would you mind taking off your shoes there?' she asked over her shoulder as she headed into the open-plan kitchen-living room. 'Freja's a bit of a stickler for not bringing outdoor germs through the place. She's a microbiologist, so she's pretty hot on that stuff.'

'Fair enough.' He followed her in his socks into the sitting room, his gaze wandering over the two blue Ikea sofas positioned opposite one another, the cushions limp and unplumped; the TV playing on mute, the gas log-effect fireplace, nail polish and cotton wool balls on the coffee table. 'Nice place you've got here.'

She reached for the wine glasses in the wall cupboard. 'We like it. It's warm, which is the main thing. And there's always hot water.'

'Crucial. We had a mains leak a few months back and they

turned off the supply for three weeks. Had to use bottled water for showers, brushing teeth, filling the kettle. It was a nightmare.'

'I can imagine,' she said, turning the oven on to preheat and tipping the popcorn into a covered pan.

'How long have you lived here?'

She unscrewed the cap and poured the wine, all the while wondering whether or not it would be an advantage to have him here if Freja did return tonight and found the dress was no longer hanging on her wardrobe door. (It was hidden at the back of Darcy's closet. She couldn't even bear to look at it.) Would it stop her from screaming, throwing Freja out? 'Um . . . since August.'

'Nice.'

She came over with the wine. 'Shall we sit soft . . . ?'

'Great.' He was still nervous, she could tell.

They settled down on the sofa together, sitting close but not touching. Darcy tucked her legs up and angled herself to face him. Behind her, the TV still played on mute.

'Well, cheers,' he said, holding up his glass.

'Cheers.'

The silence in the room resounded as they both took a deep gulp of wine.

'So, have you had a good week?' she asked him, resting her glass on her thigh. The question sounded stiff, as if they'd just met.

'You mean, apart from feeling like a prize idiot for fumbling—'

'Aksel,' she chided. 'Forget about it.'

He rolled his eyes. 'It was decent, I guess. Although we had the dog back in – you know, the one who suffered the make-shift castration at the hands of his owner?'

'He tied the elastic bands . . . ?'

'Exactly. Well, he died. The infection took hold and we couldn't get it under control.'

'Oh no, that's so sad!'

'I know. The guy was trying to save himself some money and all he did was cause suffering to that poor animal and end up losing his beloved pet.'

'I don't know how you don't shout at these people,' she muttered. 'They're idiots.'

'Verbally abusing the clients is frowned upon, unfortunately, though some of them definitely deserve it.' He looked back at her. 'You?'

'Mm, I've had better weeks.'

'How's it going with the mystery woman?'

'She's becoming slowly less mysterious.'

'Yeah? Tell me,' he said, taking another deep glug of his wine; almost half the glass.

Darcy sighed, weary. Did he really want to know? 'Well, I know now that she went to live with the Madsens from 1915, so I've been doing a deep dive through the family's photographs and diaries, which is at least giving me some insight into her teenage years with them.' To her ongoing frustration, there was no sign Lilja had kept a diary herself. It was Lotte, as her best friend and companion, who was proving to be the best source of information on her movements and whereabouts.

Darcy looked at Aksel thoughtfully. 'Actually, you might be able to shed some light on something for me.'

'Again?' he smiled. 'I'm going to start billing for consultancy.'

She laughed, although she wasn't actually sure he was joking. 'So it appears my mystery woman had a baby boy in August 1919, and there are a *lot* of medical bills pre- and post-partum. They seemed to be getting through huge quantities of potassium bromide . . . What would that be for?'

'Well, that was the standard protocol for treating epilepsy back then.'

'Really?' she asked interestedly.

'Yes. It had other applications too, of course. You've probably heard the British Army famously gave their troops bromide tea to calm sexual excitement on the front line? Everyone knows about that.' He rolled his eyes. 'But it was the principal treatment for epilepsy till the 1910s, 1920s. We still use it now to treat epilepsy in dogs.'

'Right,' she murmured, thinking hard.

'Didn't you say she drowned? Perhaps that's how it happened? She had a seizure in the bath?'

'No, it wasn't her who was epileptic.' Darcy shook her head. 'I think it was the baby.'

Aksel winced. 'Ah.'

'Yeah, seems it was pretty bad. There were all these prescriptions that started after the birth and suddenly stopped at exactly the same time the baby died, at seven months old.'

'How sad.'

'I think it was devastating for her. The birth seems to have been traumatic anyway. I saw something in one of the entries referring to eclampsia.'

'Oh, well, that explains it. Eclampsia is very dangerous. Leads to all sorts of complications for mother and baby. She likely went into premature labour . . . Sounds like she was lucky to survive.' He took another sip of his wine.

'I'm not sure if lucky is a word I'd apply to her, sadly,' Darcy frowned. 'So why do some women get it and others don't?'

'Eclampsia?' He shrugged. 'There are a number of risk factors – diabetes, obesity, twin pregnancies, age—'

'Age?'

'Yes, if you're sitting at the extremes for child-bearing years, it's more likely.'

'Such as? What's the range?'

He considered. 'Younger than seventeen. Older than thirty-five—'

'She would have been very young. I don't know her exact age, but going by photographs at the time and her being a contemporary of Lotte, I'm estimating that she was about fourteen.'

Aksel winced again. 'Mm. Adolescent pregnancies can be high risk. Depending on the individual, the body just isn't ready and may not be fully developed. The pelvis can be too small . . . Pregnancy is a massive strain on all the organs and systems and effectively a child's body can't cope with it.'

Darcy sat back, seeing how one event had triggered a chain of disasters, each connecting to another: adolescent pregnancy. Eclampsia. Epilepsy.

A baby dead because it had been born too soon, to a mother too young.

She sighed, dropping her head as she tried to remember Viggo's calm perspective on Lilja as a child bride: *Different times, Darcy.*

But it still made her angry.

Beside her, Aksel finished his drink and shifted position. 'Just to change the subject quickly – what are you doing on Friday night?'

She tried to think. 'No plans yet, I don't think. Why?'

'You know it's St Lucia's Day?'

'Oh. No, I didn't know.'

'Yeah, it's a pretty big deal. There'll be processions all

over the country, except here – in the city – we do it a little differently.'

'How?'

'The procession's on water. Everyone goes out on kayaks. We start at Nyhavn, sing some carols, have some food and drink, paddle round to the next stop, do the same. Rinse and repeat. There's always a huge crowd – both on the water and on the banks, but it's more fun on the water. Fancy being my date?'

'I've really not kayaked that much.'

'You don't need much experience. It's in the canals, so there are no tides or currents.'

'Is it safe?'

'Very – it's well lit and there are security marshals every-where. If you went in or under, I guarantee you'd be hauled back out in seconds.'

'Chilly, though.'

'I'll keep you warm,' he said flirtatiously, reaching out a hand and covering hers. 'Plus, we'd hire you a wetsuit as well as the kayak.'

She was already anticipating that invoice.

'What do you say? Are you in?'

She swallowed nervously. '. . . Okay sure, why not?' She had nothing else on her horizon to which to look forward.

He beamed. 'Great! You'll love it. I know you will.' He grabbed her hand and held onto it and she saw his stare deepening, the mood between them changing.

He leaned over and kissed her lightly, once, twice . . . She closed her eyes, not stopping him but not falling into it either. She wasn't sure how she felt, stuck in her head and not her body. She was hardly an innocent, but this just didn't feel like the right time. But how could she tell him that when the ghost of the other night still lingered? She sensed they were only going to get past it by overwriting it. His ego needed to settle this doubt once and for all. The kiss grew deeper, his enthusiasm – and wine-fuelled confidence – surging as he began to take control. He broke away to take the wine glasses out of their hands and Darcy watched dully as he set them down on the table. He resumed kissing her again, both hands now free and beginning to wander, pulling her closer to him.

The kiss was good but her mind was fractured on other things and when he began unbuttoning her shirt, finding her braless underneath, she didn't feel the same quickening of lust but simply a nervous flicker that she was going to have to do this sober.

He pulled back to remove his hoodie, the t-shirt coming off with it, although whether that was intentional or not, she wasn't sure. 'So hot suddenly,' he grinned, suddenly half naked in her living room.

He began kissing her neck, pushing her back on the cushions – but the sudden sound of small explosions made them both start. They looked up like meerkats, trying to identify the noise.

'Oh! The popcorn!' she remembered, trying not to sound too grateful for the distraction. 'I'd better take it out before it burns!' She slid out from under him and walked over to the oven. She put on the oven gloves and lifted the pan out. Inside, the corn kernels were popping as wildly as her nerves.

'. . . Do you want me to get that?'

She looked up to find Aksel pouring himself another glass and nodding his head towards the front door. 'Huh?'

'Someone just knocked.'

They had? Oh God!

She froze, the pan held between her gloved hands. Freja was back and this was going to happen way sooner than she had anticipated. This was it.

She felt panic shoot through her veins again as she looked back towards the bedrooms. Should she just come straight out with the dress and explain? Wouldn't it be worse to have Freja go in and start looking for it . . . ?

'Darcy?'

She looked back at him, still motionless. 'Uh, yeah . . . yeah, if you wouldn't mind. It'll be my flatmate, Freja . . . She's always losing her key.' That wasn't quite true. She'd lost it once.

'Ha. I do that too,' he said, getting up from the sofa, glass in hand, and disappearing out of sight into the stubby little reception hall. 'Hi . . .'

Darcy waited, eyes closed, for the sound of her flatmate's surprise on being greeted at her own door by a handsome, but shirtless, stranger.

But it wasn't Freja she heard. '. . . Hi,' she heard Aksel say in a questioning tone.

'Aksel? Who is it?' she asked, putting the pan down on the trivet and hurrying over. She rounded the corner, her oven gloves still on—

'. . . Max?' The word was little more than a breath, like it had been knocked out of her.

Aksel was holding up a long clothing bag. It was white with a familiar black font. *Valentino*. He turned back to her with a bemused expression. 'Apparently this is for you?'

But Darcy didn't look at what he was holding out for her. She couldn't take her eyes off Max. She couldn't comprehend what she was seeing, even though it was also, somehow, perfectly obvious.

Max stared back at her with that distant, shellacked look she was beginning to know well and it was obvious from the scene before him – her hair dishevelled, shirt unbuttoned; Aksel topless at the door – that he perfectly understood what he was seeing too.

In that one moment, she felt the intimacy that had bloomed between them for a few brief moments last night, close up again; tenderness balled up within a fist. The memory of what he had done for her, rescuing her from public humiliation, had sat inside her like a hot coal, refusing to cool. Try as she might to hate him, he kept shape-shifting, inciting her lust, sympathy, gratitude . . .

'But . . . how did you . . . ?' she faltered. She couldn't understand how it was possible that he was here at her door, much less why he should have done this for her. Too many questions clamoured to her throat but she knew anything she said would be inadequate, ungracious. Aksel's presence complicated things; they had an audience and she couldn't speak freely.

'Don't make a thing about it. I just made a call.' Max's voice was clipped and toneless.

'I . . . I must pay you back,' she said, trying to say something, anything, that could convey her relief. He had saved her!

'No need. It was a gift.'

Her mouth parted. She couldn't accept a five-thousand-euro dress as a gift!

'Uh . . . what's going on?' Aksel asked, looking confused, looking between them, his gaze coming to rest upon her.

It felt like minutes before Darcy could bring her attention onto him. She was trying to work out how Max even had her address, but of course Christoff had dropped her back here last night. Slowly, she dragged her eyes onto her guest; the man whose hand had been on her bare breast just a few moments ago but couldn't touch her soul. '. . . I, uh, spilled wine on a dress I was wearing to a work event last night. Except the dress wasn't mine . . . Max is saving my skin.'

'That's very nice of him,' Aksel said with a wary note.

The two men's eyes locked for a moment in silent communication before Max's slid back to her again. 'It was nothing to do with me. My girlfriend has a contact there. She gets given dresses all the time. I'm just the messenger . . .'

'Right. Wow,' Aksel nodded, leaning against the doorframe with a familiarity that suggested he was here all the time.

Max stiffened ever so slightly. Almost imperceptibly, but Darcy clocked it. 'Anyway, I should go,' he muttered.

He turned to leave and Darcy felt alarm leap through her at how all of this was unfolding – her stilted response in front of Aksel. But she couldn't say anything that would make Max stay. She couldn't thank him for what she knew had to have been a giant effort on his part, no matter what he said to the contrary, to get this dress here to her. She didn't believe that the dress had been given for free. She didn't believe it hadn't been a problem. Even if Veronique – or Angelina, or Natalia – were house models there, even if they closed the couture shows, it was still a Sunday. *How* had he got it?

She bitterly wished now that she hadn't hung back all day from texting him to thank him for getting her home last night without further indignity. Every time she had picked up her phone to call, she had put it back down again, telling herself he had been kind in a crisis but that crisis had passed now and her problems weren't his. They weren't friends, even though he'd helped her.

Was still helping – even though he was looking at her now like he barely recalled her name. He hadn't smiled once. Every thank-you was rebuffed. They could never connect; only their punches landed.

And yet, she remembered the steadying beat of his heart against her ear and how his eyes had closed as he kissed her hair.

No hello. No goodbye.

And yet . . .

Chapter Twenty-One

23rd June 1920

I felt a change in myself when we drove through the gates at Solvtraeer this morning. I had forgotten how it feels to be away from the city. I suppose I have become too used to the constant busyness of the place – people coming to visit every day, parties and luncheons. Even a stroll in the park is a social occasion. And then, of course, there is the noise. The traffic grows daily, it seems.

But here, you can actually hear the wind in the trees and the songs of the birds. The clock hands always seem to tick more slowly in Hornbaek. It is Henrik's first visit but he loves it here already, I can tell. Lilja was very gracious about the news of our engagement and I could see she was trying to be happy for us. She looked better than I was expecting. When she left Copenhagen, she was like a rag doll that had had the stuffing pulled from her – so tiny and limp – but there is a very little roundness now to her cheeks and she has some colour back. She says that is down to her walks on the beach every day. When we arrived, she was standing barefoot on the lawn, talking to Old Sally as he dug up the weeds, and I must admit it was a curious sight to come upon; but we must remember things are different here to the city, and it is precisely this being at ease which Doctor Beck said would help salve her spirit.

I hope this place will do its work quickly. Mama has the wedding arrangements all in hand and the minister will marry us in the cathedral three weeks from now. Lilja is my sister in spirit and law, and I couldn't bear to think of her not being there, but she is still so fragile, it is hard to believe she will be strong enough to attend. I am going to mention her in my prayers from tonight to help her rally. Casper will be coming back from London especially and after all the sadness they have endured, any opportunity to celebrate would be healing for them both.

I know Mama feels it isn't right that Lilja should be spending her convalescence here without a companion; in that regard, my engagement is terribly timed. But she and Papa are so taken up with their commitments in the city that it's almost impossible for them to get away either. Lilja assures me the solitude suits her very well but she has always been a stoic. I am resolved to try to come down here at least two more times before the wedding. If I can.

14th July 1920

Summer is in full blaze at Solvtraeer! Lilja is taking a nap and I finally have a moment to set down these precious memories. We are just returned from a walk on the beach, which gladdened my heart. I always forget how the sun carries in the wind here and Lilja had to remind me to bring my parasol, lest I should walk down the aisle with burnt cheeks, five days from now!

She cares not herself whether she is as brown as a berry and she has taken now to wearing her hair in a braid, as we did when we were very young girls. She says it is easier than struggling to shape a bouffant in the sea breezes and I must admit, my combs required repositioning on our return, but it seems to me a shame to fall back into girlish ways when we spent so long yearning to be fashionable young women.

Her convalescence appears to be coming along well, however. She reads and paints and sews most days; Papa has decided to have a *pianoforte sent down here as a surprise so that she might play at her leisure. She used to enjoy it when we had our lessons together and as Mama always says, any house becomes a home when it has music within it.*

This has been the first time in years that Solvtraeer has been inhabited continuously through the colder months. The old place usually has a neglected, forlorn feeling when we visit in summer but it almost feels as though the house has woken from a long sleep and is breathing deeply again. Lilja has become quite adept at flower-arranging. Old Sally brings baskets of flowers through into the cutting room every other day so that there are now posies and bouquets in every room in the house. The fragrance is quite astonishing, and I am resolved to do the same in our new home in Toldbodgade after the wedding. Henrik is keen that I should pursue some hobbies, so this shall please us both, I think.

However, I cannot put a brave face on everything. As feared, my dearest sister shall not be coming to the wedding. It is not that she does not wish to but that Dr Beck has advised against it. Her constitution is not yet robust and the melancholy is proving difficult to lift. Some days she does not remove from her bed at all and Mrs Sally has to bring her food in on a tray. Lilja says those days are increasingly rare but that when they come – and she cannot predict when they will – she is quite helpless. It is frightening to think of her like that and I know it troubles my brother that he cannot support his wife in the way he would like, but we must remind ourselves it has only been a few months. Better days are coming.

'What are you doing sitting in the dark?' Viggo asked as he came down the stairs into the oval office. He was carrying a bag of groceries for his dinner; he had bridge club tonight and there would be no time for shopping later.

'Oh, just flicking through a million and one slides of how the other half lived in the 1920s,' she sighed, twisting and tipping back on her chair to see him. She was in the west wing beside the glass cabinet, the lights off. The slide projector was positioned to shine onto the bare expanse of white wall at the end there, the small remote in her hand.

'Comparison is the thief of joy, Darcy, always remember that,' Viggo counselled, hanging his coat on the stand and checking the kettle for water. 'Found anything interesting?'

'Define "interesting". It's an assorted mix, managing to show everyone *but* the two people I want to see: there's pictures of the new Madsen mansion; their dogs; Lotte and Henrik's wedding; some photos of Bertram and Gerde at some horse race—'

'Probably the Trotting Derby at Charlottenlund. A very prestigious event.'

'Mm. Well, I've just moved on to what I'm *hoping* are pictures taken at Solvtraeer. So far, there are lots of garden and beach pictures, so I think I'm on the right track.'

'What are you hoping to find at Solvtraeer?'

'It seems Lilja pretty much relocated there after her baby died. It was the Madsens' summer place on the coast.'

'Yes, I know, in Hornbaek. It's an hour from here.'

'Well, Doctor Beck advised plenty of fresh air and exercise and according to Lotte's diaries, it seemed to suit her far better than the city.'

'It probably felt more like home to her there, too, if the girls were based there during the war years.'

'Oh yes, I hadn't thought of that.' Darcy pondered for a moment, remembering the picture of them both in the garden, on the picnic blanket. June 1915. '. . . You know, I have a bad feeling that she never saw her parents again. I think she died before they were released.'

'*If* they were released,' Viggo shrugged. 'I'll put the kettle on.'

She turned back and flicked to the next slide. It showed a slender woman in a long white cotton dress on the beach, standing by the water's edge. Her back was to the camera as she stared out over the sea.

Darcy gasped, immediately leaning forwards for a better look. Even without a face, without words, the photograph spoke to her.

'That's definitely her,' she murmured, still scrutinizing the image as Viggo came back down the corridor with their coffees several minutes later.

'How can you tell for sure?' he asked, handing one to her.

'See her hair?' She pointed to the braid. 'Lotte mentions it in her diary. She thought it was a backwards step for Lilja not to style her hair up as per the ladylike fashions of the day. But the poor girl was grieving her baby. What did she care for hairstyles?'

Darcy stared at the young woman's back. Even from behind, she looked so young. She could only have been sixteen, maybe seventeen, here. Already, to all intents, an orphan. Already a wife. Already a mother. Already bereaved.

She wondered who had taken the photograph. Lotte? Casper? Had they seen, too, in that moment, her broken spirit – a heart that could never heal?

She turned back to Viggo, remembering something. 'Viggo.'

He turned at her questioning tone. 'Yes?' he asked warily. They both knew they were not supposed to collaborate.

'Do you know anything about the circumstances in which Lilja died?'

'Yes. She drowned.'

'I know – but do you know *how* it happened? Was she in the bath? Swimming in a pond?'

Viggo hesitated. 'Does it matter? The outcome is the same.'

'Maybe it doesn't,' she shrugged. 'But if I'm writing her biography, I ought to know the specifics, don't you think?'

He looked uncomfortable and for the first time, she could see he was hedging a reply to her.

'Viggo?' she pressed. 'Please tell me. It's just a matter of fact, surely?'

His clear-eyed gaze met hers. 'Not necessarily.'

She frowned. 'What do you mean?'

'The death was recorded as an accidental drowning.'

'. . . But?' she prompted, hearing it hang in silence.

'There were rumours—' He looked pained. '. . . That she walked into the sea.'

'Lilja killed herself?' Darcy gasped. She fell still as he nodded. '. . . But that can't be.'

'Why not?'

She thought back to the certificates she had laid out: one marriage, two births, three deaths. 'She'd just had another baby.'

'Exactly why they wanted to stop speculation.'

Darcy stared at him. 'So you're saying the Madsens hid the truth?'

'I'm saying they didn't reveal the whole truth,' he said carefully. 'These were different times—'

Like a pubescent age of consent? Arranged marriages between young girls and older men? Adolescent pregnancies resulting in death and trauma? Those different times, Darcy wondered? Were any – or all – of those reasons why Lilja might have done it?

'You have to understand, there was a certain stigma around suicide in those days,' Viggo went on quickly. 'Great shame was attached to the act back then. They had to think about what was best for the baby – what she would learn, growing up. Not to mention, when Casper died just a few days later, the family knew their high profile meant the double tragedy would become the subject of salacious gossip, not just in the capital but *nationwide*. It was bad enough that they had lost two young members of their future generation. They needed to grieve. If the whole story had been known, shame added to tragedy . . . It would have followed them everywhere.'

Darcy couldn't imagine the level of despair it must take to wade into the waves and hold oneself under the surface. To leave a baby without its mother . . .

'At the end of the day, the poor girl drowned. How or why she died was no one else's business.' He looked at Darcy. 'Do you see?'

She nodded. *Never underestimate the importance of reputation.* Otto had told her that.

She looked away, bothered by what she had learned and knowing she would need to consult with Otto on it. Whatever the family's best intentions had been back then, revealing the truth of Lilja's death was surely the right and honourable thing to do now? Although she could well imagine Helle Foss's response to this discovery.

She clicked onto the next slide, staring blankly at the image of a garden in full bloom.

'It's such a shame these pictures aren't in colour,' Viggo said. 'It would look like Giverny, I'm sure. Old Sally knew what he was doing. They don't make them like him any more. He could make anything grow, they said.'

Darcy rallied herself back to concentration. 'Old Sally's the gardener?'

'Yes. He worked at Solvtraeer for over fifty years. His son worked with him too, when he came back from the Great War.'

'. . . I thought Denmark was neutral?' she frowned.

'Yes. But the Sallys were from Schleswig, close to the German border. A more complicated picture there. They felt it was their duty to fight.'

'Oh.'

'Little Sally came back when it ended and stayed at Solvtraeer for the rest of his life. Never married. They were loyal sorts and excellent at what they did. The garden came to be regarded as a sort of attraction in the area. So many people would come by and stand at the gates to look in, that eventually Sofie Madsen – Frederik's wife – decided to charge a fee for them to enter the grounds for an hour each morning, from May through to July.'

Darcy arched an eyebrow. 'The rich lady charged a fee for people to look at her flowers?'

He smiled. 'The money went to charity.'

Darcy looked just as sceptical. 'The Madsen Foundation charity?'

Viggo laughed and she grinned, feeling her mood improve again as she flicked through the next images. There were many of the garden – blowsy flower beds, wheelbarrows filled with heaps of earth, baskets of cut flowers. Darcy wondered who was taking all these slightly chaotic snapshots that stood in such contrast to the stylized, formal images she had seen taken of the family in Copenhagen.

She found her answer in one image. It looked to be almost a misfire, showing just thick, lush grass, but the hint of a bare foot – pretty toes, shell-like nails – in the lower edge, strongly suggested it was Lilja who was trigger happy.

Darcy thought again of the fragile-looking young woman staring out to sea, her hair roped behind her, toes burrowing in the sand. She had been trying to find happiness in nature.

Beauty outdoors.

Joy in the small things.

Darcy still hadn't seen her face clearly, but she could feel Lilja's spirit beginning to creep up on her, making herself known at last.

Chapter Twenty-Two

'Well, it wasn't pretty – but I'm in,' Darcy said, throwing her arms out haplessly. Getting the wetsuit on in the tiny cafe toilet had been like trying to wrestle an octopus, but against the odds, she had prevailed. 'I have to say, it's not my most festive look.'

Aksel looked back, grinning at the sight of her standing there with her hands planted on her hips. 'Well, we can do something about that. Here, put this on.' He was holding out a lifejacket for her to slip her arms into. Darcy stood like an obedient child before him as he zipped her up. 'Safety first.'

'Now I feel like a Michelin man in a corset,' she murmured.

He laughed. 'You don't look like one! Wait till I add my finishing touches.'

She watched as he pulled a string of red tinsel from his backpack and criss-crossed it around her torso. He reached into his backpack again and she saw the wink of a gold bottle cap inside. 'And for the win . . .' He set a pair of reindeer antlers on her head and then another pair on his own. 'See? They flash,' he said, switching them on.

'Oh my God,' she groaned, grinning. 'I'm glad no one I know can see me right now.'

'*I* know you.'

'No, you don't. And if you think you saw me here, no you didn't.'

He reached over and kissed her, just a peck on the lips, but there was a growing familiarity in the gesture now. He didn't need to ask with his eyes first. He was beginning to claim her as his and there was an unspoken expectation now that tonight would be 'third time lucky'. Their impromptu date on Sunday had been delivered a second and fatal death blow when Freja had come home mere minutes after Max's departure – by sheer dint of luck, Darcy had immediately put the replacement dress on Freja's wardrobe door straight after Max had left; she had needed a few moments to herself to process what had just happened. But Freja's disconsolate expression as she had come into the apartment had sent Aksel making his excuses almost immediately – Tristan hadn't proposed in Amsterdam after all. Freja hadn't known just how much she had wanted him to ask, until he hadn't.

Darcy looked around. There were hundreds of people milling about, mostly trying to find a spot to stand on the banks, their fellow kayakers walking through with backpacks and oars. 'So, what's the plan?' she asked nervously, rubbing her hands together.

'We get on the water, paddle round to Nyhavn, sing some carols; paddle on to Christianshavn, do the same. Repeat through Blox and Højbro before ending up back here again.' He shrugged. 'It takes about an hour and a half and there's mulled wine and *aebleskiver* at the carol stops to help keep us warm. Then they serve bouillabaisse and bread rolls back here for dinner.'

'Okay. Sounds fun.'

'It is. It really kicks off the Christmas spirit.'

'Well, I could definitely do with some of that. We haven't

even got our Christmas tree up yet,' she said, shivering and jumping up and down on the spot a few times.

'Cold?'

'What gave it away?'

'Here, have a glug, it'll warm you from the inside,' he said, pulling a hip flask from his backpack.

'What is it?'

'Brandy.' She could feel from the weight of it that it was only half full.

'Hah,' she winced as she took a sip, feeling it burn her throat. It did warm her a little – but it mainly burned. He took it from her and had a long, deep slug himself. No shiver. No wince, it just slid down.

Someone with a speaker began making announcements and Aksel listened in as the first kayakers made their way to the steps and began getting on the water.

'Right,' he said, screwing the lid back on and returning it to his bag. He zipped it closed. 'Wait here. I'll put these in the lockers,' he said, and she stood obediently as he checked in their backpacks and coats at the kayak bar.

'Oh, I'm a bit scared,' she said, slightly jittery, when he came back a few minutes later.

'You'll be fine,' he said, slipping what looked to be a small grey, waterproof pouch over his head. 'I've put both our phones in here,' he said. 'Just in case.'

She grimaced. If her phone was to fall into the canal . . . 'You're sure it's watertight?'

'I'm certain. I use it all the time . . . And that's your song sheet,' he said, handing her a small pamphlet. 'With the lyrics. Tuck it into the front of your lifejacket.'

She copied his actions, shivering all the while. Even in a wetsuit, it was a freezing cold night.

'Oh . . . that's us,' he said as more numbers were called. 'Follow me.'

He led the way over to the steps and the organizers lowered the next kayaks into the water. Aksel got in his first – so much for ladies first, she thought, waiting her turn.

One of marshals held the prow of the boat as she lowered herself in carefully, trying not to look at the black water sloshing just inches away from her now. She couldn't imagine what the water temperatures must be.

It rocked side to side precariously and she squealed with fright as she sat down quickly, really not convinced this was any way to get into the Christmas spirit. A mince pie worked far better in her opinion.

'Feeling okay?' Aksel asked, as she was pushed away from the steps and found herself floating alongside him.

Admittedly, now she was squarely loaded and on the water, she did feel safer. Each kayak had been threaded with fairy lights so that the canal was brightly illuminated. Above them, on the banks, the trees and ship masts were lit up too so that Darcy felt she could see every single face peering down at her. In front of them, and behind too, sat the multitude of kayakers already buoyant and just waiting for the command to go.

'This is amazing,' she beamed, wide-eyed. 'I've never seen anything like it.' Some of the kayakers had tiny Christmas trees strapped to the backs of their kayaks; others were wearing velvet cloaks and crowns, as if they were kings travelling to Bethlehem.

The backs of their kayaks were gently butted by the newcomers coming up behind them and they were in turn pushed into the backs of the people sitting ahead of them – but it didn't matter. She felt safe. The atmosphere was relaxed and happy. No one was in a rush to get anywhere.

Soon enough, a command was given and like a very, *very* slow Mexican wave, oars were angled out of the water and they began to move. The crowds cheered as the illuminated kayakers began to glide down the canal, a vast body of light slinking through the city's waterways.

Darcy laughed as they went. It was crazy but brilliant! There was simply no possibility of something like this happening on the Thames. The Serpentine lake in Hyde Park, perhaps? But that was tiny compared to this route, and there was nowhere else to go there but round and round.

Aksel grinned, looking over at her as he paddled with ease. She had never seen the city from this perspective. She had thought it would feel cold and dark, but it felt as bright as if they were standing around a bonfire. Everywhere she looked, people were talking and laughing, paddling with easy strokes, as if this was a perfectly normal thing to be doing on a Friday night in December.

She was happy – until they pulled away from the protected wharf, into the wider, more open water of the harbour. Hadn't he said there were no tides? There was a light wind blowing in, whipping up small waves that felt big in a kayak; it was darker, too, as they had only the lights on the kayaks now to throw out a glow, and she was grateful for the large body of people surrounding her. She reminded herself there was safety in numbers, although it made it hard to keep track of Aksel. He had pulled ahead of her, not quite realizing his superior stroke-rate.

'Aksel,' she called, not too loudly. Not wanting to appear frightened in front of all these people. He didn't hear her but she managed to keep him in her sights, his flashing antlers making it easy for her to find him in the crowd.

She decided to paddle in time with the kayaker in front of

her – it seemed like a logical thing to do – but by the time they pulled into the famous Nyhavn harbour twenty minutes later, she was out of breath, blisters beginning to rise on one hand.

Lights shone again, basking them in a golden glow, and the contingent stopped paddling as one, everyone letting their arms rest as the crowds gathered on the bank cheered their arrival. It had been harder work than she had anticipated.

'Darcy! Hey, over here!'

The shout carried over to her and she saw Aksel waving. He was seven kayaks away from her, width-wise, and it was difficult to navigate across to him now everyone was stationary.

'Sorry . . . sorry,' she winced apologetically as she bumped and nudged her way over to him. She could see people giving her irritated looks as they had to help her round them.

'So? What did you think of that?' he asked brightly as she finally got to him. 'There was a bit of a headwind so it was a little harder work than usual.'

She looked back at him in disbelief. 'Aksel, you went ahead without me!' she hissed, trying not to betray the extent of her upset. 'You left me behind!'

'Did I? I thought you were right behind me,' he frowned.

'How could I be right behind you when I've had to get past all these people just now?'

'Oh . . .'

She tried to keep her fear out of her voice. She didn't want to sound whiny or needy . . . 'Aksel, I've never done this before and I told you I was nervous about it . . . You can't abandon me.'

'I didn't *abandon* you!' he protested, a little too vehemently. 'It's not like you can make a wrong turn or get lost! We're all heading in the same direction. You probably wouldn't even need to paddle and the momentum of everyone else would carry you along.'

She looked away at his scorn. If he was trying to reassure her, he was failing. She saw people on the banks looking down at them. Could they tell they were arguing? She felt embarrassed that they were being watched, so conspicuous out here.

She felt her kayak pulled back slightly, bringing her alongside him; they had drifted apart again a little. '. . . Hey, I'm sorry,' Aksel said. 'I really didn't mean to leave you behind like that. I just get so into it, sometimes I forget.'

'It's fine,' she murmured, but her blissful mood had soured somewhat, something of the joy lost now. Could she trust him to look after her on the next leg or was he going to disappear into the night again? All these minor breaches of etiquette that she kept trying to brush off as unimportant suddenly felt so much more pertinent in an environment where she felt unsure of herself. She needed to be able to trust him, but he didn't really make her feel safe.

'Oh – you're glowing,' she said, pointing to the pouch around his neck.

He looked down. 'Huh . . . Well timed.' He unzipped it and reached inside, pulling out his phone.

Only it wasn't his phone that was glowing.

He looked back at her. '. . . It's yours. Do you want it?'

She hesitated. They were mere inches from the water. One fumble . . . 'Can you just see whose name is up?' If it was her mother, or Freja . . .

'Sure, it's . . .' She waited as he peered at it. 'Otto.'

'Otto?' Why was Otto calling her on a Friday evening when all of Denmark was engaged in processions? 'Shit.' She rolled her eyes. 'He's my boss. I'd better take it.'

Aksel passed the phone over and Darcy called Otto back. It felt somewhat surreal to be sitting in Nyhavn, on a brightly lit kayak, in the dark water, making a phone call.

'Otto, hi, you called?' she said quickly.

'Darcy, you need to come in.' He sounded slightly breathless, as if he was walking at pace.

She rolled her eyes. *Another* emergency? 'Otto, I can't this time. I'm sorry.'

'Why not?' he snapped. 'Have you left the country?'

'No, of course not, but—'

'Then you have to come in. They've released the backing.'

'*What?*' She was so shocked, she almost dropped the phone. 'But . . . that's so far ahead of schedule.'

'I know. Everyone's heading over to the Academy now. Get over here as soon as you can. You need to be in this meeting.'

'But—' She looked around her. This couldn't have happened at a worse time. She looked across at Aksel, seeing the apprehension bloom on his face as he watched her. 'Otto, I'm in Nyhavn. On the canal. I'm in a kayak, on the water.'

'Then get out of it and get a cab! Keep the receipt.'

'But Otto—' she protested. '. . . Otto?'

He had hung up.

'Bad news?' Aksel asked in a flat tone.

'He's at the Academy. He's insisting I go over there right now . . . They've managed to release the portrait.'

His shoulders slumped. 'Right this minute? Can't it wait an hour, at least?'

'I'm sorry, they're calling a meeting. I have to be there.'

He was quiet for a moment, then he shrugged. 'Well, sorry, no. You can't go.'

She stared at him, not sure she'd heard correctly. 'What?'

'I said you can't go. They'll have to wait. We've got plans . . .

302

Look at us!' He pointed to their all-too-evident predicament on the water.

'I know, Aksel, I told him that – but I still have to go.'

'And I'm saying no.' He stared at her with a level expression.

She gave a disbelieving laugh, really not sure if he was being serious or not. It wasn't like she wanted to leave, but he couldn't honestly think he had the right to detain her here against her will either? 'Are you . . . are you messing with me?'

'Do I look like I'm messing?' His stare had grown cold, those eyes she had thought soulful now looking back at her blankly.

There was a long pause.

'I'm sorry,' she said finally. 'I'm sorry to leave to you here like this but I really don't have a choice. I'm needed there.'

'Fucking unbelievable,' he muttered, shaking his head.

She was taken aback by the level of his resentment. '. . . What?'

'There's so much *drama* with you, Darcy. Emergency meetings that can't happen without you! Depressed housemates who simply have to talk to you alone! Hostile dress couriers who want to punch my face in.'

She stared at him. Where was this coming from? 'You turned up at my door, uninvited! And as I recall, *you* were the one creating drama earlier in the week.'

A flash of anger tightened across his face. 'Oh, there it is! I knew it would come out sooner or later! You've just been waiting for a chance to throw that back in my face!'

'That's not true,' she gasped, seeing the scale of his rage. 'You're the one—'

'Just go, then! Fuck off!' he blurted suddenly, reaching over and roughly shoving her kayak away from his – but he caught her at an awkward angle and she wobbled wildly, having to grab the sides to stop from falling in. She cried out in terror, certain she was about to plunge into the black water.

'Hey! Hey!' She looked up to find a marshal pointing at them both. 'Stop that! You know the terms of conduct!'

'What the fuck are you doing, man?' another guy in the kayak beside her shouted, looking straight at Aksel. 'You almost knocked her in!'

Darcy tried to catch her breath, deeply shaken by what had just occurred. All around them, people were staring, frowning, watching them. There were children here. Families . . .

She felt her cheeks burn, shock and fright swirling and making her shake. Everything had escalated so quickly. She couldn't believe he had forcibly tried to push her into the water!

She glanced across at him and he was glowering at her with an expression that chilled her blood. In a flash, she understood; she needed to get away from him. '. . . C-could I get out, please?' she called up, desperately.

The marshal stared at her, glancing at Aksel before looking at her again. Did she look – sound – as frightened as she felt? He nodded, beckoning for her to paddle in towards the steps.

She didn't look back again at Aksel as she paddled past him and he made no move to stop her, nor to apologize. She just wanted to get away from him and back onto terra firma as quickly as possible. She was deeply shaken by his flash of temper. There'd been no inkling he could turn like that, and she didn't want to think what he might have been capable of if they'd been alone.

Someone shouted around the harbour and there was a shuffling of paper as she made her way towards the docking platform. All around her, everyone began to sing 'Silent

Night', their voices echoing over the water so that it sounded cathedral-like.

The marshal reached out as she approached, grasping the prow and guiding her alongside the jetty. 'Everything okay?' he asked, leaning down to secure the boat with one hand, grasping her wrist with the other and helping pull her ashore.

'. . . It is now,' she said shakily.

'What happened?'

'I – I just said something he didn't like.' She shouldn't have said it, she thought to herself. She should have known it would be a touchy subject. No man wanted to be reminded of his failure to perform.

'Do you need medical attention? First aid?'

'No, nothing like that . . .'

'Do you want to file a report against him?'

'. . . No.' She squeezed her eyes shut and took a breath, trying to remain calm. Composed. She just wanted to get away from here. 'Uh, what should I do with the kayak?'

'Don't worry, we'll deal with that,' the man said with a concerned look. 'They all go back to the same place.'

'Okay.' Darcy glanced back, finding Aksel alone in the crowd, bobbing on the water. He wasn't looking her way, but was staring ahead with a dark look. How could she have got him so wrong? She was trembling a little, her breathing shallow from the shock. She had a fierce urge to cry.

'You can't stay here, miss,' the marshal said kindly. 'You'll need to get up on the bank.'

'Okay, y-yes.' Darcy turned and made her way up the steps to where the crowds stood ten deep, people shuffling a few paces to the side as she tried to slink through inconspicuously even though she was bulky and unwieldy in her protective gear.

Her phone buzzed – another message from Otto, telling her to hurry up.

She looked back one last time, but the canal – and Aksel – was hidden from her sights. She tapped on the Uber app and made her getaway.

She squeaked as she walked. The security officers had laughed at her as she gave her name at the door. It felt ridiculous walking through such a hallowed institution gloved in neoprene and tinsel.

Heads turned as her inelegant approach was heard. Margit Kinberg did a double take; Helle Foss's eyes narrowed; Otto frowned as if he'd not in fact been told she was sitting on a kayak in Nyhavn when he had called.

'Please, don't dress up on our account,' Helle quipped.

'My things are still in the locker,' Darcy replied in a quiet voice. The upset from their fight on the water had settled into her bones now and she couldn't quite shake it. She felt subdued and just wanted to crawl into her bed. 'We'd already left when you called and there was no time to get back there.' She hadn't even taken off the lifejacket. There was nowhere to leave it and she only risked losing it; she would have to go back over there in the morning to return this kit and pick up her things.

She glanced at Max. He was staring at her as if she was a riddle (or perhaps a joke). Too late, she remembered her antlers, still flashing on her head. Could he guess she'd been on a date? Did he know it was with the same guy who had stood, bare-chested and drinking wine, in front of him at her door? She knew he couldn't possibly imagine what had just happened with the kind vet with the soulful eyes who turned out to have problems with anger, performance and alcohol.

He looked away again in the next instant; he was wearing jeans and a sweater. Weekend Max. Had he not had any plans tonight? He didn't celebrate Christmas, of course, but did he not even have a St Lucia's party to go to? A model to pick up? He hadn't responded to her thank-you text on Sunday evening; nor had he picked up on Monday when she had called, determined to pay for the dress. He was ghosting her.

'I got here as soon as I could.' She felt tearful, and perhaps there was a suggestion of that in her voice, because Otto put a hand on her shoulder.

'It's quite all right, Darcy. We were busy inspecting it ourselves anyway. This is the first time we've drawn breath . . . Take a look.'

He stepped back, creating a space for her around the table, just as he had a couple of weeks ago when she'd received a similar call – but this time the UV lamp was turned off, no longer needed. Instead *Her Children*, delicately held up in a specialist clamp, had been turned around and there, affixed on the back, lay Lilja Madsen's portrait.

Darcy gasped as she laid eyes upon it – upon *her* – unobscured for the first time. Her hands flew to her mouth as she took in the painting clearly now. Immediately she looked at everyone else in surprise – did they see it too? – but they were all watching her with blank expressions.

'Have a good look, Darcy,' Margit instructed. 'We need confirmation if it's her.'

Darcy hesitated. Were they serious? Couldn't they see . . . ? But she wasn't going to disobey the director of the National Gallery and she bent forward, wetsuit squeaking ignominiously, so that she was at eye level with the portrait.

The colours were far more vivid than she had expected – the

flesh tones suffused with yellow ochre, as per Vermeer, to add luminosity and imbue a sense of flushed radiance and youth. Lilja's dress was green with delicate pink buds and had a narrow lace frill at the neck. The red necklace lay behind it, winking through the lattices, only the gilded central bead clearly visible front and centre at her throat. And on her shoulder, Darcy saw now what had been indistinct before – not a dead fox stole, as Otto had speculated, but a robin, beautifully fat, with a tomato-red chest.

The background was unfinished but the impasto looked deliberately done, as if reinforcing the point that the painting's only focus was this young woman's face. The strong brushwork in green earth suggested trees: an exterior sitting.

'So there you are,' Darcy whispered, looking into her eyes at last. They were round and light brown, flecked with gold. She had freckles too, and a tan, and though her hair was pulled back in a loose braid, wisps of baby hair sprouted from her temple, as if she'd been caught in the wind. Had she just come in from one of her beach walks?

It was a startlingly lovely rendering. Now that she could see details and not just shapes, the painting offered so much more narrative. She could tell that the Lilja who had been painted here was different to the Lilja standing in the photograph by the water's edge; she had filled out, yes, but more than that, she had survived something terrible. She had lived through unimaginable pain and loss. The tilt of her head had always been distinctive even in silhouette, but now Darcy was able to see the look in her eyes, she could see this was an older, wiser, stronger Lilja. She would have been around eighteen here but she had already endured so much. The girl had become a woman. She was coming into her own.

. . . So what had happened that made her walk into the sea? Darcy saw a date lightly traced in the bottom right corner: *August 1922.*

Darcy frowned; Lilja had been dead by the month's end.

Someone – Max? – cleared his throat impatiently, as if reminding her to get on with it; this was everyone's Friday night. Slowly, Darcy straightened up. 'Yes. That's definitely Lilja Madsen.'

Margit's look of displeasure showed it was not the answer she had hoped to hear. 'How can you be so certain?'

'The necklace, for one – we have photographs of her wearing it. Her hairstyle, for another.'

'. . . What about the hairstyle?'

'Lotte Madsen's diaries tell us Lilja wore hers in a braid. It was distinctive for its lack of refinement for a married woman and indicative of her inability to function beyond a subsistence level while she was unwell.'

Margit sighed. 'I see. Anything else?'

'Yes – the robin.' She glanced at it again, as if checking her thoughts. 'Lilja was left physically weakened by her son's birth and she was severely depressed after his death. She was sent to convalesce at the Madsens' country retreat in Hornbaek. Sea air and beach walks were her prescription, but it appears the garden became a real refuge for her. She took many photos of it while she was there.'

'But why should the robin indicate this is Lilja?'

'Because the robin is well known as the gardener's friend. I believe it's being used here as a motif to indicate the garden as her source of strength during recovery.'

Darcy watched as Otto and Margit swapped silent looks. She could feel Helle and Max listening intently.

'I see. Thank you, Darcy.' Margit's face was pinched.

Darcy looked from her to Otto. She looked at Max, too; for once he appeared to have nothing to say.

She gave a small, astonished laugh, as no one appeared to be asking about the elephant in the room. 'Um? So, are we going to address the main revelation, now that we can actually see the painting . . . ?'

Everyone looked back at her, their expressions closed. Surely they couldn't seriously *not* see it?

'This isn't a Johan Trier painting!' she said bluntly.

'We don't know that for sure,' Helle said quickly.

'Uh, we do,' Darcy argued, looking at her in utter disbelief. 'His figuring is completely different, not to mention his brush-work—'

'He was well known for trying different styles.'

'He *never* used smalt pigment and there are no other portraits by him done in an outdoor setting,' Darcy continued, unabashed. She knew she was right. 'Johan Trier did not paint this and it will take any reputable assessor all of three minutes to prove that.' She looked around at everyone, not under-standing their lack of consensus on what was clearly obvious.

'Well, this is clearly a rolling situation,' Helle said quietly. 'It is good to have a confirmed subject, if not artist. We are pleased this is a portrait of Lilja Madsen, but clearly we all would have preferred this portrait to be by Trier's hand.' Helle's gaze ran sceptically over Darcy's reindeer antlers and tinsel-strapped chest, as if they somehow threw her profes-sional opinion into doubt. 'Your work to this point has been helpful, Miss Cotterell. Thank you.'

Darcy frowned at what sounded like a dismissal. 'You're not abandoning the research, are you?' she asked Margit. 'Whether or not it's a Trier, that portrait is part of *Her Children*'s legacy now. Visitors will still want to know about it. Unless . . .'

She startled at the thought. 'You're not intending to cover it up again?'

'Absolutely not. The announcements have been made.'

'So, then, I'll need to continue as before,' she pressed. 'We need to find out who painted it, if not Trier. How it ended up boarded to the back of this painting. Why was it put there?' *They think now the portrait went in wet.* 'We need to give it the full art history treatment.'

'We must be realistic. If this portrait is not Trier's work, then public interest will be markedly less,' Helle shrugged. 'Margit can't justify spending—'

'That's fine, Darcy,' Margit interrupted. She looked furious. 'Continue as you were. You're working on *our* behalf, after all. Not Madsen's.' Margit looked pointedly at Helle until the other woman turned away.

Darcy frowned, baffled by Helle's newly dismissive attitude towards the portrait, as if it was inconsequential now. She looked again at it, for some reason loving it even more, even though – without Trier's signature – it was almost inherently worthless. There was something alive in Lilja's gaze; it captured Darcy and drew her in, as if Lilja's whispers were trapped in the paint, a past still beating within this present.

'I imagine the possibility of this portrait being the work of another artist will be a complication for your restitution claim?' Margit said coolly to Max.

'Possibly. We'll take advice.'

He was being unnaturally quiet, Darcy thought, watching as he shook Margit's hand, preparing to leave. He seemed in a hurry to get away.

Otto, beside her, turned towards the window and stood looking out into the dark courtyard with a troubled expression. Darcy went over to him.

'Otto, will my expenses cover a research trip up to Hornbaek?'

He looked at her. 'Why do you want to go there?'

'I think I should visit. Solvtraeer was an important place to Lilja. She lived there for her last few years and she died there. I think it's most likely where the portrait was painted. Obviously, Trier was based in the studio and painting *Her Children* up there that summer, so there may still be a link between him and it. I do think it would be helpful to go there myself and I can be there and back in a day. I appreciate the house may no longer be standing . . .'

'No, it's still there.'

'It is?' She was surprised. 'Well, great. I'll knock on the door and see if the owners would mind me looking in the garden – but even if I can't go in, just to see it and get the feel of the place would be useful.'

Otto glanced over her shoulder. 'Would that be possible, Max? For Darcy to visit Solvtraeer?'

'Oh – does the Foundation still own the estate?' It had never occurred to her.

'Not the Foundation, no,' Otto said. 'But Max does.'

Darcy looked at him. *He* owned the house Lilja Madsen had lived in?

'His grandmother was a Madsen. Didn't you know?' Otto asked.

'Thank you, Otto, for the family history,' Max said sharply.

Darcy took a breath as she absorbed the news. It made sense – the quiet wealth, the air of entitlement, his trustee status and big job; his over-interest in anything to do with this family. *His* family, it turned out.

A beat pulsed as she awaited his verdict. She would hardly be the most welcome houseguest.

312

Helle stepped forward. 'What's really to be gained from thi—'

'If she wants to see it, she can,' Max said flatly, bringing his attention onto Darcy at last. 'The house and gardens are largely as they were, although I don't know what you expect to find there.'

She shrugged. Neither did she.

'I'm driving up tomorrow. I was actually heading up there tonight when the call came in for this.'

'. . . Tomorrow would be great.' She swallowed. 'I'll get the train up.'

There was a pause. 'Fine.'

His eyes were cold. He was looking at her like she was nothing to him, even though he had stood in her hallway and saved her with his gift; he had held her to him and given her his heartbeat to follow when her own had lost control. He had shown her, despite his best efforts to prove otherwise, that he was flesh and blood too; just a man.

But it was hard to believe, standing here now in their enemy camps. He was so far away from her that he might as well be on the moon.

'Fine.'

Chapter Twenty-Three

'Freja? Are you here?' Darcy called, pulling her key from the door. She had seen the lights shining through from the kitchen. 'I thought you were going out with Tristan?'

There was no reply. No music playing, no voices on the TV, not the bang and clatter of pots, nor the sound of running water from the shower.

'. . . Frey?'

Darcy stopped in her tracks as she rounded the corner to find Freja standing in the kitchen, the two red Valentino dresses hanging from cupboard knobs at either side of her. Beauty and the beast.

Her flatmate twirled her hands out questioningly. 'Anything you want to tell me?'

'I . . .' Darcy felt the blood pool at her feet. Oh God. '. . . I can explain.'

'I thought you might say that.' Freja folded her arms across her chest, waiting. Darcy had never seen her look so forbidding. 'Go on, then.'

Darcy took pigeon steps into the room, oblivious now to the fact that she was still wearing a wetsuit and lifejacket. 'It's not what you think . . .'

'No? You mean you didn't steal my dress and ruin it?'

'. . . Yes, but . . . not *blithely*. I didn't just take it because I wanted to! There was a crisis while you were in Amsterdam. I tried to contact you, to explain, to ask if . . .' She held her hands out appeasingly. Pleadingly. 'I called you six times, Freja.'

'So it's *my* fault?'

'No!' Darcy said hurriedly. 'I'm not saying that at all. Things just . . . developed quickly. There was no time; I was in the situation before I knew what was happening. I was trying to help Otto out, and I said yes to him, thinking I could wear the black velvet dress. Only . . . you had it. Which was totally fine, of course. But by the time I realized I had nothing to wear, the car was on its way over here to get me, and . . .' She blinked. 'I swear, I would gladly have worn my pyjamas if I possibly could have, but it was a royal event. The King and Queen were there!'

Freja's eyebrows raised a little at that. '. . . Go on.'

Darcy stared at her with wide eyes. 'I am *so* sorry for taking it. I shouldn't have done – I should have called Otto back and said I couldn't make it. I hated wearing a dress that I knew had such huge emotional significance for you.'

'And yet you still did.'

'I swear on my life, I was being so careful. I lay flat in the car on the way over so I wouldn't crease it at the hips. But this man who was talking to me . . . someone jogged his arm, and his wine went all over me.' She gazed pleadingly at her friend. 'Freja, you have no idea how sick I've felt about it all. It's been on my mind every day since. It was awful not telling you.'

'Was it though? You had got away with it. You got another one.'

Darcy bit her lip as Freja's eyes narrowed.

'. . . *How* did you get another one so quickly? I was back the next night.'

Oh God. This was getting worse.

'Darce!' Freja snapped. 'Answer me.'

Darcy swallowed. 'Max came round the next day with a new one.'

'*What?*'

'I know, that was my reaction. I never asked him to. I couldn't believe it when . . . He said his girlfriend has a contact there.'

'His girlfriend?'

Darcy shrugged. 'One of them.'

'So you're telling me Valentino just opened up for him on a Sunday, and he came round with an identical six-thousand-euro gown—'

Six? 'He said they gifted it.'

'Valentino doesn't *gift* evening gowns, Darcy! To Bella Hadid, maybe!'

Darcy felt herself crumple. 'I know!' she protested. 'That's what I thought too, but he won't let me pay him back! He won't even talk to me. He's ghosting all my messages.'

Freja frowned, a silence lengthening as one crisis was superseded by another. 'Why? Why do all that and then blank you?'

'I don't know,' Darcy shrugged.

Freja's eyebrows shrugged back. 'I don't believe you. Clearly something had to have happened.'

Darcy bit her lip. 'There was an unfortunate sequence of events when he brought the dress over.'

'Unfortunate how?'

'Aksel opened the door to him. He was in just his jeans. It was pretty clear we'd been . . . interrupted.'

'So then he's jealous?'

'No!'

'He's jealous!'

'No! The man only dates models.' Darcy groaned, slapping her hand over her forehead and rubbing it down her cheek. She felt too drained for this conversation. 'I've yet to see him with the same girl twice.'

'And yet he kissed you.'

'He was using me! He was making me work at his place so he could spy on me and see what I was discovering about this painting he wanted to buy.'

'*Spying* on you?'

Darcy sighed. She'd had a long day and an even longer night; this was not what she needed right now. 'There's stuff going on at work I can't talk about. Legal stuff. But he and I are on opposing teams and it's not pretty. He plays dirty.'

'Yeah – clearly anyone who kisses your hair and comes all the way over here with a designer dress to save your skin must be a complete fucking monster.'

'Exactly,' Darcy muttered. Then she frowned. 'Wait.' She looked at Freja. '. . . How do you know he kissed my hair?'

Freja held up her phone, a cunning look in her eyes. 'Three million likes and counting.'

'What is?'

'How do you think I found out in the first place?' Freja asked, turning her phone to show a paused TikTok on the screen. She pressed play and the image panned from a *LADIES* sign on the door of a hotel bathroom to the push plate. Filmed through a narrow opening, a man in a black dinner suit stood with his back to the camera, his phone to his ear and his other arm holding something out of sight.

Darcy felt her blood run cold, already knowing what she was going to see. She could feel Freja's stare upon her, gauging her reaction.

Max returned the phone to his pocket, said something inaudible, dropped his head momentarily to hers, then slowly started turning towards the door. As he came around, he saw the phone, looking straight into the screen just as Darcy herself came into shot, wiping her cheeks. For three seconds, the full extent of the damage to the dress was clear as Max broke away from her and moved ahead to the door. The camera pulled away suddenly, the door closing before he could get to it; there was a flash of carpet, and then it was turned off.

Darcy was stunned. She had no idea who had taken this, but written in bright white type across the top was the Gen Z-favourite caption: *If he wanted to, he would*.

'You didn't know?'

'No,' Darcy whispered. 'Of course not. Who would . . . who would do that?'

'A fairy godmother it appears,' Freja shrugged. 'Someone who saw what you and he seem blind to – that he cares about you, Darcy. Whether he wants to or not.'

'. . . He's a player.'

'Well, then, the player got played.'

Darcy didn't reply. It was everything she wanted to hear, and yet . . . she'd seen the coldness in Max's eyes again tonight. In spite of what this TikTok suggested, she knew he wouldn't let her close. If they kept falling together, he also kept pushing her away and he wouldn't stop until she didn't come back.

He was alone, and that was exactly how he wanted it. A few tears began to slide down her cheeks.

Freja's eyebrows arched to a point. '. . . Hey, don't look so sad. I'm sorry for being a bitch. I was just shocked, you know?' She walked over and curled her arms around Darcy in a hug.

'And you were right to be. You shouldn't be the one being nice to me,' Darcy sniffed. 'It's just been a shit day. Everything's gone wrong. Max hates me, and Aksel, well he basically tried to push me into the canal.'

'*What?*' Freja pulled back.

'I was so wrong about him. He turned on me because I had to cut our date short. When I tell you he's a nasty piece of work . . .' She rubbed her eyes, not caring that she was giving herself panda eyes. 'I think he might have a drink problem. I'm not sure. Anger issues, definitely.'

Freja's grip tightened around her. 'Jesus,' she murmured, the two of them standing in silence together. 'He looked so sweet too.'

After a few moments, Darcy found Freja's hand and she squeezed it. '. . . I really am so sorry for what I did. I'll never forgive myself.'

'Yeah, well,' Freja sighed after a minute. 'What did you really do?'

'I stole your dress.'

'Because you were panicking.' She shrugged. 'I'd have done the same.'

Darcy pulled back to look at her. 'But it was special! You'd bought it for this really precious moment.'

'Which didn't happen.' Freja made a face, beginning to pace. 'I didn't even go in the end.'

'What?' Darcy was stunned. 'You didn't go to the awards thing?'

'I pretended I was sick and went back to my parents' for the night. I needed to think.'

'You couldn't think *here*?'

Freja rolled her eyes. 'I didn't want you to see me being so pathetic.'

'But you were upset about Amsterdam. That's not pathetic! You thought he was going to propose to you. It's a big thing!'

'I don't know why I can't just let it go?' Freja said, throwing her hands out. 'We're obviously not as far down the road as I had thought. The stupid thing is, I didn't even want to get married until he *didn't* ask! . . . I just got ahead of myself and now I feel like an idiot.'

'You are not an idiot. You are just in love, and that makes you a fool. Different thing entirely.'

'Ha.'

Darcy was quiet for a moment. 'At least you've still got a lovely Valentino dress hanging in your wardrobe.'

'So do you now,' Freja said, giving her side-eye.

'Not the same!' Darcy laughed. 'It looks like I went to war in it!'

Freja winced. 'Can you get it dry cleaned?'

'I'll take it in and see what they can do but I don't think it'll ever look right. A dress like that has to be flawless and I'm sure some marks will remain.'

'Even so – give it a go. Take it in tomorrow and see what they can do.'

'I can't tomorrow. I'm going to Hornbaek for the day. More research.'

'On the weekend?'

'I'm going to the Madsens' old summer house, and I can only get in while the owner's there.'

'Oh.'

Darcy took a breath, not wanting to keep any more secrets. '. . . Max being the owner. Turns out his grandmother was a Madsen. He's going up there for the weekend and he said I can pop in and have a look around.'

'Oh!' Freja said, a smile beginning to play on her lips. 'Well, that's very decent of him.'

'Yeah.'

'Reckon he'll be spying on you?'

Darcy cracked a grin at her sarcasm. 'Obviously.'

'Yeah.' Freja grinned back. 'Well, I'm sure it'll be as uneventful as my weekend in Amsterdam and *nothing will happen*.'

Darcy met her eyes. 'We can but hope.'

Chapter Twenty-Four

The train pulled into the single-track station, coming to rest outside a red-roofed, white building. *Hornbaek* was written on a plaque. Darcy disembarked, waiting for a couple with a toddler and a pram to go ahead as she got her bearings. The station sat immediately on the street and it took her only a few seconds to locate the direction of the sea, for the wind was blowing hard: salt in the air, a few gulls wheeling on the thermals high above. An hour further north than Copenhagen, it was bitterly cold and distinctly more exposed. The temperatures had to be several degrees colder than the capital and she was beginning to feel her padded running coat wasn't quite sufficient. (She had picked it up, along with her bag, from the kayak bar this morning as she returned the wetsuit and lifejacket; she'd told the guy to charge the overnight extra day's rental to the card Aksel had used to pay the deposit. If he dared to invoice her this time . . .)

She headed straight for the beach, wishing she had packed a hat. According to Google Maps, Solvtraeer was set along the coast road, just out of the village, and she figured she couldn't go wrong if she made for the water and took a left. Max had sent through an address but no directions or cab numbers, and had made no offer to come and collect her.

Not that she needed him to. She was a big girl. Here to work and get straight back to the city again.

The town was smaller than she had expected and very quiet. She looked around nosily as she walked down the streets, peering into the low buildings, most of which were painted black on the outside and white on the inside. There were very few people about. It was a seasonal resort, like Cornwall in England or the Hamptons in the United States – heaving in the summer months, deserted for the rest of the year. But she caught glimpses of the high season, pressed on pause: plastic buckets and spades tucked into corners of small gardens, children's trikes toppled onto their sides from high winds, dinghies and small boats sitting on axels on driveways, covered with tarps. She could tell the year-round properties from the holiday homes by the state of the pot plants on the sills and whether there were lights on in distant rooms. It wasn't yet lunchtime but light was scant, thick grey clouds rolled out like cotton wool wadding over a wide sky.

Within a few minutes, as she turned right and then left, she could feel the breeze pick up and the tall masts of the boats in the marina came into view above the low roofs. She passed a chandlery and an ice cream parlour, some boarded-up cafes. It always felt poignant visiting a place during its hibernation, as if life had been suspended: *Please come back later.*

But Darcy wasn't trying to imagine the town as it would be during its summer peak; she was trying to see it as it might have been a hundred years ago. Had this tree been here? That house? What had Lilja Madsen seen as she walked along the sand, mourning her child, while her own parents were trapped over a distant border? Had she missed her husband, sent abroad to build upon the company's fortunes while she grieved here alone?

Almost to her surprise, she found herself standing on the coast road. The town ended abruptly, fronting onto a wide, golden beach. Across the water were the distant mountains of Sweden, just purple shadows from here.

To her right she could see the fishing boats in the harbour, sleek yachts, and a large, grand hotel squaring over the marina. It had a modern edge with cafes and restaurants, chalked blackboards and boutiques, and she knew it was the beating heart of summer living here. To her left the beach spun away in a vast arc, empty and timeless, with shallow sloping dunes at its back. Her long hair was blown back off her neck as she watched the white horses gallop over a battleship-grey sea, indolent waves slumping on the shore, long grasses bent low in prostration. It had always been like this. It would always be like this. It was the view Lilja would have known, the one that had restored her – for a time, at least.

Until it hadn't.

Darcy walked slowly, shivering as she tried to take in her first moments here. She couldn't say exactly why she had wanted to come, only that she had felt compelled to make the journey. Otto didn't understand it; his academic stance was dry and factual – dates, places, achievement – but Darcy needed more than that. She had to see the characters she studied as living people; she had to find their pulse to capture their soul. And if Lilja's likeness was about to be revealed to the world after almost a century in the dark, the very least Darcy could do was shine a light into the deepest corners.

She saw two figures on the sand in the distance and what appeared to be a dog chasing after a ball; they were little more than black dots from here and Darcy watched, seeing them enjoy this simple pleasure as the man threw the ball and the dog chased it. Humans, for all their advancements, were still

simple creatures, repeating the same behaviours of their fore-
bears: walking barefoot on beaches, shouting secrets into the
wind. It had all been done before. And as she saw, in her
mind's eye, Lilja's body rolling in the shallows, she knew there
was nothing unique in that either. Humans were really quite
predictable, when pushed.

It was the same, but different. The sea lay at Darcy's back,
closer than she had imagined, as she stood at the brick pillars
and looked in at the garden that had become so familiar to
her eye in recent days. Of course, the trees were stiff-fingered
and bare of their leaves, no flowers in bloom at this time of
year, but the dense clusters of narrow silver birch trunks –
affording glimpses of the land and house beyond – were still
the same. The estate sat a short distance from the town,
enclosed within woodland. She imagined the villagers and
tourists gathering here to admire the famous gardens, the
bow-armed orchard trees heady with blossom, flower beds
thick with scent and colour, butterflies weaving through the
long meadow grasses speckled with poppies and clover and
drifts of forget-me-nots.

She saw the gracious curve of the drive meander left and
up towards the house, a sleek dark grey car sitting in front of
a garage to the left. It wasn't the car Christoff had driven her
home in, or in which she'd travelled with Max the day of the
Christmas market; this was sportier, smaller, low-slung.

She took a few steps in, feeling herself caught in a tension
between now and the past. Her mind wanted to stay on Lilja:
what she must have seen and felt as she walked barefoot and
bereft on the grass. Had she been happy to see Lotte, her
sister-in-law, as she looked up from talking with Old Sally,
that day on the lawn?

But there were lights on in the house, and Darcy couldn't pretend she wasn't distracted knowing that Max was in there. Was he waiting for her? Was he looking out?

The house came into view as she moved past the trees. It was a handsome red brick, diagonally strapped with black timbers and topped with a thick thatched roof with five humped gables. Smoke was puffing sedately from a chimney, another sign someone was inside. It was a large, substantial house, yet it had a comforting feel too. It was homely, not grand. She could see exactly why Lilja would have loved it here.

The car, she saw now, was an Audi R8. What had sat here in its place when Lotte and Henrik had come to stay, or when Casper had returned from London? She remembered a pony trap that had just edged into view in some of the pictures. Had Lilja enjoyed going out for rides on that?

A door opened – not the front door, but one at the side – and Max appeared. Saturday Max. Jeans, another cashmere jumper. Socks.

'You found it, then.'

No hello. Obviously.

'Yes. I had a nice walk along the beach,' she said, drawing closer.

'Nice? If you say so,' he said, looking out at the dreary weather. '. . . Were you warm enough?' He looked sceptically at her short jacket.

'Yes,' she lied.

'You should wear a hat.'

'. . . Okay, Dad.'

She stopped in front of him and there was a moment in which they both hesitated as the tension – from the meeting last night, the other morning, last weekend – lingered. Then he allowed a reluctant half-smile.

'You'd better come in.'

She followed him in, through a brick-floored boot room with deep blue-grey wainscoting – coats hanging on pegs, welly boots on sticks – and into the kitchen. It had pale wooden strip floors that looked to be original, black wooden cabinets and open shelving. The walls were lime-washed and a large black range that looked like an Aga, but wasn't Aga, dominated the back wall. There was a large old prep table in the middle of the space with copper pans underneath, but unlike in Max's Copenhagen house, here there was only a small round dining table, set before double doors that opened onto the garden. No island. No bar stools. It managed to be somehow both a period room and contemporary at the same time.

'Oh,' she breathed as her gaze cast around. '. . . It's so lovely.' Instinctively she walked over to the doors and looked out. The lawn swept down and away from the room, like a bridal veil fanning from a tiara. The deep flower beds flanked the doors, pushing out in ergonomic curves as if jostling for more space.

Ah, that's what it is, she thought to herself.

'What?' Max was standing by the back counter, watching her, one ankle crossed over the other.

She realized she'd spoken out loud. 'I was just thinking about how there are no straight lines out there. Everything's curved and natural . . . It's what makes the garden feel so soft.'

'Soft?' Max considered her words. '. . . I guess so. I've never thought of it that way before.'

She turned back into the room, embarrassed by her observation.

'. . . Coffee?'

She nodded. 'Sure. It'll warm me up.'

'So you are cold,' he said, over his shoulder. 'Go and stand by the range.'

She did as she was told, watching as he poured water into a Bialetti moka pot.

'Have you eaten?'

'. . . Yes,' she fibbed.

He looked back over at her. 'You're an appalling liar.'

'You say that like it's a bad thing.'

He made no comment. In his world, it probably was.

She watched as he made the coffee just the way she liked it. He knew that about her now. She didn't know it about him, though. Everything was one-sided. His terms. His coffee. His homes.

'Thanks for letting me pop by today. I appreciate it.'

He shrugged.

'I had no idea Solvtraeer was yours.'

'And I suppose if you had, you wouldn't have come?'

She swallowed at the sarcasm. 'What I mean is – I didn't know if this house was even still here.'

'Where would it have gone?'

'I don't know. It might have been bulldozed,' she shrugged. 'Torn down for some mega glass cube in the noughties.'

He seemed bemused by the thought. 'We're not really that sort of family.'

'No.' She watched him, understanding that meant the house had always been in their possession. 'I also had no idea you were a Madsen.'

'It's not something I tend to lead with,' he muttered. 'Besides, I'm not. I'm a Lorensen. My great-grandmother, Lilja, was the Madsen.' He glanced over at her, as if checking his words had registered.

'Lilja was your great-grandmother?' she echoed. She remembered his shocked reaction when Lilja had first been identified. He had looked stunned, in fact. But even when she had learned he was a Madsen, she had presumed he was a distant relative. Madsen Minor.

'And her daughter, Emme, my grandmother – she was a Madsen too, until she married a Lorensen and had a son, my father. And here we are.'

She was quiet for a moment, absorbing this news. 'I feel like I should have been told this sooner.'

'Why? How is it relevant?'

She looked around the room again. 'I don't know. I just feel like it is, somehow. Like maybe that's why you've been so . . .' But her words trailed away as he set the pot on the gas and turned back to her.

'So – what? Interested in what you're doing? It's my job.'

'Actually, I was going to say aggressive.'

He looked surprised. 'You think I'm aggressive?'

'Professionally, yes. Not . . .' She stopped herself, not wanting to stray into what she thought of him personally. 'But maybe that's the wrong word.'

'What's the right one, then?' he challenged.

She stared back at him, seeing the vast expanse of space between them. He couldn't get any further away from her without leaving the room. '. . . Defensive.'

'How have I been defensive? I've given you unrestricted access to our archives. I've let you come up here.' He shrugged. 'I'm making you *coffee*.'

She swallowed, knowing he was right – and yet, she wasn't wrong either. He was frustrating to argue with. 'I don't know,' she sighed, trying not to show her frustration. He could twist words. 'I just feel like you're always very . . . watchful. Like you're watching me closely.'

'Yes, I know what watchful means, thanks.'

She rolled her eyes, not quite sure how serious he was being. His humour erred on the extremely dry side. *Brut.*

'Well, now that you've confirmed, once and for all, that the portrait is of my great-grandmother, I guess I'm going to be even more interested. Aggressive. Defensive. Watchful . . . Delete as appropriate.'

She looked down. Without Otto or Margit's mitigating presence, she was no match for his careless sarcasm. An awkward silence grew between them.

He cleared his throat as if seeing her retreat. '. . . If I'm watchful of you, Darcy, it's only because I think you're beautiful,' he said quietly. 'Nothing more sinister than that.'

She looked up, taken aback by the unexpected compliment – his honesty could be disarming at times – but he had already turned away and was reaching for some cups.

Neither of them spoke again until the coffee was poured.

'So what is it you want to see here?' he asked, coming over and handing her a cup. Closing the gap.

'I'm not entirely sure. I just had a feeling that I should see it.'

He looked sceptical again. 'Is your work often directed by "feelings"?'

She ignored the sarcasm this time. 'Not usually. But I have some questions my mind keeps snagging on. I thought it would help to come here.' She had no intention of mentioning to him the various discrepancies she had noted.

He watched her, as if he could read her every thought. 'Well, you're welcome to look around, I guess.'

'Thanks. Are there any photo albums here?'

His eyes narrowed. 'Only more recent ones. Nothing that concerns the Foundation's work or needs to be in the public eye.'

She nodded, wondering if this defensiveness concerned his brother. '. . . Do you come up here often?'

'Pretty often. I like it best at this time of year, when it's quiet. The crowds get a bit much in the summer.'

'Yes. I can imagine.' She watched as he wandered over to the fridge and pulled out a stock pot. He couldn't seem to stand still, or certainly he couldn't stand near her. For the first time, she wondered if her presence here made *him* nervous.

'Soup. Which I didn't make,' he muttered, as if to deflect any intended compliments. He put it in the range, in the oven beside her. It was funny, somehow, seeing him with oven gloves on. Domestic Max.

'Will you come up here over Christmas?'

'Yes. I always do.' He pulled off the gloves, tossing them casually onto the counter. 'You? What are your plans?'

'Working through.'

He frowned, seeming surprised. 'You're not going home?'

'My sister's travelling on her gap year, so my family are going to join her for ten days in Asia. I'd go, but I'm really behind on my thesis. I can't afford to spend ten days on a beach.'

'That's a shame.'

'Yeah.'

'Where's home for you?'

'Berkshire. Sort of west of London.'

'I know it,' he nodded. 'I've played golf at Sunningdale.'

Of course he had. She sighed, looking out at the garden, knowing her father – a resident there for thirty-eight years – would give his eye-teeth for an opportunity like that.

'That wasn't intended as a name-drop. It's just my only reference,' Max muttered, seeing her irritation.

She looked back at him but he was crossing to the far side

331

of the room again, running his hands through his hair with a sigh. They were talking at cross purposes again, it seemed.

'Look, it's your Saturday and I'm intruding,' she said, putting down her coffee. 'I'll just do what I came to do and get out of your hair. Do you mind if I wander around the garden?'

'No . . . But you'll need to put on a better coat.'

'I'm fine in mine.'

He ignored her, walking back to the boot room and bringing back a padded Canada Goose parka. Men's.

'That looks enormous.'

'Yes, well I don't have any women's things up here. But at least it's warm,' he argued, holding it open for her to slide her arms into. 'I'm not sure if you realize it's trying to snow out there? This is Scandinavia, not Surrey.'

'Fine.' She slipped it on, the shoulder seams coming to halfway down her biceps, the cuffs dangling several inches past her hands. 'Who does this belong to? The Hulk?'

He grinned, that rare half-smile. 'It's *warm.*'

'Mm-hm,' she sighed wryly. He opened the back doors and a frigid block of air fell in. He shivered, but she was protected in the coat. '. . . Is there anywhere you don't want me to go?'

He looked at her, shaking his head. 'Access all areas.'

Their eyes met briefly. She noticed that he had golden flecks in his, and faint – really faint – freckles on his cheeks. Was it through him that she sensed Lilja?

'Okay, thanks.' She stepped out, pulling the coat around her as she walked around the flower bed off to the right. She looked into it, remembering the profusion of texture and colour in the photographs – such as she could make out in a black-and-white image; but there was nothing to see today except mud and sticks, a few bamboo canes and some chicken wire around what looked like the skeleton of a hydrangea. She lifted her gaze to the sweep of the land, admiring the way it undulated gently, as if the sea rippled beneath the grass.

The woodland that bordered the lawns grew thicker around the back, standing darkly with a carpet of mulched leaves, mushrooms popping up everywhere like little white thumbs. She walked around the perimeter of the lawns, stopping as she saw several small wooden crosses in a scattered area by some trees. One looked to be reasonably recent – certainly from within the past ten years, the word *Bella* still distinct – but the others were weathered, the names almost eroded from sight, the wood rotting and flaking. Pet graves?

She walked through the trees, her hands trailing on the trunks as she wove her way around the perimeter, looking back up at the house from all different angles. There was an outbuilding with a ride-on lawnmower beside it. She wandered up, peering in and finding an impressive arrangement of garden tools inside, hanging on the walls and arranged on shelves – shears, a leaf-blower, rakes, spades, some plastic trugs. It smelled of grass cuttings and she wondered how many gardeners it took to maintain the grounds. Just from what she could see, there had to be five acres here, maybe more.

She came out again. Beyond was the greenhouse. It was huge and appeared to be original, with a sharply steepled roof and a metal fretwork. She walked up to it and looked in. The smell of moss, mud and tomatoes was immediate. There was an old waxed apron hanging from a hook, elbow-length gloves and a tatty, nibbled straw sunhat. On the shelves lay countless flower pots and seed trays, but they were empty; there was a terracotta rhubarb forcer in the far corner.

She closed the door carefully again, feeling frustrated. She had wanted to somehow feel what Lilja had felt here, and she could sense flickers of energy, like glimmers of light, but she couldn't quite catch hold of anything. She was visiting at the wrong time of year, she knew. Life was dormant. On hold. There was nothing to see here after all.

Everything was still hiding below the surface.

'Well timed, I was about to call you,' Max said, looking up as she came back in through the back doors. He was carrying two bowls over to the small table. There were already plates set out, with buttered rolls and water glasses. Napkins, too. It was all distinctly more homely than the Geranium lunch they'd shared in his townhouse. 'Any luck?'

'No. The garden is sleeping,' she said, pulling off her muddy boots.

'One way of putting it.'

She stepped into the kitchen, slipping off the jacket. 'Are those pet graves down in the trees?'

'Yes. Various dogs and one guinea pig.'

She turned back to hang the jacket in the boot room, but he took it from her and did it himself. '. . . Thanks.'

'Sit.'

They sat together at the small table and she felt aware of his legs near hers as he began tearing at his roll and dunking it in the soup.

She smiled, amused.

'What?' he asked after a moment with a suspicious look.

'Nothing.'

'. . . You're smiling when there's nothing to smile about.'

She shrugged. 'I just didn't take you for a soup-dunker.'

'Soup-dunker?'

'Is it considered polite over here to dunk your bread in your soup?'

334

His eyes flashed up to hers. 'There's a time and a place for etiquette. This isn't it.'

'Ah.' She tore off a piece of her bread and dunked it too, remembering he had dined with royalty. 'But you wouldn't do this sitting beside the Queen?'

He paused, his hand almost at his mouth. 'There are many things I might do with you that I wouldn't in front of her.'

The comment took her by surprise but he carried on eating without a wink or a smile, no moody stare, seemingly wholly unaware of any innuendo.

'You know, while we're on the subject of that night—'

He shook his head, once. 'Don't.'

She looked at him. 'Don't what?'

'Don't thank me. I already told you, it was a freebie. Veronique arranged it.'

She watched him eat, so determined not to be thanked. 'And if I don't believe you?'

'Then you don't believe me.'

She was silent for a moment. 'Well . . . then will you please thank *her* for me? I'm incredibly grateful. What she did was so kind and wholly unexpected. I don't really know why she would go to such trouble when, to be honest, she's never given any indication that she even likes me—'

He paused eating again, stopping her with a mutinous stare. He knew exactly what she was doing.

'I'd text her myself but I don't think she'd read anything from me.'

'Enough.'

She bit back a smile. 'I also didn't realize *she* was your girlfriend. I thought it was Angelina. Or was it Natalia?'

'Yeah? And how long have you been with your boy-friend?' he hit back, tearing apart his bread roll. 'Because he wasn't the guy waiting for you on the steps the other week.'

He remembered Erik? She fell quiet. Aksel was the last person she wanted to discuss.

'Hm? Cat got your tongue?' he asked, looking up at her, satisfied to have scored a point.

'He's not my boyfriend. Never was.'

Max's eyebrow arched as he heard her abrupt tone. 'What happened? Weren't you with him last night? *Kayaking*.' He made no attempt to disguise his scorn.

'It doesn't matter.' She looked back at her soup.

He frowned then, seeing that she wasn't joking any more. '. . . Something obviously happened.'

'Nothing.'

'Tell me.'

She looked at him. 'You know, you're very nosy. I don't pry into what's going on with your girlfriends – plural.'

'Because they're not my girlfriends.'

'What are they, then?'

'You know what they are.' His eyes flashed. 'I don't date. No one's under any illusions.'

She looked away but he crouched lower, catching her eye. 'What did he do?'

'How do you know it was him at fault and not me?'

'Call it a hunch.'

She sighed, knowing he wasn't going to let it drop. Now she could see why he was a lawyer – and why lawyers were called sharks. He had an instinct for blood in the water. 'It turns out he has a temper and . . . he took it out on me yesterday when I told him I had to leave early.'

She saw his expression change. 'Took it out on you how?'

'He just shouted at me and said some stuff and then he

sort of struck at my kayak and almost sent me into the water—'

'*What?*'

'But he didn't,' she said quickly. 'Someone else stepped in, and the marshals saw and they got me out. And that was the end of it. I'll never have to see him again.'

A silence pulsed. 'I should have punched him when I had the chance,' he muttered, the anger glittering in his eyes.

'Because that would have really helped things.'

'He couldn't kayak so easily with a black eye.'

'Then it would have happened another time,' she shrugged. 'Listen, I'm fine. It's done.'

He sighed, looking stressed. 'And that's when you came to the Academy, straight afterwards?'

'Yes. Why?'

He watched her, giving a small shake of his head. 'I thought you were quiet. I just didn't realize.'

'Well, why would you? It's not your problem.'

He was still for a moment, before dropping his spoon onto the plate and sitting back in his chair with a sigh. 'Fuck, Darcy,' he said, staring at her hard. 'How could you be with someone like that?'

'Because I didn't realize he was like that till it was happening! He was perfect on paper and I ended up missing a few red flags.' She rolled her eyes. 'I let myself turn a blind eye because he's kind to animals.' She rolled her eyes.

'Kind to animals?' Max frowned.

'He's a vet.'

'Oh.'

'But don't worry. I'm going to follow your example and swear off dating for a while. I'm too busy with work anyway.'

'Right. So then you get it,' he said, picking up his spoon.

'Yeah. Hookups are the answer.'

He looked sharply at her. 'No!'

'Why not? It clearly works for you.'

'That's not funny.'

She wanted to laugh. It actually was funny. It appeared that what was good for the gander was in fact not good for the goose.

At least they'd moved out of the awkward stage, she supposed.

'Just let me eat in peace,' he muttered.

'I didn't know I was disturbing your peace.'

'You've been disturbing my peace since we met, and you know it.'

She was quiet for a few moments. She did know it. But she also knew something that would *really* disturb his peace; something he had a right to know. 'Are you aware we've gone viral?'

'. . . I wasn't aware we're a "we".'

'I'm afraid so. You haven't seen it on TikTok?'

'I don't have TikTok.' He'd stopped eating now, a look of mild alarm crossing his face. 'What's gone viral?'

She swallowed. '. . . Someone filmed us in the ladies' at the fundraiser.'

'What?' The word was a bark, breaking through his carefully controlled composure. '*Why*? What was there to see? You'd got wine on your dress! Why is that interesting to anyone?'

'It's just social media nonsense. This is what happens. I'm not happy about it either.'

He stared at her, looking stunned. 'Show me.'

'Maybe I shouldn't—'

'Darcy, show me! I have a professional reputation to consider.'

She brought it up on her phone and stared at the table as he watched. He played it through several times before flinging himself back in his chair, his hands in his hair. He clearly understood the intimation upon them. How the caption was casting him: the way he'd held her as he called for his driver; how he'd kissed her hair; the protective body language as he'd turned for the door . . . He was no longer Max Lorensen, corporate law titan, but the poster boy for *If he wanted to, he would*.

'Four million people have watched this?' He was incredulous. Mildly panic-stricken.

'If it makes you feel better, it's probably just ten teenage girls who have watched it four hundred thousand times.'

To her surprise, he gave a small laugh. '. . . Fuck,' he groaned.

'I know. I'm sorry.'

'Why are you sorry? *You* didn't film it and post it.'

'No, but if I hadn't—'

'If you hadn't been flirting with that guy, your dress wouldn't have ended up ruined and I wouldn't have had to go after you?'

'You *didn't* have to go after me. And besides, I wasn't flirting with him. We were talking.'

He shrugged. 'Looked like flirting from where I was standing.'

'I wasn't aware you were even looking.'

His eyes flashed. 'I'm watchful. Remember?'

'. . . Ha-ha, very clever.' She looked away, feeling her heart pound. The conversation between them could veer from awkward to intense so quickly, it made her head spin.

They were quiet for a few minutes, drinking and eating, but from the way his eyes kept going to her phone, she knew he was preoccupied with what he'd just seen. Would he be professionally embarrassed?

She sipped another spoonful but slightly over-rotated the spoon so that a bit of soup dribbled down her chin.

'Oh God,' she muttered. 'Can't take me anywhere.' She went to grab her napkin but he was faster, instinctively reaching over and smudging it away with his thumb, his hand pausing on her face as his eyes locked with hers.

In that single, unguarded moment, she saw his secrets – emotions he usually managed to hide so well shining back at her as if they'd been caught in the sun. It was as if time itself slowed. She had thought all along he had been calling the shots – deciding where the boundaries were; everything on his terms. Only now did she realize the power lay with her. *He* was running from *her*, fighting this.

But surely he knew he couldn't run for ever? She leaned slightly into his hand and felt the pressure from his fingers increase, holding her—

He pulled away, as if only just realizing what he was doing. 'Darcy.'

'Max.'

A silence bloomed and this one felt heavier. Loaded.

'Darcy . . .'

'Yes,' she breathed, hearing how his voice cracked on her name. He heard it too and looked away, as if he'd betrayed himself somehow. He hesitated and she felt her heart pause with him. '. . . There's something I want to ask you.'

She swallowed as she watched him, waiting. 'Okay.'

He looked back at her, but she saw that in that moment of reprieve, the shutters had come down again. The sun had gone back behind the clouds.

'. . . Do you really think I should get a dog?'

Chapter Twenty-Five

He gave her the tour, the house breathing quietly as they walked through its rooms in socked feet. It felt completely different to his townhouse. That was all moody colours and striking statement pieces but this felt gentler and less self-consciously beautiful. It had the air of inheritance to it, an old soul that had seen much, the worn comfort of a jumper he'd pinched from his father: the fireplaces had coloured tiles, there were finger-wide gaps between the floorboards and some of the sofas needed patching. The curtains in some rooms looked so old, the patterns had been sun-bleached so that only faint shadows remained.

The paintings were different here, too. Fewer large-scale extravagant oils and instead, galleries of quieter, humbler sketches and watercolours. Darcy stopped before a grouping on the stairs. They were botanicals – larkspur, lavender, daffodils. 'L. Madsen,' she said, reading the artist's signature in the corner. She looked up at him on the steps above her but he shook his head, knowing what she was thinking.

'Lotte.'

'Oh.' She wondered how he could be so sure.

She followed him up the stairs. He seemed different here, too; the more he moved into the private areas of the house, it was as if his hard edges were knocked off. He stopped outside a bedroom, his arms folding over his chest, and she somehow knew this had been his brother's room. Exposed timbers striped the ceiling; the walls were air force blue, with ticking curtains and old pine furniture. Any artefacts from their childhood had been, seemingly, long since packed away, but there were some photographs on the surfaces, some school sports photos on the walls.

'Peder's?' she asked.

'This was his,' he nodded. '. . . All of it.'

She looked at him, picking up his meaning. '. . . The house?'

'The bulk of the Madsen fortune passed out, a couple of generations back, to our cousins – Frederik's side. This place was slim pickings compared to what they inherited, but this was all we would have wanted anyway,' he shrugged. 'We always loved it here. Our grandmother and father both grew up here, and we spent our summers here until our parents died.' A small spasm flickered in his jaw. 'We got sent to live with our aunt, inherited some shares in the company and some honorary positions. I inherited the townhouse and Peder got this . . .'

His voice trailed off and she knew what he was thinking: that he never should have had both. It wasn't supposed to have been this way.

She felt his aloneness radiating from him. He had lost everyone he loved. His entire family. She couldn't begin to imagine how that must feel. She may not see her family on a daily basis but they always messaged and shared memes, laughing, joking and teasing as if they were in the same room. The thought of having no one in the world to care about her, to check in on her . . . 'Max, I'm so sorry.'

He glanced at her, but it was as if the emotion in her voice was threatening to him – a knife glinting at his throat – and she saw that inscrutable gaze blink back at her. It was like a mask he could slip behind, keeping the world at bay. He had already come close to revealing too much at lunch, but instead of drawing them closer, every slip now only seemed to push him further away from her.

She swallowed, recognizing the pattern. He would never let her in. He didn't want an emotional connection with her, or anyone.

He turned and carried on down the hall, his back to her, pointing out the bedrooms. Darcy trailed after him. The ceilings were reasonably high but they sloped sharply in the gables, making the rooms feel cosier. The views onto the garden were far-reaching as the lawns fell gently away and the sea was visible above the treetops from some of the rooms on the west side. All the beds were pristine, every sheet wrinkle smoothed out as if it was a White Company catalogue. It looked like no one had ever touched them, much less slept in them.

She supposed most of the bedrooms – if not all but his – were now guest rooms. And yet the small table in the big kitchen suggested he didn't entertain on any large scale here.

'When was this taken?' she asked, stopping in front of a pair of large photographs on the wall. Both looked to be weddings held here at the estate, bride and groom surrounded by family, just outside the kitchen doors; one photograph, the older one, was black and white, but the other was in colour and for the first time, she understood what Viggo had been telling her about the Sallys' talents. In contrast to the starkness outside right now, the garden was a profusion of textures, a riot of colour. It made her want to walk through the grasses, run her hands against the heavy flowerheads . . .

'Those are my parents' and grandparents' weddings. It was a bit of a tradition getting married here back then.'

'I can see why,' she murmured. 'It's heavenly here.'

He didn't reply. It didn't need to be spelled out why there had been no weddings since.

They came to a room at the end of the corridor. It was smaller than the others, with a window set in the back wall that looked down the drive towards the clumps of silver birches and the beach beyond. There was an iron bedstead, a faded flat-weave rug, a small desk. And in the nearside corner was a large easel, grubby with paint marks.

'This was Johan Trier's room, when he stayed here,' Max said, looking in dispassionately. 'Out of all the rooms, it's probably the one that's been touched least. I suppose we were always too aware of the importance of the connection with him to dare doing much in here.'

Darcy felt the hairs on her arms stand on end. 'You mean, this is where he stayed while he was painting *Her Children*?'

He nodded.

'And you didn't think that would be of interest to me?'

He shrugged. 'It's just an old bedroom.'

Was it though? She paused for a moment, realizing, for the first time, that the connection between Trier and the Madsens really was something more than just an academic fact or commercial advantage. Johan Trier had slept in that bed; he had woken in this room . . . He had created the greatest work of his lifetime, and of Denmark's past century, while staying right here. Suddenly Max's argument that *Her Children* belonged at the Madsen Collection didn't just feel like legal jousting or good PR prior to a public listing. He might actually have a point.

She felt a green shoot of hope break through the frozen ground. The past was stirring . . .

'Which was Lilja's room, do you know?' she asked, looking back down the hallway.

'We're not quite sure, but we think probably Peder's. It was the smallest, and as Casper was the younger brother too . . .' His jaw pulsed, as if he was pained by the logic of the younger brothers always receiving less. Smaller room. Smaller real estate.

Darcy tried to imagine Lilja sleeping down the hall, her new baby in the cot beside her . . . August 1922. She had been living here for two years by then; what had been a temporary suggestion to recuperate from her bereavement had gradually become a new life. She had recovered here and never gone back to the city. Her husband – working in London – and in-laws had been infrequent visitors; so how had she felt about having a newcomer – a brilliant, famous artist – sleeping down the hall? Had it been an intrusion? Or a welcome return to wider life?

'Were there staff?'

'Yes, the Saalbachs. Mrs Sally, as she was known, was our cook and housekeeper, and her husband and son, Ernest and Arne, were the gardeners-slash-drivers.'

'Old Sally and Little Sally. Viggo's mentioned them.'

'That's right. Although Little Sally was six foot three, so that was something of a misnomer.'

'And where did they sleep?' she asked, counting that there were five bedrooms up here.

'There used to be a small staff lodge house, where the garage now stands.'

'Ah.' So not in the main house, then. 'And did Trier have a studio here?'

'Yes, also long since gone. It was more of a glass lean-to at the back of the house. It was supposed to give him lots of natural light but it was too hot in the summer and too cold in the winter.'

She looked back in at Trier's bedroom again. 'May I?'

'Sure.'

She stepped in, looking around carefully and trying to observe her own reactions to what she saw and felt. It felt as if she was trying to inhale the past – as if Trier had left something of himself behind in here that she could capture. She was looking for something, but she didn't know what.

There was another old photograph on the wall. This one was sepia-toned and mottled with dust mites trapped between the paper and the glass, so that small dark patches bloomed in several areas. But she knew immediately who she was looking at. Johan Trier was standing by his easel. He was as recognizable by his long, pointed beard as by his painter's smock, a paintbrush held upright in his hand like Cruella de Vil's cigarette holder.

To his left stood a man in a pale suit and tie. He had an imperious look about him, with a neatly trimmed beard and his chin up as he gazed straight towards the camera. His hand rested on the shoulder of a young woman beside him. She was holding a baby wrapped in a blanket and was barefoot, her dark hair worn in a braid. To the right of the easel stood another two men – one middle-aged, the other young; unlike the bearded fashion of the day for gentlemen of the upper classes, they were clean-shaven and their clothes cut from hemp. Slightly in front of them stood a middle-aged woman in a dark dress and pristine apron, her hands clasped before her.

'That's the Sallys,' Max said, as Darcy peered at the image. 'Johan, obviously . . . And as you'll no doubt recognize, my great-grandparents, Casper and Lilja. She's holding my grandmother there.'

She was also wearing the necklace. It was a clean, clear image and Darcy took a good look. There was no longer any doubt at all that the necklace was Lilja's, nor that it was her in the painting. Her head was tipped at the same angle – chin sightly down, lips parted, gaze up.

'What did you say was your grandmother's name?' she asked, her gaze settling on the baby bundled in Lilja's arms. *Two births.*

'Emme.'

'Emme,' she murmured. 'That's pretty.'

'This was taken in August 1922. They were all living here that summer.'

'All of them? Casper, Lilja and Johan? . . . That must have been intense.'

'Why?' His voice was immediately defensive.

'An artist in the midst of greatness – and a newborn? How thick are the walls in this house?'

He conceded the point. 'Not thick enough.'

Had there been arguments? she wondered, looking again at Casper and Lilja; they stood stiffly, as if carved from wood. By this point, Casper had been in London heading up the family office there for almost three years and Lilja had settled into permanent residency here. They must have been like strangers by then, surely? There were no letters between them that she had found – which struck her as odd – and from all she had read in his sister's and mother's diaries, Casper's trips back to Denmark had been infrequent. Not only that, she hadn't been able to find any comment, anywhere, about their relationship, so she had absolutely no sense of its temperature. Stone cold or hot? Had they fallen passionately in love when Casper had returned from his war business to find this beautiful young girl living with the family? Or had it been a marriage of convenience, as Viggo had posited? Good families, merged fortunes, old allegiances and favours . . .

She looked at Trier . . . then at the baby in Lilja's arms again. 'When did Trier come to Solvtraeer to start working?' she asked lightly.

'I don't know exactly. Sometime in the late spring, I think.'

Had he been down the summer before? She would need to go back to his diaries again. She had stopped concerning herself with his movements as soon as she acquired Lilja's name, but perhaps their fates had become more intertwined than merely through a painting?

She looked again at the people on the other side of the image. The Saalbachs had kindly faces with appled cheeks, but there was reserve in their eyes and she sensed tension in the photograph. Were they uncomfortable with this presentation of a happy family? What secrets did they know that Casper didn't? Darcy glanced down the corridor no one would have monitored at night: the Saalbachs across the drive, unable to hear the creak of a floorboard, the squeak of a mattress coil . . .

'The Sallys look nice,' she mumbled, knowing she was staring too hard, too long, as suspicions formed in her mind.

'They were. And incredibly loyal. Mrs Sally became a mother figure to Lilja during her convalescence here. She helped with the birth.'

Darcy smiled at that. For some reason it comforted her to think that Lilja – practically an orphan, barely more than a child herself – had had someone looking after her after all.

'My grandmother would tell me and Peder stories about how Old Sally would let her help him with the flower beds. And Little Sally taught her to fish and would take her foraging and truffle hunting in the woods around the back.'

'You can grow truffles here?' She was surprised. 'I thought they only grew further south, in Italy and France.'

'No, it's ideal conditions here. To the extent that some of

the so-called garden visitors who came to enjoy the grounds were interested in more than just the flowers.'

'They tried to steal the truffles?'

'They're valuable. It happens,' he shrugged.

She stepped back from the image, looking again at Trier. There was a large canvas on the easel in the photograph. This one beside her here? She reached a hand out to it. It certainly looked the same.

'Is that *Her Children* on the easel there?' Its back faced the camera.

Max looked at her and nodded. 'We believe so.'

She could see how all this added to his claim. 'So why isn't this photograph hanging in the gallery with the others?'

He shrugged. 'Because it's in poor condition and there's plenty of other ones of Trier with the family for people to see. This one just feels a bit more candid and private – Lilja's not wearing shoes, she's just had a baby, she's not formally attired . . . And besides, we can't put out everything that we have just because we have it.'

'Yes,' Darcy agreed. But something had snagged in her mind, an echo that made her look again at the photograph. She could feel a tiny itch in her brain that she couldn't quite scratch as she stared at the gathered faces. One was unexpectedly familiar . . .

With a frown, she followed after him as he left the room, walking back down the corridor, past the family wedding photographs again, past Peder's bedroom that might once have been Lilja's . . .

She saw from the bedroom windows that it had begun to snow lightly, dusting the ground like a lacy veil. Light was beginning to fade, the garden starting to glow a soft violet. Dusk was falling.

They came downstairs in a silence that seemed to grow thicker with every step. Max was just ahead of her, and she stared at his back, at the slight dark-blond curl at the nape of his neck. For all his offhandedness, she couldn't deny he had been generous in opening his home to her today when he had no obligation to do so. He had let her look around without suspicion. He had fed her and made sure she was warm. He had answered her questions . . .

Now what?

'The snow really is trying to settle out there,' she said as they walked through the hall, back towards the kitchen.

'Scandi winters.' He stopped by the prep table, unusually quiet.

Things had become stilted between them again now that her reason for being here had been satisfied. '. . . Back home, that would be enough snow to have all the trains cancelled and flights grounded.' God. Small talk.

'Mm.' He looked away, his hands in the back pockets of his jeans, and she took it as the cue that he wanted her to go. It was his Saturday afternoon . . .

Her boots were by the back door and she walked straight over to them, pulling them on. She saw her jacket in the boot room and put that on too, wasting no more of his time.

'You don't want another coffee?' he asked, mannered as always, watching as she readied herself to make a swift exit.

She didn't look at him as she zipped up the jacket. 'Thanks, but I really should get out of your way. I've already taken up too much of your Saturday as it is.'

'It's fine.' So polite.

'There's a train at twenty past, so –' She saw on the kitchen clock that it was ten to three.

'Yes . . . I'll drive you to the station.'

'No,' she said quickly. 'There's really no need. I've got my bearings and the walk will do me good. This is the second Saturday on the trot I've missed my run, so . . .'

'Right.'

She glanced at him but, ever since his withdrawal at the lunch table, he had scarcely looked at her. No more teasing, no more jokes. Nothing personal. She sighed. Not just shut out but locked out. 'Well, thanks for letting me visit here. I appreciate it.'

He shrugged. 'I didn't do anything. I can't see what help it's been for you.'

'Oh, but it has. It's been useful being able to see where Lilja was living when the portrait was painted. It all helps build up a—'

'Feeling?'

She smiled at the tease. 'Exactly.' She swallowed, her hand reaching for the doorknob. '. . . Well, I guess I'll see you at the next friendly meeting.'

It was her turn to tease, but he didn't smile as she opened the door.

'Bye, Max,' she mumbled, walking out.

'– Don't.'

She looked back in surprise, her feet straddling the threshold. She was half in, half out. Caught. 'What?'

'Don't go.'

'But the train . . .'

'Miss it.'

She blinked. 'I have no reason to stay here now.'

'. . . You do. You know you do.' His voice was strained, though whether it was from the words he was saying, or those he wasn't, she didn't know.

'But you said—'

'I think we can agree it's not working,' he said brusquely. Still Max the Lawyer.

He clenched his jaw, looking stricken as the silence stretched. If she couldn't speak, she also couldn't move; she couldn't even look away from him.

'. . . Stay with me.'

They were straightforward words, but not for him. Not for a man who kept everyone at arm's length. He'd spent the past few weeks constantly repelling her and pushing her back, but it had only made the tie between them grow ever more taut.

He looked away, mocking himself in disgust. 'You wouldn't believe I'm usually better than this—'

'I don't want you to be better!' she blurted.

He looked surprised. 'Then what do you want?'

'More than what you're offering. I don't want to have one night with you and join your list of model hookups. And I don't want perfection. I want you to be real – a flawed, feeling man! I want *all* of you. Not someone who compartmentalizes his life like it's a sock drawer, Max.'

She came back into the room and stood before him. 'Mess it all up, with me.'

He stared down at her and she could see the strain in him as he struggled to hold back what she knew he felt. Emotions were complicated. Dangerous. She took his hand and placed it on her hip, making him touch her, bringing him into the physical realm. She felt his fingertips press into her flesh once, then again, beginning to grip her more tightly as he gave her, finally, what she'd wanted from the start: to be held by him. Kissed. Craved.

Lost, together.

*

'Five point one million,' she murmured, reading out the latest TikTok tally, her cheek pressed against his chest. He was so warm, and smelled of sandalwood and log fires. His heart rate was only just beginning to get back to normal; so was hers.

'Jesus,' he groaned. 'Why?'

'It's the hair kiss. That's up there with a forehead kiss, you should know that. What were you thinking?'

He rubbed his eyes. 'Clearly I wasn't.'

She smiled, her finger twirling a chest hair; his other arm was looped around her and stroking her waist. 'So you were running on instinct, were you?'

'Running on instinct. Fuelled by jealousy.'

She shifted position to look up at him. 'You're being very candid.'

'I have to. I need to be able to sleep. You've kept me awake too many nights lately.' He moved his head so as to get a better look at her. His stubble was coming in; it had been a long evening. His gaze was soft, enveloping . . .

'I have?'

'Mm-hm.'

She gave a sleepy, satisfied smile. 'Well, now, that's nice to know.'

He chuckled, the sound deep in his chest. 'Is it? You want me suffering over you?'

'Of course! It's what every woman wants for her lover. Abject despair.' Her finger tapped his chest playfully.

'Well then, mission accomplished. I thought standing in your hallway with a Valentino dress was rock bottom, but then you turned up to a meeting in a wetsuit with flashing antlers . . . Ripped my heart out.'

She laughed, and his arm tightened around her as he flipped her over to the other side of him. She felt the mood get serious between them again. The attraction was unstoppable.

'Did Veronique really sort the dress out for you?' she asked, looking up at him as he leaned over to kiss her.

'No.'

'And it wasn't a gift?'

'No. But I know their Finance Director and he got the manager to go in for me.'

'Why did you do all that?'

He swallowed, his weight propped on one elbow as he pushed her hair back from her face, his knee nudging between her legs. 'Because I wanted to,' he said, looking pleased with himself. 'So I did.'

'You know this counts as a date?' she said as they walked out of the wind and into the boat warehouse that was temporarily set up as a Christmas tree stand. He was doing a fine job of keeping her warm – wrapping her in hat, scarf and mammoth coat from his boot room – but it spoke to the level of coldness when the snow was settling on the beach.

He shook his head. 'No, it doesn't. A date means dinner, or . . . ice skating.' He gave a shudder of disapproval.

'Absolutely not,' she pushed back. 'That's just a template for beginners. A walk on the beach, takeaway coffees, and now buying a Christmas tree, is premium date territory.'

'. . . So you're saying I'm good at this, then?' He looked down at her with a grin as he slung his arm over her shoulder, clasping her hand.

'You're brilliant at everything; you know you are,' she murmured, as he reached down and kissed her again. He was up to eleven hair kisses and counting, although she didn't think he was aware of it.

They were oblivious to the people milling around them in the boatyard. 'I'm wishing we'd driven down here now, though.'

'Why?'

'To get you home quicker.'

'Hmm.' She grinned, relishing the prospect.

He pulled back as he remembered where they were. '. . . Not to mention getting the tree back.'

'Oh, right! And how were you going to get a Christmas tree into an R8?' she laughed.

'Good point,' he conceded. 'We'll have to carry the tree back.'

'Excellent,' she shrugged.

'It'll have to be a small one.'

'Over my dead body. This is your first Christmas tree in years. We're getting a whopper.'

'A *whopper*,' he laughed, amused by her colloquial English, 'will take two hours to carry back from here.'

She squeezed closer to him. 'Then it'll take two hours. It'll become part of our legend and we'll tell everyone all about our first date when it took us two hours to carry our first Christmas tree home.'

'I see,' he murmured, looking happy. 'I'm beginning to see that dinner would have been easier.'

'I'm not interested in easier,' she whispered, reaching a hand to his cheek and kissing him again. She wanted today to never end. Just like she had wanted last night to roll into eternity. Every moment she shared with him, she wanted to endure.

They stopped by a stand of Nordmann firs propped against a railing. Max glanced down the row, assessing size, straightness, colour . . . He went over to one and stood it upright. It had to be nine feet high at least, with wide, splayed, bushy branches all the way around.

It was enormous. Unwieldy. Heavy.

She grinned at him, shucking her hands out. 'It's perfect.'

Chapter Twenty-Six

Denmark flashed past the windows, snowflakes dashing against the windscreen as they drove through the night. His hand was on her thigh, squeezing every few moments as if checking she was real. The past twenty-eight hours had felt like a dream and she didn't want it to end. She didn't want them to be driving back to the city, to their separate homes and divided lives, and she knew he felt the same. They had remained in front of the fire at Solvtraeer for as long as they possibly could, only the worsening weather finally convincing Max they had to hit the road.

She let her head loll against the headrest, gazing at his profile as he drove. 'You're too handsome,' she murmured.

'No.'

'Yes . . . It made me hate you on sight.'

'Ouch,' he winced.

'Yeah – that profile pic. Imperious stare, saying you don't date . . . you come off as deeply arrogant. You'll have to change it.'

He glanced over, his eyes falling to her lips and making her stomach flip, just like that. She wanted him to tell her he didn't need that profile pic now, that he'd be closing his account . . .

'Well, you still swiped right. And you definitely didn't hate me the night we met.' Laughter tripped through his eyes like a skipping child.

'. . . No,' she groaned, unable to deny it. 'More's the pity.'

He smirked, his eyes on the road but knowing exactly the effect he had on her.

'There's something I want to know,' she said, studying his jawline.

'Okay.'

'Did you recognize me, the night we met? Did you know we'd matched?'

He smiled, bemused. 'Not only did I recognize you, I recognized you long before you recognized me.'

'No you didn't!'

'I saw you when you arrived. You were coming down the steps and I started making a beeline for you.'

'You recognized me straight away?'

'No. At that point I just wanted you—'

Darcy swallowed at his candour.

'But then you went over to Otto's group; I saw you being introduced to Helle and I realized, from all the interest in you, that you must be the specialist researcher they were bringing in. It felt like an unfortunate complication.'

'That's why you hung back?'

'Yes.'

'But you kept staring at me.'

'No law against that,' he shrugged, unapologetic. 'I was on my way out, *trying* to resist temptation, when I checked my messages and saw that the hot girl I'd matched with, who was turning down my kind offer of a drink, was right in front of me. There's only so much a man can take.'

'So you decided to wait and try your luck again?'

'Well, you'd turned me down on the grounds you had plans. Given I was at those plans, I figured I now had a good shot.' He winked at her. His logic was impeccable.

'But if you knew we were going to be working together . . . ?'

'There's always an exception to the rule, Darcy.' His hand squeezed her leg. 'And besides, it wasn't like we were going to be in the same office. As it was, I had to manufacture ways to see you.'

'Like making me work at your house?' she grinned, feeling vindicated. 'I knew it!'

He grinned back. 'I liked having you around.'

'You make me sound like a pet.'

'You were even cuter than that. So *principled*. I could barely get you past the door,' he chuckled.

'Yeah, well – it was just great being introduced to all your girlfriends.'

'Not my girlfriends,' he said with a simple shake of his head. 'They only ever stayed the night. You're the only one I ever wanted to stay for the day.'

'Charmer.' She reached out and stroked his cheek again; it was impossible to stop touching him. 'So, if you were looking for reasons to see me, why did you come to the gallery the day after we met to "establish boundaries"?'

'To see you again.'

'You dumped me – in order to see me again?'

'Technically I couldn't dump you when we weren't together – but yes. And also because I was angry with you.'

Her eyes narrowed gleefully. 'Because I had a date?'

He shrugged again.

'You get so jealous,' she smiled, remembering how he'd ghosted her after meeting Aksel too.

'Not usually.'

She watched him. 'So then, if we didn't really need to work closely together, we *could* have just dated?'

'No. Because I don't date . . . Didn't date.' He looked ahead at the road. 'I realized you were different; that's why I was trying to keep a distance.'

'That didn't work out so well for you, huh?' she murmured, taking his hand and sliding it up her thigh a little. She saw how he swallowed before he glanced over at her, with a look she had grown accustomed to over the past day and night. 'You're a confusing man,' she whispered.

He shook his head. 'I've always been straightforward. No false promises. No leading anyone on.'

'Never letting anyone close.'

'We all wear armour, Darcy. Even you.' His grip tightened on her thigh.

She stared at him, hating how badly he made her want him. It wasn't good. She shouldn't be falling so hard, so soon . . .

'Don't,' he murmured, the small half-smile playing on his lips as she continued to stare.

'Don't what?'

'Ask me what we are.' He glanced at her again. 'You're the exception.'

'And you're telling me we're supposed to sit in meetings now, pretending to be the enemy, when we've just done all these *unspeakable things* to one another?' She took his hand and slid it even further up her inner thigh, seeing the smile curve on his lips. He looked at her hungrily. 'Do you think they'll be able to tell?'

He shook his head. 'No.'

'How can you be so sure?'

'Because we're both professionals. And because you're almost done on this project, and then our private life won't matter one way or another to anyone else.'

Our. She smiled at the word. It felt precious, coming from him.

He glanced at her hopefully. '. . . You are almost done, aren't you?'

She wrinkled her nose, giving a little sigh. 'Well, not nearly as done as I'd like to be.'

'What does that mean?' he frowned, looking puzzled. 'You've confirmed it's Lilja in the painting. You've got unrestricted access to our archives, you've seen private family photos, we've made love in the very rooms she walked through . . .' He winked, destroying her. 'What more do you need? Just write up her bio and deliver it. Everything will be a lot simpler once we can sign this thing off. Then we won't have to pretend anything.'

'I know.' She bit her lip as she shifted her weight and looked out of the window, feeling suddenly pressured. Questions kept coming to her mind that felt wrong to ask.

'Darcy? . . . What is it?'

'Nothing.'

'It's obviously something.'

She dropped her head back, running her hands over her face as she tried to clear her thoughts. 'I just feel like I'm missing something important. It's staring me in the face but I can't see it. I feel like I'm not seeing the wood for the trees.'

He sighed. 'Look, Lilja was my great-grandmother. I never knew her, obviously, but without wanting to do her down, it's not as if she lived a life of international mystery. She was a privileged woman of a certain class. How much is there really to say about her?'

Never knew her . . . Darcy flinched, staring into the darkness suddenly. '. . . That's it.'

'What is?'

She didn't reply immediately, allowing her thoughts to run,

untrammelled. 'It makes no sense why she would have done it,' she murmured.

Max frowned. 'Done what?'

She angled her knees towards him, her brain shifting gears, facts and theories beginning to move into new positions. 'Max, you know how she died, don't you?'

His jaw pulsed at the sudden, unwelcome turn in conversation. 'Of course. She drowned.'

'Yes – but do you also know it wasn't accidental?'

He glanced at her with a guarded look. She took it as confirmation. 'Where are you going with this?'

'Viggo told me she walked into the sea and killed herself – but it doesn't make sense that she would do that.'

'Doesn't it? She had been living in Hornbaek for years by then. She was depressed, Darcy.'

'That's just it – she wasn't. She had been completely broken by her son's death but she'd gradually recovered. She'd just had another baby. Emme, her daughter. A daughter that she never got to know. Why would she have killed herself when she'd finally got the one thing that could heal her? It makes no sense that she would have done this.'

'Doesn't it?' he asked, his voice suddenly cold. 'You don't think depression is insidious? You think it just miraculously disappears when one good thing happens? . . . Having the baby could well have made things *worse* for her. Postnatal depression?'

Darcy pulled back. He was right, of course. That also made sense. She looked across at him, realizing she shouldn't have articulated her theory out loud. Not to him. Lilja's great-grandson. 'Max, I'm sorry, I was just hypothesizing. I didn't mean to—'

But it was too late. She had crossed a line. She could see

his knuckles were white around the steering wheel as he drove. 'What exactly is it you want to find, Darcy? Do you *want* sensation? Do you want terrible things to have happened to my family so that you can launch some kind of exposé when the painting's revealed? . . . Is this about trashing my family's reputation so that you can make yours?'

'Of course not!' She was appalled. How could he think such a thing?

'No?'

'No!'

He shook his head as the temperature between them dropped to freezing. 'Well, it sure as hell looks like you've got an agenda from where I'm sitting.'

'You're back!' Freja exclaimed, coming outside in her Ugg slippers and heatless curling ribbons, the bin bag in one hand as Darcy stood on the pavement, watching Max's tail-lights disappear up the street. 'A whole day later than planned. I *wonder* what could have happened?' she asked in a wry voice.

Darcy heard the bin lid slam down and the slap of Freja's slippers on the path as she came and stood by her. Someone had already cleared the snow to the sides.

'. . . That's him, is it?' Freja asked, when Darcy didn't reply.

'Yeah,' Darcy breathed, watching the indicator come on. A right turn, and he was gone.

'Darce?' Her flatmate put a hand on her shoulder, seeing her subdued manner. 'What's happened?'

'He trusted me. He finally started opening up and I . . . I just threw it back in his face.' Darcy turned to look at her, tears skimming her cheeks as a sob burst from her at last. '. . . I think I've just messed everything up.'

Chapter Twenty-Seven

'Good night, Darcy. Don't stay too late.'

'Night, Viggo,' Darcy mumbled, hearing him climb the stairs. It was poker night. The man had a better social life than she did.

She checked her phone for the umpteenth time: double ticks. Grey.

He was ghosting her again. She had triple texted and left a short voice note saying she was sorry, could they please talk? But there had been no reply.

Freja had checked in hourly for updates all day, remote monitoring Darcy's responses. She was allowed no more than three 'aired' messages. 'You can show him you're prepared to swallow your pride, you can show contrition – but there's also a hard limit,' she had said sternly at the bathroom mirror as they applied their make-up that morning, Darcy trying to conceal the under-eye bags that revealed another night of no sleep (this time for the wrong reasons). 'You might lose that man, but you will at least keep your dignity.'

She stared at her screen. She had started writing her copy on Lilja's biography, but it was a sparsely feathered nest. Strictly speaking, she could have done it at the apartment, or in the university library, or at the Academy, or at Paludan, but she was here because there was comfort to be found in the muted confines of the archive. The background murmur and hum of visitors upstairs, Viggo's footsteps in the background, coffee on tap . . . the possibility that Max might come here unannounced, as he had before, against his better instincts.

He hated her for probing into his great-grandmother's death, but she had been skating on the surface of Lilja's life and there were glaringly obvious suppositions she couldn't ignore. Max had been right that Emme's birth could have triggered a profound postnatal depression in an already fragile young woman, and that might explain why she had walked into the sea. But it also might not. No matter what he said, Darcy couldn't ignore the fact that in the photographs she had seen of Lilja in those final months, she had looked stronger and decidedly content – so different to the reports of her physical and mental condition when she'd arrived in Hornbaek in 1920.

Which posed the question: why? What had happened to make her so happy? Was it falling pregnant with her daughter, or something else? Some*one* else.

Had she had an affair with Johan Trier? It was the obvious question and Darcy couldn't discount it without consideration, not if she was to do her job. She had to look at the circumstances of Lilja's life leading up to that last summer if she was to convey the background to a portrait of a woman in love.

Because she had been. It was the quality Darcy hadn't been able to pinpoint before: Lilja's direct eye contact was not so much provocative as intimate, the parting of her mouth sensual . . . She had been looking at her lover.

And if she was to take this hypothesis to its logical conclusion, then she couldn't disregard the next question it posed, either: was Casper the father of Lilja's baby, or was it Trier? The artist, being twenty-seven that summer, had been significantly closer in age to Lilja. With her husband so often absent, building the family's fortune abroad, might an affair not have been almost inevitable between them, living in that house together? If theirs had been a marriage of convenience, she and Casper might both have found passion elsewhere. Darcy had seen the Sallys' silent disapproval in the photograph – the family forced into being reluctant keepers of secrets as their employer's son returned for the summer, an unwitting cuckold.

It all made sense. On arrival this morning, Darcy had gone straight to the artist's files and looked for Trier's 1922 diary, but there wasn't one to be found in any of the boxes. She had checked against the red ledger too, and gone into the family files in case it had been inadvertently left there, but that was just more medical invoices for bromide and household accounts.

The diary's absence was glaring. Trier had been a committed and disciplined diarist. He had kept a journal for every single year that she had looked at so far – it made no sense that there wasn't one for arguably the most important year of his life, when he had created his masterpiece – and become a father?

Had he destroyed it? Or had he known better than to leave a written record – evidence – of his affair with the daughter-in-law of his patron?

She had read through his 1921 diary; that, at least, had been where it was supposed to be. She'd scanned through the summer months for mentions of Hornbaek, Lilja, Solvtraeer . . . even if he had just visited fleetingly, it might have helped to officially cast doubt on Casper's paternity. But she had found no entries detailing life beyond his return from Italy to Copenhagen. She was at a dead end. She had only suspicions without proof, and she couldn't – she wouldn't – include anything speculative.

She checked her phone again.

Nothing. She groaned, dropping her face into her hands, knowing for a fact that Max wasn't going to call. She was no longer the exception, but the rule. What to her was professional rigour he saw as betrayal – even though she knew he wouldn't hesitate to do the same in his own job, or if he was in her situation.

The hypocrisy of it angered her, but she also knew he was reverting to type. His walls had come down and he had enveloped her with a depth of feeling that had taken her by surprise – and perhaps him, too. He had made himself vulnerable to her and, in his eyes, this was how she responded?

She couldn't bear it, being cast out like this. If she could just talk to him, explain . . . But she didn't even know where he was. In his office? On a plane to Munich? At home?

Home . . .

She remembered something. She got up, strode towards Viggo's desk and opened his drawer. The key was still there. Viggo was supposed to have returned it by now, or Max should have collected it, but she pressed it into her palm, pleased either way, and grabbed her coat.

Outside, the roads were treacherous. The fallen snow hadn't thawed but nor had it settled into thick banks, and as the evening temperatures dropped sharply it formed a thin, icy veil underfoot. Hardly anyone was cycling, which was always a sure sign.

She stayed on the park side of the road as she walked in the bitter cold, bright headlights shining straight at her, traffic heavy as people headed for home. It was nearly the last week before Christmas and everyone was busy tying up loose ends.

Across the street, lights were glowing from the generous windows of the townhouses, extravagant Christmas trees behind the glass decked with lights and ribbons, plush wreaths hanging on the doors. Christmas was nine days away and the city felt swollen with festive cheer. It was a time for happy endings and new beginnings: families coming together, lovers making memories . . .

But as she drew nearer, she saw Max's house sitting in darkness. No merry-making here. No tree, no wreath. No sign of life.

She rang his doorbell three times anyway.

The key was warm now in her palm and she squeezed it, reminding herself of the intentions that had propelled her here. She had a key. She knew the code. She could let herself in and make him dinner. She could let herself in and climb, naked, into his bed.

Or . . .

Or she could turn around and leave again before he came back.

Fear gripped her as indecision kicked in outside the dark house. She could have her dignity or him.

But not both.

'Darcy?' Max asked, stopping on the pavement and looking up at her. Behind him, the car door closed and Christoff pulled away.

Darcy looked up from her crouched position on the top step. She could no longer feel her backside; she felt like a stone statue. How long had she been sitting here? Twenty minutes? Thirty? More?

'Max.' She was stiff and shivering but determined not to show either.

'What are you doing here?' His tone was flat, his face expressionless.

It was exactly the question she had dreaded: polite disbelief she should be here. Embarrassing herself. Embarrassing them both.

'I wanted us to talk,' she said, watching him slowly ascend the steps. His body language was closed, his mood hostile. 'And to return this.'

He looked at the key, then back at her. 'If you had that, why didn't you let yourself in, instead of sitting in the cold? It's sub-zero out here.'

'As if I was going to do that.' Didn't he know he could trust her not to breach his privacy?

He took it from her, not meeting her gaze. 'How long have you been here?'

'Not long.'

His expression showed he clearly didn't believe her, but he looked away and down the street, staring sightlessly into the traffic. He sighed. 'Look, I'm sorry you've been waiting in the cold for me out here, but I can't invite you in. I don't think us talking is a good idea.'

'Why?' She was calm. So far, so avoidant.

'Because it isn't going to change anything. My mind is set.'

'Your mind is set, even though forty-eight hours ago you were telling me we couldn't go on pretending we didn't have feelings for one another?'

He took a breath. 'Darcy . . . I don't want to hurt you, but it was a mistake.'

His voice was even; she could only imagine how many times he had said those very words to countless other women over the years. But although his delivery was flawless, she saw a shadow pass through his eyes, as if his spirit was turning over. Restless and disturbed.

'No,' she said quietly. 'It wasn't a mistake. It was the best thing to happen to either of us in a really long time. And I'm sorry I ruined that by pushing too hard with questions about your family. I shouldn't have let work come between us. The fact that Lilja was your great-grandmother is irrelevant. If I need to find information, it can't be through you. I understand that now. What's between us is strictly personal.'

He stared at her, a silence beginning to stretch out as she challenged him with the truth. She could see he was fighting her in his head. He looked tired.

'Well? Aren't you going to say something?'

His gaze fell to her mouth. 'Your lips are blue.'

'I didn't mean . . .' She sighed. 'I don't care about my lips right now, Max.'

'No, but I do.' He leaned forward, kissing her lightly, a gentle press of their lips. Momentary comfort. Fleeting tenderness. But his hands remained by his sides, their bodies apart. Resistance lingering.

He drew back, refusing eye contact as he recovered himself. Headlights washed over them both as the rush-hour traffic skulked past. 'You should go.'

'I'm cold.'

His eyes flashed up to hers, recognizing her defiance; her refusal to give up. He wanted to keep her at arm's length but she wouldn't let him. Clearly they couldn't stay out here. Without a word he reached for the lock, slid the key in. He opened the door and walked through into the dark hall, switching on the lights as the alarm pips beeped. He entered the code. 'Come in.'

She stepped into the familiar, beautiful space as he closed the door behind her – shutting out the sound of the traffic, cutting off the rest of the world so that it was just the two of them again. Instantly she felt the tension ratchet between them, as it always did. He looked at her and she knew that what was coming was inevitable. The genie was out of the bottle and it couldn't be put back in again. She saw the defeat come into his eyes and he reached for her, pushing her against the wall and kissing her hard this time. He was angry and desperate all at once. His hand reached for her thigh, pulling it higher as she wrapped her leg around him. He groaned as she unbuttoned his fly.

Resistance was futile.

They slept in the spare bedroom. Not his, with the massive emperor bed that had been the scene of a thousand seductions, but the smaller room across the hall where the Sorolla hung. It was even more beautiful than she had imagined and she lay wrapped in his limbs, looking up at it in wonder – until he made her look at him again, and she was lost.

'Don't get up,' he whispered the next morning, laughing quietly as he came back from the shower to find her sitting up in bed, her hair mussed, head nodding sleepily. It was still dark. Middle-of-the-night dark. 'I've got an early meeting. Go back to sleep.'

'Are you sure?' she mumbled, offering no resistance to the idea.

'You're not a morning person, are you?' he grinned, kissing her forehead and lowering her gently back into the pillows. 'I'll call you later.'

'Wait . . .' Her hand reached for him blindly. '. . . I need a clean shirt.'

'Right-side closet in my room.' He kissed her temple.

'And . . . charger . . . my phone,' she sighed. It was so hard to have to *think*.

'Next to my bed. I'll put it on for you now so it's ready when you get up.'

She smiled into the pillows as he picked up her phone, kissed her temple again and walked out. She was asleep before he reached the front door.

When she awoke, it was almost light. She could hear from the low drone of traffic that the day had started in earnest now and she blinked, wondering what the time was. She stared at the Sorolla – how could it be that she was able to gaze upon such mastery without even getting out of bed?

Max's bedroom was off-white, with chocolate-brown linen sheets that hung loosely to the floor and fitted wardrobes upholstered in tobacco leather. A Barcelona chair and stool sat in one corner and there was a huge Slim Aarons print above the bed. The room was chic but assuredly masculine. Presumably any feminine accents would be provided only by visitors: lacy knickers on the floor, a lipliner in the bathroom drawer . . . She tried not to think about it.

She showered, choosing a blue shirt from his wardrobe and putting it on like she'd won Capture the Flag. She had just enough make-up in her bag to make herself look presentable and she walked over to the bed to get her phone. It was charged to 92 per cent.

She sat on the edge of the bed as she checked her messages: her brother – *'go halves on this White Company shirt for Mum's Christmas prez??'* Numerous texts from Freja – *'Where are you? What's happening?? You need to callll me.'*

She pressed dial. 'You are so dramatic,' she said before Freja could shriek at her.

'Oh my God, where are you?' The words fell out in one jumbled breath. Freja sounded like she was jogging. 'I've been trying to get hold of you since last night!'

'I know, I've just seen your thirty-nine missed messages!

Honestly, Freja, I was with Max. Surely you could guess, if I wasn't returning your calls?' She went downstairs. Her coat was draped over the newel post and she smiled at the memory of them in the hall last night, shedding clothes, desperate for skin upon skin.

'But how was I to know for sure? Where are you now?'

She shrugged on her coat. 'I'm at his place right now. I'm just leaving, in fact.' She entered the alarm code and pulled the door closed behind her.

'Is he there too?'

'No, he had an early start,' she said, beginning to walk at a brisk pace along the road.

'Okay, so tell me everything then, and leave out nothing.' Freja's feet pounded rhythmically in the background. She was definitely running.

'He was doing what I should have realized he'd do: freaking out. This is new territory for him. He doesn't do relationships.'

'And what if he freaks out again?' Freja panted lightly.

'Then I keep showing up. But he won't. We talked it out—'

A police car suddenly shot past, lights flashing, siren blaring, and Darcy realized a moment later that she could hear the siren coming down the line too. 'Hey, where are you right now?'

'Me?'

'Yes – where are you running?'

She could hear Freja's grin in her voice. 'Actually, I'm about two hundred metres behind you.'

'*What*?' Darcy spun round to see a familiar spry figure jogging towards her. She laughed as she stopped walking and waited. 'What are you doing all the way over here?' she asked into the phone. Freja worked at the university on Tuesdays.

'I thought I'd come and catch you on your way in to work, seeing as you weren't picking up last night.'

'Oh my God, Freja!' Darcy laughed. 'That's ridiculous! I'm completely fine! Did you really think I'd come to harm?'

'No,' Freja panted. She was only twenty metres away now, and Darcy hung up.

'So then what are you doing over here?' Darcy asked as Freja ran up to her, looking fresh.

Freja just grinned. 'I had something to tell you that can only be said in person.'

'What?' Darcy asked, before she suddenly gasped, her hand flying over her mouth, as she saw the delight in her friend's eyes and immediately understood. '. . . Oh my God, he *didn't*!'

'He did!'

'You're *not*!' Darcy shrieked, her body already coiled to leap.

'We are!' Freja cried back, holding out her hand to show a marquise diamond on her engagement finger. They began hugging and jumping excitedly, so that people in passing cars looked at them in alarm. 'He asked me last night!'

'Oh my God, Freja! And I wasn't picking up!' Darcy shrieked. *'No!'*

'I know! I'd murder you if it wasn't for the fact that I need you as my bridesmaid!'

Darcy gasped again, falling still. '. . . You want me as your bridesmaid?'

'Well, who else, dummy? You're the closest thing to a sister that I've got.'

'Oh, Frey.' Darcy's fingers pressed against her mouth.

'So that's a yes?'

'Of course it's a yes!' They hugged again in the middle of the street, oblivious to the dog walkers and kindergarteners waddling past bundled up in boots and winter coats. 'Oh Freja, I can't believe this has happened, especially after the non-event last weekend.'

'I know. When I tell you I was *so* shocked . . . I'd put all thoughts of it out of my mind!'

'How did he do it?'

'We were in bed, just cuddling, and he asked. No showy proclamation.'

'You mean no flash mob?' Darcy asked with mock horror.

Freja grinned. 'No.'

'No petals on the bed?'

'No petals.'

'Please tell me there was a balloon.'

'Not even. It was just quietly us being us, and it was perfect. Get this – he said he *had* intended to ask me in Amsterdam, but he saw another other couple getting engaged in the spot where he'd intended to do it, and he thought it was too cliched.'

'So you hadn't got ahead of yourself after all, then?'

'Apparently not.'

'Show me the ring again,' Darcy demanded. 'I need to study it.'

Freja held her hand out as Darcy cooed over the glittering stone. 'It's stunning. That is a big diamond!'

'I know.'

Darcy heard the note of worry in Freja's voice and looked up to see her biting her lip. 'You don't think it's a bit too fancy for me, do you?'

'Too fancy?'

'Yeah. You don't think the diamond's too big?'

'Freja, there is no such thing as a diamond being too big! That concept does not exist. Why would you even say such a thing?'

'I don't know. I'm just quite a . . . humble girly. I guess I always anticipated having something more modest?'

Darcy opened her mouth, ready to argue again, but Freja's

words prompted a sudden shift in her brain, like a gear being levered into place. Suddenly everything made sense. The truth had unlocked and one newly revealed fact led on to another, exposing a past she had stared in the face.

She couldn't believe it.

She had looked straight at it! Everything had been right there, in front of her – but she'd added two and two together and come to five.

Chapter Twenty-Eight

Otto stood with her in silence, waiting, as she stared at the portrait on the easel. On his orders, the conservation team were taking a long coffee break as she stood motionless, allowing her mind to fall into a deep dive. For weeks now she had been recording the high and low points of Lilja's life as if she were plotting a graph – only now did it acquire a three-dimensional shape.

'You're going to have to bear with me in this, Otto,' she said quietly. 'I'm still trying to join the dots. There's a lot to go at . . . but if we can just talk it through . . .'

'Okay. Why don't you start by telling me what's tripped your thoughts?'

'It's the necklace,' she said quietly, unable to take her eyes off Lilja's likeness. 'It's wrong.'

'How can a necklace be wrong?'

'Because it's wooden. Home-made. Far too humble for a woman of her class. She would be wearing pearls in the daytime, or at the very least, paste.'

'I see,' he murmured, narrowing his eyes as he looked at the portrait with a fresh gaze. But he passed no comment. He wouldn't lead her thoughts, only listen to them.

'I think it was her lover's gift to her.'

'Her lover?'

She leaned forward, pointing. 'Look at her expression, the tilt of her head – it's intimate, like this is a shared, private moment. She's in love . . . And see how the gold bead is positioned directly front and centre. It's like a north star, drawing the eye. She's wearing the necklace as a signal, using it to say she is still her lover's property, even if she can't show it publicly. Even if her husband has returned.'

'Had he?'

'Yes. The baby had been born – a little girl, Emme – and Casper was back from London.' She reached for her phone and showed him the photograph she had taken of the picture in the end bedroom before she'd left. 'This was taken at Solvtraeer in August 1922. It shows Lilja holding Emme, with Trier, Casper and the Saalbachs – or the Sallys, as they were known. They were the Madsens' longstanding housekeepers-cum-gardeners. Trier was staying in the house that spring and summer, painting *Her Children*.'

Otto's brow furrowed as he looked back at the portrait again, his own brain beginning to make connections. 'And you think Lilja was having an affair with Trier?'

'I did,' she nodded. 'But now I don't.' She pointed to the robin. 'I think it was Arne Saalbach, the gardener's son. Little Sally.'

Otto's eyebrows slid up. 'Explain.'

'Originally I thought the robin was just a motif for her love of the garden, a symbol of her return to health. Now I think it was a way of proclaiming that *she* was the gardener's friend. She was head over heels in love with him, Otto, and I think this painting was her gift to him. I think it was a self-portrait.'

'*She* painted it?'

'We know Trier didn't. And she was an accomplished artist, even if she never took it too seriously. Lotte's diaries tell us she and Lilja took fine art lessons together for years and there are some paintings at Solvtraeer which are signed L. Madsen; Max said they were by Lotte, but I think they just as easily could have been by Lilja.'

She hoped that had been an innocent misdirection on Max's part, but she couldn't be certain.

'There are artistic similarities, definitely, between those paintings in Hornbaek and this,' she continued. 'And the botanical watercolours I found – misfiled – in Trier's documents are, I suspect, also hers; they never looked like his work, even if he was experimenting. They're much lighter and finer stylistically, and thematically they coalesce to her interests in the garden.'

Otto looked unconvinced. 'Tenuous, though. And highly speculative.'

'Yes,' she agreed. 'But there's more that points to a relationship between them. There's a cabinet in the Madsen archives with some clays: garden tool miniatures – spade, trowel, wheelbarrow, that sort of thing. But there are some lovely main pieces, too: life-size heads of fishermen.'

'Specifically fishermen?'

'Well, they're all wearing sou'westers. But here's the thing, Otto. There aren't any miniature clay pieces of fishing kit – no nets, pots, hooks, not in the way that there are gardening tools. And all the clay heads have the same face. They're of the same man.' She enlarged the screen to show Otto a closer image of the young, tall, dark-haired gardener in the photograph. 'Arne. She disguised him – figuring no one would recognize the gardener in a fisherman's hat. She hid him in plain sight, Otto.'

She brought up the photo again, showing the Sallys' guarded demeanours. They had been the keepers of secrets after all, just not the one she had first thought. 'What if their son, Arne,

378

was the father of her baby? She could never publicly admit it, even if they were in effect living as man and wife most of the time – except for when Madsen family or visitors came to stay. Which was rarely.'

Otto pinched his cheeks between finger and thumb as he contemplated everything she was saying. It was a lot to take in.

He began to pace. 'Okay. Well, let's go with that, for argument's sake. Let's say he is the father to the child.'

'All of these things are love notes: a bead necklace around an aristocrat's neck; a self-portrait of a private look; models of his head because she loved his face so much; clay doodles as she sat in the grass beside him as he worked . . . They all *scream* affair when you see it. But it could never be allowed to come to light. Can you imagine the scandal – the gardener and the lady of the house? It would have been unthinkable for a family so ambitious about its social prospects.'

Otto nodded. She could see he was with her. That the evidence – disparate though it was – stacked up when put together. 'So, did someone find out about them? Did they get caught?'

Darcy closed her eyes, moving effortlessly through memories of a house she herself had slept and made love in. 'I think we definitely have to consider that possibility. Trier was in the house by spring onwards, and we know Casper came back in the summer around the time of the birth, meaning it would have been difficult for Lilja and Arne to move with the same freedom they had probably been accustomed to.'

She thought of stolen looks across the lawn, hands brushing lightly as they passed by the greenhouse.

'I imagine it would have been difficult for Arne to see his

child in another man's arms, not to mention the woman he loved sharing a bed with her husband again,' Otto posited, running with it.

'Exactly. Tensions might have escalated. There could have been a confrontation, or a fight . . . If Casper uncovered the truth about her and Arne, he might have threatened to fire him and send him away. Or worse, said he'd take the baby from them?' Darcy blinked. 'That would send any woman walking into the sea, much less one who had already lost a child. She would have had nothing more to live for.'

They were both quiet, thinking hard.

'I agree it sounds plausible, Darcy, but without concrete proof . . .'

She nodded, knowing what he was saying.

'Tell me more about the marriage. Was it a good one?'

She shook her head. 'It was blighted by tragedy, and I'm not sure how close they ever were. There was a large age gap.'

'Ah,' he said knowingly. 'Well, we all know those only ever fall in two directions: either they're a great love story or a horror story.'

A horror story? Had it been?

If she stopped casting the Madsens as Lilja's saviours, for just one moment; if she looked at the facts without that bias . . . *Had* it been a marriage of convenience? A favour between two families . . . ?

Or something altogether more sinister?

She had never found anything on Lilja's marriage – not a wedding photograph, nor a letter of correspondence. Suddenly she understood why.

'Oh,' she gasped as another context was finally applied and the facts sifted in her mind, the heaviest settling at the bottom and underpinning everything.

'Tell me.'

She looked at him. 'I think it was a forced marriage. I think Casper sexually assaulted her and it was arranged to cover for the pregnancy that resulted.'

Otto frowned. 'Elaborate.'

She closed her eyes, recalling what she had read. 'He had come back from his war profiteering to find this beautiful, but very young, fourteen-year-old girl living with them . . . The Madsens threw a party that December . . . I think it probably happened then.' She thought back, trying to remember the details of Lotte's diary. 'Lotte said that Casper danced with Lilja, gave them both champagne . . . she was distraught that her parents hadn't returned from Germany; later on, Lotte said she could hear Lilja crying . . . Plus, he had been paying her undue amounts of attention before that.' She remembered the car rides and the shopping trips.

'And when was the child born?'

She bit her lip. 'The end of August, but I think it was a premature birth. She had eclampsia – hence the complications to her baby. Her body was too young to cope with the pregnancy.' She looked at Otto. 'Casper was sent away to London, ostensibly to head up the Madsens' growing business interests there. But what if they were keeping him away from her? Putting a lid on any scandal?'

'London would be suitably far, without raising questions.' Otto inhaled deeply, a sombre look on his face.

'It might also explain why he appears to have been largely written out of the family legacy. There's almost nothing on him. I think Helle would scratch him from the record altogether if she could.'

'Indeed, it's not at all the sort of thing they would want getting out. They've built their reputation on philanthropy and high-minded cultural ideals, and with the public listing in the offing, it's a reputation stain they could do without.'

'It makes sense, though, doesn't it?' she said, looking straight at him. 'They covered up Casper's crime by marrying Lilja to her rapist. No wonder she couldn't recover! She was traumatized . . . Hornbaek must have felt like the only place she was safe.'

'Except Casper went up there too.'

'Yes, but only for very occasional visits. I suspect appearances would have needed to be maintained to some degree. They couldn't let people start to talk . . .'

Darcy tried to imagine eighteen-year-old Lilja's horror as her abusive husband came back into her life. Her bed.

A door opened at the far end of the room and Ida stuck her head around. 'Ah, you are in here . . . Otto, your seminar group's arrived. They're in your office.'

Otto gave a small sigh. He looked at Darcy. 'I'm sorry. Terrible timing. We'll have to pick this up later.'

'Sure.' She looked at him. 'But just tell me, is this making sense to you – or am I too close to it? Have I lost my perspective?'

He looked back at the portrait, Lilja watching them in painted silence as they conjectured over her fate. 'Darcy, sadly, I think there was always going to be a dark reason why this painting was hidden behind another one. It was no accident that it was put there . . . These secrets have been kept for a long time – so keep going. We owe it to Lilja to tell her truth.'

Darcy watched him leave. Was he right? Did they owe it to Lilja to tell the world about her trauma, her love affair, her decision to leave a newborn baby to grow up without her mother? Was that to be her lasting legacy, immortalized for ever as a victim?

She walked over to the window, rolling out her neck and swinging her arms. Her mind was stuck on Lilja's desperation in her final weeks – her husband and her lover, all together at Solvtraeer . . . emotional anguish so bad it drove her into the sea . . .

She leaned on the sill and looked down into the courtyard. It was trying to snow again, the Christmas tree glittering majestically – reminding her that this was a time for goodwill to all men – as tourists walked past with shopping bags. A glossy black car was parked on the cobbles almost immediately below the window. She could see the driver in his front seat, waiting. Christoff? . . .

She gasped just as the door swung open and she turned to find Max himself walking through with a bold smile.

'I just saw Otto in the hall. He said you were in here,' he said, the yellow lining of his suit flashing as he headed straight for her. Her heart lurched at the sight of him. 'I had to work not to look happy about it.'

She saw him scan the room for others, but they were quite alone and he didn't hesitate as he reached her, cupping her face and kissing her possessively. She felt weak by the time he pulled back. '. . . I've been thinking about doing that all day.'

She smiled. 'Me too.'

'Sleep well?' His tone was intimate, as if they were still in bed, talking as the moon came up.

'I missed you.'

'Even in your sleep?'

'Yes.' She lightly hooked a finger into the waistband of his trousers, drawing a weighty look from him. Memories of last night played between them and he made a small sound, pulling back as if he didn't quite trust himself. His eyes went to the door again; someone might walk in at any moment and she knew their body language would give them away, whether they were kissing or not. 'What are you doing here anyway?' she asked instead, trying to dial down the temperature between them.

He gave what almost passed as an apologetic look. 'I needed to cross-check something with someone here.'

'Oh. Something with someone.' It was to do with the restitution claim, clearly.

'You? I thought you'd be at the gallery.'

'I was actually heading over there this morning, but then I realized I needed to cross-check something with someone here too.'

He grinned. 'Oh yeah?'

He glanced over at the easel where the back-to-back canvases were clamped, Lilja's portrait and *Her Children* stuck fast to one another. Pots, jars and brushes were scattered on the neighbouring counters, the delicate business of extrication ongoing.

Someone had made an attempt at decorating the room, she noticed now: glittery paper chains were looped in a criss-cross over the ceiling and fairy lights threaded over the pinboards. A paper crown had been placed on one of the plaster casts of King Frederick VII.

He walked towards the easel, his head tilted as he took in the unobstructed view of his own great-grandmother's portrait. He had held back in the last meeting, she recalled, when everyone else had been clamouring; of course, she had been unaware then of his familial connection.

'I'd ask for an update, but I'm not sure it's worth the risk now,' he said, looking back at her with a wry smile.

'No! Although I guess I can tell you we believe the painting is actually a self-portrait.'

He looked surprised. 'Lilja painted it?'

She nodded. 'We also think she was the artist responsible for the clays in the glass cabinet in the archives.' She remembered they had been marked A.S. on the bases. The presumption had been they were the signings of the artist, but now she believed the initials were identifiers of the subject, not the maker.

Viggo had told her the artist was an unknown, Anna Saalbach. Had it been a deliberate attempt to head her off – or had she misheard? Anna and Arne weren't so very different, especially to a non-native ear.

'The clays? . . . Really?'

'She was very accomplished,' she said, trying to stick to the positives, even though they were few and far between. If her theories bore out, there really wasn't much from this that was going to cast the Madsen family in a good light. 'She had a natural talent. It's a shame she never got to do more with it.'

'No. She died before she could get going.'

Dead at eighteen, in fact. Darcy bit her lip as she watched him stand before his great-grandmother's likeness, his hands in his trouser pockets. There was one thing she needed to know. Something only he could answer. She was nervous to ask the question, to open up a line of conversation on this, after the disagreement it had led to last time – but, as she saw it, she really had no choice. He was the only one left. Last man standing.

'. . . Max, can I ask you something?'

He turned to her, hearing the hesitation in her voice. 'Okay.'

'Did your grandmother suffer from epilepsy, do you know?'

'Emme?' He frowned. 'Not that I've ever heard.'

'Is there a family history of it?'

'No.'

'Okay,' she murmured, trying to appear unaffected by his replies.

'Why?'

'Oh, I'm sure it's nothing,' she demurred, wishing he had answered in the affirmative. A small silence bloomed between them. In spite of their best efforts to keep things personal, they were back to business again.

'Evidently it's not nothing, or you wouldn't have asked.' He came and stood in front of her. 'I've answered your questions; it's only fair you answer mine.'

She looked back at him. Was she talking to her lover, Lilja's descendant, now – or to her professional adversary? The boundary kept shifting.

'Lilja's son, her first child, had severe epilepsy. The family doctor prescribed regular dosages of bromide until his death at seven months.'

'Okay.' His eyes narrowed, waiting for the next part. 'So . . . ?'

'So, a household ledger shows some more was bought again a few weeks before Lilja died. That coincides with just after Emme's birth, so I wondered if it was for her . . . But you say she didn't have epilepsy, so . . .'

She felt the gears shift in her brain. Facts levering into position.

'. . . It must have been for someone else?' he shrugged.

She nodded, but turned away, her mind already beginning to race again. For need of something to do, she crouched down at the side of the portrait; tiny, hair-thin wires had been inserted between the back of the *Her Children* canvas and the portrait, keeping them fractionally apart where extrication had been achieved. But she didn't see them. Her thoughts were caught on the bill for the bromide, and something Aksel had told her.

All I Want for Christmas

In the context of what she now suspected about the Madsen marriage, there was another possible application for the bromide: had Lilja drugged her husband's tea when he went to stay at Hornbaek? It was one way she could have kept him away from her, even if – for appearance's sake – they had shared a bed. She wouldn't have been able to fend off a full-grown man – Lilja had been slight and certainly weakened after the birth – but if he was rendered impotent . . . ? Threat neutralized.

Had it worked? One time? Every time? If they hadn't been intimate – quite possibly ever since the attack at the party: his relocation to London and her severe depression must have thwarted numerous opportunities – then they alone would have known the baby wasn't his.

Casper would have known he had been cuckolded. Had he also discovered what she was doing to him?

One marriage. Two births. Three deaths . . . What had happened at Solvtraeer that the two of them should have ended up dead within days of one another? Because everything told her it wasn't a broken heart Casper had died from.

'Darcy?'

She realized he had been talking to her; said something she had missed. 'What?'

'You're very distracted.'

'Sorry.' She blinked, running a hand through her hair, feeling her heart pound.

He watched her closely. 'What's going on? Talk to me.'

'No, I . . . I shouldn't say . . . at least until I've spoken to Otto.' She reached for his hand. 'I'm still working through theories, that's all.'

He made a small groan. 'Fine. I'm not keen for a repeat of the other night.'

'No,' she agreed. Neither one of them wanted to go back there. It had been a catastrophic end to what had been a perfect weekend and she hated that it sat like an inkblot on their fresh, clean sheet together.

But . . . *The other night*. Darcy frowned at the words, falling very still as she realized she had overlooked something conspicuous in the car the other night, in the dark.

She looked at him, her conscience urging her to speak, her heart telling her to stay quiet . . .

His eyes narrowed, seeing the conflict running over her face. 'Darcy— What?'

'. . . Why were you so challenged in the car, when I suggested Lilja's death might not have been suicide?'

He tipped his head back and sighed. 'Why are you asking me that? We've literally just said we don't want to go back there.'

'And I don't want to!' she agreed. 'But it makes no sense; it's contrary, in fact. Most people would far prefer to think their great-grandmother's death had been a horrible accident; that it was not her actual choice to walk into the sea, leaving behind her baby, her longed-for child.' She stared at him, remembering what Viggo had told her. 'And yet, that's what the Madsen Foundation would seem to prefer people think. A deliberate death instead of an accidental one.'

He made no move to reply, as if waiting for more. She could see his guard was up again.

'Was it a double bluff?' she asked. 'Deflection strategy?' If the marriage itself had been a cover-up for a crime, why not Lilja's death? 'Was an accident too open to speculation?'

There had to have been gossip in society circles about the state of the marriage: Casper in London, Lilja up there in

Hornbaek – strangers but for infrequent reunions. The birth might even have raised more questions than it answered . . .

'Darcy—'

'An accident was too open to speculation, so hustling public opinion into whispering about suicide shut down other wonderings instead – right? Lilja's depression allowed the family to control the narrative.'

There was a pause.

'Darcy, you know I have feelings for you,' Max said in a steady voice. 'But you're mistaken if you think I'll let you defame the Madsen name.'

'I'm not defaming anyone. I'm actually trying to honour your great-grandmother's memory.'

'By sacrificing her husband's?'

She caught her breath as she stared at him. '. . . Who said anything about her husband?'

She watched as Max turned away. She could see the tension in his shoulders. She could read his body now. 'I'm only interested in revealing the facts of what happened,' she said more quietly. 'It's not for me to judge.'

'But Casper is obviously the villain in your story,' he said after a moment. 'You want to sacrifice his reputation—'

'Is it worth saving?' she cried. 'Why would you defend him over her? *Why*, a hundred years later, is your family still putting his interests before hers?'

He turned back on his heel, angry now. 'You wouldn't understand.'

'Wouldn't I? He was a Madsen, as are you. Isn't it the same reason now as then? You're doing damage control, Max. You're making sure I don't get too close to the truth. A lot of people are about to get very rich when the company is listed, and *this* is not the sort of scandal they want to get out.'

'There's no scandal. You're overplaying this.'

'No. I'm not,' she said, shaking her head as she saw from his stricken look that she had hit upon a truth more terrible than she could have foreseen. 'Because it strikes me that if Lilja's death wasn't an accident, and it wasn't suicide, then there was only one other thing it could be.'

'Darcy –' A desperate note came into his voice. 'Don't—'

'Lilja didn't walk into the sea. She had too much to live for. I think Casper killed her and put her there.' She felt her heart break as she watched his response to her words: no surprise; just defeat. '. . . But you already knew that.'

Chapter Twenty-Nine

Darcy lay in the dark, watching the figures revolve: reindeer and fir trees and snowflakes writ large on the walls of her bedroom. For the past few nights, she had fallen asleep to the gentle whir of the carousel, feeling her spirit soothed as the figures glided in serene silence. It was the only thing that made her feel better, even if it was inextricably linked with the man responsible for making her feel so bad.

There was a gentle knock on the door and Freja peered in, checking on her again. 'Hungry?' She was holding a bowl of ramen.

'Not really. Sorry,' Darcy said apologetically.

'You have to eat something. You'll get sick.'

'I'll eat tomorrow.'

'You said that yesterday. And besides, tomorrow is the party and if you don't get something inside you today, you'll be a hot mess within five minutes of sipping a cocktail.' She came further into the room and switched on the lights, drowning out the shadows playing on the walls.

'Hey!' Darcy protested.

'Relax, I'll turn them off again in a minute and you can go back to rotting in bed. Just eat something first.'

Darcy gave a groan as she reluctantly pulled herself up to sitting, Freya tucking herself under the duvet to keep warm while she waited. It was snowing every day now, but not so cold that they would allow themselves to turn up the thermostat.

'So – is everything ready for tomorrow night?' Darcy asked flatly, blowing on the ramen. It smelled delicious and she wished she could conjure an appetite.

'Pretty much, although the naked waiters came in at more than we expected—' She burst out laughing as she saw Darcy's expression.

The engagement party had been pulled together at impressive speed, given they were now just days before Christmas; Tristan had contacts who were pulling out the stops for him. Darcy wished she could conjure an appetite for that, too. For her friend's sake, she had to try.

'And you? Did you hit your word count?' Freja looked hopefully towards the laptop on the desk. The screen glowed, bright white and blank.

Darcy kept trying to work, but the flashing cursor mocked her as it took root in the top left corner and did not budge. She knew she had done her job: she had found Lilja, identified her and researched her. All that was left to do was write it all up. She had done the hard bit, cracking the story; telling it was supposed to be the easy part, and yet for the past two days she had been unable to sleep or work. Neither would come – not oblivion, not words.

Otto kept pressing her for updates following their discussion and she kept stalling him, but time was running out. Her deadline was Monday, four days from now.

'Tomorrow for the win. Definitely,' Darcy sighed, seeing how Freja looked back at her pityingly.

'. . . Why don't you talk to him?'

'And say what?'

392

'You've got a job to do and so does he. But it's just business. You respect each other's professional commitments, but that doesn't mean it has to bleed into your private life together.'

'How can it not? He doesn't trust me and I don't trust him. I don't even think I *like* him now. What does it say about his moral compass that he's fine to just live with what happened to his great-grandmother? She's his own blood, but he'll sweep her death under the carpet? That makes him no better than Casper, or Frederik and the rest of them who covered it up.'

'Well, when you put it like that,' Freja sighed. '. . . But it was all such a long time ago—'

'Exactly! And no one seems to care that for over a century, that poor woman's fate has been covered up by lies. Her reputation was sealed as being weak, broken, depressive. Her daughter grew up thinking her mother didn't love her enough to stay alive . . . Just think about that for a moment, Freja. You'd think maybe a hundred years later it was time to right the wrong? But no! The Madsens are still in damage control mode. They're a brand now. Reputation is everything.'

'But would this hurt them, *really*? I know it's all unpalatable, but it's not like anyone alive and working *now* was involved with it.'

Darcy pinned her with a look. 'All they care about is the money. And there is no way the shareholders are going to let it come out that Bertram Madsen's son murdered his own wife and the whole family helped cover it up. That company trades now on a public image of making products that save lives.'

Freja sighed, giving up the debate. 'So then what are you going to do? Reveal the truth, the whole truth and nothing but the truth? Sink them before they can float?'

Darcy shot her friend a wry look at the pun. 'I have to, for Lilja's sake. If her portrait remains fixed to *Her Children* and goes on show at the National, it's going to be seen by millions of people. I can't allow a false story to be put up about her . . . lies perpetuated for evermore.' She blinked. 'I have to pay witness to the facts, regardless of whether *I* like it or it causes a scandal. It's not for me to filter the reality of someone's life and death.' She sighed. 'What happened to Lilja was abominable. She was betrayed over and over again by the people who were supposed to protect her. At the very least, she deserves to have someone defend her now, after all this time.'

And yet it was easier said than done. Every time she tried to write, every time she thought of that eighteen-year-old girl floating in the sea, she saw Max's face in the long room as she had pulled the shroud off his family's darkest secret. He hadn't looked angry, as she had feared. It had been worse than that.

He had looked alone. That was what haunted her.

'Well, you know I'm on your side no matter what,' Freja said loyally, nudging her legs under the duvet. '. . . Will you have to see him again? Any more meetings?'

Darcy stared into space, feeling the pain spread in her body at the prospect of never seeing Max again. 'Probably not. I've done all I can do in terms of research . . . although I do need to go back to the archives and see Viggo. I can't not say a proper goodbye. He must have been wondering where I've been all week.' She hated the thought of him down there alone now. Their leisurely chats and hourly coffees had become an unexpected joy for her.

'And have you thought any more on my offer? I can't bear to think of you being alone here for Christmas, like this, when there's a spare place at my parents' table.'

Darcy shot her a loving smile. 'The original plan still stands, otherwise I promise you I'd be booking the first flight to Bali. No, come next week I'm going to be living my best life here:

the flat all to myself, endless conversations with Miss Petals, powering ahead on my thesis, all while wearing ruined Valentino. No one can tell me that's not living.'

Freja chuckled. 'Well, it's certainly something. And I suppose it's no terrible thing to rededicate yourself to the serious business of becoming Professor Cotterell.'

Darcy's phone buzzed with a text – a spur to her heart, making it quicken as she checked the name.

'Oh, talk of the devil,' she murmured. 'It's Viggo. His ears must have been burning,' she said, clicking on it and reading the message.

'Oh yeah?'

'. . . Hm, that's strange.'

'What is?'

'He wants me to meet him at University Old Library on Fiolstræde at eight a.m. sharp tomorrow morning.'

'What for?'

'He doesn't say.'

Freja met her gaze. 'Think Max is sending him as his messenger?'

'Well, if *he* couldn't talk me out of doing my professional duty, I don't know why he thinks Viggo would be able to.'

'You have got a soft spot for the old guy.'

'Not that soft . . . And besides, I'm not sure Viggo would do it. He's not driven by money. He's there for the love of the work. He's got these things called *principles*?'

Freja rolled her eyes. 'So then I wonder what he wants to see you for, if not emotional blackmail? You really can't think?'

'No.'

'Will you go?'

'Of course. It's Viggo.' Darcy bit her lip. '. . . I trust him.'

Chapter Thirty

Darcy stood at the bottom of the library steps and looked up. Viggo was bundled up in his heavy overcoat and scarf, his hat on, reading the opening times on the wall plaque. Was there anyone else left in this city who still wore a trilby? she wondered.

'Morning, Viggo,' she said, shivering in the cold and rubbing her hands together. Two paces to her right, a couple of empty wine bottles had been left standing politely against the wall, traces of last night's festivities in the student quarter.

He turned. 'Ah, Darcy, I'm glad to see you here.'

'Are we the only people up?' The city felt as if it was still asleep. The bike racks were empty, birds silent in the small trees clustered in the courtyards. All the shop shutters were still pulled down – even Paludan was at rest – and their only company was a stray cat padding silently over the cobbles with a mouse in its mouth.

In the distance, several streets away, she could hear the clatter of bins being emptied into refuse lorries, commuters disgorging from Nørreport station and heading to their office buildings; but there was an aura of suspension still in these back roads, the city balancing on the tines of night and day.

'It does appear the Christmas getaway may have begun,' he agreed, peering around at the handsome Victorian brick buildings she knew well. If the university was her world, these were her temples.

'And what are *we* doing here, so bright and early?' she asked.

'I thought we should do this together.'

'Do what?'

The lights inside the building switched on, falling through the windows onto the street in huge golden tiles, and they heard the sound of bolts being drawn back. A lock turned and one of the arched doors opened.

'Oh! . . . Good morning,' a woman said, looking out and seeming surprised to find them standing there.

'Good morning,' Viggo replied, with an almost leisurely air. 'We're here for the unsealing of a bequest.'

'. . . Oh,' she said again, stepping back. 'Well, come in. You're very early.'

Viggo motioned for Darcy to step through first into the impressive pale brick hallway. A huge turning staircase lay immediately before them like a sleeping dragon, set behind arches and lit by high-set round windows. The entrance to the library lay off to their right, and Darcy let Viggo lead the way. She knew the space well – she often worked here – but he was the only one who knew what they were really doing here today.

The space was double height and majestic, an aisle running through a central colonnade with book-lined chambers flanking off on either side. There was a round window at the very end of the central aisle and huge arched windows sat at the end of each book stack, sucking in natural light. But for the books that lined every wall, floor to ceiling, it could have been a grand church.

They walked through, footsteps sounding out of step on

the stone floor. A librarian was standing at the large black desk in the middle of the aisle, tapping on a computer. He looked up at their approach, seeing that they were not typical students.

'We're here for the unsealing of the Johan Trier bequest,' Viggo said quietly.

Darcy's head whipped round to look at him. The what?

'Ah . . . you're ahead of me,' the man said, tapping something into his screen. 'It's still . . . Yes, it's still in the vault. We weren't anticipating a rush.' He looked back at them, curious that they should be so keen. 'If you'd like to take a seat in the reading room at the end down there, I'll bring it through to you?'

'Thank you,' Viggo said, removing his hat and slowly making his way. They moved past the reeded columns, in and out of the shadows on the ground, past the thousands of books that lent their powdery, slightly almond-like scent to the dusty floors and old timbers.

They sat down together at a table in the small room at the end. It was no different to any of the other chambers, save for a glass wall that partitioned them from the open space and provided some privacy.

'So, Johan Trier made a bequest?' Darcy murmured, unzipping her jacket but not removing it. It would be a while before the central heating made itself known.

'Indeed. He made a gift to this library in 1923, but the bequest was granted on the condition it was not to be opened for fifty years following his death.' Viggo shrugged. 'And he died on the nineteenth of December 1974, aged seventy-nine. So here we are.'

Darcy tried to come up with a reason why 1923 would have been a notable date in Trier's life. *Her Children* was completed and sold . . . He had been on the cusp of leaving

Copenhagen as the work dried up . . . Lilja and Casper were dead, of course.

'What is the bequest – letters? Sketches?' she asked.

'No one knows,' he shrugged. 'But we'll find out soon enough.' He looked across at her, changing the subject. '. . . I've missed you this week.'

It was a simple statement but Darcy crumpled at it, dropping her head. 'I'm sorry, Viggo. I haven't been avoiding *you*.'

'Oh, I know.' He watched her, seeing how she fiddled with her fingers. '. . . It must have been quite a showdown between you both—'

Darcy looked up at the comment. What exactly did Viggo know about what had happened? And how did he know it had been between her and Max?

'I didn't expect him to react like this.'

She swallowed. 'Like what?'

'I thought he'd dig his heels in harder. Normally he likes the fight. I assumed you would be the last person he wanted to see this – but bringing you here was his idea.'

'He wanted me to know about the bequest?'

'Seemingly so.'

She frowned. 'Does Helle know?'

'By good fortune, she's skiing with her family in Sweden now. Max assured her he'd oversee this in her absence. He's the family's representative, not just a corporate lawyer.'

Darcy was quiet for a moment. If that was so, she couldn't understand why – having tried deflection and distraction strategies for all this time – he should suddenly choose to bring her in on this. Johan Trier had been both a friend and a foe to the Madsen family, so who knew what they were going to discover here today? Max knew she already knew enough about their complicity in Lilja's death to besmirch the family's good name. Was this the white flag of surrender? Or a favour he would somehow call in?

'. . . How long have *you* known about it?'

'Oh, decades.' He gave her a knowing look. 'Officially, since Trier died and the bequest was revealed during the reading of his will. Unofficially, since 1961.'

Darcy blinked. Officially? Unofficially? The date registered with her. '1961 was when the Madsen Foundation was formed, wasn't it?'

'Correct. It's also when Arne Saalbach died.'

'Arne?'

'Yes. And when he died, he left a letter for Frederik Madsen, revealing his relationship with Lilja and his paternity of Emme.'

'He confessed it?' Darcy's eyes widened. 'And you knew?' It stung that Viggo had kept this from her when he knew how relevant it was to her research. She had discovered the truth of Arne and Lilja's relationship herself, the hard way.

'If Helle had had her way, once you identified Lilja, I wouldn't have let you down the stairs, Darcy. But I made it clear to her that I would do my job with you, as I would for anyone else. I would assist without leading.'

Darcy bit her lip, knowing it was a fair position to have taken; they had both been trapped in a power struggle between more powerful figures. She nodded in acceptance. 'Why did he wait until after he died to publicly claim her?' she asked instead.

'Partly because when both Lilja and Casper died, he found he couldn't actually prove he *was* her father. Back in the 1920s, it wasn't like it is now – sending off a hair from a comb in the post. Not to mention, he would have had no rights, certainly no power, against a family with resources like theirs. If the Madsens had known Casper wasn't the father, they might have disinherited the child. And if they'd known Arne was the father, they could have sacked him – and his parents – and taken Emme away . . . Whatever they liked.' He shrugged. 'He was in an impossible position.'

'So, what did happen?'

'With all the notoriety around Lilja and Casper's deaths, it was agreed the Saalbachs would raise Emme at Solvtraeer, "out of the way". But in truth, neither Lotte nor Frederik had much interest in their orphaned niece.'

'So Emme ended up being raised by her own father and grandparents anyway?'

'Yes. It worked to their advantage to simply continue as the faithful servants.'

Darcy gasped at their audacity and sheer good luck. 'And the Madsens never suspected?'

'They had no reason to. Arne hid all evidence of his relationship with Lilja. He only held onto the clays she had made of him, and no one guessed they were of him. And by the time he passed away, Emme was grown and had made a good marriage; she had already come into her inheritance at twenty-one. Arne's own parents were long since dead by then, so they faced no repercussions.'

'So he wrote the letter as an official act of claiming her as his?'

'Yes. Every father desires that. It was important to him to have it on record, if not publicly then at least with the family that had destroyed the woman he loved. An act of revenge, perhaps.'

'But it was still risky, surely? If Emme was revealed as not being a Madsen by blood, they could have revoked her inheritance.'

'Not without having to explain why. The sensation around the Hornbaek deaths was still fresh enough for many in polite society, even as late as 1961.'

Darcy absorbed all this, remembering how Max had told her most of the family fortune had been diverted to his cousins but for the country house, and some shares and honorary positions within the company. Their branch of the family – the illegitimate line – had been as disinherited as far as was possible without attracting public notice.

In the wake of such tragedy, she would have thought it almost impossible that happiness could flourish for Arne and his secret daughter again; and yet, somehow, it had. Quietly, out of sight and out of mind. 'It's nice to think Emme got to grow up there, in the place where her mother was so happy.'

'Yes. Emme lived her whole life at Solvtraeer. She was married there, had her son . . .'

'I saw her wedding photograph when I was up there.'

'And did you see how Arne honoured Lilja's memory? . . . He planted all the flower beds full of lilies. He never loved anyone else after her.'

She gave a quizzical smile. 'Viggo, how do you know all this about Emme?'

'It's in her diaries.'

Darcy blinked. She had never got that far along – and likely never would have, either. She had made the mistake of assuming that Lilja's story had ended with Lilja's death.

'So then Arne's revelations . . .' she mused, coming back to their original point.

Viggo chuckled. 'Came as quite a shock to the old boy, yes; Fred Madsen was in his late seventies by then, but he was still a shrewd operator. He immediately understood the damage that would be done to the family name if the truth were to come out about Emme's parentage – it would lead straight back to Lilja's death and Casper's culpability. Business had to be seen to continue as usual.'

Seen? Darcy's eyes narrowed at the semantic hedging. 'What does that mean?'

'In the letter, Arne revealed his affair with Lilja – but also how he had concealed it from them for all those years. The night Casper died was chaotic; the family were already en route, travelling up to Hornbaek, having been in Sweden when Lilja had drowned. Arne realized they had to get any and all evidence of the affair out of the house before the family arrived.'

'They?' She looked at him, understanding suddenly that Arne hadn't acted alone. 'And the portrait would have revealed the affair?'

'Supposedly she had written an inscription on the back of it. Trier only remembered it was still drying in his studio after the police had arrived when Casper was found dead. He concealed it in the back of *Her Children* and sealed it. He had promised the painting to Bertram, of course, but the next day, a German tourist visited the gardens and he sold it to him to get it off the estate, right under the police's noses.'

This, Darcy knew, was the apparent betrayal that had ended Trier's lucrative relationship with the Madsens.

'And Arne's letter told them all this?'

'Not exactly. He was careful not to specify which painting it was hidden behind; that would have been an unwarranted kindness, telling them exactly where to look. He only said that it was hidden in the back of one of Trier's paintings.'

Viggo arched an eyebrow at Arne's sly game.

'So that's why the Foundation was set up right after his death – they've been assiduously buying the entire Trier portfolio, trying to find it.' Darcy's brain was working at triple speed. 'But surely they must have suspected it was in the back of *Her Children* – given it was what Trier was working on at the time?'

'Of course. They just couldn't be certain.'

It accounted for their aggression, though, trying to acquire it, she thought to herself.

'Remember, they were only learning all this forty years later. Who, by then, could say with any real certainty what other works had been in the studio at the same time?'

'Wow,' she murmured. 'Revenge really is a dish best served cold.' For the past sixty years, the family that had covered up Lilja's death had been scrabbling to keep their tracks hidden. They'd spent tens of millions on the hunt for the portrait, only to have to stand on the sidelines as it was finally found and she, of all people, was drafted in.

Had they underestimated her? Darcy remembered Helle's cold, assessing stare at the National Gallery drinks reception – clearly trying to decide whether Darcy was a threat. She remembered how Max, too, had hung back, holding back his personal inclinations as he realized the role she was about to play in his life. She remembered the stunned look on his face as they had found the necklace and first uttered Lilja's name. He must have realized that from there it was a game of dominoes . . . It was why they'd come in so hard, so fast, on the threats of legal action. Desperate bullying in the hopes of a quick surrender.

'And so now we're here for the unsealing of Johan Trier's bequest,' she said. 'Is it a letter admitting what he did and where he hid the portrait?'

Viggo shrugged. 'Your guess is as good as mine.'

She was quiet for a moment. 'It's strange, isn't it, that Trier helped Arne that night? . . . Don't you think it's slightly curious that he chose helping the Saalbachs over his patrons?'

'Yes. I think it's very curious. I've often wondered about it.'

Darcy looked back at him, the keeper of secrets. For four

generations, the Madsens had been bracing for a bomb to go off, the family forced into a waiting game, counting down the years, hours and minutes for this bequest to be unsealed. It was finally happening – and yet Max had invited her to watch?

'Apologies for the wait,' the librarian said, drawing her from her thoughts as he came back in with a black folio box and wearing white protection gloves. '. . . So here were are.'

He opened the box and lifted out a brown package, wrapped and sealed with fine steel straps. Beneath it was a small cream envelope, with handwriting in black ink: *Bequest of Johan Trier, January 1923*. Darcy recognized his sloppy cursive, but this looked especially dashed and urgent.

Darcy watched, her breath held as the librarian opened the letter. She thought he might read it out loud, but after glancing at it, he simply laid it flat on the table.

Viggo and Darcy immediately leaned in to read.

Enclosed here the diary of Johan Trier. I swear on my honour that everything written in these pages is a true and honest account of events as I witnessed and experienced them. Strictly not to be opened till fifty years to the day of my death.

Witnessed?

Viggo and Darcy swapped glances as the librarian clipped off the security straps with wire clippers. Darcy had to remind herself to breathe as he slipped the diary out of the envelope onto his palm: it was burgundy tooled leather, like all the others.

Innocuous. For a bomb.

For several moments everyone just looked at it as it was set down on the table. Johan Trier's 1922 diary. The one she hadn't been able to find in the archives.

'May we . . . ?' Viggo asked.

'By all means,' the librarian shrugged, oblivious to the significance of what he had handled. 'I'll be just outside if you require assistance.'

They watched him go in silence.

Viggo touched the cover lightly before thumbing through into January. He began to read aloud: 'The first day of the year, and already I am made melancholy by the northern light . . .'

He looked up at Darcy. They were both far too familiar with the artist's grumblings, and it wasn't his life they were interested in.

'Go straight to August,' Darcy urged.

Carefully, Viggo flicked through the pages to September, then leafed back carefully towards the date Lilja had died – but even at a high-level glance, they could see the artist's distinctive sloping scrawl had, in these entries, become smaller, denser, more tightly bunched.

Panic.

Trauma.

'Ready?' Viggo asked, smoothing the page flat.

Darcy nodded, taking a deep breath, as together they leaned forward and began to read.

Chapter Thirty-One

'Well, given you only had three days to pull this together, it's not *too* shabby,' Darcy said as she and Freja looked out at the sea of glamorous guests. The two-storey space was filled with people mingling around small tree-planted islands, subterranean gardens and a blonde ceiling that was speckled like shagreen. The Opera Park was set on a man-made island in the harbour and was an oasis in the city with six parks around it; there wasn't a right angle to be found anywhere, the 360-degree curved glass walls set beneath a huge overhanging flower-shaped grass roof. Beyond, the lights of the city glittered across the water – so many lives being lived alongside one another, all with different plans, different hopes.

'It's like partying inside an amoeba,' Freja giggled, her champagne glass pressed against her lips.

'It's incredible, is what it is. Do you even know these people?'

'Maybe . . . ten of them?' Freja shot her a grin.

'Ten out of a hundred. Great!'

'Most of them are Tristan's uni friends, colleagues, industry contacts . . . But remember, I'm marrying an older man – he's had more time to make friends! Plus, he's rich, so everyone wants to be his friend.'

'Uh-huh.'

Freja squeezed her arm. 'So long as *you're* here, it doesn't really matter.' She scrutinized Darcy closely. Darcy was wearing the black velvet dress again, her hair worn in a half-up, half-down do and make-up on. For no one but Freja would she have made this effort; an evening of small talk was the very last thing she needed. She had tried to get hold of Max when she had got back from the library but, to her dismay, had discovered he'd blocked her number. The revelation had floored her. Things had ended badly between them at the Academy on Tuesday as they retreated to their opposite corners of the ring – but surely he had spoken to Viggo by now and saw that, with the unsealing of Johan Trier's bequest, everything had changed again?

'I thought I heard the tippity-tap of fingers on keys through your door earlier. I looked in, but you had your headphones on and I didn't want to disturb your flow. Do I take it your early-morning rendezvous was a success?'

'Illuminating, certainly.'

'And you've started writing?'

'I've made a start,' Darcy nodded, forcing a smile even though her body still thrummed with the aftershocks of what she had learned. Everything had pivoted again and she wasn't sure how to feel any more. Nothing was absolute.

'So then the block's unblocked!' Freja said, too brightly. 'Now you can close the door on the whole thing and move on!'

'Exactly,' Darcy replied with some equanimity. This was neither the time nor place to give the final post-mortem on her situationship. It was Freja's moment and she refused to put a downer on her friend's joyous mood.

They both stared into the crowd, watching the sophisticated guests glitter and sparkle. Elegant receptions were becoming something of a norm for her these days, it seemed.

'Freja!'

Tristan was calling her through the crowd, his face split into a happy beam as he motioned enthusiastically for her to come over.

'Come with me? Let's see if he's got any hot single friends.'

Darcy rolled her eyes. 'Hard pass.'

'But—'

Darcy smiled, shaking her head. 'I'm fine. You go! You're the hostess. And I need another drink. I'll join you in a bit.'

'Promise?'

'I promise.'

'I'll come looking if you don't,' Freja warned, squeezing her hand before slipping into the crowd. '. . . Hey, baby,' Darcy heard her say as Tristan looped his arm around her.

Darcy turned away and headed for the bar, weaving between the bodies and avoiding eye contact as interested stares landed upon her. She figured another hour here, tops, before she could make a French exit – and she could spend half of that hiding in the loos.

'A champagne, please,' she said to the bartender.

'. . . Make that two.'

She turned, stunned by the sound of a voice that had no place being here.

'What are *you* doing here?' she breathed as Max stared back at her, one hand in his trouser pocket, his tie off and top button undone. He looked exhausted, no sign of his usual anima in his eyes.

'Tristan's a contact. We've worked with his labs on a few things.' He looked down at her, his eyes narrowing fractionally as he clearly recognized her dress from the night they had met. 'You?'

'Freja's my flatmate.'

'Ah,' he breathed. 'Well, I guess that trumps me. Don't

worry, I won't linger. I'll head off as soon as I've offered my congratulations.'

'You don't have to go on my account.'

The bartended handed over their drinks.

'Thank you,' she murmured, her heart pounding at this surprise encounter. Of all the people she hadn't expected to see tonight, he was top of the list.

Quickly, she took a sip of her champagne. It tasted colder, fresher, sharper than usual, another small jolt to her shocked body as she tried to gather her composure. Their last meeting had ended so abruptly, with such finality . . . And yet seeing him again, she remembered only the weight of his head upon her breast, his hand on her hip.

'I'll leave you in peace.'

Darcy watched in shock as he turned to go. That was *it*? He'd blocked her online and he had nothing to say to her face?

'Haven't you spoken to Viggo?' she asked to his back.

He stopped and half turned back. 'Not yet. I've been in board meetings all day.'

'Well then perhaps you should.'

'Viggo would alert me if there was anything I needed to know.'

Unless Viggo was leaving it to her? He clearly wasn't blind to what was going on between her and Max, and after what they'd discovered today . . . 'There is.'

He sighed. 'Yeah? And what further surprises await?'

She swallowed at his flat sarcasm. Viggo had been right; he wasn't acting to type. It was as if he had completely checked out. Acceptance of his fate. The Madsens were the villains of this piece and he was one of them. Right? 'Johan Trier was there the night Lilja died; he was a witness. He put it all in his diary. That was the bequest.'

There was a long silence as Max digested the news. Outwardly, he appeared not to react, but she saw the tension in his mouth, the unnatural stillness in his body. 'Did he detail what happened?'

She nodded.

He walked back over, standing right beside her. 'Tell me,' he said in a low voice, not wanting anyone to overhear.

'. . . They had all gone to bed when he heard an argument down the corridor. Casper was shouting. Lilja was crying. Johan could hear her pleading with Casper, saying he owed her this happiness. Trier thought he heard things being thrown and he debated going through and intervening – but he didn't.'

Max blinked, saying nothing.

'I assume he felt that as a guest in his patron's house, it wasn't his place to interfere in domestic disputes – although he was clearly conflicted. From the earlier diary entries, it's clear he and Lilja had become friends over the summer.' She bit her lip. 'Eventually it seemed to die down. Everything went quiet and he fell asleep. But then he woke up later in the night. He needed the bathroom and said that as he was walking back to his bed, he saw Casper through his window, coming up the garden. He was fully clothed but soaking wet, as if he'd just gone for a swim. Apparently he'd had a lot to drink at dinner so it wasn't . . . completely inexplicable.'

Max looked away, his jaw clenched.

'Trier went back to sleep. It was only in the morning, when Casper started shouting for Lilja, that he realized something was wrong. The baby was crying, needing to be fed, and she was nowhere to be found . . . It was Johan who ran down to the beach and found her.'

'Jesus,' Max muttered through clenched teeth, closing his eyes momentarily as he sighed, the sound weary and dark.

It was a moment before he looked back at her. 'So then it's exactly as we thought. Trier's given us confirmation – but no surprises.' It was a deliberate dig, echoing her accusations at their last meeting that he had known all along what Casper had done.

'No.' She shook her head. 'Because he wasn't just a witness . . . He became an accomplice.'

'By hiding the portrait?' he asked sceptically. 'That would hardly meet the threshold for obstruction of justice.'

'No, not that crime. He realized what he'd seen the night before and told the Sallys – he knew all about Arne and Lilja; he knew they were in love. Arne was destroyed by her death. He had known there was no way Lilja would leave him or Emme. So when he heard Trier's account . . . he went after Casper.'

Max's eyebrows raised. 'Arne killed Casper?'

'Trier too. They all did.'

'But how? There was no evidence of foul play.'

'Not externally. Mrs Sally served him a lunch of ham, eggs and mushrooms. The mushrooms had been freshly foraged that day by Arne and his father. They collected them from the woods at the back.'

She looked at Max with an expression that made him frown, detecting subtext. 'They fed him poisonous mushrooms? They poisoned him?'

She nodded. 'It took seven hours for the first symptoms to appear. Another day and a half before he died. He was already unresponsive by the time the Madsens arrived from Sweden.'

'But the police wouldn't have just bought the story that he coincidentally collapsed and died within hours of his wife.'

'They did, because Casper had already given them a show. He had had to give a statement after Lilja's body was found.

Trier heard him telling them that Lilja was a depressive and that she'd threatened to do this before . . . Apparently his act of distress was so convincing that the doctor had to sedate him. By the time he was called back to the house late the next day, Casper was too sick to speak and there was nothing left at Solvtraeer to disprove Casper's own cover story of his wife's suicide. The doctor and the police had seen his anguish first hand, so there was no suspicion when the doctor recorded a broken heart as his cause of death.'

Max couldn't reply. He looked confounded.

'Max, this changes everything,' she said quietly, willing him to look at her. 'What happened to Lilja didn't go unpunished after all. She was avenged by the people who loved her. Johan Trier never forgave himself for not intervening that night, but he proved himself her friend by bearing witness in the diary to what he'd seen, and by agreeing to keep the affair secret so that Emme could stay with her real family.'

'Testing, testing.' Tristan's voice suddenly carried through the room, the slight whine of a microphone switching on.

Darcy ignored it, focused solely on Max. Didn't he see what this meant for him? Them? Casper Madsen wasn't even his biological relation; his true great-grandfather, Arne Saalbach, had prevailed over him, against almost overwhelming odds.

'The problem I have now is that if I reveal Casper's crime, I also have to reveal the Saalbachs' . . . And they were good people. They don't deserve to be vilified.'

He looked sharply at her with a mildly incredulous expression. 'So what – *now* you want to whitewash this? You told me it wasn't your place to judge either way.'

'It isn't! It's just—'

'Complicated? Don't you think I know that better than anyone? My entire family history has just been rewritten and there's still no happy ending. Did it ever occur to you I might actually be pleased to hear that Lilja's death was avenged? That as far as I'm concerned, Casper had it coming?' Anger blazed in his eyes. 'Yes – the family had suspicions about what he might have done, but there was never any proof; only two dead bodies and a baby that needed a home.' He stared at her, his eyes blank. 'But you – *you* assumed I wanted him to get away with it.'

'Max, I—' she stammered.

'That's what you think of me; that's the kind of man you think I am. Because – what? – my grandmother was a Madsen? Because I'm good at my job?'

'No!'

He shook his head fractionally, his stare cold. 'I've been waiting for this day my entire life. My father warned us that Trier's bequest was a threat, that the missing painting could destroy our lives; that no matter what good *we* might ever do, it could all still be swept away. And you proved he was right. You were the first to believe the worst.'

'Max, please—' She thought of the work he did in his brother's name, raising millions for the paediatric hospital. *The sins of the father are visited upon the children.* None of this was his doing; it was just coming to pass on his shift.

'The truth is out now,' he shrugged. 'And I've simply swapped one murderous great-grandfather for another.' He gave a small snort of contempt. 'So for the avoidance of doubt, I'm glad Lilja was avenged, Darcy, but *I* don't win either way.'

He was right. She had let him down, too quick to believe the worst. 'Can't we just go outside and talk?'

'Thank you, everyone! . . .' Tristan's voice echoed across the room, making everyone turn and fall silent as their host commanded attention. 'Where's my . . . ? Freja, come over here, darling,' he said, standing centre stage, his arm outstretched for Freja to curl into. 'Look at her – isn't she beautiful?'

A cheer went up, everyone clapping loudly, and Darcy reluctantly dragged her eyes off Max to watch as her flatmate gave a small curtsey while blushing furiously.

'Now, I know what you're thinking: what the hell is she doing with an old man like me?'

Everyone laughed. Everyone but them. Darcy glanced back at Max, feeling the hostility radiating from him. He was staring dead ahead, not listening to a word. He hadn't touched his champagne; he was standing completely alone in this crowded room.

'Well, I'll have you know not all love stories look like a Hollywood rom-com. In fact, not all love stories even have happy endings; sometimes the most powerful love stories don't get the endings they deserve. But I have always been a lucky man . . .'

Max moved suddenly, turning to go, as if the words pained him. 'Where are you going?' she gasped, catching his fingers in her own.

'I can't stay here. I have to call a meeting with the board and let them know what's coming. You're not the only one who has a job to do.' He slipped his hand free, a muscle flexing in his jaw as he looked back at her with resentment and blame.

'Max, I'm sorry!' she whispered desperately. 'I wish everything could be different, but . . . Trier's eyewitness account is in the public sphere now. Anyone can read it. Someone was always going to uncover the truth.'

'I know that,' he said, and she saw something like regret flicker through his eyes. 'But why did it have to be you?'

Chapter Thirty-Two

Darcy stood at the brick gateposts, shivering, the house at her back. The R8 was parked outside the garage but there was no smoke puffing from the chimneys, no lights on in the house. She had walked around to the kitchen doors that gazed upon the lawn and peered in, cupping her hands around her eyes. The Christmas tree they had bought together (in between kisses) and carried home (in between kisses) stood quietly in the corner; they had dressed it with the decorations Max had brought down from the attic, but the lights were off. There was a newspaper on the kitchen table, left open on the football pages; a new bag of coffee beans on the counter.

They were the signs of life she had hoped to see, but no one was here now. She crossed the road and looked down the expanse of the beach, blowing on her hands as the wind lifted her hair and made it fly wildly. Had he gone into town? Gone to get food?

There was snow on the sand, a crunchy crust dotted with footprints, a solitary dog and its human walking in the distance from the opposite direction. Sweden was nowhere to be seen, the low-lying clouds sucking in the horizon and painting the sea a battleship grey.

She walked down to the water's edge, clutching her arms around her body as she stared into the shallows where Lilja's life had ended. Though not her story. That had continued to beat through Emme, her son, Max . . .

A sharp, piercing whistle zipped through the air, startling her, and she heard the man give a shout. She looked up and saw the dog, a caramel-coloured spaniel, begin to hurtle at full gallop along the strait. It shot past her before doubling back and careering up to her legs, sniffing her shoes excitedly.

'Hey,' she cooed, holding her wind-whipped hair back with one hand as she looked down, seeing the delight in its eyes, tail wagging so hard it could almost take off.

'Sorry!' the man called, jogging towards her, holding a hand up appeasingly. 'Sorry! She's friendly, just a bit hyper—'

His voice tailed off as they recognized each other. '. . . Darcy.'

Max was carrying a rope lead in his hand, a dog whistle on a string at his neck.

'You got a *dog*?' she asked, stunned, as he stopped a few feet away, staring back at her like he was the one who couldn't believe his eyes.

'. . . She's, uh, a rescue,' he said finally. 'I've only fostered her for the holidays. She's . . . not used to open spaces yet. She just runs any time she's let out.'

'Oh.' Darcy hated the thought of this sweet animal in a crate. 'Well, who can blame her?' she asked, watching as the dog ran happily around them in figures of eight, seemingly still nowhere close to tiring. 'What's her name?'

'Luna. She's four.'

'She's adorable.' She crouched down, holding her arms out, and the dog ran into them, curling like a comma. Her tail wagged dementedly as Darcy squeezed and hugged her; she laughed as the dog began sniffing her neck, tickling her. 'Oh, you're too cute . . .'

'What are you doing here, Darcy?' His tone was flat and

her brain briefly flashed through the justifications that would preserve her dignity: she had come to share the good news she had received from Otto this morning – that the portrait had been successfully released from *Her Children*. That she and Viggo had had an idea for a new exhibition at the gallery: give up the claim for *Her Children*, buy the portrait and put it out alongside Lilja's clays, her garden drawings and the family photographs showing Arne's famous lily displays. Show the love, not the hate, and let them finally rest in peace together.

But it wasn't in her to pretend and she felt the tears press behind her eyes as she saw the distance that lay between them, even as they stood at arms-length. 'I came to tell you I'm sorry,' she said thickly, standing up again. She had spent the past week willing him to call, knowing he wouldn't, until finally she had broken and come up here hoping she could make him see that the conflict between their jobs had no real bearing on their feelings. But for a man who had spent the past decade making his job his identity, his life . . . his worst fears had been confirmed. 'You were right, I did assume the worst about you. I thought you would do anything to protect the Madsens ahead of the public listing. I never thought about how any of it would impact you personally.'

Her words were met with a short silence.

'I appreciate that,' he said stiffly. 'But you needn't have come all this way . . . It doesn't change anything.'

'I don't deserve a second chance?'

He shook his head. 'I just can't trust you.'

'That's bullshit and you know it,' she said quietly. 'You're as fastidious about your job as I am about mine. If the boot was on the other foot, you'd have done exactly the same.' She stared at him, wanting to shake him out of this torpor. Where was his anger, his fight? 'But you and I both know this isn't about Lilja, or Casper, or my mistaken presumptions.'

'No?'

'No. You're just using it as an excuse to push me away – and if it wasn't that, you'd be looking for something else instead. You let me get too close and now you're looking for reasons to reject me.'

He said nothing back, refusing even to argue with her, and she felt her heart fold at his intractability. Even if she was right, he had checked out from her, long before she had stepped onto this beach.

She looked away, watching as the dog continued to tear along the beach, but only ever going a hundred metres before looping back to them, as if understanding that he – they – were her anchor.

'Will you be able to give her back?'

He didn't hesitate. 'Yes. Those are the terms I agreed with the home.'

Ever the lawyer. 'Well, I guess I can see how that would work for you.'

Max shifted his weight. 'What does that mean?'

She looked back at him. 'Just that it's your standard MO: you get to give her some affection and exercise and then hand her back afterwards.'

His eyes narrowed. They both knew perfectly well that she wasn't talking about the dog.

'It's better not to get too attached, right?' she asked.

'In my experience, yes.'

She stood before him, staring into those blue eyes that were so good at making women fall – but they were voids, as beautiful and as empty as the sky. He had lost everyone he ever loved and he knew how to detach in a way that she didn't.

'Well,' she said finally. 'I guess that makes perfect sense when all you know are endings.'

He frowned. 'What?'

'. . . When all you know are endings, there's safety in sticking to beginnings. And we've had our beginning, haven't we?' she asked quietly.

He hesitated, then nodded.

She nodded too, feeling a searing pain that flashed white behind her eyes. This really was it. 'Yeah,' she whispered. '. . . I guess I just needed to hear you say it.'

Luna ran a figure of eight between them, having her best day, and Darcy took a step back, trying to step out of his sphere. She truly was the rule and not the exception after all.

'Bye, Max.' She shrugged and took another step back, seeing how he didn't stir, knowing she had to leave before the tears fell. She turned and began to walk away, but Luna gave a bark and ran up to her again, jumping so that her paws rested on Darcy's thighs.

'Goodbye little one,' Darcy murmured, ruffling her head and kissing it again, stroking her behind her long silky ears. 'You deserve better,' she whispered, pressing her cheek against Luna's fur and feeling her tears absorbed as she squeezed her eyes shut.

She remained like that for several moments, the dog sensing her despair in a way that Max did not. At last she straightened again, letting Luna resume her sprints. She looked back at him, standing frozen as he watched them.

'I know you can give her back without a backward glance,' she said stiffly, her hair flying around her face and hiding another solitary tear that had somehow escaped her guard and was sliding down her cheek. 'But it might actually be kinder not to let her get attached to you.'

Max flinched at the comment but she didn't wait for his defence; she just turned and walked away, holding her head up as she strode over the hard sand. The wind was in her face now and she felt the tears streak across her cheek like raindrops on a windscreen.

She didn't turn back. There was nothing more to be said. He'd told her, almost without any words at all, that it was done. He was too entrenched, or she was too inconsequential after all, for him to break the chains that bound him.

She could feel her shoulders rising as she walked, the tears beginning to come harder as her heart pounded with the exercise and devastation. She just had to get back to the station; she could fall apart when she was on the train. It had been almost empty on the way up, everyone deserting the City for Christmas.

Luna shot past her like a golden arrow again, doubling back and coming to trot alongside her. She barked and jumped up, trying to nose Darcy's palm as she walked, not understanding that she was leaving.

'No, Luna . . . no, you can't walk with me . . . Go back,' she said, pointing behind her. But when did a dog ever look in the direction of a pointed finger? Luna nosed her hand again. '. . . Go back.'

Still the dog walked to heel, a faithful companion already, refusing to leave her – or be left.

'Luna, go back.' Uselessly, she pointed again, but the dog only seemed to cling closer. At this rate, Luna would be getting on the train with her. '. . . Please.'

Darcy looked up and away out to sea as she walked on, deciding ignoring Luna was probably the best option. If she didn't engage, the dog would lose interest and go back to Max.

421

If he'd just blow the whistle, or call after her . . . Or was he so avoidant he'd actually just let the dog *go*?

She stopped abruptly and wheeled round. 'Max! Could you just call h—'

She gasped as he almost ran into her, having to step into a sort of straddle around her so as not to mow her down, his hands grabbing her to hold her up.

For a moment, they stood there in a shock embrace, and she saw him see her wet lashes and cheeks; he saw her see the desperation in his eyes.

His fingers pressed against her arms, his breath coming hard as he brought her back to upright. '. . . I thought I could do it. I thought I could let you go,' he panted. Her hair was being blown into his face and he swept it back, clasping her head with both hands. 'But it's too late.' He swallowed, looking like a confession was being dragged from him. '. . . I'm already attached. Was from the very first night, when I had to leave you on the steps to go on your *date*.' Jealousy flared in his eyes at the memory.

It was a moment before she could find her voice. 'As I recall, you set up your own date too.'

But he shook his head. 'I blew her off. We had gone two blocks before I told Christoff to turn around and drive back to the gallery.'

'You came back for me?' Darcy gasped.

'You'd gone of course, but it was too late – you were already in my head. I knew I couldn't have you, but that only seemed to make me want you more. I told myself to stay away but still I somehow found myself making up ways to see you. So I fell back on my old tricks. I figured if I couldn't keep myself away from you, I could at least make you want to stay away from me. But that didn't work either.' His voice broke on the words and she knew, from the look of panic that darted through his eyes, that he'd never spoken to anyone like this before.

'Because I didn't want to let you go Max,' she said urgently. 'I still don't.'

'Good.' His grip tightened. 'Because . . . because I love you, Darcy.'

'I love you back,' she whispered, feeling her body thrill as he bent down and kissed her.

Her lips were salty with tears, his cheeks cold. Luna was barking excitedly as she ran around them in circles. Darcy felt the dog's wet paws paddling on her thighs until eventually they were forced to pull apart and give her some attention. Max scooped her up, bringing the dog's warm body between them. 'You just can't bear to be left out, can you?' he asked the animal, kissing its head affectionately.

Luna nuzzled their necks, her cold, wet nose tickling them both and making them laugh.

Darcy looked back at him, an idea beginning to form in her mind. '. . . Oh God,' he groaned as he immediately caught her drift.

'Well, she loves you too,' she smiled, ruffling Luna's silky head. 'And you do need a bit of chaos in your life.'

He arched an eyebrow. 'I thought that was you.'

She shrugged happily, her hand stroking his cheek. 'I wasn't so confident of my mission up here that I dared to get you a gift. She could always be our Christmas present to one another.'

'But I don't do Christmas.'

'Liar. You've got a tree . . .' she murmured, tracing his mouth with a finger. 'And I've got stockings . . .'

His eyes glittered at the intimation, his gaze falling to her lips. 'Well, when you put it like that,' he grinned, squeezing her tightly, '. . . Happy Christmas.'

Acknowledgements

Well, the Pan Mac SWAT team had their work cut out with the early drafts of this story. As is the worst-case scenario for any writer, I didn't quite know what it was all about until I got to the closing pages – and the tight deadlines of my two-books-a-year schedule meant the first submission was a horror. Huge thanks to my editor Gillian Green for not panicking and, more importantly, not showing it to anyone else until I had time to work on it. My reputation was on the line. . . ! Thank you also to Lucy Hale for constant support and cheerleading when my bottom lip was wobbling.

I am forever in debt to Stu Dwyer for making sure the finished product ends up in every key bookstore up and down the country – let me tell you, that man has contacts! – and to Chloe Davies and Natasha Tulett for making sure you all know about it. So many people are involved in the process from start to finish I don't want this to read like a wedding speech but I must give particular mention to Ellah Mwale, Lucy Grainger, Claire Evans and Leanne Williams. Most especially, I'd like to give a resounding shoutout to James Annal for producing this stunning cover. Copenhagen has never looked prettier.

Finally, I must thank my agent Amanda Preston for her

tireless support, especially over the last few years which have been difficult for me personally, and my beautiful daughter who was my research assistant on the trip to Copenhagen. She was amply paid in new clothes and hot chocolates.

There's a Karen Swan book
for every season . . .

Have you discovered her winter stories yet?

www.panmacmillan.com/karenswan

Discover Karen Swan's
sweeping historical series set on the wild, remote Scottish island of St Kilda

Read on for an extract of

The Last Summer

The start of a major new series by Karen Swan

'**Powerful writing and a wonderful premise make this a novel you'll simultaneously want to savour and race through**'
Jill Mansell

Summer 1930 on St Kilda – a wild, remote Scottish island. Two strangers from drastically different worlds meet . . .

Wild-spirited Effie Gillies has lived all her life on the small island of St Kilda, but when Lord Sholto, heir to the Earl of Dumfries, visits, the attraction between them is instant. For one glorious week she guides the handsome young visitor around the isle, falling in love for the first time – until a storm hits and her world falls apart.

Three months later, St Kilda falls silent as the islanders are evacuated for a better life on the mainland. Effie is surprised to be offered a position working on the Earl's estate. Sholto is back in her life but their differences now seem insurmountable, even as the simmering tension between them grows. And when a shocking discovery is made back on St Kilda, all her dreams for this bright new life are threatened by the dark secrets Effie and her friends thought they had left behind.

Available now

Chapter One

13 May 1930

The dogs were barking on the beach. The old women came to stand at their doors, looking out with hard frowns across the curve of the bay. The tide was going out and there'd been a testy wind all day, whipping up the waves and making the birds wheel with delight.

Effie didn't move from her position on the milking stone. She had her cheek to Iona's belly and was filling the pail with relaxed indifference. She knew it could be another twenty minutes before a boat nosed around the headland, though it would probably be sooner today, given these winds. Her collie Poppit – brown-faced, with a white patch over one eye – sat beside her, ears up and looking out over the water, already awaiting the far-off sea intruders, though she wouldn't leave Effie's side.

She watched the movements of the villagers from her elevated perch. The milking enclosure was a good third of the way up the hill and she always enjoyed the view. It was a Tuesday, which meant washing day, and she could see the younger women standing in the burns, skirts tucked up and scrubbing the linens as they talked. They wouldn't like having their sheets flying in the wind if visitors were coming. None of the tourist boats were scheduled to come this week, but if it was a trawler, it wouldn't be so bad; most of the captains were friends.

The indignity of airing their linens before strangers was taken seriously in a village where privacy was merely a concept. The layout alone meant anyone could see the comings and goings of the villagers from almost any point in the glen; it was shaped like a cone with smooth but steep slopes two-thirds of the way round, leading up to towering cliffs that dropped sharply and precipitously on the other sides to the crashing sea below. The cliffs only dipped, like a dairy bowl's lip, on the south-easterly corner, skimming down to a shingle beach. There was nowhere else to land on the isle but here. The seas were heavy and torrid all around but by a stroke of luck, the neighbouring isle, Dun – no more than a bony finger of rock – almost abutted the shores of Hirta, creating a natural breakwater and rendering Village Bay as a safe haven in the churning grey waters of the North Atlantic. During some storms they had as many as twenty ships taking refuge there.

Trawlermen, whalers, navy men, they all rhapsodized, as they took shelter, about the welcoming and cosy sight of the village tucked beneath the high-shouldered ellipse, chimneys puffing, oil lamps twinkling. The grey stone cottages – interspersed with the older traditional blackhouses, which had been steadily abandoned since the 1860s – sat shoulder to shoulder and fanned around the east side of the bay, bordered by a strong stone dyke. Looking down from the ridges on high, they were like teeth in a jaw. Giant's teeth, Effie's mother used to say.

The village's position afforded the best protection from winds that would funnel down the slopes at speeds that lifted rocks and tore the steel roofs from the stone walls (at least until the landlord, Sir John MacLeod of MacLeod, had had them strapped down with metal ties).

The Street – and there was only one – was a wide grassy path, set between the cottages and a thick low wall that topped the allotments. It was the beating heart of island life. Everyone congregated there, protected further from the wind by their own homes and able to bask in the sun on fine days. The old women sat knitting and spinning by their front doors; the children ran along the wall, cows occasionally nodding over it. Every morning, the men would meet outside number 5 and number 6 for their daily parliament to decide upon and allocate chores; and after tea, the villagers would amble down it to pick up from their neighbours 'the evening news'.

In front of each cottage, across the Street, was a long, narrow walled plot that ran down towards the beach. It was here that the villagers planted their potatoes in lazybeds, hung their washing and allowed their few cattle to overwinter. During the summer months, the cows were kept behind the head dyke, whilst the many sheep were grazed on the pastures of Glen Bay, on the other side of the island. Separated from Village Bay by a high ridge, Am Blaid, Glen Bay spiralled down to a sharply shelved cove. There was no beach to speak of over there, for the northerly waves were relentless and though the villagers kept a skiff there for emergencies, heading out and coming ashore were only possible on the rare occasions when the prevailing wind switched and the sea lay fully at rest.

Iona stopped munching and moved with a twitch of irritation. Unperturbed, Effie reached down for the pile of dock leaves she had picked on her way up and wordlessly passed her another few. The cow gave a sigh of contentment and

Effie resumed milking. This was their usual morning routine and both were accustomed to its gentle rhythms.

A few minutes later, the pail was almost full and Effie sat up, patting Iona on the flank. 'Good girl,' she murmured, standing up off the milking stone and looking down the slope. As predicted, the prow of a sloop was just nosing round the headland of Dun.

She watched keenly as the ship slipped silently into the embrace of the bay and threw out an anchor, sails drawing down. Not a trawler, then. The women would be displeased. This vessel with its slim-fingered triple masts and low curved hull was a finessed creature, more likely found in the azure waters off France than the outermost Hebrides.

'Friend or foe?!'

The question echoed around the caldera.

The crew were just black dots from here but she could see the locals already readying the dinghy; the men would need to row powerfully against waves that were pounding the shore. The passengers aboard the sloop had chosen a bad day to sail. The open water would have tossed them like a cork and although Dun's presence granted mercy, it was no free pass; a south-easterly made the bay's usually sheltered water froth and roil like a witch's cauldron and there was no guarantee they would be able to disembark.

Only one thing was certain: if the men were able to land them, no one would be coming back dry, and the villagers knew it. Already faint twists of grey smoke were beginning to twirl from the chimneys, people rushing in and out of the arc of low cottages that smiled around the bay and taking in their washing, sweeping floors, putting on shoes, moving the spinning wheels to their prominent positions so that their visitors might watch.

They all knew the drill. Catering to the tourists had become a quietly profitable sideline. It couldn't help feed them – with not a single shop on the isle, they had little use for money on Hirta itself – but it was useful for asking the more familiar captains to bring back treats when they were next passing, or to give as extra credit to the factor when he came wanting the rents. Or in Flora's case, to purchase a brightly coloured lipstick she'd once seen on one of the well-heeled lady visitors – even though it would be wasted on the three hundred sheep she was currently herding in Glen Bay for the summer.

None of the villagers understood quite why the world at large took an interest in them, but the postmaster, Mhairi's father, Ian McKinnon, had been told by colleagues on the mainland that a St Kilda-stamped postcard was now considered desirable, if not valuable. Their way of life, they were told, was being rapidly left behind by the rest of the world. Industrialization meant society was changing at a more rapid pace than any other time in centuries and they were becoming living relics, curiosities from a bygone age. Some people pitied them, perhaps, but the St Kildans cared naught for sympathy. They had learnt to play the game to their advantage – Effie chief among them.

She lifted the pail and began to walk down the slope, her eyes never fixing off the black dots as they transferred from one heaving vessel to the other. Once they'd dried off and recovered from the swell, she knew they were going to want a show. And she was going to give it to them.

'Where'll they do it?' her father asked gruffly as she finished with churning the butter. He was standing by the window, looking out, his pipe dangling from his bottom lip.

'Sgeir nan Sgarbh, I should say,' she replied, closing the lid of the churn and going to stand beside him. 'It'll be more protected from the wind round there.'

'Over the top, aye, but will they get the dinghies round on the water?'

'Archie MacQueen's got the arms on him,' she murmured.

'Just not the legs.'

'No, not the legs.' She watched a trio of men walking down the Street. One she recognized by his distinctive gait – Frank Mathieson, the factor, their landlord's representative and the islanders' de facto ruler – but the other men were strangers. They were wearing well-cut dark brown suits and wool hats, but from beneath one of them she caught the gleam of golden blonde hair and a tanned neck. She willed him to turn around, wanting just to glimpse the face that went with that hair and elegant physique; but the path curved, taking them out of sight.

The group that had come ashore had been disappointingly small – a private contingent, Ian McKinnon had said with his usual authority. It meant the tips would be meagre. If the women were to take their sheets in, there had to be good reason for it and two men alone could hardly reward everyone. The captain had been put up in her Uncle Hamish's cottage and the other two men would stay at the factor's house, for it was the largest on the isle. She didn't envy them having to endure Mathieson's hospitality.

'I'm just going to put this in the cool,' she said, lifting the churn onto her shoulder and walking out, Poppit trotting at her heels. She could see the visitors further down placing pennies into the palm of Mad Annie as she sat carding the wool and telling stories about broomstick marriages and snaring puffins. Unlike most of the village elders her English was good, but that didn't mean the others couldn't communicate, and Effie gave a small grin as she saw Ma Peg make a play of bustling and hiding from their camera, even though those days of shock at the new technologies were long past. More coins crossed palms.

She went round the back of the cottage and a short way up the slope that led to the plateau of An Lag, where they herded the sheep into stone fanks in bad weather. Beyond it, Connachair – the island's tallest mountain – rose majestically like a stepping stone to heaven. For some it was. Many had met their fate over the precipice, tricked into distraction by the summit's rounded hummock on the village side and caught unaware by the sheer cliffs – 1,400 feet high – that dropped suddenly and vertically to the sea, as if cleaved.

The lush grass was speckled with buttercups and thrift and felt springy underfoot as she moved past the countless identical stone cleits to the one where she and her father stored their butter and cream. She ducked down as she stepped inside and set down the churn. It was the very store her family had been using for this purpose for over three hundred years. There may have been over 1,400 of the hump-topped, stacked-stone huts on the island, but she could identify every single one that belonged to her family – this one below An Lag for the dairy; that one on Ruival for the bird feathers; that on Oiseval for the fulmar oil; that on Connachair for the salted carcasses, that for the peats . . . There were plenty that lay empty, too, but they also had their uses as emergency larders, rain and wind shelters, hiding places for courting lovers . . .

She came back down the slope again, jumping nimbly over the rocks nestled in the grass and seeing over the rooftops that everyone was beginning to gather on the beach, preparing for the visitors' exhibition.

'Are you joining them, Effie?' a voice called.

She looked over to find Lorna MacDonald coming out of the postmaster's hut, fixing her auburn hair. She worked there sometimes with the postmaster.

Effie skipped over, Poppit beating her by two lengths. 'Aye,' she grinned. 'You never know, there might be some pennies in it for me.'

'And more besides,' Lorna said with a wink.

'What do you mean?'

'He's a fine-looking fellow, the young one. A smile from him would be payment in itself,' Lorna laughed, her brown eyes twinkling with merriment.

Effie gave a bemused shrug. 'I only caught the back of him.'

'That's pretty enough too, I should guess.'

Effie chuckled. It was a wonder to her that Lorna was their resident old maid – all of thirty-three years old and still unmarried – for she was a terrible flirt. Alas, the visiting men never stayed for long and the St Kildan bachelor nearest in age to her was Donnie Ferguson, who had no interest in a wife seven years older than him, cleverer than him and almost through her child-bearing years.

'Who are they, anyway?'

'Rich,' Lorna shrugged. 'If that ship's anything to go by.'

Lorna knew about such things. She wasn't a St Kildan by birth but a registered nurse from Stornoway who had chosen to make her life here; she had seen another world to this one and what money bought.

'Good,' Effie sighed, catching sight of the men beginning to head up the hill with their ropes, the dogs running ahead in a pack. 'Well, then I'll still aim for some pennies from them and you can have the young gentleman's smile. What do you say?'

'Deal,' Lorna winked as Effie took off again and darted back into the cottage to grab their rope. It was thickly plaited from horsehair, supple and rough in her hand. Her father was sitting in his chair by the hearth now – he could never stand for long – tamping his black twist tobacco.

'Well, I'll be off then.'

He looked back at her. His eyes had a rheumy look, the whites yellowing with age, but they still revealed a strong man within an infirm body. He gave a nod. He wasn't one for sentimental farewells. 'Hold fast, lass.'

'Aye.' She nodded back, knowing those had been his last words to her brother too.

For a moment she thought he might say something else; the way he held himself, it was as if an energy for more words lay coiled within him. But the moment passed and she left again with just a nod.

Some of the men were already walking the slopes, ropes slung over their shoulders too. As she'd predicted, they were heading for the easterly cliffs. A small rock stack just out in the water provided enough of a break from the broadside waves for the dinghy to rope up in relative comfort whilst the show was put on.

She ran and caught them up, listening in as they chatted about the visitors and the news from 'abroad', meaning Skye.

'. . . friends of the landlord,' David MacQueen, Flora's eldest brother, was saying. 'So we're to make it good.'

'Shame the wind's up or we could have gone further round,' her cousin Euan said.

'There'll be no tips if they're sick as dogs,' Ian McKinnon replied.

'But the cliffs are lower here.'

'This will do them fine. It will all be high to the likes of them.'

She fell into step with Mhairi's older brothers, Angus and Finlay.

'What are *you* doing here?' Angus asked with his usual sneer.

'Same as you,' she shrugged, slightly breathless as their longer legs covered more ground than hers.

'We're not fowling. This is just for display.'

'Aye, so there'll be tips.'

'Then knit them some socks!'

'You know I'd get a fraction of what I can get up here and the agreement is whenever you're all on the rocks, I'm allowed to be too.'

'You're a pain in my side, Effie Gillies,' Finlay groaned.

'And you're a pain in mine,' she shot back.

They rolled their eyes but she didn't care. Her brother's friends, her friend's brothers, they had been teasing her all her life and she knew to give as good as she got. They had all grown up playing hide and seek in the cleits as children, learnt to read together in the schoolroom beside the kirk, and kicked each other during the minister's sermons.

But she couldn't ignore that things were changing. Or had already changed. A tension existed now, a low-level hum, that hadn't been there before. Her brother's death had profoundly affected them all and she was no longer John's little sister to them – or anyone but herself; sometimes she caught them looking at her in a new way that made her nervous. Finlay's eyes seemed to follow her wherever she went and Angus had tried to kiss her as she cut the peats one evening; he hadn't yet forgiven her for laughing.

For visitors wanting to take in the view – and they always did – this would be a forty-minute to hour-long walk, but she and the men did it in under thirty and were already spread across the top and looping out the coils of rope by the time the dinghy appeared around the cliffs. Birds whirled and

screeched around them, feathers lilting on the updrafts. From
this height, the boat looked no bigger than a bird either. Effie
glanced down a few times, scanning the rock face for the line
she wanted to take, then casting about for a rock with which
to drive in her peg.

Looping the rope around the peg, she leant back, checking
its firmness and tension. It vibrated with pleasing freshness
and she wrapped it around her waist in the St Kildan style.

She looked down the drop once more. Cousin Euan had
been right; it really wasn't so high here. Seven hundred feet?
Half the height of Connachair. A single drop of the ropes would
take them maybe a third of the way down. Still, they were
merely going to be playing up here today. No bird hunting,
no egg collecting, no saving stranded sheep. Just playing.

'You're looking peely-wally there, Eff,' Angus drawled.
'Sure you're up to it?'

She looked back at him with scorn. Angus prided himself
on being the fastest climber on the island. He had won last
year's Old Trial, a climbing race among the young men to
prove they were worthy of providing for their families – and
future wives. If he had wanted to prove anything to her, the
point had been well and truly lost. Effie was certain she could
have beaten him (and the rest) had she only been allowed to
enter too. But as a girl . . . 'Actually, I was just wondering
how quickly I could get down there.'

A smirk grew. 'You think you can do it *fast*?'

'Faster than you.' She pulled her fair hair back, tying
it away from her face in a balled knot. The last thing she
needed was a gust of wind blowing it about and blinding her
on the route.

'Ha! You're all talk and no trousers, Effie Gillies.'

It was her turn to smirk. 'Well, yes, even I won't deny

there's not much in *my* trews.' Angus McKinnon might be the fastest man on the isle, but he wasn't the brightest. As if to make the point, she hitched up her breeches at the waist; they had been John's and were the only suitable attire for climbing, but she didn't wear them purely for reasons of practicality.

Finlay blushed furiously. 'Ignore her,' he said. 'You know she's only trying to rile you. Everyone knows you're the fastest, brother. Just give the rich people a show. This is an exhibition, not a race.'

Effie shrugged as if she couldn't care less either way, but they all knew the gauntlet had been thrown down. She – a girl! – was challenging Angus for his crown; the competition could happen here between the two of them. Why not? It was as good a chance as any. She watched him looking down the cliff as the islanders did final checks on their ropes and took their positions on the cliff edge.

Effie kept her eyes ahead, her hands already around the rope. Waiting. Hoping—

'H'away then!' Archie MacQueen cried. Flora's father, he had been an experienced cragger himself, but he left these shows to the younger ones these days; already lame in one leg, his grip wasn't what it used to be either. Besides, someone had to stay up top in case anyone needed hauling up.

It was the cue to go, to perform, to show off their derring-do and the skills that made the St Kildans famous around the world as they all but skipped and danced over the cliffs. Without hesitation, Effie leant back and stepped over. She felt the swoop of her stomach as her body angled into open space and the rope tightened. She pushed off, allowing the rope to swing on a pendulum, her bare feet already braced for contact with the rock face, ready to caper across it in a bold defiance of gravity. A visitor had once told them it was like watching spiders drop from the top of a wall. She herself loved the sound of the ropes under tension – a *huzzahing* – as she and the men scampered and sprang from side to side.

'First to the boat then?'

She looked across to find Angus on his rope, staring straight at her. She smiled at his tactic – finishing the race at the boat, not the bottom, when neither one of them could swim . . . 'Aye. But I'll wait for you, don't worry.'

Angus's eyes narrowed at her insult, but she was already off. Abandoning the acrobatics, her foot found a toehold and she brought her weight to bear on it as the other foot searched. The St Kildans never climbed in boots, always bare feet. The cliffs were too unyielding to give any more than a half inch to grab and there was nothing that compared to skin on rock. Shoes and boots – the hallmarks of civilization – had no place on a granite cliff.

She left the older men to the games, their powerful arms and legs flexed as they made a point of playing on the rock faces, bouncing off with their feet, reaching up for a fingerhold and pulling themselves up like lizards, before repeating again. Others scrambled sideways, scuttling like crabs over the rocks.

Effie just focused on going down. She could see the boat between her legs, far below her, as she descended on the rope, her arms braced as she lowered herself, hand over hand. She didn't have biceps the size of boulders to help her, but as she always said to her father, she didn't need them. She was wiry and light, skinny even, but that didn't mean she was weak. The less there was of her, the less she had to support. She wouldn't tire so quickly. She was more nimble, more flexible . . .

From her peripheral vision, she sensed she was already ahead of Angus, but only just. He had power, height and gravity on his side.

Soon enough she was out of rope. Balancing on a narrow ledge, she unwound the rope's end from her torso.

'What are you doing?' Ian McKinnon called sharply down to her as she began to free climb.

'Winning! Don't worry. It was Angus's idea.'

It always felt different scaling without the rope and she knew it was reckless, but there was something about the intensity it brought – her brain and eyes seemed to tune into hyper-focus, the adrenaline refreshed her muscles – that meant she could remember her mother's eyes and smile, hear again her brother's ready laugh. Somehow, by thinning the skein of life, it seemed she could almost reach the dead.

Down she went, agile and sharp until the horizon drew level, then hovered above her, and the crash of the waves began to intrude on her concentration. White splashes of cold sea were beginning to reach towards her, spraying her bare brown calves, but she didn't care about getting wet or cold. She just had to win. She had to know – and crucially, Angus had to know – that she was the fastest and the best.

She saw the dark sea, ominously close. She was less than thirty feet above the waves now, but the cliffs just sliced into the ocean depths, and as she scaled ever downwards, she realized that the only place where she could stand and pivot was a narrow ledge perhaps six feet above the surface, no wider than her hand's span.

For a moment, she felt a visceral spasm of fear. This was madness! If her father was to hear of the carelessness with which she was treating her life . . . Or maybe that was the point of it. Maybe she wanted him to hear of it. His heart had been broken by death too many times, and she was the only one left. He couldn't – or wouldn't – love her in case he lost her too. Was that it? If she was to slip, to go

446

straight down, under the waves . . . would he weep? Would she be mourned like the others? On the other hand, if she won, would he be proud? Would he see that she could be enough?

There was no time to think. Everything was instinct. Her feet touched down and her arms splayed wide as she hugged the wall, gripping its surface with her fingertips, her cheek pressed to the cold, wet granite. Breath coming fast, she gave her muscles a moment to rest. They were burning, but she knew she wasn't there yet.

She glanced up. Angus was only a few feet above her. What he lacked in nimbleness, he made up for in power. In a few more seconds . . . She looked carefully back over her shoulder and saw the dinghy tied to a rock just a short distance away. Her Uncle Hamish, skippering, was frowning and watching her intently, the way Poppit had watched for the boat earlier. He saw her movement and seemed to understand she wanted in; that she was going to launch herself towards it, one way or another. If he was alarmed, he didn't hesitate nonetheless. Not in front of the guests. Quickly he pulled in on the rope, hauling the small dinghy as close as he dared to the cliff wall, knowing that if he went too far, the swell risked tossing them against the rocks.

A nervous flinch inside the boat betrayed someone's nerves as her intentions became commonly understood. Effie knew she would have to time the next wave and then leap. She hugged the wall as she watched and braced for the next break – just as Angus landed beside her.

A blast of white water broke upon them both, making them gasp with the shocking cold as they were soaked. She didn't care. As she felt the draft pull back, she twisted and leapt blind. Death or glory then!

For one stunning, protracted moment, she felt almost as if she could fly, like the very birds that soared and wheeled and sliced around her in this island sky. Then gravity took hold, and she landed – half in the dinghy, half in the water. She took a hard knock to her chest but her arms gripped the prow as the boat rocked wildly, water slopping over the sides. But it was flat-bottomed and made for heavy weather; it righted itself almost immediately, and she laughed victoriously as her uncle Hamish hastily got a hand to her waistband and dragged her aboard in one swift movement like a landed salmon.

'I didna' know you had decided to make it a race to the bottom,' Uncle Hamish said to her with a stern, disapproving look. It was the most he would reveal in front of the tourists, but she already knew he'd be telling her father about this. There would be trouble to come, most likely a hiding; but it was worth it. Effie's eyes were bright. She'd beaten Angus McKinnon! The fastest cragger on the isle. Not just that – he could make no further claims now of providing for her when she herself had beaten him.

'It was Angus's idea,' she panted, scrambling to her knees and looking back to find him still clinging to the ledge. With her leap to victory, he now stood frozen in place and was becoming more soaked with every breaking wave. He either had to jump too or climb back up, but he couldn't stay there.

With an angry sigh, he jerked his thumb upwards, indicating the latter. He had lost. What good was there in riding back with them now? She would only crow her victory at him.

Uncle Hamish nodded, understanding perfectly what had just happened between them. It was a man's look, the kind

448

that cut her out, but what did she care? With a satisfied smile, Effie sat on the bench, pulling out her hair tie and wringing her long hair. Seawater puddled in the dinghy floor.

'Heavens above!' a voice said. 'It's a *girl*?'

She twisted back to face the visitors properly at last. In all her ambition to beat Angus, she'd forgotten who they were trying to impress in the first place. The three men seated towards the back were staring at her in wide-eyed amazement: Frank Mathieson, the factor, and the two men she'd glimpsed from behind earlier.

'Well, I can't climb in a skirt, sir,' she grinned, wringing out her tweed breeches as best she could.

'It wasn't just your clothes that fooled me. The speed! I've never seen a spectacle like it. You scaled that cliff like a squirrel down a tree!' It was the older man speaking. He was portly, with a dark moustache, lightly salted. Spectacles made it difficult to see his eyes past the reflection, but he appeared friendly as well as impressed. 'Do you mean to say females climb here, too?' he asked their skipper.

'Only this one,' Uncle Hamish said with a resigned tone, untying the rope from the mooring rock and beginning to row. 'This is my niece, Euphemia Gillies.'

'Effie is Robert Gillies's daughter. They live at number nine,' the factor added, as if that information was somehow enlightening. 'How are you, Effie?'

'Aye, well, sir, thank you for asking.'

'Becoming bolder, I see.'

'If by bolder you mean faster.'

He laughed. 'Allow me to present the Earl of Dumfries and his son, Lord Sholto,' he said. 'I'm sure you will be aware that they are great friends of Lord MacLeod.'

'Ah,' she said blandly, although she was aware of nothing of the sort. Who their landlord kept as friends was no business of hers, though it confirmed Lorna's observation that the visitors were rich.

'They were visiting his lordship at Dunvegan when they heard I was planning on making the voyage here—'

'It's been something of an ambition of mine to get over here,' the earl said brightly, interrupting. 'I'm a keen birder, you see, and Sir John very kindly agreed to my proposal that we might sail Mr Mathieson here ourselves. Two birds, one stone and all that.'

'Aye.' She could feel the younger man watching her keenly as she talked, but for as long as the others spoke, she had no such opportunity to cast her gaze openly over him. 'So will you be staying for long, then?'

The factor inhaled. 'Well, a lot will depend upon the wea—'

'Certainly a week,' Lord Sholto said suddenly, allowing a dazzling smile to enliven his features as she finally met his eyes.

'A week?' Effie smiled back at the blue-eyed, golden-haired man. Finally she could see his face at last. And she liked it.

'Miss Gillies.'

She turned to find the factor hurrying up the beach after her. Uncle Hamish was tying up the boat, the distinguished guests having been appropriated by the minister again the moment they'd set foot on shore.

'Mr Mathieson.' She tried not to show her impatience, but her tweed breeches were soaked from her half-swim and she wanted to get back and change. Their progress round the headland had been slow as they'd met the headwinds and she was shivering now.

He stopped in front of her, slightly downhill from where

she stood, so that she was aware of standing taller than him. He wasn't a tall man, stocky but not conspicuously short either, and the consequence of not standing out in any way seemed to work to his advantage; many times an islander had been caught saying things they shouldn't, not realizing he was within earshot. His relationship with the St Kildans was highly taut, for as the bringer of supplies every spring, and the collector of rents every autumn, he was both carrot and stick to the island community. He could smile and be charming when it suited him, but no one could ever quite forget that the power he wielded over them was almost absolute, and few – apart from Mad Annie – would clash with him. He wore finer suits than the village men and affected the manners of his employer, but reddened, pitted cheeks and the forearms of a wrestler betrayed him as a fighter first.

'Well, that was quite a display,' he said.

Effie wasn't sure this was intended as a compliment. 'That's the idea,' she replied vaguely. 'They always like it.' A sudden gust blew her long, wet hair forward and she had to use both hands to pin it back. The sky was growing ominously dark.

'Indeed.' He gave what she had come to learn over the years was his customary pause. It preceded a direct contradiction of what came after it. 'Although I'm not sure such daredevil antics require the added *novelty* factor.'

It took a moment to understand his meaning. 'Of a girl climbing, you mean?'

He shrugged. 'I understand your obligations to your father impel you to undertake men's work in a regular capacity, but when it comes to making a good impression on visitors . . . '

'But they seemed to like it.'

'Well, they're polite, of course, but things are quite different

451

in the wider world. I know it's not your fault that you don't know any differently – why should you? – but decorum and good taste are held in high regard. Women scrambling over cliffs like monkeys . . . ' He pulled a face. 'No. It's important to think about the impression you make on these visitors and how you and your neighbours will be conveyed in their onward conversations. I'm sure you wouldn't want to embarrass Sir John, would you?'

She had never met Sir John. '. . . Of course not.'

'Very well, then. So we're agreed there'll be no more fits of vanity on the ropes. We must strive to make sure the guests are not made to feel uncomfortable by what they witness here. Best foot forward, yes?'

She stared back at him, shivering with cold and anger. '. . . Aye, sir.'

He looked over her shoulder, along the Street. 'How is your father, anyway? Still lame?'

Her eyes narrowed. 'And always will be.'

'Which only makes him all the luckier to have you,' he nodded, oblivious to her terse tone. 'But please tell him I shall need to find him later and discuss the rent arrears.'

'Arrears?' Alarm shot through the word.

'As I recall, you were short thirteen Scotch ells of tweed last year. Your uncle picked up some of the slack, but you were also down nine gallons of oil and seven sacks of black feathers.'

'It'll be fine this year,' she said quickly. 'We were only short because I twisted my ankle and couldn't walk for ten days. It was just bad luck that it happened when we were fowling.'

The factor looked unconvinced. 'I'll need to reappraise the quota with him. You will remember I extended a great kindness in not reducing the oatmeal bolls after your brother's accident and as a result you have enjoyed more than your share for nigh-on four years now—'

Effie looked at him with wild panic. What he said was true, but it still wasn't enough. The past few winters had been hard ones and their harvests had all but failed, save for a half-dozen potatoes and those oats that were only half blackened by frost.

'—I have been both generous and patient, but it's not fair to expect others to compensate for your shortfalls. Accidents will always happen, Miss Gillies. You cannot expect to be fit and well every day of the year.'

'But I do. And I will,' she said urgently. The factor didn't know it yet, but she and her father had lost four of their sheep over the top this year already, so they were already down on their wool yield. Her father had bartered 100 extra fulmars instead with Donald McKinnon and it had been a rare endorsement of Effie's climbing skills that both men believed she was capable of bagging the extra haul, on top of the usual harvest.

'Miss Gillies, you don't need me to remind you that you are a girl doing a man's job. The odds are already grossly stacked against you.'

'But I'm eighteen now, and I've grown this last year. I can do anything they can and I'll prove it to you. I'll show you, sir.'

The factor looked at her keenly. 'You receive more than you are due and you deliver less than you owe. You see my predicament? I must be fair, Miss Gillies. Why should I make – and keep making – exceptions for you? If the others were to know—'

'But they won't. I'll make sure we're square and level come this September.'

'So you're saying you want me to keep this a secret?'

'Secret . . . ?' Behind him, the reverend and the two gentlemen guests walked past on the path back to the village, the minister holding forth on the repairs made to the manse. Lord Sholto glanced across at them talking as he passed by and she found herself smiling back at him, as though he'd pulled it from her on a string.

'From your neighbours? And your father too?'

She looked back at the factor in confusion. He was watching her intently. '. . . No, please don't tell him. I don't want him to worry. I can make the quota this year, I know I can.'

He tutted. 'I don't know why I allow you to manipulate me, Miss Gillies—'

She frowned. *Did* she manipulate him?

'A "thank you" doesn't pay the fiddler, now, does it?' he sighed. 'Still, I have sympathy for your predicament and although I have a job to do, I believe in being a friend in the hour of need.'

Effie bit her lip – she had to – to keep from laughing out loud. What? There wasn't a person on the isle who would have considered the factor a friend. He bought their feathers at five shillings a stone and sold them at fifteen, and the supplies he brought over – oatmeal, flour, sugar, tea and tobacco – cost them three times what he paid. Was it any wonder the villagers tried to bypass him with money they earnt from the tourists and could spend directly themselves?

'Talking of which, I have brought you something, again.'

'For our studies?' She had finished her schooling four years ago, but he never seemed to remember this.

'I've left it in the usual spot. Just . . . be discreet, please. I can't oblige these sorts of favours for everyone.'

Favours? Secrets? 'But—'

'Good day, Miss Gillies,' he said briskly, assuming his usual manner as he noticed the three men now ahead of him on the path. 'I must get on. Our visitors will be requiring some refreshments after the afternoon's . . . excitement. Just remember what we discussed. We shall have to hope first impressions don't stick.'